HIS FEAR WAS REAL

HIS FEAR WAS REAL

ZACHARY GOLDMAN MYSTERIES
BOOK SIXTEEN

P.D. WORKMAN

 **PD WORKMAN**

ISBN: 9781774685501 (KDP Paperback)
ISBN: 9781774685518 (KDP Hardcover)
ISBN: 9781774685525 (Large Print)
ISBN: 9781774685532 (Lulu Paperback)
ISBN: 9781774685495 (ePub)
ISBN: 9781774685549 (Accessible Audio)

ALSO BY P.D. WORKMAN

FIND MORE BOOKS AT PDWORKMAN.COM

MYSTERY/SUSPENSE:

AND MORE AT PDWORKMAN.COM

For those whose stories are written on their skin.

T his is nice!" Tyrrell looked around the restaurant, his eyes pausing momentarily on one of the TVs showing the game. "Great to have a 'bro night' now and then."

Zachary nodded his agreement. He didn't want to bring up anything serious yet. He would let Tyrrell get comfortable. Make sure that he was calm and relaxed. See whether he could spot any red flags.

The last time, Zachary had been too casual about it. When Tyrrell had told Zachary that he was a recovering alcoholic, Zachary had thought that he was talking about a long time ago. That he had drunk as a teenager or young adult. Tyrrell had seemed perfectly normal and in control of his life and Zachary hadn't inquired further to find that he had never been sober for more than a year or two at a time, that he had destroyed his marriage and much of his relationship with his children with drink, and that, due to his history, he was working dead-end jobs despite having a college degree.

Things were better now. Zachary and Kenzie had helped Tyrrell through a recovery program after his last setback, and Kenzie had helped to get him a better job at her family foundation that used some of his skills. All of the signs indicated that Tyrrell was doing well. He assured them that everything was going great. He was enjoying his job, attending meetings, and trying to repair his relationship with Alisha and Mason. They were glad to have Daddy around again, as long as he wasn't drinking, and Zachary thought it was especially good for Mason, whose extreme ADHD behaviors reminded Zachary of himself at that age, only without the trauma of losing his family after a house fire and growing up in foster care.

But the call from Hillary, the woman who ran the Kirsch family foundation, had raised alarms. She had been very happy with Tyrrell and his work for them. Things had worked out very well in the beginning. But she had expressed some concerns.

Tyrrell had been more forgetful lately. Not doing jobs he had been assigned or not completing them to her satisfaction. He didn't have to show up at work at a specific time since most of his work was done remotely. Still, he did go to Burlington occasionally to do physical filing and have admin meetings with Hillary, and his attendance those days was beginning later and later.

Zachary and Tyrrell loaded their plates with food from the buffet and returned to their table. Zachary's wasn't quite as full as Tyrrell's, but he could eat more since his meds had been changed and he wasn't so nauseated. He'd put on weight, which pleased his doctors and Kenzie. But he still didn't eat huge amounts, even at the all-you-can-eat buffet where it was expected. He wouldn't finish what was on his plate, but he'd give it his best shot. And while he wanted to keep his weight at a healthy level, he didn't want to go too far in the other direction and end up overweight.

The way that his cheeks and the hollows under his eyes had filled in as he gained weight meant that he and Tyrrell looked even more alike than they had before. Both had the same dark hair and eyes and similar bone structures. Zachary kept his hair very short, which was easier to take care of and made it less noticeable if he did forget to comb it one morning. Tyrrell's was longer and a bit wavy. Zachary had cleaned up his three-day scruff of beard before going to the restaurant so that he would look respectable. When he was surveilling someone, following them or spying on them in a crowd, it was better to be unshaven. People avoided looking at him, figuring he was homeless and might ask for money or start talking to them about drunken delusions if they met his eyes. They automatically skimmed over him and wouldn't remember him later.

Tyrrell was looking good. Zachary saw no signs that he had started drinking again. If he was, it wasn't enough yet that he had stopped eating and was living primarily on liquids. He, too, was clean-shaven. His eyes were bright with no side-to-side movement.

"What's up?" Tyrrell asked, apparently noticing Zachary's scrutiny. Zachary dropped his eyes to his plate and pretended to be busy with his meal.

"Just wondering how you are. Everything going good?"

Tyrrell nodded. "Fantastic," he declared, but his face did not take on any animation to match the word. "My life is good, Zach. Life is good."

"How are things going at the foundation?" Zachary cut into his slice of ham and had a couple of bites, pretending that he was not watching Tyrrell and analyzing how long it took him to put an answer together.

"They're good too."

"You're still enjoying it? Not getting bored with all of the filing and computer work?"

"Nah. I love that part of it. After working on construction sites or road cleanup and other jobs I've had the last few years...? I enjoy working indoors, filing everything away neatly, doing searches and data entry to pull together profiles on the companies that we deal with. Making suggestions about social programs the foundation might want to be involved with. It's great. Really."

Zachary nodded. "No problems? You get along with Hillary?"

"Yeah. Hillary is great." Tyrrell looked at Zachary, brows drawn down. "Where is all of this coming from? You think something is wrong?"

Zachary cleared his throat and considered the best way to confront the issue. But he'd been trying to figure out what to say ever since he had talked to Hillary, and he still didn't know. There wasn't any way to make it sound better.

"Hillary has some concerns."

Tyrrell put his fork down on his plate and stared at Zachary. "What do you mean, she has some concerns?"

"She said… that you have seemed distracted lately. Forgetting to do things or not finishing them. Showing up late. She knows your history and we're all concerned about your welfare."

"I'm not drinking."

Zachary searched Tyrrell's face for signs that he was lying. He'd been fooled the last time. Tyrrell had denied it then, too, but Zachary and Kenzie had been right to be suspicious. Would things have turned out differently if they had been more persistent? If they had not let it go once he said that he hadn't had anything to drink?

"I'm not," Tyrrell insisted. "You want to have me tested? I'll do it any time you like. Pee test, blow in one of those personal breathalyzers, hair samples, whatever you like. I'm clean. I have not fallen off the wagon."

His voice was loud enough that some people at nearby tables were looking over to see what was happening. Covert, concerned expressions. Curiosity written on their faces. It was always entertaining to see someone flip out at a restaurant.

"If you say you're not… then I believe you." Maybe he shouldn't, but what kind of relationship could he have with Tyrrell if he didn't take him at his word? He couldn't go around suspecting him all of the time, checking up on him, asking questions about his behavior. How many more "bro nights" would they have if he did that? If Tyrrell was drinking again, he needed his relationship with Zachary more than ever. He needed a strong community of supporters around him, holding him up and cheering him on.

"I told you I'm not."

"Okay." Zachary went back to eating his meal, slurping a forkful of Jell-O.

"Okay?" Tyrrell repeated. "Okay? Is that all you've got to say?"

Zachary nodded. "Yes."

"No more probing questions?"

"No. Do you want me to ask more probing questions?"

Tyrrell grinned suddenly, some of the confrontational attitude falling away. "No. That's quite all right. No apology?"

"Apology for what? Asking you if you're okay? Following up on concerns that you could be drinking again? Why would I apologize for that?"

"Because I didn't do anything wrong. I'm sober. I haven't had a drink."

"Good for you. I'm glad. Let me know if you have any trouble or need any help."

Tyrrell picked at his food, dragging a couple of fries through his salad dressing before eating them.

"There *is* something you could help with."

2

Zachary's shoulders tensed and his heart sped up. He took long, deep breaths and tried to relax his muscles.

"Of course. What can I help you with?"

"It isn't anything to do with recovery. This is… something different."

"Sure. Anything."

"I know I've been making mistakes lately at work. Not because of substance abuse. Just because I've been… distracted. Like you said."

"And not sleeping well?" Zachary guessed. There were shadows under Tyrrell's eyes. Not as bad as the ones Zachary usually sported. But visible if he were looking for them.

"No. Insomnia. Laying awake for a long time before I can get to sleep. And then I sleep in, because I don't *have* to be up at a certain time. With the foundation job, I don't have to check in and out at certain times. I can do what works for me. So, it's okay if I start late as long as I get the work done."

Zachary nodded.

"And I know I haven't been getting all the work done," Tyrrell admitted. "But that's just part of… being distracted."

"So why are you distracted? What's going on? Something to do with the kids?" Zachary guessed.

"No. You know that case that you had? With your friend from school?"

Zachary shrugged. He couldn't very well forget it. It had occupied all of his time for a couple of weeks and had resulted in his being kidnapped. So it wasn't exactly a case that would fade from his mind in the near future.

Was Tyrrell lying awake at night worrying about Zachary? Zachary knew that the abduction had bothered Kenzie. Even though she said that it helped her to face what had happened to her, there had been an increase in her nightmares. Maybe that just meant she was dealing with her own trauma instead of suppressing it. Maybe it was a good sign. But Zachary worried about her. And now, about Tyrrell.

"Is that what's bothering you?" he asked. "It all got resolved, and I'm okay. It was just one of those... freak things."

"Yeah, I know. Not sure I like it, but I didn't know you'd even been kidnapped until it was all over, so...?" Tyrrell grimaced and raised his shoulders an inch. "Okay. That's just my big brother's life. Being the hard-boiled detective."

Zachary laughed. He was anything but. He was nothing like the private investigators in the TV shows and books featuring gun-toting, hair-trigger, hard-fighting, womanizing, but ruggedly handsome private eyes. He didn't even own a gun.

"So...?" He invited Tyrrell to fill him in on what his case with Jennifer, an old school friend, had to do with Tyrrell's distraction.

"What was it like, meeting her again? A friend from way back then?"

"It was nice..." Zachary wasn't sure what Tyrrell was looking for. In actuality, meeting Jennifer had been hard. As nice as she was and as good a friend as she had been back then, she'd brought back memories of a difficult time in his life. A time when he had lived in a group home, he had been off of all of the meds he needed to function, dealing with bullying and all of the crap that teenagers had to deal with at school and abusers within the walls of the home. Jennifer had been a bright light in his life, but it had been a very dark time.

Tyrrell was studying Zachary closely, trying to read all of this. Zachary decided he needed to be more truthful if he hoped to get honesty from Tyrrell.

"She was nice to me then, helped me out at school. She was the only real friend I had for the time she was around. But it was a tough time. And she came to me at the hardest time in her life—after losing her teenage daughter suddenly. So it wasn't exactly a happy reunion for her either."

"You must have had other friends."

"The way that I got moved around, and with the stuff I was going through? No, not really. It was a struggle to get out of bed every morning and get to school. I slept through lessons, couldn't concentrate on the work when I was awake. Was hypervigilant. Even if some guy had *wanted* to be friends with me, I would probably have frozen him out, figuring he was just out to gaslight me."

Tyrrell nodded. Maybe he had experienced some level of the same thing. He had been luckier than Zachary. One of the younger children in the family, he had been through less abuse, and had been removed from an unsafe environment earlier in life than Zachary had. He had been able to stay with Vince and Mindy, the two youngest children, and all three had been adopted together. But he had still had to go through that trauma, and obviously still had the ADHD genes that Zachary did, and their father's addiction issues. He had dealt with his troubles in his own way.

"With Jennifer… she was in the same group home as I was, so we had contact that way, and she was willing to help me with my schoolwork at home at night. And stood up for me at school. So… I let her in."

"It must have been good to see her again after all that time," Tyrrell said. "Especially if she was your best friend."

Zachary tried to think of a way to encourage Tyrrell without actually lying and saying that he had enjoyed meeting with Jennifer again. "It had been a long time," he said finally, and looked at Tyrrell expectantly. It was Tyrrell's turn to contribute and explain his thoughts. What had been on his mind so much that it was disrupting his sleep and work. Maybe if it could be addressed, Tyrrell would be able to move forward rather than falling back on the behavior that had worked before—turning to the bottle.

"I had a friend in school," Tyrrell said, staring past Zachary. Zachary didn't think he was watching the TV this time, but replaying his memories. Searching for something.

"Who? What were they like?"

"Robbie. Robert Elder. He was great. Like with your friend, he was the only one I felt like understood me. Everyone we went to school with, even Vince and Mindy... they were normal. You know, white middle-class middle-income folks who had grown up in the neighborhood, lived with one or two of their parents, were going to graduate high school and go on to college and something better in life... like being a doctor, and they would pay their parents back for all of the school bills and everything..."

Mindy had told Zachary that Tyrrell had insisted on paying his own way in college, so that there would be enough money for the younger kids to go to school. Zachary was proud of him for that. He had looked after his younger siblings the best he could, even though he hadn't been in a situation where he had to. And things had been rocky for Tyrrell. It was an accomplishment that he had gone on to college and graduated with a degree, let alone paid for it himself.

"But Robbie was different?"

"Yeah. He was... I didn't know his situation, but I think he was in foster care. Or maybe an aunt had offered to look after him. I knew the people he lived with weren't his parents, and they had a lot of strict rules that seemed pretty unfair to me at the time. I should know more, but I was a teenager. Pretty self-centered. I never asked him all of the details of how he had gotten there. We must have talked about the family he had come from because I knew that it had been a pretty volatile home."

Zachary understood. "Like ours."

Tyrrell nodded. "So, we had that in common. This other life we had lived. The fact that we weren't living with our biological parents. He understood that not everyone lived in this middle-class situation where everything was…" Tyrrell shook his head slightly, trying to find the words. "Clean and pressed. That there was an ugly world out there. And we were going to have to face it again someday. By ourselves."

Zachary picked at his food, nodding, waiting for Tyrrell to get to the point. What did any of this have to do with today? With slipping up at work? With not being able to sleep at night?

"We hung out together," Tyrrell said. "Were troublemakers. I'm sure people wished they could just get rid of us. That we would drop out of school and do our thing without bothering everyone else. The principal would lecture us," Tyrrell rolled his eyes and stared up at the ceiling, remembering. "How the younger students looked up to us. Especially Vince and Mindy. That they would copy our bad behavior. He didn't even try telling us how we were going to ruin our own futures. I'm sure he didn't think we had any."

"Well, you showed him."

"I guess I did."

Tyrrell wasn't smiling about it. He looked much like Zachary had felt discussing things with Jennifer—pulled into a dark vortex of unhappy memories. He sounded alone and isolated. So like Jennifer, Robbie had gone on to bigger and better things. He had left Tyrrell behind, to his own devices. Whether it was his own choice or something he had no control over. Tyrrell had felt abandoned.

"What happened to him?"

Tyrrell looked Zachary in the eye, then away again. "What do you mean, what happened to him?"

"Uh… where did he end up? The two of you lost track of each other?"

"Yeah. Do you think… you could find him? I've been thinking, since you had that case, about what it would be like to see him again. Catch up on all the bad old days."

"I could look for him, sure," Zachary agreed, relieved that Tyrrell had finally gotten to the point and suggested something he could do. "It probably wouldn't be too hard to find someone you went to school with. There are name changes and all of that, but most people don't do that. Even if they do, it's public record."

Tyrrell chewed on his lip. "You would do that? And you think you could find something after this long? It's been decades."

"I do have some experience in tracing people."

"And you solved Heather's case." Tyrrell referred to their older sister. She had been assaulted years before, and Zachary had been able, mostly through luck, to figure out who had done it and to get him charged. Heather could finally open up and live her life again without worrying that her rapist was still out there somewhere, stalking her or her children. The world became a livable place again, and Heather had blossomed.

"Well, I did," Zachary admitted. He didn't want to take all the credit for solving the case. Heather had provided parts of the solution herself. It had been a joint effort. And Tyrrell wasn't asking him to solve a cold case, just to trace someone he had lost track of over the years. High school grad committees tracked down alumni. It didn't take a lot of skills.

"If I hired you, you could try to find out what happened to him?" Tyrrell pressed.

"You don't have to hire me. I'll do it as a favor."

"No, I should pay you. You and Kenzie are already doing so much for me. I should stand on my own two feet and cover the cost myself. I mean, it isn't something I *have* to do. It's just something I want to do. A... discretionary expense."

"Let me see how long it takes," Zachary said, putting him off. "It will probably amount to nothing."

Tyrrell shifted in his seat and looked around. "Okay, I suppose," he agreed.

Rather than seeming reassured by Zachary's agreement, he seemed more agitated. He fingered his soft drink glass, no doubt wishing he could order something stronger to take the edge off.

"Why don't you give me his details," Zachary suggested. "All of the vitals that you can remember. Name, birthdate, where he lived, his foster parents' names if you knew them, all that kind of thing."

"Robert Elder. I don't know if he had a middle name. We never shared them." Tyrrell tentatively remembered the street Robbie had lived on. And, of course, the school they had gone to. Zachary would check with the alumni committee. They might already know where Robbie was.

"And do you know what years he lived in that house?"

"Months," Tyrrell corrected. "He wasn't there the whole school year. I think he'd been there from September and then disappeared in March… maybe April…"

Zachary looked at him. "Disappeared? I thought he was moved to a new family."

"I don't know. One day he was there, and then he was gone. Not there anymore. Not in any of my classes. When I went to his house to find out what had happened, he wasn't there."

"And they told you he had been transferred to a new family."

Tyrrell shook his head. "No."

3

Zachary picked up a barbecued rib from his plate and gave it his attention while he gathered his thoughts.

It was going to take some time to tease the story out of Tyrrell. He had presented it as just someone he used to know that he would like to get in touch with again when that was apparently not the case. A disappearance from twenty-some years before would be a lot more challenging to sort out than just someone Tyrrell had lost track of. Though, of course, sometime during that twenty years, he might have shown up again. If he had run away, he would eventually stop running and begin a new life, probably with the same name or some version of it. Adult missing persons usually showed up again somewhere near home, sometimes just a mile or two from where they had disappeared. Tyrrell's friend had not been an adult, but an older teen, not that far from adulthood.

"So, what did they tell you?" he asked finally when Tyrrell offered no further details.

For some reason, Tyrrell looked surprised that he would ask that. "They said... that he had not come home. Wanted to know when the last time was that I had seen him, like I might have something to do with him disappearing. It wasn't like he was hiding out at my place. My folks wouldn't have allowed it. They thought he was a bad influence."

Of course they did. They had rescued three children from a bad situation and had been working hard to raise them to overcome their rough beginnings, and along came some delinquent determined to take the oldest from them, leading him off down some garden path.

Or dark alley.

"What did his guardians say when you said you didn't know where Robbie was? That you hadn't seen him?"

"They were kind of casual about it. Said that he would show up again when he was good and ready. Probably slept over at someone's house or was drunk."

Zachary nodded. "But he didn't show up?"

"No." Tyrrell looked like he was going to leave it at that, forcing Zachary to keep digging away to get the story, but then he went on. "They eventually did call the police and report him missing. But they weren't too worried."

"The police or his parents?"

"Any of them. He had run away before and they figured it was just voluntary, and he would show up sooner or later if he was in trouble or got tired of it. They didn't do much to investigate it."

"Did the police talk to you?"

"Uh… yeah, briefly. Came by the house. I think it was just to see if he was there. They didn't ask me very much. Just when I had seen him last and if I knew anyone he might be staying with."

"Did you have any idea where he might have gone? Other friends who might put him up? Back to his biological family?"

"No. There wasn't anyone. He didn't have anyone else. It was just him and me and maybe a few other guys who hung out sometimes. He wouldn't have been able to stay with any of them. Not for more than a day or two. And his bio family… I don't know. I never really knew the situation, but he didn't sound like he wanted to go back there. He figured he was better off with the folks he was with, even if they did have too many rules."

"At least they cared enough to try to keep him safe." Zachary could see things from a different perspective now that he was older and those teen years were long behind him. He had been in homes where the rules were unfair and coercive, but he had also lived in homes where he could see now that they had just been trying to keep everyone safe and on track.

Tyrrell shrugged. He sipped his soft drink. "You probably won't be able to find him, will you? Or to find out what happened to him?"

"I don't know," Zachary said honestly. "Until I start looking, I have no idea what I might find. He might be easy to find. Might not have gone far and still be using the same name. Kids escaping from foster care usually go back to their biological families. His bio family might know where he is regardless of where he went back then. He might easily have gotten in touch with them since then."

"What if he's dead?"

Goosebumps made Zachary's skin crawl. He tried to ignore the sensation and shook his head. "There's no point in jumping to that. If the police never found his body, then chances are he is alive somewhere. He just never went back to the foster family or the school you went to. He might have been found and sent to a different family or group home. The foster parents wouldn't be likely to tell you anything about it. You might try to visit him and disrupt things."

"Yeah. I guess."

"Give me some time to look into it. I'll let you know what I figure out."

Tyrrell blew out his breath. "Okay. Thanks, big bro. I appreciate it."

4

Kenzie opened the door as Zachary walked from the car up the sidewalk to the house. She must have heard him slam the door or had been looking out the window and seen him pull up. She stood waiting for him, rubbing her arms at the nip in the air, but still wearing her bedtime shorts and t-shirt. Her dark spiraling hair bounced when she moved and her lips looked as if she had just reapplied her favorite red lipstick. Maybe she was planning some romance before bed.

"Hey," Zachary greeted her, giving her a quick kiss as he reached the doorway. "How are you doing?"

"I'm good," she said a little impatiently. "I want to hear how things went with Tyrrell."

Zachary had invited her to join them, but she had thought that Tyrrell would probably be more open if it were just Zachary, and he agreed. Tyrrell loved Kenzie and was very grateful for the opportunities she had given him, but he wouldn't necessarily want to talk about a relapse in front of her. That was better addressed in private, just between Zachary and Tyrrell.

"He's fine," Zachary assured her. He could get into a longer explanation once they sat down, but he wanted to ensure that she knew everything was okay from the beginning. "He isn't drinking again, as far as I can tell."

There was a loosening of tension around Kenzie's eyes. She nodded gratefully. "I'm really glad to hear that. Are you sure? Last time he *told* us that he wasn't drinking again…"

"I can't be one hundred percent sure. But as far as I can tell, he is telling the truth."

"Good." Kenzie looked out at the quiet street for a moment before closing the door after Zachary entered. He turned and looked out as well. He couldn't spot any surveillance cars or anything out of place. Everything looked safe and normal. But they both knew that things could change. They had dealt with break-ins and intruders before, and neither one of them could be complacent about it.

Eventually, Kenzie shut the door and rearmed the burglar alarm. They both watched it blink on and give its three-beep "armed" alert. They walked to the kitchen. Kenzie already had coffee on. Either she had been drinking it to distract herself from the fact that Zachary was not home yet, or she had anticipated his arrival with great precision.

Which could have something to do with her checking her phone app to see where he was throughout the evening. She would be able to see when he left the restaurant. She might even have an alert set to notify her when he was on the move. They both needed the reassurance of knowing where the other was and that they were safe.

Zachary did not comment on this line of thought and poured himself a mug of coffee. Caffeine wouldn't keep him awake, but she had probably brewed decaf anyway so it wouldn't keep her up. They sat at the kitchen table to discuss Zachary's evening with Tyrrell.

Kenzie frowned at Tyrrell's explanation and shook her head. "You really think that anything to do with this old friend could be causing him problems at work? Could it be that much of a distraction? If it happened twenty years ago, how can he still be worried about it? That doesn't make sense."

"He didn't say that it's been bothering him for twenty years, just that it has been on his mind. Ever since I took on Jennifer's case, I guess that my meeting with an old high school friend made him think of *his* old high school friend, and he started to wonder what had happened to him. How he had ended up."

"I don't know. That sounds like a cover story to me."

Zachary thought about it, sipping his coffee. "Well, put that way... I guess it's possible. But it sounded genuine. He *is* concerned about Robbie and wants me to see if I can find him."

"Are you going to?"

"Sure. I'll see what I can find. I'm hoping it won't even be hard. Robbie should be past whatever he was running or hiding from back then. Why would he still be hiding now? He's probably in contact with his biological family. Probably using his real name. It should be a cinch."

"Is it ever a cinch?"

Zachary smiled. "You don't hear about all of my routine cases. There's not much point in telling you, 'Oh, I found five skips today. They took about ten minutes each.'"

Kenzie laughed. "Okay, yeah. You probably wouldn't bother telling me you found everyone you were looking for without a problem. Any more than I would tell you that I had a routine autopsy that didn't turn up anything and was just a natural death like it appeared to be."

Zachary nodded his agreement. "I want to hear the medical mysteries and surprises. Not just... routine deaths."

"Well, I hope you're right and this Robbie is just a routine skip, and it only takes you five minutes to track him down. And then... we'll find out whether that was really the issue or whether something else is going on with Tyrrell. Because I'm not convinced that he's just worried about what happened to an old friend. Twenty years ago."

"I know. But I have to take him at his word, at least to start with. Until he proves me wrong for trusting him. If I'm suspicious of everything he says and think it is all lies... we won't have a relationship. If I can't trust him and he knows I don't believe anything he says…" Zachary shook his head. "I have to trust him, at least to start with."

5

Zachary sat down on the couch in front of his computer, on the mobile table that was supposed to improve his posture and keep him from getting too fatigued, which it really didn't because he was sitting on the couch instead of in a proper office chair and still slumped and used all kinds of lazy postures that would have horrified his elementary school teachers. But it was what worked for him and, although he could use Kenzie's home office whenever she wasn't using it—which was pretty much anytime—he usually chose to stay in the living room, the center of activity in the house, closer to the front door and the kitchen, with a big window that looked out onto the street so he could keep an eye on anything going on in the neighborhood. He always felt shut away, isolated from the action, in the small office. Even when he was the only one home, the living room felt busier and was more comfortable.

He had written down a list of what he needed to do in his small notepad, and he kept it open beside his computer, promising himself that he would only do what was in the notebook, in the order he had written it, and not be distracted by anything else. It was easy to get distracted following rabbit trails on the computer, only realizing hours later that he had wasted half the day doing nothing productive.

He set up a project folder in the file system to corral all his notes and save any documents related to his search for Robert Elder. He took pictures of the notes he had made while talking to Tyrrell and sent them to the new folder. Then he set up a project on his project management system, where he and Heather could set up tasks for the file and keep track of his billing hours. Even though he wouldn't charge Tyrrell for the project, no matter how many hours it took, despite what he had told Tyrrell. Heather had set up these systems for him to keep him from storing everything in his email inbox, and he had to admit that it worked well. She had raised two kids with ADHD and had some good strategies to help him to keep himself on track. She stayed on top of what was in his inbox, sorting it and setting up tasks in the project management app to keep him from getting lost in unrelated tasks.

The phone rang. Zachary looked at the next line on his notebook, trying to stay focused on his list but, when the phone rang again, he looked at it. It was Heather. Zachary picked up the phone.

"Hi, Feathers," he greeted, using his childhood nickname for her.

"Hi, Zachy. What's this new file?"

He wondered whether she had a notification set up to let her know whenever he created a new project. Was there a setting in the app for that? Or had she just been looking at it when he had created the project?

"It's for Tyrrell," he explained. "Looking for a friend of his."

"I can see that," she agreed. "When did this happen? Is T okay?"

"Yes. It's old. Back when he was in high school. I don't know whether we'll be able to find anything or not, but I told him I would check it out. With any luck, the guy will be close to home, and it will just take a couple of traces to find him."

"A high school friend?" Heather's tone was doubtful. "Why is he looking for him now?"

Zachary hesitated, wondering whether he was speaking out of school by giving Heather the details. He normally tried to preserve client confidentiality and would not have told a random family member of Tyrrell's what was going on.

But Tyrrell knew that Heather worked with Zachary on cases and would hear about what he was doing. And he hadn't told Zachary not to involve her or let her know what was happening. So, he must not care. He had known the details of Heather's cold case before Zachary had, so he probably didn't mind her knowing about his case.

"He said it was because of my contact with Jennifer. That me meeting with an old high school friend made him think about Robbie and how he had disappeared. That it's been on his mind a lot lately, so he would like me to look into it…"

"Huh. If it bothered him so much, why didn't he ever look into it before this? Or ask you to do it when he first reunited with you? He was quick to tell me that I should consult with you on my case when I mentioned it to him."

"I don't know. I don't think he's telling me everything about it. But I have enough data to start a search, so we'll see where it leads. Maybe he'll open up more about it once we've got more information."

"Did he really 'disappear'? Or did they just lose touch with each other?"

"Robbie had run away before. His parents and the police figured he had again. Tyrrell never heard anything else about it, but that doesn't mean they didn't find him. Just that he never came back to that family and school."

"Do you want me to run the first few searches? I can put it ahead of my other skips today; I don't have any urgent ones."

"Uh, sure," Zachary agreed. He knew that Heather enjoyed doing the mundane database searches to track people down. He understood why. It was rewarding to find someone who had been missing. More so when it was a friend or family member who was looking for them than a creditor or enforcement agency. It would be nice if Heather could find Robbie for Tyrrell. "Do the basic searches and see if you find anything promising. I've got other things to do and will circle back to it later."

He switched over to the task management app to add a task for himself to review Heather's results later in the day, and watched tasks magically appear as Heather typed them in on her end. She was very efficient. He was lucky to have her helping him out.

"Looks good," he confirmed. "Message me when you're done."

"Will do," she agreed cheerfully. Zachary was about to hang up the call when she spoke again. "Do you think this is legit?" she asked. "I mean... is Tyrrell telling the truth about why he wants to find this guy? You really think it was someone he knew in high school and now he just wants to reconnect with him because you were talking to Jennifer?"

Zachary preferred not to examine Tyrrell's motives. Maybe because, like Heather, he was skeptical of the story. Tyrrell's description of how Robbie had disappeared sounded fine at first blush, but Tyrrell's decision to look for him now and his suggestion that Robbie's disappearance was distracting him from his work at the foundation were suspect.

Tyrrell had lied and hidden things from Zachary before. He had a habit of telling Zachary what he thought he wanted to hear and obscuring what was really going on. He told him how he had tracked down Zachary, Heather, and Joss, but not about finding out they had siblings. How he had hidden his relapse from them and denied that he was drinking again, even when confronted with the evidence. How he had disappeared on binges at various times during his life when things had gotten too difficult, dropping out of sight for weeks or months at a time with no explanation to his wife, children, or the others who loved him.

Zachary didn't want to think that Tyrrell might be lying to him again or shading the truth to make it more palatable to Zachary. Bringing up Zachary's recent reunion with Jennifer was meant to make his desire to track down his old school friend seem more normal and relevant, but Zachary wasn't sure it was really the truth.

"I don't know," he admitted. "And right now, I don't want to know. Let's see what we find, and then we can decide how to handle it."

"Roger," she agreed. "I'll let you know what I find."

6

Zachary was not surprised when Heather reported that she had been unable to find any trace of Robert Elder. It wasn't an uncommon name, so there were several Robert Elders on social media platforms that they could look into further, but none of them appeared to match the details that Tyrrell had given to Zachary. As far as the various government databases, creditor checks, and phone directories went, there were no matches.

"No Robert Elders in the old neighborhood," Heather said, going down her list of searches. "No Robert Elders with that birth date or anything close to it. No Robert Elders with a previous address in the neighborhood. I've requested public records to see if Tyrrell might have remembered any of it wrong, but I don't see any sign that the guy lived in Vermont or any of the nearby states any time in the past twenty years. I've requested courthouse records in case he legally changed his name. I'll have to comb through the social media stuff and national searches to see if I can match anything up, but… it doesn't look like he ever went back home."

"Okay. You can dig deeper into those, and I'll start tracking down people who knew him. See if I can find more information about him that would help point us in the right direction."

"How will you find people who knew him?"

"I'm going to see what Vince and Mindy remember. Dig into any high school alumni stuff I can find. Yearbooks, reunion committee, that kind of thing. There will be people in the neighborhood who remember him."

Zachary figured Mindy was probably the best source for information initially. Even though she was the youngest, she had been the one who was the most helpful when he had talked to her and Vince after Tyrrell's disappearance.

It had been his first conversation with them since they were separated as children. Before that, Tyrrell had kept them separate, saying that Mindy and Vince were not ready to meet Zachary yet. But they hadn't been upset when Zachary had called and had been happy to meet with him and provide whatever information they could to help Zachary track down Tyrrell and ensure he was okay. It wasn't the first time Tyrrell had disappeared.

Mindy had been more talkative than Vince. Less careful of what she said. She was the one who had revealed the existence of their DNA half-siblings.

Zachary wondered briefly whether Robert Elder could be related to them but, after considering it for a few seconds, rejected the idea. The chances that another unknown sibling had ended up in the same school as Tyrrell after they had entered the system seemed extremely unlikely.

Mindy answered the phone after a few rings. Because it had taken her time to get to her phone or to wipe her hands clean, or because she had been trying to decide whether to answer Zachary's call?

"Zachary. Hey, how is it going?"

"Hi, Mindy. I'm good. How about you?"

There was a slight hesitation before she assured him she was fine and waited to see what he wanted.

"I'm working on a job for Tyrrell," Zachary told her. "And I wondered if you could remember some stuff from back when you guys were in high school. Or junior high."

"Junior high." She blew out a breath. "Well, that's asking an awful lot," she told him with a giggle.

"I can remember some stuff from high school and I'm *much* older than you are," Zachary teased.

"Well, I can't promise anything, but… I'm willing to give it a go."

"It has to do with a friend of Tyrrell's. Do you remember Robbie Elder?"

"Robbie. Yeah, I remember him. He and Tyrrell hung out a lot."

At least that part hadn't been a lie. Tyrrell wasn't looking for Robbie for another reason and pretending they had been friends to get Zachary to help him.

"Do you remember what happened to him?"

There was silence as Mindy considered this. "Man, it was so long ago, Zach… and he wasn't my friend; he was Tyrrell's. I don't think Mom and Dad liked him. Probably figured he was a bad influence on us younger kids."

"Was he that type? In trouble a lot?"

"Yeah, that was the impression I got, though I don't know if he actually had a juvie record or any convictions. He had that kind of rep. A troublemaker. Bad boy."

"Did he get Tyrrell into trouble?"

"They probably both got each other into trouble. Tyrrell wasn't exactly an angel either. I don't know what kind of stuff they got into together, but Tyrrell was drinking, staying out late. I don't know if he was into weed or any other drugs. I don't think so. But Robbie, I got the feeling that he was into *all* the drugs."

"But you didn't know anything for sure."

"No. Probably just bits of overheard conversations or him bragging about all the stupid stuff they did, showing off to the younger, naive siblings."

Zachary had seen that type of dynamic.

"Do you remember anything about Robbie disappearing? Or what might have happened to him?"

"Robbie disappearing?" Mindy echoed. "Uh… yeah, I guess I kind of do. I remember the police showing up at the house asking about him."

That confirmed another piece of Tyrrell's story.

"But Robbie wasn't staying with you?"

"No. No way. Mom would have freaked."

"And Tyrrell couldn't have been hiding him? Letting him sleep in the spare room or basement without telling anyone?"

"No. We would have known that. It wasn't a big house. He couldn't have kept a secret like that. And Tyrrell was really upset. I don't think he could have put on an act like that."

Having seen Tyrrell lie, Zachary doubted that. "An act like what?"

"I remember him yelling at the cops that they had to find Robbie. That something had happened to him and they needed to find out what. He was… probably drinking a lot. I remember him being very emotional. Mostly anger in front of the adults, but… I saw him crying in his room too. When he thought he was alone."

Zachary had to concede that it probably wasn't just an act. Teen boys, especially ones who drank and hung out with tough friends to make themselves feel better, did not want people to see them crying. Tyrrell wouldn't have cried to get attention or convince people that he didn't know where Robbie was. Tears in private meant that he really had been upset or worried about what had happened to his friend. Or that he was feeling sorry for himself for his loss.

"And none of you ever heard anything about what had happened to Robbie? Whether he was found and went back to his parents or another foster home? You never saw him around the neighborhood or heard any rumors about what had happened to him?"

There was a hesitation or period of consideration before Mindy answered. "No. He never came back. I never heard anything like that."

"But...?" Zachary prompted.

"Nothing. Just... I mean, there were rumors. There are always rumors. Kids make stuff up. Teenagers like drama; if they don't have any, they'll create it."

"And there were rumors about what had happened to Robbie? Or where he went?" Zachary thought back to his school experiences. It was true; there were often rumors after someone moved away. Reasons they had left, where they had gone. Some were probably true, but others were more bizarre or unbelievable. Teens were creative. They were good at making stuff up.

"I don't know," Mindy said, backtracking. "I'll have to talk to Vince about it. See what he remembers. I wasn't in the same school as Tyrrell, so I didn't hear anything from people who actually knew him. Junior high gossip about what happened to a high school kid... it was probably wrong."

"You might as well tell me what you heard. I can follow up and see if I can get any verification."

"No. I'll wait. I want to see what Vince says about it."

If Zachary knew Vince—and really, he couldn't say that he did, he'd barely met the man—he would tell Mindy to keep shut and not say anything about it. That it wasn't any of her business and she shouldn't go around spreading rumors.

"Now you've got me curious," Zachary persisted, hoping to coax Mindy into telling him about it. "I understand that it's just a rumor, but... what did you hear in the junior high?"

He could picture her sitting back, shoulders squared, and shaking her head. "No. I'll tell you later. Maybe. See what Vince thinks."

He was glad that Vince and Mindy had each other and that they had a good relationship and could rely on each other. But he couldn't help wondering if maybe Vince and Mindy were too close and Mindy relied upon Vince a little too much. She needed to develop some independence and make her own choices without going back to Vince. They weren't teenagers anymore. Mindy should have her own life and opinions by now.

"Okay," he conceded, wanting to keep her on the line longer. If he argued, she would probably just shut him down. "I wonder what else was going on around that time. Anything in Tyrrell's life especially. Why was he so close to this guy? How did he deal with it when it became obvious that Robbie was never coming back again? It sounds like they were pretty close. Not just guys who happened to go the same places and hang out some of the time."

"They *were* close. I don't remember Tyrrell having very many friends as we were growing up. He fought a lot. Not just at school, but with everyone. He fought back against Mom and Dad and any rules they tried to enforce. Against school teachers and administrators, and Mrs. Pratt, our case worker. He was always pushing everyone else away."

"You and Vince too?"

"Sometimes. He was usually pretty good to us. Protective. Helping us or giving us things that he thought we needed. But sometimes he fought us too. Told us that we were babies and to leave him alone. That he didn't want us around. Getting mad at us for following the rules and doing what Mom and Dad said. Said that we were... brown nosers, whatever other words kids use to criticize someone who sucks up to authorities. But we weren't," Mindy's voice changed slightly. Higher, wanting to plead her case and make sure that Zachary understood. "We were just... we were kids. We tried to do what we were told and follow the rules, but we weren't suck-ups or too submissive. We just loved our mom and dad."

"Like you're supposed to," Zachary agreed. "It was different for Tyrrell. I know he was only a few years older than you, but he'd been through a lot of stuff in those developmental years. It's not his fault that he was so... rebellious. No more than it was yours because you attached to your adoptive parents. You just had different life experiences. You got out in time... Tyrrell didn't."

"I guess. It's hard for me to see it, because I just hear the things that Mom and Dad said about him. That he needed to get his head on straight and start making some good choices. That he could behave if he wanted to. That he just needed to try harder."

"He didn't get the therapy that he needed. If it would have

helped at that point. They didn't know much about how to treat trauma yet... I went through the same thing. They just thought that I needed stronger discipline. But that just..." Zachary shook his head. He thought the rest instead of saying it out loud. That the discipline, the efforts to force him to behave like the normal kids, the kids who grew up in homes where they were loved and protected, just traumatized him further. Force was no way to heal a kid who had been abused and neglected.

"Well, anyway," Mindy said abruptly. "They tried to help him. They tried to do the right thing. When Robbie disappeared... T was going through a rough patch. Drinking a lot, getting in trouble, mouthing off, not going to school or doing what he was told. A 'troubled kid' is what they called him back then. And maybe they didn't have the right kind of therapy back then, but they tried. They sent him away to one of those boot camps."

Zachary's stomach clenched at the thought. He had managed to avoid getting put into a program like that. He had been withdrawn rather than angry and rebellious. But he knew kids who had been through boot camps or other programs designed to break kids down in order to build them up into properly conforming members of society. He'd heard about the kinds of abuses that went on in those camps. Camps that sometimes ended up killing the kids they were trying to save.

He swallowed. "How long was T away?"

"I don't know. I think maybe six weeks, a couple of months. Something like that."

"And when he came back?"

"What?"

"What was he like? Had things changed?"

"Well... I guess. I mean, they always dried him out, and I think that was the main thing. He always behaved better if he wasn't drinking. But then he'd go back to it again when things got stressful. He was... kind of aloof. He was nice to us and didn't yell or tell us what to do. But he didn't talk to us anymore, either. He wasn't like the same Tyrrell who went away. He wasn't close, trying to protect us. Just... some guy who lived there."

They'd managed to break his only attachments, his ties to his brother and sister. Zachary could picture zombie Tyrrell, an empty shell, walking around empty and doing what he was told to, just waiting for his chance to escape. If he hadn't lost that desire too.

"Was that... it must have been pretty close to graduation for him. And then he started at college?"

"Umm... yeah, that sounds about right. He worked over the summer. Had some kind of construction job. Something outside. But it made good money, enough to set him up for school fees for at least the first semester."

"Did he have any supports when he aged out? Did he stay at a dorm?"

Mindy's tone was puzzled. "Aged out?"

Zachary remembered belatedly that Tyrrell hadn't been in foster care like he had. Turning eighteen didn't mean that he was dumped on the street.

"I mean... did he stay home? Or did he go away to school?"

"He stayed home. He couldn't have afforded to pay for board as well as school itself. He had a couple of really good years. College was better than high school. He wasn't fighting. He went to his classes. He took some remedial classes because he hadn't learned everything he was supposed to in high school, but he upgraded, worked hard, and got his degree."

Zachary wondered how well Tyrrell had really done during that time. He had held things together and had managed to stay sober and complete his schooling, but how had he been emotionally? Had he stayed distant, as Mindy had noticed, or had he been able to put whatever had happened to him in boot camp behind him?

"And did you ever hear him talk about Robbie again? About what had happened to him? Did he want to know if he had been found when he got back from... that place?"

"No. I had kind of forgotten all about Robbie. It was just sort of... a blip in our lives. Tyrrell had been friends with him for a few months, and then he was gone. There was a lot of other stuff going on. I remember him, but I don't. He was never allowed to hang out around us."

Zachary jotted down a couple of notes. He should have written more during their conversation. But then, not much of it was anything to do with Robbie and what had happened to him.

"Will you get back to me after you talk to Vince? I'd like to hear what some of the rumors were after Robbie disappeared. Some of them might have a thread of truth."

"Sure," Mindy agreed, but she didn't sound very committed. Maybe she would, but most likely he would have to call her back.

7

Heather had uncovered records of Robert Elder's birth, which gave them the names of his biological parents. Zachary still suspected that Robbie probably went home at some point. He would try to return to his parents if things got too hot for him in Clintock, where Vince, Mindy, Tyrrell, and their parents, the Millers had been living. Or at least back to the old neighborhood, where there had been someone else who could help him out. An old schoolteacher who had befriended him or someone who had said that they would help him out at some point.

But it wasn't a conversation to be held over the phone. Zachary checked the time and called Kenzie at the medical examiner's office.

"Hi, Zachary." She sounded tired but cheerful. Not a day that had been too stressful. "How has your day been?"

"Been working a bit on this new case for Tyrrell. Mostly dead ends."

"That's too bad. Are you going to be able to find him? Or has he really gone off the grid?"

"I'm not sure at this point. Too early to say for sure. We've got a number of inquiries out that might take a few days before they produce anything. Public records, microfilm, that kind of thing is always slow. Assuming the original records weren't destroyed by a flood or black mold."

"Right. Well, I hope something turns up."

"I've got a line on his biological parents. I was thinking... that I might go talk to them today. But it's getting a little late, which means I won't be home for supper. But hopefully... back early evening so we can still spend time together."

Zachary listened for any change in her voice indicating whether she was upset about the suggestion.

"It's not like it's urgent," Kenzie pointed out. "He's already been missing for over twenty years."

"Well... yes, that's true."

"Why don't you leave it until tomorrow? What's the hurry?"

"I just figured they're more likely to be home during the evening than the workday. If I try to set something up for tomorrow, they probably won't be able to do it until later in the day anyway. So, then I would be away for supper tomorrow instead of today."

"Or maybe the weekend."

"Maybe..." Zachary didn't like seeing it getting pushed out further into the future. "Tomorrow is supposed to be date night, so it would be better if it were tonight."

"Or next week."

Zachary opened his mouth to protest, then heard the warble in her voice. Teasing him. Knowing that pushing it out further and further would get him more anxious about it.

"I guess if it has to be tomorrow, we'll just have to cancel date night," he told her. "Too bad, because I was planning something really nice..."

Of course, he didn't have anything planned yet. They usually decided on something last minute. Now he was going to have to come up with something good.

"Fine," Kenzie laughed. "Do it tonight, then."

"Are you sure? If you really want to have dinner together tonight..."

"Go on. Go today. Get it done, so you don't have a stroke trying to schedule it."

Zachary just hoped that Robbie's parents would be home. He would be pretty embarrassed if he went to all of the trouble to make sure that it was okay with Kenzie and then was not able to do it.

8

A man of around Zachary's age answered the door when he rang the doorbell, expecting it to be opened by George or Kathy Elder. And someone Zachary's age was not old enough to be the parent of someone Tyrrell's age. Zachary immediately started going over the details that had led him there in his mind, trying to figure out where they had made a mistake.

"Yes?" the man asked a little forcefully when Zachary didn't immediately say what he wanted. "If you're selling something, we're not interested."

"No, sir. I was looking…" Zachary looked around at the neighborhood, evaluating it, trying to decide if he'd gone to the wrong address or if this Robert Elder had been a different Robert Elder from the one they were looking for.

"Looking for what?"

"Sorry," Zachary refocused on him. "I was looking for George and Kathy Elder. I had this address, but…"

The man nodded. He looked Zachary over. "What do you want them for?"

"I had some questions… are they here?"

"Some questions about what?"

"I'm not sure I want to spread this around. If I could talk to them and see if they want to talk to me about it, that would be better."

"You're not seeing them without talking to me first. What are you? Vacuum salesman? Security systems?"

"No." Zachary could catch only a glimpse of the front hall. "But they really *should* invest in a security system. They're not badly priced for something basic, and they provide a lot of peace of mind…"

"And you just happen to have a recommendation."

"No. Call someone local. They can give you a good recommendation."

"Then who are you?"

"I had some questions… about their son."

The man blinked and his jaw tightened. "I am their son."

Zachary was startled. He had not expected that. "Robbie?"

"Robbie? No. I'm Aaron."

"Oh." A sibling. "Sorry. You surprised me. I had some questions for them about their son Robbie."

Aaron shook his head, brows drawn down. "Questions about Robbie? No one has seen Robbie in decades. Where did you even hear his name?"

"He was friends with my brother."

"Your brother." Aaron looked Zachary over and decided he was at least the right age to have a brother who had been friends with Robbie. He shook his head again, but motioned Zachary to enter.

He led Zachary into a small living room. The room was dominated by an oversized easy chair, which was occupied by an overweight, white-haired woman. There were a couple of side tables within easy reach of the chair, littered with tissues, books, glasses and mugs, plates empty of all but crumbs or smears of jelly, and other detritus Zachary didn't immediately identify. The woman looked across the room at a small TV. An old-style one, not one of the modern flat-screen TVs most people had now. She looked at her son and then at Zachary.

"Who is this? You didn't say that you were having a friend over."

She said it as if Aaron were eight or nine years old and had brought home a friend without asking first. Zachary shifted uncomfortably.

"No, he's asking for you. He said he has questions about Robbie, Mom."

She looked back at Zachary, her watery blue eyes large. "About Robbie? No one knows about Robbie anymore."

Zachary nodded apologetically. "I'm sorry to disturb you. I know you're probably having dinner soon. But I was hoping that you'd be able to answer a few questions about him."

"About Robbie? What do you want to know about Robbie?"

"He was friends with my brother back when they were both in school. I know this probably seems very strange, but do you think I could talk with you about him?"

Mrs. Elder studied him for a moment, her brows drawn down. Then she finally motioned to the couch, which was pushed to the side as a less-important piece of furniture in the room, sort of an afterthought. It looked very old, like something Zachary might have seen in one of his foster homes as a child.

He perched on the couch, trying to find a position that allowed him to face Mrs. Elder comfortably.

"Who are you?" she asked him again as if she hadn't understood.

"My name is Zachary." He paused momentarily, hoping the name would sink in and he wouldn't have to keep repeating it throughout the conversation. "My brother is named Tyrrell, and he was a friend of Robbie's when he was living in Clintock."

He paused again, waiting for Mrs. Elder to acknowledge that Robbie had lived in Clintock. She didn't say anything.

"He lived there with another family?" Zachary suggested. "With a relative or in foster care? Tyrrell didn't know the situation, just that the people Robbie was living with weren't his parents."

"He'd been having some difficulties," Mrs. Elder acknowledged. "He couldn't live here with us."

Aaron was still standing nearby, listening in, openly curious about the situation. He didn't jump in with any further explanation.

"Tyrrell was going through a tough time, too," Zachary told the older woman. "He'd been in some trouble. Acting out. Drinking. We didn't have an easy time growing up. So even though he was with a good family, people who I think were good parents, they weren't able to control him."

"I know how that is," Mrs. Elder sighed. She folded her hands over her ample stomach. "We gave Robbie everything he needed. We didn't raise him any differently than the others. But he was always wild. Always broke the rules and acted out, and there was nothing we could do about it. He was that way right from the time he was a little boy. People would look at us like we must be monsters or that we were completely inept parents because we couldn't stop him from acting that way." She shook her head, lips pressed together. "They could see that the other children were just fine, couldn't they? Did they think that we treated him differently? He was just..." she trailed off, unable to finish the thought.

Zachary wondered what she had intended to say. He was just a bad kid? He was just different? He was just broken? How did she see him?

"That must have been very difficult for you as parents."

"It was. He broke my heart. I couldn't do anything for him. No matter how many times I pleaded with him to listen, cried myself to sleep, went to the police station to pick him up. He just wouldn't change. He didn't want to change; he had no desire."

Zachary made another murmur of understanding.

"We had to do something. We needed him out of the house, away from the other children. I didn't want him to influence them to do bad things or to do anything that might hurt them. There was really no other choice."

"So, you found him another home."

She nodded. "They were good folks, and they were willing to try to straighten him out. They said they would make sure that he had strict rules and that he followed them. They could be tough with him when I couldn't be. They didn't have any other children in the home, so they didn't need to worry that he would hurt anyone."

"What was the name of the couple? Tyrrell couldn't remember. If he had ever known."

"Ernie and Jeannette Weylund. They were a family my sister knew. They went to her church. They had taken in troubled youth in the past and had good success with them. I hoped they could get Robbie turned around."

She stopped and looked down at her hands, fidgeting. Her knuckles were swollen and knobby with arthritis. Zachary thought she couldn't be much older than Mr. Peterson, the only foster parent he had ever kept in touch with. But Mr. Peterson, though balding with a white fringe of hair that was getting progressively whiter and thinner, did not act like an old man. He was still active and had hobbies and interests other than sitting in front of the TV. He must have some health problems with his advancing age, but he never talked about them. He complained about getting older, but he still acted like he was in the prime of his life. And his younger partner, Patrick Parker, seemed like he would never slow down. He was in better shape than Zachary.

Much better shape.

"Can you tell me what happened to Robbie?" Zachary suggested tentatively. He didn't want to upset her, and he had no idea how things had ended up. Not happily ever after, with Robbie going home and deciding to live out his life the way his conservative parents expected him to, with a family and a steady job and a mortgage. But that didn't mean that he had entirely disappeared from their lives. He might still go home occasionally, even though "no one asked about him anymore."

9

You know what happened," Mrs. Elder said bitterly. "Robbie never came home. I sent him away to live with strangers—people who would discipline him and be tough on him. I wanted them to turn him around. And he never came home. One day he disappeared, and they said that he had run away and maybe he would come back here because kids often ran back home. But he didn't. I waited, and I left the light on for him, and he never came home."

"I'm so sorry." Zachary had been hoping to hear better news. He thought of Mrs. Elder leaving the porch light on for her son night after night, maybe for weeks or even months, waiting for her wayward son to return. And he never had. "You never heard from him again? Not on the phone, no rumors or anyone else who had run into him and mentioned it?"

"No." She shook her head. Her eyes glistened with tears. "No, I never heard from him. Heard of him. Nothing."

"And the police... they investigated it, right? Did they have any thoughts? Any idea what had happened to him?"

"They said he was a runaway. He didn't want to be found and was close enough to being an adult that they didn't do anything about that. There would be no point in bringing him home if they found him, because he would just run away again. I don't think they looked. Not really."

"They asked my brother if he had seen Robbie. Went to his house to see if he was hiding out there."

"Did they?" She nodded. "Well, that's nice. At least they did that." She looked at Zachary after a moment of silence, meeting his gaze. "And your brother? How did things turn out for him?"

"He's had some rough times. He still struggles with addiction issues. But he got a college degree. Had a family, though he's divorced now. He's working for a charitable foundation, one that does a lot of good. For now... he's doing well. I hope he stays that way."

"You're very lucky. Things could have turned out differently."

"Yes, I know. We didn't grow up together, we just reunited recently, and I'm glad to have him in my life." With a lump in his throat, Zachary found it suddenly difficult to talk. "I hope he manages to stay on the path he's on now... and be happy."

"Children can cause you so much grief. I don't even know what happened to him. If he died, or if he's still out there somewhere. If he did run away, or something happened to him. He hung around with bad people." She shook her head sadly. "I don't mean your brother. I don't know him. But the people he used to spend time with... they were dangerous. We didn't want him associating with bad characters. Getting ideas in his head. Getting involved in anything criminal."

"Who were these bad people? Do you remember?" Zachary's heart quickened at the thought. Maybe she did know something after all. Even though she didn't realize it.

"I don't know. Gangs. People who commit crimes. Violent, nasty people."

"Adults? Or kids his age?"

"Other boys, I think. I don't know. I didn't meet them. The police warned me about him getting involved with them, but I could never keep him home. Never keep him out of trouble."

"And they didn't come to the house here."

She shook her head, eyes widening in horror. "Oh, no. We would never have allowed them in the house."

Most likely, they were just boys, then. Mr. and Mrs. Elder would not have been able to keep adult thugs out of their house just by telling Robbie he wasn't allowed to bring them home. If they had wanted to come into the house, they would have forced their way in. Maybe to see Robbie some day when he slept in and didn't show up somewhere he was supposed to be. But they apparently never had.

Zachary nodded sympathetically. He looked around the room. "Is your husband still..." he trailed off tactfully.

"He hasn't been around for a long time, dearie," Mrs. Elder told him. "It's just me and Aaron now. And my younger children, but they don't live here anymore. We keep each other company." She tilted her head to indicate Aaron.

Zachary looked at Aaron. "That's good of you. I don't suppose... you remember much about Robbie?"

It had been a long time and he had been pretty young at the time. Zachary assumed he was also younger than Robbie, not older.

"I was twelve when he left. I remember him... but he was older than me. We weren't good friends."

"You must have been... about five years apart?"

Aaron nodded. "Yeah. Five years. When you're a little kid, that's a long time. I thought he was a grown adult almost as far back as I can remember. By the time I was five, he would have been ten, and he was mature for his age. As far as I was concerned, he was a grown-up."

"Funny to think of that now," Zachary said. "I can remember when thinking a teenager or twenty-something was old. And now I look back and think..."

"Ten is practically a baby. When I look at ten-year-olds now, they're so tiny. So immature."

It was a good reminder for Zachary. He had been ten when he had burned down the house and been put into foster care. He had carried immense guilt with him ever since for all that had happened to his siblings. Finding out what had actually happened to Joss, Heather, and Tyrrell during that time had made that guilt worse. He had felt responsible for everything that happened to them. He had been trying to do something good. He tried to take care of his younger siblings and keep them safe and, instead, he had been the cause of the family's dissolution and the horrible things that had happened to them.

But he had been ten. A child. Not the monster or criminal that his mother had made him out to be. Incorrigible? Hopeless? He had let her put those labels on him and had carried them with him throughout his life, had believed them even while he fought them. But ten... as Aaron said, ten-year-olds were tiny and immature. How was Zachary supposed to protect his siblings at that age? How was he supposed to keep them safe from angry, abusive adults? To be responsible for their care? His therapists speculated that he had been suffering from PTSD even before the fire. All the neglect and abuse had made his home a war zone, and he had lived moment to moment, never sure where the next blow would come from. Was it any wonder that by age ten, the damage had already been done and nothing could reverse it?

"That's quite a gap in your ages. Were there other children between the two of you?"

"No." Aaron looked at his mother. "Robbie came before Mom and Dad knew each other."

"He had a different father," Mrs. Elder confirmed.

Zachary held himself back from asking who Robbie's father had been and whether he had been part of his life. Was there a previous marriage, and Robbie had grown up in an abusive home for those first few critical years? Or had it been an assault and he had never been a part of their lives, and Mrs. Elder had raised him as a single mother until Mr. Elder came along to marry and support her? Robbie might have come by his behavioral problems naturally, from a man who'd been violent and had poor impulse control, or from abuse or neglect in the early years.

And by the time Mr. Elder came along, it might have been too late for him to be able to reform his behavior.

"Well... thank you for meeting with me today, Mrs. Elder. I appreciate it."

"Are you looking for him?"

Zachary nodded. "I am. I don't know whether I'll be able to find him, but I'm doing my best. It's still early stages."

"Will you tell me? When you know what happened?"

Zachary nodded. "Yes. I'll let you know."

"I'll walk you out," Aaron offered.

Zachary didn't object that he could find his own way. Clearly, Aaron already knew that and had something he wanted to say to Zachary. They walked slowly to the door, and Zachary stepped out onto the front step but waited to see what Aaron wanted.

"Do you really think you're going to find anything?" Aaron asked.

"Impossible to tell right now."

"Mom has... well, she's romanticized this whole thing. Remembers the best in Robbie and says how nice it would be to have him back. I don't think that she really remembers what it was like. How it was like... a war zone."

Zachary was startled to hear his own thoughts fed back to him. Like a war zone. He had never actually gone to war, and probably Aaron hadn't either, but the way that they had grown up had been traumatic. And violent.

"When your mother said she had to send Robbie away to protect the rest of you children..."

Aaron nodded, waiting for Zachary to go on.

"Was that because she didn't want you following in his footsteps and getting into the things he was into, or because she was afraid of physical harm toward you?"

Aaron stared at the blue sky, not saying anything at first. Zachary waited, giving him time to think things through.

"I remember a lot of hitting," he said finally. "Not torture. Not beatdowns that left any of us crippled or sent us to the emergency room. But... it was definitely more than brothers bopping or wrestling with each other. He was explosive. And if he didn't get his way, well, you would hear about it. Or feel it."

"Sorry you had to deal with that."

"Mom and Dad were right to send him away. I know it didn't turn out well and Mom regrets it, but I don't see how he could have kept living here. He was getting bigger and angrier. The people that he went to, the Weylunds, they didn't have any kids. There wasn't anyone there for Robbie to take his anger out on. It was a better situation."

Unless the Weylunds had done something to Robbie. They could be the reason he had disappeared. There had certainly been other cases of foster parents or caregivers going too far on discipline and killing their wards. It was too early to discount that scenario.

"They did the right thing to protect you," Zachary agreed. He held his hand out to shake with Aaron. "I will let your mom know what happened to Robbie if I find out. But he won't be coming back here. That time of his life is long gone now."

Aaron grimaced and gave an embarrassed laugh. "I guess that's true. It's a bit late for him to come home to live with Mom." He rolled his eyes. "Even though I am."

"Well, you're not as old as he is," Zachary assured him, smiling. "I think that it's nice you're living here with her. It's good for her to have company and have one of her kids close by. Whatever the reason for it is."

Aaron didn't offer up whatever catastrophic life event had led to him returning to live in his childhood home. Or whether he had been living there all along. That was his own business. Zachary didn't need to pry into it.

10

D r. B had recommended that Zachary and Kenzie do something other than just ordering in and watching a movie on the TV for date nights, which was pretty much what they did the rest of the week and had suggested that they instead get out and see some sights together. Visit some of the tourist locations around the state, visit museums or other cultural centers, and open themselves up to some other experiences.

Zachary remembered being dragged around to all of the finest establishments by Bridget when they had been married and didn't tell Dr. B and Kenzie that he had already seen all of that stuff and would rather not. If Dr. B thought it was good for them to get out of the house and expand their horizons, she was probably right. Zachary didn't want to enable Kenzie withdrawing from outside activities after her kidnapping. It was nice to be home and spend time together there, but extroverted Kenzie needed to have opportunities to interface with other people in a relaxed atmosphere to help her to get through her newfound anxiety in public spaces.

Even though Kenzie said that she knew she wasn't in danger of being kidnapped every time she went out, her jumpy reactions showed that she was still very anxious about what could happen to her out there. Even if she knew logically that she wouldn't be kidnapped, her brain had turned on extra pathways just to be sure, and she couldn't just will herself not to be anxious when she went out.

So, he found himself wandering through an art museum in Burlington Friday night, trying to show polite interest in the various forms of art that they walked by, even though there was nothing there that interested him in the slightest.

"What do you think of that?" Kenzie asked, indicating a tall, skinny figure carved from a dark wood.

Zachary studied it and let his eye fall to the tag with the title and description on it. "It's uh... too skinny."

"Said the pot to the kettle," Kenzie laughed.

It was one of those metaphors that Zachary had never really understood, but he knew it meant he was guilty of accusing the sculpture of the very thing he was guilty of. "Hey," he protested good-naturedly. "I'll have you know that this is the fattest I've been since my twenties." He pressed his shirt against his belly and did his best to push it out and make himself look potbellied.

"That's pretty pathetic," Kenzie teased. "I probably weigh twice what you do."

"Twice?" Zachary knew she was nowhere near that heavy, but she had been concerned about gaining weight lately. "The day that you're twice as heavy as me is..." He couldn't think of a way to finish the sentence.

"Yes?" Kenzie prompted, waiting.

"Umm... I don't know. If you weighed twice as much as me, would I be able to do this?" He put his arms around her and kissed her, then tightening his grip, lifted her off the ground a couple of inches. "You see?"

"Put me down!"

Zachary let her feet rest back on the floor. Kenzie kissed him back, laughing. "You're crazy, Zachary Goldman."

"So they say," Zachary agreed.

"That sculpture happens to be representative of..."

He tuned her out. Even though he knew he was supposed to listen carefully and respond to her points about the sculpture, he couldn't focus on it. His mind went immediately back to his investigation.

He didn't like the fact there was no sign of Robert Elder anywhere in Vermont that he could find. He might still be there, under another name, or he might live in a neighboring state, or even halfway across the world and still be alive and well, but the lack of results did not bode well. Maybe not everyone his age was active on social media, but not showing up on a credit search or through any phone directory was unusual. It did not bode well. Many people in witness protection were not able to cut off ties that completely.

Not that he thought that Robbie was in WITSEC. Such a thing was highly unlikely. Robbie had been a teenager. He wouldn't have known anything worth testifying about. As common as witness protection was as a TV trope, it was rarely used in real life, and then only in the most extreme cases. Not for someone like Robbie Elder, juvenile delinquent.

"Zachary?"

Zachary came back down to earth and looked at Kenzie. She gazed at him, a half-smile on her face, eyes dancing.

"Sorry, what?" Zachary hoped he hadn't looked too glazed during her explanation. He didn't want her to know that he hadn't picked up a single word of her lecture.

"I asked you if you're finished looking at this one. Maybe we should go on."

"Oh." Zachary cast one last look at the tall, skinny sculpture. "Yes, definitely."

11

I t was their weekend to visit Lorne Peterson and Patrick Parker for Sunday dinner, a ritual that Zachary greatly enjoyed. It helped to keep him grounded and connected with his chosen family—the men who had been there for him for so many years before he had been reunited with any of his biological family. Dark years as a teen as he had been trying to get along in group homes and other living situations, the initial bright, warm days with Bridget before things had gone all wrong. Difficult Christmas seasons and watching Pat's tulips blossom in the spring.

It was still warm enough to take Kenzie's convertible, and he had driven the last time, so it was her turn. As much as Zachary wanted to drive himself, enjoying the calming effect of highway driving, he tried not to let his disappointment show and let Kenzie take her turn. She loved driving her beautiful cherry red "baby," which was one of the few luxuries she had splurged on. Kenzie came from money, but she was quite frugal, normally living on her earnings at the medical examiner's office rather than the family money she had access to.

"It's a beautiful day," Zachary commented. It was sunny and warm, but they had experienced a few cold nights, resulting in the first leaves of the season changing color. Before long, the leaf peepers would be out in full force, snapping pictures of the riotous fall colors. Zachary picked up the camera which almost always rested on his chest and took pictures of the trees in their last days of green. Change was in the air.

"It is," Kenzie agreed, resting her head against the headrest and stretching her body as she drove. "I love the late summer and early fall."

Zachary could have ridden along with his nose stuck a couple of inches from his phone the whole way to the Petersons', but he kept it in his pocket, determined to enjoy the sunshine, fresh air, and hypnotic pull of the road. Kenzie glanced at him.

"Nothing to do?"

"Plenty to do. Living in the here and now."

"Wow, impressive," she told him. She adjusted her sunglasses and rested her right hand on Zachary's thigh. He put his hand on hers and intertwined their fingers loosely, so she could pull back quickly if she had the need, and enjoyed the journey.

Pat had set up for a backyard picnic, so they settled in the lush surroundings of the backyard, full of trimmed bushes, pathways, and a couple of water features. When it started to get dark, tiny lights would come on all over the yard, creating a magical fairyland effect. But it was still sunny and bright. Pat and Mr. Peterson carried out a variety of cold salads and a big pan of fried chicken. Not the fast-food stuff, but Pat's made-from-scratch crispy chicken. Zachary always went home stuffed from Sunday dinners.

"So, tell me what's been going on lately," Mr. Peterson prompted, as Zachary knew he would. "You take on any interesting new cases?"

He was looking at Zachary, of course, because he didn't want to hear about interesting medical examiner cases. Too gruesome for the dinner table, and neither Lorne nor Pat enjoyed a good autopsy discussion like Zachary and Kenzie did.

"I'm actually working on a case for Tyrrell."

They had both met Tyrrell before. He'd been over for a number of family dinners and, in fact, Zachary had been at the Petersons' the first time he had met—or been reunited—with Tyrrell.

"What are you doing for him? I hope you're not charging him too much. I know he's working now, but he needs to pay child support for those two kids of his."

"I'm not charging him," Zachary assured him, "even though he is expecting me to. I'm just doing a favor. I have enough in the bank and on routine paperwork to cover things, so I don't need to worry about it."

"You made a good amount on the Godfrey case," Kenzie pointed out.

"Yes. Helps to work for millionaires."

"So, what is this case?" Pat asked.

"It's about a man—a boy Tyrrell knew when he was a teenager. He disappeared. Back then, more than twenty years ago. It's been on Tyrrell's mind lately and he asked me if I would look into it. See if I can find him anywhere."

"After twenty years?" Mr. Peterson asked. "That seems like a long shot."

"I guess it is, but a lot of people who go missing return home or never go far from their neighborhood, so I thought I might be able to find him close by, just living quietly in one of the nearby towns."

"But no luck so far?"

"Not yet. But I've only just started it. We've done a bunch of electronic searches, ordered public records, and I talked to his mother on Thursday. She's quite grieved at never having seen him again after he disappeared. I hoped he'd been in contact with her, but no such luck."

"Do you think he was a runaway?" Pat inquired, topping up everyone's lemonade glasses, "Or do you think something happened to him?"

"The police thought it was voluntary. He had run away before. He was a rebellious teen and was not living with his parents, and they figured he would show up on his own."

"They were obviously wrong," Kenzie inserted.

"Right... so we can't rely on their judgment. I'll be asking for access to their file on Monday. See if there were any leads that weren't followed up on. Anything that might mean something different to Tyrrell than it did to them."

"Will you be able to see the police file? I didn't think they would share anything from an open investigation."

"Well, they don't... but I can talk them into letting me have a peek sometimes. Or get an interview with one of the cops who originally investigated it. If they still have their notes to refer to, it can be better than looking at a file. A file isn't alive."

Even though cops could be grumpy and terse, Zachary still felt like he got more out of them than he did out of paper. He read faces much better than print.

12

I wondered whether I could ask you some questions about it," Zachary told Mr. Peterson. "You helped out with Ben Burton's case, because he had been in foster care at the same time as you and Mrs. Peterson were still fostering."

"Was Tyrrell's friend a foster child?"

"I'm not sure if he was officially a foster or not. It sounded like it might have been a more informal situation. Looking after a friend or family member's child at their request."

"They probably wouldn't have been a part of the foster care network, then. I doubt I would have heard any gossip about them."

"I know. I'm just thinking through scenarios. His parents—or his mother and stepfather—had to get him out of the home, away from the other children. They didn't want him disrupting their lives and setting a bad example for them, and he was sometimes violent toward them."

Mr. Peterson nodded, looking concerned, even though they all understood it had happened decades before. "Yes. You have to consider the other children in the home. You can't ignore the possibility of harm being done to them."

Zachary had a brief flash of memory. Mrs. Peterson saying that she wanted Zachary out of the house because he was putting the other children at risk. Of course, Zachary had never been a danger to them. But he had already been accused of trying to light a fire at the school and had hit one of his school teachers and, to Mrs. Peterson, that meant that he was, in fact, a risk to the other children the Petersons were fostering. He hadn't been able to stay there for long.

"So they gave him to a friend to look after. To see if they could get him turned around."

"An untrained friend," Mr. Peterson deduced.

"Yes. They wouldn't have to have any home study or background checks, no training in how to deal with the behaviors they were likely to encounter. No oversight by a case worker."

As much as Zachary had hated being in the system and having to deal with social workers all the time, there had at least been someone keeping an eye on things. Someone to act as a resource or to spot red flags if she thought that things were breaking down and children were at risk.

"Not ideal," Mr. Peterson said, nodding slowly. "Some people are very good at dealing with children and knowing how to handle discipline and behavioral issues. It comes to them naturally, or they have developed the expertise over time, maybe in the family they grew up in. But without anyone monitoring the situation, things can get out of control pretty quickly."

Zachary had been in foster families and group homes where the caregiver wielded an iron fist. Sometimes quite unfairly. He'd been hurt. Sometimes children ended up with injuries that needed to be seen by a doctor. But no one in any of the foster homes Zachary had been in had been killed.

Little Annie in the Bonnie Brown children's home, but no one in his foster homes. Bonnie Brown was a different story on many different levels.

"You hear about children being killed in foster homes sometimes. In 'therapy' sessions or accidents during discipline," he said.

Mr. Peterson looked at Zachary, who hadn't actually asked a question.

"I don't recall any children who died in foster care while we

were fostering," he said slowly. "There was talk of it in other juris-
dictions. In the news sometimes. Or things that had happened
back in the bad old days, before we started fostering, when they
didn't know as much about dealing with children with severe
behavior problems. I remember one of our caseworkers telling us to
call her if we ever felt like things had become a power struggle or
we didn't know how to deal with a child without physical punishment or restraint. Or if we couldn't reach her, to call the police.
Better to have the child removed than to end up injuring him."

Zachary shifted uncomfortably. "Did she tell you that
about me?"

Mr. Peterson looked at Zachary and shook his head. "I never
felt like there was a need to beat some sense into you. You always
tried to do what you were told."

And failed miserably at meeting their expectations. But
Zachary was glad that Mr. Peterson's recollections matched his. He
hadn't been the kid who always fought back. He'd been in constant
trouble, but it hadn't been because he was angry and defiant.

"But that was not the case with Tyrrell's friend, I gather?" Mr.
Peterson nudged Zachary's train of thought back onto the proper
tracks.

"Not according to his mother and brother, no."

"I would be very hesitant to put a violent child into a home
where the parents hadn't been properly trained in how to deal with
him and who to call if there was a problem." Mr. Peterson shook
his head. "That's just asking for trouble."

"You would have had Robbie removed if he had been in your
care?" Zachary asked. "If you had a child who was violent?
Wouldn't listen to you, drank, stayed out nights?"

"Yes. We generally dealt with younger children. We didn't take
on the most difficult cases. Mrs. Pratt convinced us to take you,
despite the accusations against you, because she felt like you were
not the hard case that you looked like on paper. And she was right.
It didn't end up working out, as you know... but I think we would
have tried for longer if there had not been other children in the
home."

"But not with an older child."

"Sounds like he was old enough he could have been put into a group home, and probably should have been. Yes, we would have asked for him to be removed."

"Did you ever have any runaways? Have to deal with a kid who didn't come home at night?"

Mr. Peterson chuckled. "Yes, of course. Everybody gets a runner at some point. If you're lucky, they are located in under an hour, returned home, you have a good chat and cry with them, and they go to bed. But when it takes longer..." He shook his head. "You don't know the panic you feel, even though it is not your own child, and you know they have run away and been returned safely before."

Zachary could feel sympathy toward the family trying to take care of Robbie. It must be terrible to lose a child and wonder what was happening, whether they were safe or not. The fact that the Weylunds had not called the police until later the next day, figuring that Robbie would be back, meant that it was not the first time he had disappeared overnight. They'd probably had to go through it several times before then. And when things had turned out the way they did, and the police had not found Robbie and he had not returned... it must have been heartbreaking, even when it was not their own child.

"What would happen once you reported a child missing?"

"Well... first call goes out to the police and the next one to their social worker. If it's a kid who is a chronic runner, they don't deploy a lot of resources. They search the house. Check out the places they have run to before, anywhere you think they might be hiding out. Talk to a few friends. See if they show up at school. A surprising number go to school after staying out all night. It's normal, and they don't know where else to go. That's where their friends are. If they don't go to school, their foster family, best friend, or back home to their biological family... things get more serious. The police start asking about suspicious vehicles or people who have been in contact with the child."

"To consider whether it was a kidnapping," Zachary said, and then glanced toward Kenzie, knowing that the topic would be difficult for her. She stared down at her plate, picking at the salads, and gave no indication she was listening.

"Stranger abductions are rare, but runaways are vulnerable. And if it took several hours to report the child missing, and then the police have not treated it as an abduction, but as a runaway, then it might be twenty-four hours or more before they start looking in that direction."

"And they say the first forty-eight hours are critical."

Mr. Peterson nodded. "We never had a child gone that long. As I said, we didn't take the most difficult cases and generally fostered younger children, not teenagers, so we never had one gone for more than a couple of hours. But I saw it happen to others, and it was tragic. A very difficult situation."

And as far as Zachary knew, there had never been any sign of Robbie or hint of what had happened to him. He had just disappeared into thin air. The fact that there had never been a body found was encouraging, but not being able to find any sign of him, no mention of him in over twenty years, was not. Zachary had to wonder if something had happened to Robbie rather than just having run away.

_____

13

Z achary had dealt with the police in Clintock about a cold case before. Heather's assault case, in fact. He had dealt with a number of people there, and wondered whether any of them would be helpful now that he was looking into another cold case.

He could put in a freedom of information request, but when he finally got the information he asked for—probably two years later—it would be heavily redacted and likely useless. He had to be more creative.

Detective Able seemed like the best bet. He was the detective who had helped Zachary out when he had been trying to track down not only Heather's file, but the evidence that was supposed to have been kept for later use. The evidence had been destroyed, the shortsighted bureaucrats unable to foresee the advent of DNA testing and faced with limitations on storage space.

"I'll pull what we have," Able told him tersely on the phone, "but there really isn't any point in you coming here. You're not going to be able to access it directly."

"I'd like to do it face to face anyway," Zachary negotiated. "You let me look at Heather's file…"

"That was different. She was the victim and authorized you to look at it. In this case… you don't have any kind of standing. It's just a cold case that has nothing to do with you."

Zachary didn't bother explaining what his connections with the case were. Because Tyrrell looking into his best friend's disappearance wasn't a special circumstance. Tyrrell didn't have any official standing and, therefore, Zachary didn't either.

"I'd still like to come to talk to you," Zachary urged.

"Well, come have a coffee then, but I won't tell you anything."

Zachary knew that was the best he would get, so he accepted quickly. Monday afternoon, he sat in the police department lobby until Able came out to get him. He was much as Zachary remembered him. Overweight, probably sitting too long chained to his desk. Close to retirement. Hair salted with more gray than Zachary remembered from the last time. He offered Zachary his hand, and Zachary shook, a little surprised that Able was showing him so much respect. Zachary had solved Heather's case, but a PI solving a case that a police detective should have broken didn't exactly recommend him to them. PIs were a pain in the butt.

Able led him to a small meeting room, similar to the one Zachary had seen there before, but not the same one. A thin file already lay on the table. Able sat down in front of it, motioning Zachary to the coffee carafe and cups on a sideboard. Zachary filled a cup for himself and a fresh one for Able, even though he had one half-drunk cup already on the table. Probably stone cold. There was certainly no steam rising from it.

Able took the cup with a grunt of thanks and found a second coaster to sit it on after having several long swallows.

"You were asking about the missing person report for Robert Elder," Able said, checking the label on the file folder.

"Yes, that's right."

"Over two decades ago."

"It was never solved."

"Which is why I can't release it to you."

"But you can confirm facts for me."

Able shrugged. No promise that he would.

"Robert Elder was seventeen when he disappeared? Is that right?"

Able nodded. "Yep."

"So, he was still a minor."

"He was."

"And the people he was living with were not his parents."

Able flicked through pages of the report. "Parents were apparently in Kingsley."

"And the people he was living with, were they official foster parents? Or just friends?"

"Not foster parents. Carers. They had joint guardianship with the parents."

"My brother knew Robbie. He said that the carers didn't report him missing right away. They waited to see if he would come home, first."

"That's what the police would have encouraged them to do. When you've got a delinquent like Elder, the detectives don't want you calling in to report him missing every time he gets home late. Wait at least twenty-four hours. Or call if you have some concrete reason to believe something has happened to him. Call around to friends and the hospital on your own. Then if he doesn't eventually show up..."

"Who were the investigators on the case?"

Able looked at the faded copies. "Robertson and Delaney. Robertson was the senior. He died of cancer a couple of years ago. Don't know what happened to Delaney. Haven't heard his name in a few years. Left the department, as far as I know."

"Delaney?" Zachary wrote it down. If the detective still had his personal notes to assist with recall, he might be able to answer some questions. "First name?"

"Harold. Hal."

Zachary nodded.

"Did they ever find any sign of Robbie? Any trail? Rumors?"

"There's not much on the file. It doesn't look like they got very far. Or this file has been purged and just the important stuff retained. Searched the home. Called the legal parents. Checked in with friends or usual hangouts."

"Were there any concerns that it might have been more than just a routine runaway?"

Able leaned back in his chair. "Hard to tell from the file how concerned they were at the time. Having looked through it, it sounds like Young Mr. Elder was a chronic runaway, so this wasn't a big surprise or priority. I'm sure it became more of a concern as time passed without finding any sign of him. But there is nothing to suggest that there had been any violence or suspicious circumstances." He shrugged. "What do you do? You have to prioritize your investigative time. A kid who keeps running away but doesn't appear to be in any trouble...? You don't spend a lot of resources on a case like that. I know you might question that years later, looking back and knowing that he was never found, but you need to understand what they were contending with at the time."

Zachary nodded. "I'm not criticizing the investigation. Just trying to see how far it went and if there is anything I can pick up on. Was there any physical evidence gathered that might be tested now? Who were the acquaintances they talked to? What places did they actually physically check out?"

"No evidence. The kid just walked away. What do you expect? A bloody baseball bat? There was no sign of violence."

Zachary waited for more.

"Known acquaintances... your brother was Tyrrell, you said?" He scanned the papers in front of him.

"Yes."

"Miller?" Able's brows drew down in a questioning frown. Did he think Zachary was making up their relationship, hoping it would get him somewhere?

"He was adopted by the Millers. He's gone back to Goldman now. I don't know if he ever actually went by Miller but, legally, that was probably the correct name at the time."

"He's down here as a known acquaintance. Some other boys. A Thomas Brown. Benjamin Russo." He shrugged. "Known troublemakers, from the sounds of things. Your boy was running with some bad kids."

"I don't think they were involved in anything too serious, were they? I got the feeling from Tyrrell that there was underage drinking, disorderliness, not anything serious. He doesn't have any criminal convictions."

Zachary realized after saying this that he didn't actually know that was true. He knew that Tyrrell had a police record, generally for things like drunken driving or public intoxication. But Tyrrell could have had more serious convictions that Zachary didn't know about. Especially if they had occurred while he was a teenager and were therefore sealed.

Able shook his head. "Known to police usually means more than just underage drinking. I'd have to pull up each of their files, and they're minors, so they'll be sealed."

"Did the police decide that he had run away or that there had been foul play?"

"Runaway. Nothing to indicate that it was anything else. Investigated for a few days and then shuffled to the bottom of the pile."

And eventually, to file cabinets or boxes where it was forgotten. Still officially open, but with no one looking at it.

"They exhausted all of the leads," Able said. "Nothing else to pursue."

"Do you think he was just a runaway?"

Able pursed his lips. "The fact that he never showed up again, that his family and friends never heard of him again from any quarter... that would suggest that it was more than a rebellious teen running away. But a lot of things could have happened to him. He might have driven off a mountain or into a lake. Sometimes they find these wrecks years later. He could have ended up as a John Doe in some morgue somewhere. Or he might have changed his name and not seen any reason to return to his old family or life. Some people completely cut ties. Start over again with another name in another state or halfway around the world. They just found a woman last week who had been missing for thirty years. She was working as a missionary in some third-world country. She had dementia and started talking about her former life for the first time. DNA tests proved her original identity. But what good does that do her or her family now? Her mind is gone. She's locked down in some end-of-life facility. If her family showed up there, they wouldn't know her, and she wouldn't know them. Better if she was dead."

"Would you reinvestigate Robbie's disappearance?"

"To find what? All leads were chased down. No one is going to remember anything important anymore. Witnesses have moved or died. And no one knew what happened to him at the time. How are they going to know now?"

Zachary had to concede the point. He wasn't making a lot of headway, and the police wouldn't either. They could run a few general searches and, when nothing showed up, put it back away.

"Were the parents ever looked at as suspects?"

"Suspects in what? The boy's disappearance?" Able shook his head. "What would they have had to do with it? They were the ones who reported him missing."

"You know as well as I do that parents kill their kids and then report them missing or abducted."

"But they weren't even his parents. If they didn't want to deal with him, they could just send him back to the parents. Kick him out."

"There wasn't anything suspicious in their behavior? The police who investigated it didn't see or hear anything that didn't feel right? Not even the slightest suspicion?"

Able shook his head. "You would have to talk to the detectives who investigated it. Hunches don't make it to official reports. If they had a bad feeling about the parents, but no evidence they had done anything to him, it would not have made it to the file." He closed the folder, symbolically closing their discussion.

"Would you have suspected the parents?"

Able pressed his lips together. "Maybe," he conceded finally. "With what I know now about how often parents are involved in their own kids' abuse or disappearance... I would have given them a pretty hard look. But back then...? I don't know if they would have. Robertson and Delaney might still have had a fairly idealistic viewpoint of loving caregivers."

Zachary sighed. "Well… I appreciate the coffee and you taking the time with me. I know there wasn't much to share, but at least I have the official word now."

"Sorry I couldn't be of more help."

"You did everything you could. You didn't have to meet with me about it. I appreciate that."

Able nodded. He stood up, pushing himself up from his chair. "Let me know when you solve it, Mr. Goldman."

Zachary laughed. "I'll be sure to do that."

14

Ernie and Jeannette Weylund agreed to meet with Zachary, but there were complications. For one thing, the two were no longer married. But they both agreed to meet. Although Zachary suggested two separate meetings, they preferred to meet him together. For moral support, Zachary assumed. Or for each of them to keep an eye on the other and ensure they did not say anything they shouldn't.

After some negotiating, they all agreed to meet at Jeannette's house in Clintock, which happened to be the home they were living in when they had been looking after Robbie. Zachary hadn't dared hope to be able to get into the house that Robbie had disappeared from, so he considered this a huge stroke of luck. Hopefully, they would allow him to look around a little and get a feel for the place, and both of them being there together would help them to remember what had happened around the time that Robbie disappeared.

The house was pretty much the same as any other home in Clintock. A bungalow with white siding and a fenced yard. No kids' toys, of course. Flower borders suggested a retired woman with time to work on her garden. The two boring sedans parked in front of the house signaled that they were both still driving, but were not in the midst of any mid-life crisis that inspired them to drive an unnecessarily showy new car.

Zachary walked up the sidewalk, looking around the neighborhood in his peripheral vision. Were there others on the street who had lived there as long as the Weylunds? People who would remember Robbie from his few months spent there? He wasn't sure anyone would remember him after such a brief stay. But maybe they would, since it was unusual. The Weylunds didn't, he assumed, usually have troubled young men staying with them. And one who had disappeared might raise eyebrows and give them something to gossip about and remember.

No one appeared to be paying him any special attention as he approached the house. Zachary paused on the front step, trying to get his script straight in his head and to make sure that no one was watching. But the door opened before he raised his fist to knock.

"Mr. Goldman?" A woman with graying hair stood looking at him. It might once have been red or strawberry blond. She was about Zachary's height and looked him over curiously. "You *are* Mr. Goldman, aren't you?"

"Yes. Sorry, yes, that's me. I was just..." Zachary motioned to the doorbell, embarrassed. "Sometimes it's hard to think of what I am going to say when someone opens the door. To introduce myself and what I'm there about." He gave a nervous laugh.

She shrugged and waved him in. Did she already think he was a complete nut? Not a great way to introduce himself to the couple.

The man sitting in the living room waiting for them was tall, with a pressed blue shirt, a chiseled face, and completely gray hair. His ramrod-straight posture made Zachary wonder about the possibility of time spent in the military.

"Mr. and Mrs. Weylund, thank you for agreeing to meet me. I really appreciate you setting some time aside for me. And both of you meeting me together helps to save time and conduct this investigation more efficiently."

There was no point in telling them that he would have preferred to meet them separately to test their individual recollections. He would have to settle for meeting them as a unit. He could always follow up with phone calls later if he had to. Asking each one of them directed questions. But some people disliked talking on the phone and refused to divulge anything.

"It seemed to make the most sense," Mr. Weylund said forcefully. "Come in and have a seat. My wife will bring you some coffee."

Mrs. Weylund made her way into the kitchen. "Not your wife," she reminded him, without turning back to address him.

"Not my wife," Mr. Weylund repeated, rolling his eyes. "What am I supposed to say? 'My ex-wife' sounds rather awkward."

"Say Jeannette," she suggested from the kitchen. "I'm not your possession."

"Okay, Jeannette," he agreed grudgingly. "And you must call me Ernie."

Zachary nodded. "And Zachary," he agreed, touching his chest to indicate himself.

"Zachary. Not a name you hear a lot anymore. Good, solid name."

"Thank you, sir." Zachary figured that the older gentleman would appreciate the *sir*. Especially if Zachary was right and he had, at some point, been a military man.

Zachary looked around the living room as Jeannette prepared the coffee. It was a pleasant room, but it definitely looked like an older woman's home. Pastels and earth tones, handcrafted fabrics, and furniture that was styled like antiques but was new and mass-produced. Nothing masculine about the place. He tried to imagine what it would have been like when Robbie lived there. More masculine touches, teenage detritus, things not put back where they were supposed to be. Untidy, but more homey. A place where a young man could be more comfortable.

Though they were, as far as he could tell, a childless couple, so maybe they hadn't done anything to make it feel welcoming or homey to him.

Jeannette walked into the living room, moving her feet slowly as she carried a tray with coffee cups, sugar, and powdered creamer.

She set it down on the coffee table. "Please help yourself." She stopped herself before saying anything like "I'm not anyone's servant," but it was certainly implied.

"Thank you," Zachary told her sincerely. "This looks great." Coffee would, he hoped, help the conversation to flow better. Rather than waiting for Ernie to take the initiative, Zachary immediately picked up one of the cups of coffee and added a little sugar and cream, even though he didn't normally take them. He resumed his seat, sitting forward on a Queen Anne chair. He waited while Jeannette served herself, and then Ernie picked up a cup, drinking it black.

"So, if I understand what you said yesterday, you are looking for information on Robbie Elder," Jeannette said finally, after they had each had a sip of coffee.

"Yes."

"Why?"

"As I told you, I'm a private investigator, and I'm looking into his disappearance."

"All those years ago."

"Yes."

"What is the point in that?" Ernie demanded. "Who cares now where he went twenty years ago? It wasn't like anyone cared particularly at the time."

"Ernie!" Jeannette remonstrated, shaking her head. "Really!"

"Well, it's true. Kathy and George weren't bent out of shape about it. He'd run away from them before, too. It was no great shock for anyone. That's why he was living with us, to try to get him straightened out."

"He had friends. People who missed him."

"He didn't," Ernie disagreed. "The boy had burned all his bridges. In every direction. He didn't have a soul in the world who cared what he did next. Hopefully, he hopped a train across the country and started somewhere fresh. There was no point in sticking around here."

"My brother was Tyrrell Goldman—Miller, I mean. They were friends. Tyrrell was quite upset when he disappeared."

"Tyrrell," Ernie meditated on the name. He stared at Zachary, as if trying to connect him with anyone he had known all those years ago. "Yeah. I remember the Millers had an older boy. About Robbie's age. He didn't spend any time around here."

"No, I don't think they spent much time at either house. They had other…"

"Other places to make trouble?" Ernie suggested. "I imagine they did. He never spent a lot of time here. We tried to get him to follow a curfew, to get him settled down, keep him off the streets when he could be causing trouble. But getting him to come back here anytime was… challenging. He didn't see it as much more than a place to change his clothes."

"We tried to make it a home," Jeannette raised her voice in a protesting tone. "It was a safe place where he could do his school work and sleep and there was always something nourishing to eat…"

Not the things that a teenage boy cared about. Food, yes, but *quantity* rather than nourishment. A place to sleep? He could crash on a friend's couch. A place to do his homework? Who wanted to do homework? Not a kid like Robbie, who was more interested in hanging out with his friends and getting in trouble.

"How long was he with you?"

"About… six months, wasn't it, Ern?"

Ernie nodded. "About that. Long enough to wear on us. It was obvious at that point that he wasn't going to turn around. That he didn't care about second chances or starting over. He didn't do any schoolwork. We were lucky when he actually attended any classes. When he did, I think it was out of boredom. Looking for something to do."

"Did he get in trouble? Or was it mostly just not being where you wanted him to be?"

"He'd been in trouble at home, in Kingsley. His mother hoped that by getting him out of town, sending him somewhere where he didn't have any friends, with someone who could be strict with him, he would turn around. She thought that as long as you put them into the right environment, any child would flourish and turn out to be the way you wanted. If she just got him out of Kingsley, then he would be fine."

"But things didn't work out that way."

"Of course not. He could find bad seeds here just as well as anywhere else. He wasn't here three days before he was hanging out with other juvenile delinquents. Like your brother."

Zachary ignored the needle and didn't defend Tyrrell. Ernie sat back, looking slightly disappointed at this.

15

W hat can you tell me about the night he disappeared?"

"Can't tell you anything," Ernie said flatly. Zachary looked at Jeannette for her input. Surely she remembered something about that night.

"Mrs. Weylund?"

"I told you, it's Jeannette."

He nodded encouragingly. "Jeannette. What do you remember about that night? What stuck out to you?"

"Nothing particular." She shook her head slowly. "He said he was going out. We tried to talk him into staying at home to do some schoolwork and studying, talked to him about how he needed to buckle down and put some effort into it if he wanted to get his diploma. But he didn't. Laughed about it. Said that he could get plenty of money without ever getting his diploma. We tried to explain to him that employers want kids with high school diplomas, not dropouts, but he said we were stupid if we thought that was the way he was going to go."

She shrugged her narrow shoulders.

"So, he had something else in mind to make money."

"Kids always do," Ernie spoke up. "They think they know everything about how the world works. They don't think that we know what we're talking about, just because we've been on earth longer than they have. But we know the way things work. People put all of their time into chasing dreams, thinking they can strike it rich without anyone's help, without any education or references, but that's not the way it works. The people who make that kind of money, they had parents to help them along. Putting up seed money. Introducing them to people. Telling them what to go into."

He made it sound like Robbie thought he was going to be famous or start up a business venture on his own. But from what he'd heard of Robert Elder, Zachary was pretty sure that wasn't what Robbie had in mind. Or why he had left home that night. He wasn't an entrepreneur. He was hanging around with other hoods and delinquents, and their ideas for making a quick buck without any work experience would have been quite different.

"Do you know who he went out with that night?"

"Your brother. I don't remember who else. There were several boys who hung out together, but they were not allowed to hang out here."

Just like the Millers, who wouldn't allow Robbie to hang out at their house because they didn't want him and Tyrrell to be a bad influence on the younger children. So, the boys had gone somewhere else. Wandering around town, making trouble. Staying out late. And then returning to their own homes. Or not returning.

"What did the other boys say about Robbie? What they had done that night and where they had seen him last?"

"None of them were any help. They said that they had split up and everyone went their own way home. They just assumed Robbie was coming home like anyone else."

"Were there any witnesses who could put him anywhere? When had he been seen last?"

"You really think the police went looking for witnesses? They weren't interested. They said he would come back sooner or later on his own. Or be arrested for something else. But he never was. We never heard anything of him again."

"Did you follow up with the police? Ask them if they had

managed to find anything? If they had chased down all of the leads? Maybe if they thought you were worried…"

"We all knew he was going to run away for good one day." Ernie looked at his ex-wife. "Isn't that right, Jeannie? It was only a matter of time. We weren't surprised. And there wasn't any reason for us to hunt him down. He didn't want to be here. What was the point in trying to get him to stay? We figured…"

"Good riddance?"

Neither of them said anything for a moment, then Ernie gave a curt nod. "Yes. Exactly. We didn't want him here anymore. Things hadn't worked out the way we or his parents had hoped. The experiment was a failure. If he had come back after that… I don't know. We probably would have told him it was time to find his own place."

Zachary had been faced with the real world and how to support himself at not much older than Robbie. As soon as he had turned eighteen, he was on his own. It had not been an easy life, but he had been glad to say "good riddance" to foster families and group homes, too. He'd had enough.

"He was a lost soul," Jeannette piped up, apparently trying to soften Ernie's words. "There wasn't anything we could do for him by the time we got him. He was already grown at that point. If we'd had him a few years earlier, or from when he was a boy, that might have been different. But we didn't."

"Did you ever care for any other children? Was this something you did regularly?"

They exchanged a look. Zachary tried to interpret it, but failed. He waited to see if they would give him a verbal answer.

"We had other kids from time to time. Never for very long."

Looking around the living room, Zachary couldn't see any pictures of them. Whoever those kids had been, they had not been welcomed into the family.

"Did you ever consider becoming foster parents? Doing that officially?"

"There were too many rules with that," Jeannette dismissed. "You had to do whatever the social worker told you to do. There wasn't any freedom to make your own choices, to find out what worked best for each child. Someone was looking over your shoulder the whole time, telling you what you could or couldn't do."

"I guess so."

"That wasn't something we wanted to do. We helped people now and then through church or family connections. Most of the kids that we worked with wanted help. They appreciated us giving them a space to live while they finished off their schooling, or had finished out their pregnancy, or whatever. They knew that they could be a lot of worse places and were grateful for another chance."

Zachary nodded.

"But Robbie," Ernie said, shaking his head. "He didn't want another chance. He just wanted to do his own thing and didn't care who he inconvenienced along the way."

16

Zachary left the Weylunds, thanking them for seeing him. He wasn't sure how much he had actually learned from the interview. He would need to think about it some more and decide what new information they had given him about Robbie and their living situation. Had they just given up on him, kicked him out, or something worse? They certainly weren't broken up over his disappearance. Granted, it had been many years and they'd had a chance to put it behind them and divorce themselves from any guilt associated with it. That didn't necessarily mean they'd had anything to do with his leaving or disappearing. They had, at least, reported his disappearance to the police, which showed some concern over Robbie's welfare at the time. Or had they only been covering their own tracks?

He hadn't had a call back from Mindy, which wasn't a big surprise. Even though she had said she would call him, he hadn't been expecting her to. She was nervous about giving him too much information. She wasn't going to call him back to tell him that no, she and Vince had decided not to tell him any more. And likewise, she wasn't going to call him back to tell him more of the information she was reluctant to share. She hoped he would go on with the investigation and forget about her.

He dialed her number as he sat in the car in front of the Weylunds' house. She might not pick up. Not if she was that resistant to talking to him about the rumors surrounding Robbie's disappearance.

But she did. After a few rings. So, she was probably either busy or had taken a few seconds to consider whether to talk to him.

"Hello?"

"It's Zachary, Mindy. Hey, I'm in town and wondered if you wanted to go out for coffee or dinner. It would be nice to see you face to face again and have a visit."

Of course he didn't mention Robbie Elder.

But she would know that was what he was really calling about. Not that he just wanted a sibling visit. He had been trying to establish a relationship with her, but she had been fairly cool toward him so far. That wasn't going to get better when he was trying to pry information out of her. Zachary considered whether he should even pursue the Robbie Elder case any further. Not if it was going to put a rift between himself and one of his siblings. But if he dropped it prematurely, it might put a rift between himself and Tyrrell. His relationship with Tyrrell was stronger, but he still couldn't say whether it would survive a disappointment like that. If Tyrrell was really that worried about the friend who had disappeared two decades earlier, so much so that it was affecting his work and his ability to concentrate on other things, then he wouldn't be too happy about Zachary shrugging his shoulders and backing out of the investigation, telling him "Sorry, couldn't find anything out."

Zachary had promised to put reasonable effort into it, and he hadn't yet pursued all available avenues to find out what had happened to him.

"Oh, I don't know," Mindy hedged. "I have a lot of things that I need to get done today."

"You still need to eat, don't you? Let me take you out for dinner."

"That will take longer than if I just grab a sandwich around here."

"I could bring you something. Grab a burger. Just a short chat while we eat and then I will let you get back to your work."

Zachary wasn't even sure what it was that Mindy did. They had discussed work only generally. She knew that he was a private investigator, and that was what their discussions had revolved around. Both when he'd been looking for Tyrrell and now that he was looking for Robbie, the focus was on his work rather than hers.

"I don't know. I suppose," she conceded. "But I don't have a lot of time."

"What's your favorite burger place around here? Or do you want a wrap or something else? Just point me in the right direction, and I'll bring you what you want."

Burgers seemed to be just fine, and Mindy directed him toward an independent burger shop that hadn't been there when Zachary had lived in Clintock as a child. He placed the order she had requested and got himself a meal. She hadn't said anything about Vince so, apparently, he was not being invited to join them this time. That was a good sign. Maybe Mindy was getting more comfortable with Zachary. She didn't need that buffer anymore. And if Vince had told her not to talk about any rumors that had been going around when Robbie disappeared, she would have told Zachary not to come over. That she didn't have anything to tell him and he might as well go back to Roxboro.

He hadn't been to Mindy's apartment before and was curious to see it. She lived on her own, as far as he knew. There had been no mention of living with a roommate or boyfriend. The smell of the burgers filled his car as he drove over to her house, making his stomach rumble hungrily. He tried to remember whether he had stopped to eat lunch. Maybe not. He might have been too distracted by his investigation.

Mindy's apartment was on the third floor. The elevator smelled of stale sweat and garlic from someone's dinner, but it was a nice building, so maybe it didn't always. Someone had just returned home from the gym with their lunch. Sitting at their desk and eating while they got back to work. A lot more people were working from home these days.

Since he had called up from the glassed-in portico to be buzzed up, Mindy was standing in her doorway in the hall waiting for him. She nodded and stepped back, letting him in.

"I don't want to eat in the kitchen," Mindy said, glancing at the room as they passed it. The table was piled with mail, flyers, a laptop computer, and several empty or nearly-empty coffee cups. "Let's relax in here." The afternoon sun poured in through several large windows, painting the wall, ceiling, and furniture with a bright wash of light. The floor was hardwood, partially covered with a large, multicolored rug. There were large, framed photos on the wall, beautiful examples of Vermont scenery—green in the summer and brilliant splashes of color in the height of leaf-peeper season. There was a small TV on a stand in one corner of the room, along with a bookcase, which contained all of Mindy's books and DVDs.

Zachary was drawn to the photos. He walked over to them, studying the composition and looking for a photographer's watermark or print number in the corner. "Are these yours?" he asked Mindy tentatively.

Mindy bit her lip and looked like she wasn't sure what to say.

"They're fantastic," Zachary told her. "I love them."

"You do? Yes, they're mine." Her shoulders dipped down a quarter-inch, relaxing.

"I do. You didn't tell me you were a photographer."

"Just a hobby. I couldn't make a living at it."

Zachary grinned at the familiar refrain. Artists could rarely make a living in creative endeavors. Maybe working on layouts at a magazine or something of that nature, but not just by selling photographs, even ones as beautiful as Mindy had on display. He pulled the camera from his jacket pocket and displayed it to her.

"I don't go anywhere without a camera."

Mindy blinked in surprise. She motioned for him to put the bag of fast food down on the coffee table in front of the couch and reached toward him for the camera. "Can I see?"

He handed it over. He didn't bother to turn it on and launch the camera roll for her. She would know all the ins and outs of a camera like that.

Mindy sat down on the couch without looking, staring at the tiny LCD screen and starting to flip through the pictures saved on the memory card. Zachary let her look, digging into the paper bag from the burger place to get out their meals and arrange them on the coffee table while she browsed through his pictures.

"You didn't tell me you were a photographer," she told him, still immersed in the tiny pictures on the bright screen. "You just said that you were a private eye."

"Well, I'm both. I don't talk much about my hobby. But it was actually photography that led me to becoming a private investigator. I was able to help out a young woman I had taken some pictures of on the street, because my pictures established an alibi for her. And a friend suggested that although there were not a lot of professions where a photographer could make good money, private investigation was one of them. And I might want to consider it, since…" Zachary trailed off, unsure how to finish the explanation.

"Since you care about truth and justice?" Mindy asked, finally looking up from the camera.

Zachary shrugged, his ears getting hot. "Well… yes."

"What was the woman accused of? Was it a murder case?"

"No. Not as dramatic as that. Robbery. A hold-up at a convenience store. It was someone who looked similar to her—blond, same build—but it wasn't her."

"So they wouldn't have convicted her anyway."

"They probably would have. She was homeless, living in the area, known to police. She might shoplift from a place like that, but she wouldn't have held it up."

"You knew her?"

"No. I just… knew she hadn't done it."

"Because you'd seen her and taken her picture."

"Yes… and I just knew."

Mindy looked at him for a minute, then handed back his camera. "Those are really nice. I'd love some prints of some of them. I would pay you."

"I'd be happy to give you some. I don't make a living from those."

"Not the kind of thing you take pictures of as a private eye."

"Well… no."

"Do you take a lot of couples? On TV, PIs are always… getting proof of infidelity. Catching people in the act."

"No intimate photos. That's not part of what I do. If you want bedroom shots, I can show you where to get spy cams and how to set them up, but I don't do that myself. I'll get restaurant or theater pictures if they go out with someone else on the side, people meeting or sitting in cars. But no skin."

"You're a nice guy, aren't you?"

"I have ethics. I think most private investigators do, despite how you see them portrayed on TV. What you see on TV and in movies is fiction—romanticizing the profession, feeding people's fantasies. You don't see them sitting at a computer for hours doing skip tracing, following people around to see if they were actually disabled by a car accident or just faking it for insurance money, doing background checks for corporate hires, that kind of thing. Not the stuff that we really do every day."

Mindy nodded.

17

S he picked up her burger and unwrapped it. "Mmm. Love bacon cheeseburgers. I can't help it. I know they're not good for me, but every now and then…"

She was slim, so it didn't seem like she indulged in them too often. Zachary nodded his agreement. "They smell really good." He unwrapped his as well and they took the first few bites in silence, enjoying the shared repast. Zachary put down his burger, wiped his mouth with his napkin, and took a sip of his soft drink.

"So, I guess you figured out that I'm going to ask you about Robbie, and what you've decided to tell me."

"What makes you think I decided to tell you anything else?"

"Well, you let me come here. I don't think you would do that if you were going to say, 'I can't tell you anything. Finish your burger and get out.' That could be a little awkward."

Mindy snorted. "And this isn't?"

"I don't know. I'm pretty comfortable. But I'm assuming that you're okay talking with me more." He studied her. "You don't look like you're too uncomfortable, like you would if you didn't want to talk to me anymore and just wanted me to leave, so I'm assuming that you are okay with this."

Mindy nodded and wiped a bit of ketchup from the corner of

her mouth with the back of her hand. "I guess you're right." She sighed. "I didn't know what to say. Or if I should say anything at all. I don't want to get anyone in trouble."

"I'll be discreet about whatever you have to tell me."

"Like I said, I wasn't even in the same school. But there was lots of talk. Vince said it was pretty much the same at the high school, so maybe the high school kids talked to their younger siblings about it."

Zachary nodded. It was surprising how quickly rumors could spread between two schools, even twenty years before when kids did not have their own phones. Somehow, word still got around almost instantly.

"So people knew that he had gone missing and started to talk about it."

Mindy shrugged. "But I don't know how much is made up. Or if all of it is. I think even if he just disappeared in the night and no one knew anything about it, they would still have made up wild stories about what had happened."

"Probably," Zachary agreed. He had a couple more bites of his burger, waiting for Mindy to get around to telling him what she had heard.

"Well… they said that Robbie had gotten involved with some bad dudes and that he'd gotten himself shot."

"Shot?" Zachary raised his brows. "And then what? The police never found him, and that includes not finding his body."

"Then I guess they dumped the body somewhere. I don't know; kids didn't say where the body was disposed of. How would they know?"

"How did they know he was shot?"

"They didn't, that's what I'm saying. I don't know where the story came from, but you gotta figure that no one who was there and saw what happened was telling the story, right? Because either they would get shot because they were there, or they would be someone who was trusted enough not to tell what they had seen."

"Who exactly was Robbie mixed up with?"

"I don't know. Bad guys. Criminals, gangsters, I don't know.

We didn't know any of the big criminals in the area, so it was all just... shadowy identities, big bad guys. People you don't want to get mixed up with."

"Do you mean that he was mixed up with a juvenile gang? Some street gang? Or something more... significant? Like the mob, organized crime."

Mindy's eyes widened. "How would I know that?"

"Well..." Zachary pondered. "I'm not sure. Were they talking about him being killed by other kids? People who went to the high school or had graduated in the past few years? Or..."

"I don't know. I never heard any names. I never heard that it was anyone who went to the high school. I would assume that if it was, people would have known that. There would have been a name rather than just 'bad dudes.' But whether they were three years older or thirty years older, a street gang or a big crime syndicate... I don't have any idea. If someone like that wanted Robbie dead..." She shrugged expressively. "I guess they got what they wanted."

"And disposed of the body cleanly."

"Right. I guess. Since the police never found anything. But I never heard where they disposed of it. Him."

Zachary thought some more about it, picturing the kids and what they would have said or done. "So, they said he got shot... where?"

"Where? You mean like—in the head?"

"No, I mean in a car, in a warehouse, gunned down in the streets? Where?"

"Oh." She reached back in her memory. It was clear from her grimace and rolling eyes that this was not an easy question. Zachary wasn't sure he would have been able to do any better remembering crazy rumors that he had heard as a junior high student. That had been a long time ago, and he had blocked out much of what had happened at that age. Would he be able to recall any of it now?

"It was like... in a car. In a particular location, like a certain street or address. It was pretty specific. But this was before cell phones, and no one had any pictures or GPS coordinates or anything like that. No one could actually go over there and find anything. Whatever had happened had already been cleaned up."

"How do you know that?"

"Well, it makes sense, doesn't it?"

"But did you actually hear that it had been cleaned up? Maybe kids went over there for a look around? Drew chalk figures on the ground to freak people out? Some other prank to make people think that they had seen something at the scene of the crime?"

Mindy grinned. "I like that with the chalk outline. That's just the kind of thing that kids would have done. But..." her brows drew down. "I don't think I can answer the question. I don't remember... blood. Someone said that there had been a lot of blood. That he must have bled like a stuck pig. No one could have lost that kind of blood and survived. A gruesome scene."

"Who saw?"

"I don't know. Someone's brother. You know how it is. Lots of speculating, and then someone has the authoritative word. 'Joe's older brother was there, and he saw the car that Robbie was shot in, and everything was soaked with blood.'" Mindy's eyes moved around as she tried to access the memories. "He got in the car with someone. Thought he was going to pull something over on them. But then they just turned around and drilled him."

"He was in the back seat and whoever shot him was in the front."

Mindy shook her head. "If it really happened."

It made sense to Zachary. He had already been wondering whether Robbie had been killed. Why else hadn't anyone seen him again after that night? No sightings, no calls, no postcard, nothing. He hadn't used his name again after that night. He had totally broken off contact with all friends, family, and his caregivers. Zachary could see him cutting off the adults who were supposed to be in charge of him, refusing to be controlled by them. But his friends? He had never said another word to Tyrrell or the other boys that they ran with.

18

"ny rumors about what he was into with these bad dudes? Drugs? Gambling? Trafficking in weapons or sex? Dog fights?"

"I don't know. I don't know anything more than that; even that is a stretch. I don't know if it is right or not. I can't remember anything more, I swear. And that's assuming that what I was told or overheard was the truth. And how would anyone at school really know about it."

"An older brother?"

"A brother who saw it happen, saw a blood-soaked car, and got away to tell people about it? They had the sense to run but not to keep their mouth shut?"

"Kids can be stupid. Especially a kid who wants attention and doesn't think that any adults will ever hear the gossip he spreads around."

"I guess. I just don't buy it."

"And you never heard anything about it from Tyrrell? Are you sure?"

"Tyrrell? No. I knew Robbie was his friend, that they hung out together. He just said Robbie was missing. And Tyrrell was..." Mindy's voice faded. She looked away. She dug into the paper takeout bag. "Is there any more ketchup in here? They never put enough in. You have to tell them 'extra ketchup' if you want to get enough."

Zachary stood up. "Do you have some in the fridge? I'll grab it for you."

Mindy didn't say anything, but she didn't stop Zachary from going into the kitchen to see if he could find more ketchup in the refrigerator for her. It would give her a break. Time to consider what she wanted to say.

He glanced at the laptop she had left on the table, but the screen was black. He tapped a key on the laptop before opening the fridge door. Her email and word processor popped up, but nothing on the screen about a boy who had disappeared twenty years before. No email to Vince, Tyrrell, the Millers, or the Weylunds about the bit of history Zachary was trying to uncover. Just work stuff.

Looking through the shallow shelves in the door of the fridge, Zachary found a plastic bottle of ketchup and picked it up. He shut the fridge door again. "Do you need extra salt and pepper?" he called back to her.

"No, just ketchup."

Mindy smiled when she took it from him. She looked tired. She hadn't looked that way when he had first arrived.

"Mom always said I was a ketchup monster. Had to put loads of ketchup on everything. Fries, macaroni, steak," she shrugged and rolled her eyes at her own silliness. "I can't help it. I love the stuff."

"Me too," Zachary agreed. Why else had they run out of packets of ketchup? Despite Mindy's insistence that the restaurant never gave out enough ketchup, there had been what looked like a normal and sufficient amount when he had first opened the bag.

He had a vague recollection of a conversation with Jason, one of his DNA half-siblings, about wanting ketchup on his steak. An uncouth and unconventional thing to do. But it was what Zachary liked. And, as it turned out, Jason too.

"Tyrrell had a tough time after Robbie disappeared?" Zachary asked, as they smothered the remaining fries in ketchup and continued eating. "Did *he* think that Robbie was dead?"

"Well, he didn't say so…" Mindy sucked the ketchup off of one fry thoughtfully before putting it into her mouth. "Yeah, I think he did. When Robbie never came back. T just kept getting worse and worse. Yelling, upset, pushing Mom and Dad away like they had done something wrong when they hadn't done anything and were just trying to help him out… and drinking so much. They tried to keep it away from him. The house was purged of anything alcoholic, even cough medicine or mouthwash. But he would go out and get it from his friends or get someone to buy it for him. And he'd be so pi—so drunk that he'd pass out. They wanted to take him to the hospital, but the hospital wouldn't hold him. As soon as he was conscious, he would be out of there again."

"That must have been hard on them. And on you. It must have been stressful for you and Vince."

"Yeah, of course. We didn't like to see him like that. Didn't like all of the fighting and yelling all the time. It was a relief when they sent him away to boot camp. We just couldn't… couldn't deal with it."

"I guess it was the best they knew how to do," Zachary said. Increased discipline and physical punishment were not the way to help a kid who was drowning in alcohol, but it was the best that the Millers had been able to come up with. And it had worked out for them. They had kept Mindy and Vince safe, and Tyrrell had come back from the boot camp more compliant. Sober for long enough to finish his school year and get through college. The longest sober period he'd had.

Mindy rubbed her forehead with the heel of her hand, "I miss him."

"Robbie?" Zachary's mind immediately flew to all kinds of scenarios where Robbie and Mindy were friends or lovers.

"No. Tyrrell. The way he used to be. I don't remember a lot, and I'm probably looking at it through rose-colored glasses, but he wasn't the same when he came back. We didn't spend much time together as kids, but I remember him… reading me a story or tucking me in before bed. Playing horsey or other games with me. Telling us we were a family, and no one could ever take that away from us."

"You still are family. And with me, and Heather, and Joss too." He touched the hair at the base of her skull for an instant before pulling away, worried that she would be uncomfortable with the contact from a near stranger. "We're not kids anymore. Things aren't like they used to be. But we're still family."

"I know. It was just... a more innocent time."

Zachary nodded.

He had thought that Tyrrell was the same boy he had known when they had been children, just grown up. His eyes were the same and when he had first reunited with Zachary, he had seemed cheerful and open. It wasn't until later that Zachary saw the things Tyrrell kept buried—the anger, bitterness, and longing for the family that had been stolen away from him. Of course, Zachary felt all of those things too. His desire to replace his missing family had fueled his marriage to Bridget, but it had never felt the same. Being reunited with his siblings was close, but they could never experience that childhood again. A lot of damage had been done and things would never be the same.

19

o you have some time to meet?" Zachary asked Tyrrell as he drove back toward Roxboro. He'd needed the numbing effects of highway driving for a while before being relaxed enough to contact Tyrrell and take the next step.

He had a feeling that the meeting with Tyrrell would not be a happy affair. Tyrrell would try to pretend that everything was fine, because that was what Tyrrell did. But if he were distracted by the fact that he didn't know what had happened to Robbie twenty years ago, then the conversation with Zachary would not make things better. He didn't want to drive Tyrrell away, chasing him back to drink. That was the way that Tyrrell had handled stress in the past and, although he claimed to have new tools from the last rehab program that he had been through, Zachary wasn't confident that they were going to hold up.

And even if Tyrrell didn't fall off the wagon with the extra pressure that Zachary was going to put on him, his job might be in jeopardy if he continued to make mistakes at work and leave jobs unfinished.

"Sure, Zach," Tyrrell agreed cheerfully. "Does that mean that you've found something out?"

"I've been talking to several different people… and I have more questions for you. Some follow-up."

"Okay, shoot!"

"No, I want it to be face to face."

Because, of course, he hoped to be able to tell from Tyrrell's eyes whether he was telling the truth. He needed the extra clues from Tyrrell's facial expression and body language. His words and voice were not enough.

"Well, how long do you need? Should I come by the house now? Or are we talking about tomorrow?"

"I'm on the road right now, but later this evening might work. As long as you're okay with meeting with me. I don't get a lot of sleep, but if you have somewhere you need to be in the morning… if you have work you need to do…"

"I can do my foundation work any time. If I need to sleep in, I can put the foundation off until later in the day."

"You're sure you don't have anything on a deadline? And you won't be too tired to drive or to meet tonight?"

"No. If you've got questions about Robbie, I'm eager to get them squared away. I appreciate you working on this for me."

Tyrrell sounded upbeat and cheerful, not like he was worried about what Zachary would say to him.

"Okay. I'll call you when I get home, then, and we'll set something up. I'll need to make sure that Kenzie is okay with it too."

"Of course," Tyrrell agreed with a laugh. "You have to keep the wife happy! I know how that is!"

Zachary swallowed, thinking about *his* ex-wife and his inability to keep her happy. Was he doomed to experience the same failures with Kenzie? They hadn't even made it to marriage yet, not even a proposal or serious discussion about marriage. His relationship with Kenzie was good, but he worried about the future. If they had a future together.

"Okay. I'll talk to you later."

Kenzie had been prepared to join Zachary and Tyrrell in their conversation, but Zachary did his best to dissuade her. "I don't know if he's going to be very happy with what I have to say. Or… that's understating it. I know he's not going to be happy. And it's probably best if he doesn't have to try to keep up appearances in front of someone else. Or have anyone else to take his anger out on if he blows up."

"You don't think it's going to be that bad, do you?" Kenzie asked in disbelief. "Tyrrell's never shown any sign of violent behavior before."

Tyrrell's children, Alisha and Mason, had said that Tyrrell didn't hit, which was some reassurance. But they had said that he got mad, and he got mean. They didn't like it when Daddy got out of control.

"I don't think he'll get violent. I don't think he's that kind of guy. But he won't be happy, and there will probably at least be yelling and door slamming."

"I can handle that."

"I know. But… I think he would be embarrassed for you to see him out of control like that. And I don't want to… feel like I have to defend you. If it's just him and me, I can handle it. But I don't want you in the close vicinity."

Kenzie sighed. "Okay, fine. You're the best one to judge that. You're the one who knows what's going on, not me. Exactly how far away do I have to be? Can I be in my bedroom or office, or do I have to be out of the house?"

"I think just in the other room is fine. As long as you're not where he can see you, he won't think about you being there."

"Okay. If things go okay, and you want to have drinks afterward or just to give me a chance to say hi and bye, you'll let me know?"

Zachary nodded. Of course, Tyrrell might be perfectly okay with their conversation and give Zachary the information he wanted.

But Zachary suspected he would not.

20

They sat at the kitchen table with soft drinks and a bowl of chips, which was as casual and relaxed as Zachary could make it without the distraction of a game on TV or some other form of entertainment. He wasn't planning a fun-filled night.

"So," Tyrrell leaned forward in his chair eagerly. "What have you found?"

"I don't have a line on him yet. I was hoping that it would only take a few easy searches and we'd be able to track him down. But it hasn't been like that. I thought he might be back near home or one of his old haunts, using the name he had used back then."

Tyrrell nodded. "I've done social media searches a few times and haven't been able to find anyone that could be him."

"Yeah. Nothing on the more in-depth searches that I have access to either. For our work with skips and some of the other investigative work I do."

"So... you needed to look some other places, talk to some other people," Tyrrell suggested.

"Yeah. I've talked to his birth family and also the couple who took care of him in Clintock. To see what their recollections were about his disappearance and if they had ever heard anything from him after that."

Tyrrell nodded.

"But no luck there. No one ever heard anything from him after that night."

Tyrrell's lips twitched. He couldn't find anything to say.

"I think," Zachary said slowly, "That you haven't been entirely open about what happened that night. I think there are things you are not telling me."

"I told you what happened."

"No. I don't think you have."

"Zachary!" Tyrrell used a wheedling, half-joking tone. "I'm telling you. I told you everything I know. There isn't anything else to tell. He disappeared. And I was thinking, since you're good at tracking people down, you might be able to help find him."

"There is no sign that he survived beyond that night."

Tyrrell's face went sheet white. He shook his head. "What do you mean, he didn't survive?"

"There was a rumor that he was shot. That he had met with someone, maybe a known criminal element, and he was shot and killed."

Tyrrell jumped to his feet, pounding the table with his fist. "That didn't happen! He's not dead!"

Zachary remained seated, hoping that if he remained calm and didn't move, Tyrrell would take his seat again.

"What were you guys doing that night?"

"I don't know. Drinking. Messing around. Like we did other nights. Just relaxing and blowing off some steam. That's all it was. When everyone was too tired to stay up any longer, or too drunk, then we went home. Slept it off. Got together later the next day. We were just kids, Zachary, drinking too much and messing around with stuff."

"With gangs. With criminals."

"No!" Tyrrell's brow furrowed and he shook his head. "Not with criminals! Just with other guys. Just rebelling. It was harmless."

"People knew you and Robbie were doing more. Were you in an established gang? Trying to set up something of your own? Did you even know whether there were gangs already established in your area? That you might be stepping on someone else's toes with your 'messing around' and rebelling?"

"You don't know what you're talking about."

"People knew," Zachary insisted. He wasn't about to tell Tyrrell that his own brother and sister had heard he was involved with criminal elements and that Robbie might have been murdered by one of them that night. Tyrrell would be horrified to know that his little brother and sister had been aware of it.

"No," Tyrrell insisted again. "You're just trying to get me to say something. You're exaggerating and hoping that I'll tell you more."

"Then tell me what you're keeping from me."

"I'm not keeping anything from you."

"Tyrrell."

"Why would I hire you to find the guy and then not tell you everything?"

"Because you still think you can keep it a secret. But you can't."

"We were just kids," Tyrrell insisted.

"Kids can still get into trouble. And do get into a lot of trouble. So, what happened that night? What are you not telling me?"

"We weren't a gang."

"Were you hanging around with gangs? People who could have been gang members?"

"We were just kids, messing around like kids do."

"And you got yourself into something much more serious than you realized."

Tyrrell considered this. Zachary could see that he was close to agreeing. But he was still holding back.

"Did you know that Robbie got shot that night?" Zachary asked. "Did you hear something about it? Even just a rumor? Or were you with him?"

"I don't *know* what happened."

"But you had a pretty good idea."

Tyrrell was silent.

"You heard that he got shot," Zachary tried. "But you didn't know what happened after that. You hoped that he was still alive somewhere. Even though you never heard anything from him again."

"The cops never found a body. If he was dead, they would have found his body."

"Maybe. Sometimes people go missing and their bodies are never found. Vermont has lots of wilderness area. Places where it would be easy to bury a body where it would never be found."

"Don't *say* that!" Tyrrell snapped. "That's not what happened."

"You have been worried all these years that he was killed that night, because of something you guys were mixed up in. That's why it bothers you so much. That's why you wanted me to see if I could find him. You were hoping that he got away that night. That the rumors were not true. And that he might still be alive somewhere. Safe and sound."

Tyrrell's eyes were shiny with tears, but Zachary wasn't sure whether they were the result of grief or anger. Maybe even Tyrrell could not have said.

"He's not dead. If you don't want to find him, then fine, but he's not dead."

"I'll look into it more. But you might not like what I find."

"I don't," Tyrrell muttered.

"I can't guarantee the results. Just that I'll dig a little deeper. See if I can find out what really happened that night." Zachary met Tyrrell's eyes. "You could help me out. You know more about what happened than you are admitting."

Tyrrell shook his head. "When I left Robbie that night, he was alive."

Zachary waited, hoping that the silence would break Tyrrell down, that he would be compelled to fill it and tell Zachary more about what had really happened that night. But Tyrrell just picked up his glass and swallowed the rest of his drink. He was already on his feet. He looked pointedly at the clock on the wall.

"It's getting late. I have work to do tomorrow."

21

That went about as well as expected?" Kenzie questioned when Zachary went to her room to give her the "all clear."

Zachary shrugged. "You heard?"

"I couldn't hear much. Just that he was upset."

"Yeah."

"He doesn't like the results of your investigation? What's happening with it, if you don't mind me asking?"

"There were rumors that his friend was killed the night he disappeared. But T won't tell me what actually happened."

"So did he take you off the case?"

That gave Zachary pause. Of course it would have made sense for Tyrrell to fire him, to say that he didn't want Zachary to look into it any further. Tyrrell had told Zachary that he didn't have to pursue it if he didn't want to, but he hadn't told him to stop.

"Actually... no. He didn't."

"He still wants you to dig deeper."

"Yes. I mean... he could change his mind tomorrow, but..."

"Then maybe he still wants answers. Even if it is bad news. Sometimes, it is worse not knowing."

"I just hope… this doesn't start him drinking again. We both know how he reacts to stress."

"It might be coming out because he's finally dealing with it now. It could be a good sign."

"Do you think so?"

Kenzie shrugged. Of course she couldn't know one way or another, any more than Zachary could. But it was a ray of hope. Maybe she was right, and the reason Tyrrell was thinking about the past was that he was actually facing it instead of running away from it again.

But he couldn't erase the image from his mind of Tyrrell going to the nearest bar or liquor store and getting roaring drunk.

Getting information about what was happening on the street was tricky for an outsider. Especially when it was in another town and related to something that had happened two decades earlier. Zachary had a few contacts he could tap, but he wasn't sure whether any of them would actually be able to help him. And it meant facing his own past, which wasn't comfortable.

He drove back to Clintock for another round. As he drove the highway, he thought about the families of the boys involved. He had talked to Robbie's mother and to the couple who had taken care of him while he was in Clintock. And he had spoken to Mindy, and she had brought Vince into it. But he had not talked to Tyrrell's adoptive parents. Would they have anything useful to share? Zachary didn't imagine that they knew what had happened to Robbie or what Tyrrell and Robbie had been into. They might be able to tell him a little about Robbie and why they had not wanted him around the house, but Zachary already had a pretty good handle on that.

And he felt like talking to the Millers would be crossing a line. They were Tyrrell's other family, and Zachary wasn't a part of that. It would cause awkwardness between them. Tyrrell might see it as an invasion of his privacy, even if it was a logical part of Zachary's investigation.

Zachary parked at the community outreach center. It was not the most beautiful building. Probably as old as Zachary, repaired and renovated a number of times, with no landscaping to speak of. It did have a bright mural on the back wall, and any graffiti that had been applied to the other walls in the past had been scrubbed clean or painted over. It was clean and well-maintained, but it was old. As far as Zachary could remember, it had never had the staffing it needed to run its programs efficiently.

He locked the doors of the car and, after he got out, checked the handles to make sure it was secure. He glanced around to see if anyone was watching him. There were a couple of youth chatting and smoking and keeping an eye on him. But just because he wasn't someone they knew. They didn't appear to be threatening. Not gangbangers, just a couple of youths who lived in the neighborhood and accessed the services of the center.

Zachary checked the handles again and pressed the lock button on his key fob twice to arm the security system. He resisted the urge to check again and walked in through the main doors of the center.

The doors opened immediately into a large hall used for activities, lectures, and meetings of all sorts. There was a petite blond woman on the other side of the room, a clipboard on her arm, hair cut shorter than he remembered, talking to a young black man while gesturing with her free hand. Ivy Shane. She was facing Zachary and her eyes moved to him when she saw and heard the door open. She stopped talking to the man and opened her mouth to inquire of Zachary. "What can I help you with?" or some similar question froze on her lips as she stared at him. The black man looked at her with concern, then at Zachary.

"Zachary Goldman!" Ivy exclaimed, "How the hell are you?" She speed-walked across the hall to greet him.

Zachary was prepared for the vigorous hug and gave her a friendly squeeze in return. She stepped back from him slightly and grasped his face between her hands, staring into his face.

"You're looking good. What's going on? I never see you."

The young man joined them, brows raised. Ivy put her hand on his arm and gestured to Zachary.

"This is Zachary Goldman, a private investigator and old friend. And he never comes here, so this might just be a sign of the apocalypse. Or maybe the rapture. Zachary saved my life."

Zachary's face warmed. "Well, not exactly…"

"You did," she insisted. "I was arrested for armed robbery. Zachary comes along with his photographs, proving it was someone else. If he hadn't done that, I would have gone to prison."

"Juvenile."

She waved this off. "Doesn't matter. My life was basically over at that point, and you were my savior."

"Well, I'm glad to meet you," the man said, extending his hand to shake. "I'm Bruce."

"Nice to meet you."

"I don't know what we would do without Ivy," Bruce declared. "She's the only thing that keeps this place running. And the community needs it. So, I'm glad you saved her."

Zachary tried to ignore the burning of his cheeks and ears, knowing they were probably bright red.

"So, what are you doing here?" Ivy demanded. "I know it isn't just to say hello. You never come here."

"Maybe I could buy you a coffee?" Zachary suggested. "We could chat for a few minutes?"

She turned her wrist to look at a bright red fitness watch. "Sure, why not? Bruce, you can mind the store for a bit?"

"Sure thing, boss."

Ivy put her hand on Zachary's arm. "Lead the way."

He walked with her back out to the parking lot, arm in arm, like they were a couple, or she was an old lady he was escorting across the street. When they got out the door, Zachary could see the kids he had spotted earlier hanging around his car. Not touching it or trying the handles, but clearly casing it out, craning their necks to see what might be inside.

"What are you two up to?" Ivy demanded. "You don't need to

be hanging around these cars. If one of them gets broken into, what do you think I'm going to tell the cops?"

"No, no," one of them protested, putting both hands up. "We ain't touched anything. Would we do that? No ma'am, Miss Ivy. We treat the center with respect."

"You'd better! This is my friend Zachary." She looked at him. "Is this your car?"

Zachary nodded. "Yep."

"It's a nice ride," the boy told him. "They handle good, and nice stereo, huh? I didn't touch it. I swear."

"I know you didn't, because the security alarm is armed."

"Yeah, see?" he appealed to Ivy. "He knows we ain't touched it." Then he looked over at his friend, nodding. It appeared that they'd had a discussion about security systems when casing it out.

"You'll make sure no one bothers it, won't you?" Zachary asked. "You keep the neighborhood around here safe for folks."

"That's right!" The boy drew himself up taller. "We do. We know what goes on around here and we won't let nothing happen to the good folks here."

Zachary nodded. He looked at Ivy. "Is that good coffee shop still around? The one at the end of First?" He gestured in the appropriate direction.

"It is! I can't believe you remember that. Still run by the same folks, though they must be in their seventies or older now."

"They had good coffee."

"They still do."

"We may as well walk, then, and leave your friends to keep an eye on the vehicles."

Ivy nodded, giving the boys a stern look.

"We'll take care of it," the talkative boy assured her. "We'll make sure nothing happens to your friend's car, Miss Ivy."

Zachary and Ivy continued down the street.

"I see a look from you still strikes terror into the hearts of even the most hardened criminal," Zachary joked.

"Yes—but Tony and Jay are not hardened criminals. They're in the homework club and mentors to the little readers. They're not trouble."

"That's good. Glad that you're looking out for them."

"Just like you did for me," Ivy said with a contented smile.

Zachary could never convince her that he'd just done what anyone would have done. It was only serendipity that he had taken pictures of her and the kids she'd been hanging out with when the crime was committed. Ivy had been a street kid back then. Zachary had seen her a few times with her friends and envied her freedom. No parents to report to, no teachers, no case workers, no therapists. They were on their own, able to do whatever they wanted.

Of course, he hadn't thought much about all of the negatives. He'd only been on the street for very short stints himself. A day or two here and there. And he didn't like it. Didn't like the cold, and how people looked at him, or refused to look at him, didn't like panhandling or eating out of dumpsters or food that people bestowed on him, acting like he should be grateful. But Ivy always seemed cheerful and was always with friends instead of being alone like Zachary.

That had probably been a mask, even though he hadn't realized it. Her way of keeping the world at a distance, making them think that she didn't need anything from them. He was glad that things were good for her now. She was the neighborhood "mom." She had a home and the food she needed and borrowed rides if she needed a car, usually to help someone else out. She ran the center, as Bruce had said, keeping everything running smoothly.

22

_____

Ivy talked a little about what was happening in the neighborhood as they walked to the coffee shop, which looked and smelled just like Zachary remembered. It was strange to see the owners so much older when everything else looked the same. And, of course, the prices were higher.

"Do you remember my friend Zachary?" Ivy asked the old woman as she worked the ancient cash register with big noisy keys, everything manual instead of programmed.

Mrs. Ferris leaned forward, squinting at Zachary. She smiled, her wrinkled face creasing even more deeply. "It has been a very long time since you were here!" She accused. "Where have you been?"

Zachary laughed. "I'm in Roxboro now, Mrs. Ferris. I'm sorry. That's why I haven't been around."

"You should come and visit now and then. You come here in another twenty years, and I might not be here anymore!"

"You're right. I'd better come here more often."

She nodded her agreement. Zachary and Ivy collected their mugs of coffee and sat down at a small bistro table with two chairs. There wasn't a lot of seating in the old place. But Zachary had been counting on that. It meant that they were more likely to be alone and undisturbed.

Ivy sipped her coffee and set it on the table before her. "So, who are you looking for?" she demanded.

"What makes you think I'm looking for someone?"

"You're a PI. That's what you do. And you've been studying every person you walk by. I know you didn't just drop in at the center for a visit and a coffee. You're not attached to this neighborhood. It wasn't ever your neighborhood anyway. So, you're looking for someone." She pressed her lips together, thinking. "Someone who hasn't been here for a long time."

With that, she took another sip of coffee.

Zachary should have known that she would read him immediately. She always could. He smiled and shook his head.

"So, who is it?" Ivy asked.

"It's a long story. My brother, Tyrrell—"

"Your brother?" she interrupted sharply. "I didn't know you had a brother."

"We were split up when we went into foster care. He and the younger kids were adopted. I just met him a couple of years ago."

"Wow. That's really something."

"It is." Zachary's heart thumped as he remembered the excitement of his reunion with Tyrrell. The first family member that he had been reunited with. He had seen them all now, all of his siblings. He'd even seen his father, though that had not been intentional, and he didn't plan to have anything to do with him. "It was really exciting to have them back in my life again. And Tyrrell especially. We were close. Or as close as we could be. But he had a friend years ago who disappeared. Back when they were in high school."

"So that's who you're trying to find."

"Yes and no. I don't think… that he's still around. I think that when he disappeared all of those years ago, he was killed. But I don't have any proof of that, or of what happened. I was hoping to be able to find some witnesses."

"Who saw him killed?"

"Who saw something that night. Whether it was him meeting with someone else after he and Tyrrell went their separate directions that night or something went down in the neighborhood that was significant. Or… there was a rumor at the schools that he had been shot in a car, and there was a lot of blood."

"And you think it is a good idea to be asking these questions? Digging up these old crimes?"

"It happened a long time ago. I don't think it is something I need to worry about. I'm not trying to have anyone charged. I'm just trying to find out, for Tyrrell, what happened that night."

"That doesn't sound like a good idea to me."

Zachary tried to brush her concerns aside to focus on what he needed from her. "There are statutes of limitations. And evidence gets lost and people's memories fuzzy. No one is going to lay charges for whatever happened that night."

"There's no statute of limitations on murder, if that's what you think happened to this poor boy. The police will still happily put away whoever did that, if they have enough evidence."

"But that's not what I'm after," Zachary told her, exasperated.

"Fine, what is it that you are after, then?"

"I just want to know what happened. Whether Robbie is still alive, and I need to track him down somewhere else, using a different name, or whether he was killed that night, all I can do for Tyrrell is tell him that… Robbie is at rest, wherever he is."

"When was this, and what happened?"

Zachary outlined the timing for her. "What I'm hoping you can help me with is what gang activity was going on at the time, and whether any of the players are still in the neighborhood."

"Gangs. I don't know, Zachary."

"There are gangs, whether we want to admit it or not. Talking about them isn't going to make anything bad happen. Not when it's just between you and me. Who is going to know?"

Ivy stared out the window as if she were watching the people walking by on the sidewalk, but her eyes didn't focus on them.

"No one would know," she repeated. "But you're not going to

stop after you talk to me. You're going to keep digging. You want witness statements."

"I'll be careful."

They both knew that being careful wasn't exactly in Zachary's nature. Obsessive or paranoid, sure. But in the heat of the moment, too often his impulsivity overrode any care that he meant to take.

Ivy chuckled and shook her head.

"I can't believe that this is what you came back to me for. To give you gang intel on a case that's been cold for more than twenty years."

Zachary shrugged. "It's what I do."

She sat contemplating it for a longer period, staring out the window. If Zachary were a cop, he might have been impatient with her silences. But he knew Ivy and that she wouldn't be bullied into talking to him about it. She would have to work it out in her own mind first. Make her own decision about it.

"What was this kid's name?"

"Robbie Elder."

"And when did he disappear?"

Zachary gave her the date and a few more vital details.

"And who do you think he was involved with? Or what?"

"I don't know. Tyrrell won't tell me. He says that they were just out drinking and messing around. But who knows what that might mean. Messing around with who? Doing what? He says they weren't a gang or trying to form a gang, but I don't know if that's true. There were rumors that he was mixed up in gang activities, but no one has been able to tell me whether it was youth gangs or adults involved in more serious criminal activities."

"Drugs?"

"I don't think so. From what I can tell, booze was his big vice. But I don't know. If he had thought that he might be able to get into some kind of lucrative drug trade... you know what teenagers are like. They think they're going to make it big. Since he won't tell me what he was into, I can't really speculate."

"And he was shot?" Ivy asked, shaking her head. "I can't

remember anything like that happening. This is a small town. You hear about stuff like that."

"The rumor was that he was shot. No one can or will confirm it. And the police never found the body, so that's all it is. Rumor."

She nodded.

"Was there anyone around back then who is still around now? Someone who might remember?"

"Gangbangers don't live long. Or stick around in small towns. Anyone who was around then and is still around now is most likely cartel. Someone who's been in the business a long time or whose family is, and they were brought up in it. And you don't want to mess with any of those players."

"It doesn't have to be someone in a gang. Just eyes on the street. You still have some of your old contacts. Just someone with eyes and ears who might have heard what was going on at the time."

"The streets are just as bad as the gangs," Ivy pointed out. "People don't live on the streets for twenty years. Life expectancy isn't that long."

"But people who come in and out... come on, Ivy," Zachary said impatiently, "I know there are people around who would remember that far back. Or people like you who were on the street back then but have a place now, are giving back to the community in different ways. You can't tell me you don't know anybody."

She nodded, conceding the point. Zachary wasn't sure why she was blocking him so hard. Wasn't it better if he talked to one of her contacts, someone safe, than canvassing on the street and maybe ending up talking to the wrong person? Was she afraid he was going to scare her friends? Bully them?

"Okay," Ivy said finally. "I'll make a few calls and hook you up with someone. But I can't guarantee they'll be able to help you or find anyone else who can help you. That's a long time ago, especially for someone on the street. It's a lifetime ago."

"I know," Zachary said. "I don't have any great expectations. I'm just going to do what I can. When I reach the end of the road and can't find anything else... then I'll have to stop."

23

"Just tell me you'll be careful," Ivy told Zachary one last time as she said goodbye to him.

Zachary gave her a hug. "I'll be careful."

"You don't want to go stirring up old secrets. It's just not a good idea."

"I don't know how I'm going to find out what happened to Robbie Elder without turning over a few stones."

"That's exactly what I mean." She squeezed him. "You should rethink this. Sleep on it. Talk to your brother. This guy has been gone for twenty years. Do you really need to know what happened to him?"

Zachary drew away from her. He had thought about it. Had wondered just how far he should go in the investigation and what it would do to Tyrrell if he persisted or if he didn't. Either way, there could be negative consequences, but he had to assume that doing the right thing would have a better outcome. Finding out the truth was right by itself, without any other considerations.

Could he leave it? He wasn't sure he would be able to. It would eat away at him and keep him awake at night. It would distract him from his other jobs, just as it had distracted Tyrrell from his work.

"Whatever happened to Robbie Elder that night, his family and friends deserve to know the truth. For him to drop off the face of the earth… that's not how it should end. They need to have an answer."

Ivy shook her head slowly. "Your insistence on doing the right thing always was your worst quality. And your best." She kissed him on the cheek. "Take care, Zachary."

"Thanks. You too."

He met his first contact in a library. Not a librarian or someone there to read books, but a homeless woman. Zachary tried to remember Ella from when he had lived in Clintock, but she wasn't familiar to him. He didn't remember ever living in the area or having done anything there, so it was probably just a matter of having lived in different parts of town. Ella was a big woman. Zachary couldn't tell how old she was. She had gray, sparse, frizzy hair, but her face was largely unwrinkled. Zachary glanced down at her hands as they sat at one of the library reading tables together. Sometimes age was much easier to tell from the hands than the face. Her skin was thin, with thick veins bulging underneath it, but no liver spots. Maybe in her sixties. It was Zachary's best guess. And that would put her in her forties when Robbie had disappeared.

"You're Ivy's friend?" Ella asked in a slightly quavery voice.

"Yes. We've known each other for a long time."

He hadn't seen Ivy very much in the intervening years, but Zachary figured she would always consider him her savior, and therefore always his friend.

"And this boy you are looking for? Who is he?"

"He was a friend of my brother's, a little younger than me." Zachary paused, letting her look at him for a minute to get a feel for their ages. "He was just a teenager. And it sounds like he got mixed up in some business that he shouldn't have and got killed."

Ella shook her head, eyes moist with tears. "That's very sad. That's such a sad story."

"It is," Zachary agreed. "His friends and his family never knew what had happened to him, so I'm looking for people who remember what happened back then, hoping someone will have the information we need to put him to rest."

"And he lived around here?" Ella looked out the window as if she might see him walking by.

"He moved around. I'm not sure if you ever saw him. Or if maybe someone you knew saw him. I'm trying to find someone who might have heard or seen something, so if you can think of other people who were around back then... that would be really helpful."

"What was his name?"

"Robbie Elder. He was just a teenager," Zachary repeated. "So, you might not have known him or known his name... but he hung out sometimes with his friends, drinking and getting in trouble. You know how kids like that are."

"Oh, yes," she agreed with a little singsong in her voice. "Oh, boys that age do like to get into trouble."

Zachary nodded. "My brother was one of his friends. His name was Tyrrell, and he looks a little bit like me." Zachary let her look at him for a minute to see if it triggered any memories for her. She didn't respond.

Zachary told her the date and what he had heard about Robbie possibly being shot in the back of a car, and about the reports of the blood-soaked car being seen. She rocked back and forth a little and stared off into space.

"You want to talk to Freddie," she said finally. "Freddie can help you. He knows everything that was going on downtown back then."

"Freddie?" Zachary wrote it down in his notepad. "How can I find Freddie? Is he still around?"

"I haven't seen Freddie for a long time," Ella admitted. Zachary's heart sank. If she hadn't seen him for a long time, it was probably because he had died or moved on. "He used to hang out at the park that-a-way over by the school." She waved her hand in one direction. "But they've been pushing folks out of there for a while. He had to set up a new camp, and I don't think it's in this part of town. His friend..." Ella put her finger to her lips as she concentrated. "His friend is the General, who helps at the soup kitchen." Her eyes focused back on Zachary. "You know the soup kitchen?"

Zachary nodded. "Is it still in the same place as it was twenty years ago?"

She laughed. "It is. Soup kitchen hasn't moved, and the General is still there."

"I'll find him," Zachary said. "And I'll ask him about Freddie. Maybe Freddie saw something or heard about what went on back then."

Ella nodded her agreement. "That's right. That's what you should do."

"Thank you. That's very helpful. And... you never saw or heard anything about Robbie Elder? Never ran into that name or heard anything about a kid getting shot in a car downtown?"

"No," she shook her head. "I stay as far away from anyone who got shot as I can."

"Probably a good idea!" Zachary agreed. He tentatively pulled out his wallet. "Can I..." He inched a bill out, not wanting to insult her by asking, but also not wanting to offend her by walking away and acting ungrateful about the information she had given him.

"Oh, darlin', you don't need to do that. I'm happy to help a friend of Ivy's."

But she licked her finger and whipped the bill out of Zachary's wallet so fast that it was only a blur in front of Zachary's eyes. She *tsked* and tucked it into an inside pocket. "You're a nice boy," she told him. "I can see why Ivy likes you."

24

The soup kitchen that Zachary remembered was in one of the big old churches downtown. It was constructed of red brick and white siding and, to Zachary's eye, looked exactly as it had when he had lived in Clintock. He hadn't gone there very often, but for an eighteen-year-old trying to start life on his own, it had been a godsend the days he couldn't raise enough money to cover both his meager rent and groceries.

It was too early for the soup kitchen to be serving yet, but Zachary stopped in anyway. He didn't have much else to go on and didn't see any point in driving aimlessly around Clintock.

The door to the hall was unlocked and he walked in and looked around, his footsteps echoing off the walls and floor in the empty space. A few minutes later, he heard a voice from the other side of the large room where the church offices were located.

"Can I help you?"

Zachary looked at the tall man standing there and, despite his plain work clothes, recognized him as a clergyman. He just had that bearing. And that resonant voice, honed through hours of speaking over the pulpit. Zachary shifted awkwardly, feeling like a kid again. Caught somewhere he probably shouldn't have been, because he was looking for something more. Not just somewhere to eat or receive services, but something he longed for to fill the other kind of emptiness inside him.

"Oh... I'm sorry, Father. I didn't mean to disturb anyone. I'll come back later."

"You're not disturbing anyone just by being here. The soup kitchen doesn't open until suppertime, though. Do you need something?" The pastor walked slowly across the floor toward Zachary, his footsteps not making as much noise as Zachary's had. His eyes went over Zachary, evaluating him.

"No. I'm not hungry. I just need to talk to someone, if he's helping with dinner. I know I'm too early."

"Who is it you're looking for?"

"The General?" Zachary tried not to make it sound like a question. He knew who he was there to see and knew that the General was supposed to be there for dinner. He didn't need to sound so tentative.

"Ah," the priest nodded. "Well, you are in luck. He's in the kitchen, talking with Mrs. Bridger and planning everything for the rest of the week."

"Oh! You don't think I could talk to him, do you? I don't want to interrupt what he's doing. It's very important."

"I'm sure he can talk to you while he peels potatoes," the priest laughed.

"Well, thank you. That would be great."

"This way," the priest motioned for Zachary to go along with him and, when Zachary fell in beside him, touched him briefly on the back to encourage him forward.

"I'm Father Henry," the priest said on the way to the kitchen. "I don't think I've seen you here before."

"Zachary. No. It's been a long time since I was here. Long before your time. But I used to come sometimes when I couldn't make ends meet. It's an important service."

"He told us to feed the hungry," Father Henry said simply.

Zachary glanced at him and accepted this.

"Do you know the General?"

Zachary shook his head. "I don't think so. Maybe I'll recognize him when I see him. I don't remember everyone from back then, and I wouldn't necessarily have known his name or what he went by. People keep their names to themselves. Or change them. Ella told me that I would find him here."

"Oh," the priest's voice was warm. "How is Ella?"

"She's doing pretty well. Looks good. Seems energetic."

"Good. Glad to hear it. I haven't seen her for a while."

"She must be keeping herself okay."

They reached the kitchen, a large industrial one with lots of floor and countertop space, several stoves, and walls lined with supply cabinets. A few people were there, bustling around, chopping vegetables and discussing plans. Heads turned to look as Father Henry escorted Zachary in.

"This is Zachary," Father Henry introduced cheerfully. "He's looking for the General."

An older man with a buzz cut of gray hair and a thin, craggy face looked him over. He gave a nod. "You've found him, son. What can I do for you?"

Zachary searched his memory. The man was familiar, but it had been a long time since Zachary had been a part of that community. He had undoubtedly aged in the past couple of decades.

Zachary moved in closer. He didn't want to yell over the noise of the kitchen or for everybody to be part of their conversation. "Is there somewhere we could meet privately?"

"I'm making battle preparations right now," the General advised with a tight-lipped smile. "If you want to talk, you'll have to talk here."

"Okay... well..." Zachary inched a little closer, but he didn't want to get in the man's space. And he had his own comfort zone. The priest's touch as he had escorted Zachary to the kitchen had triggered his aversion to being touched by strangers, and he didn't want to be close enough to the General for him to make contact, even in a friendly, nonthreatening way. "I'm actually looking for Freddie, and Ella said you are the person to talk to." Zachary hesitated. "She said she hadn't seen Freddie for a long time, so maybe he isn't around anymore, but if he is..."

The General nodded and didn't indicate one way or the other. "What do you want Freddie for?"

"I'm looking into something that happened a long time ago. More than twenty years. It's hard to find people who might have been here during that time. Who might have seen or heard something or know about the rumors that were going around then."

The General picked up a potato and started peeling it. "Seen or heard what?"

Zachary was silent. Ella hadn't said the General would know anything except where to find Freddie. And Zachary wasn't sure he wanted it spread too far and wide. Not after the warnings from Ivy.

Zachary took another step back. "Is Freddie still around?" he asked. "If he isn't, then I'll just go…"

The various people in the kitchen exchanged looks, but none that Zachary could interpret for sure. They knew who Freddie was, but that didn't mean that Freddie was still in the neighborhood or alive, or that they would tell a stranger who just showed up asking for personal information.

"I was talking to Ivy Shane," Zachary tried dropping another name. "Stopped by the center earlier to have a chat with her. She's the one who pointed me toward Ella. Ivy and I… go way back."

"Ivy is good people," the General admitted. He chewed on his lip as he peeled the potato. Then he picked up the next one. "She knows what this is all about?"

"Yes." Zachary shifted restlessly. He looked around the kitchen, eyeing his escape routes, and then looked back at the General. "It's to do with my brother."

"Who is your brother?"

"You wouldn't know him. But I'd appreciate the help. You can call Ivy if you think I'm scamming you. I'm not."

"I don't know how much Freddie could help you," the General said finally. "He's not really seeing anyone these days." He pondered, letting several seconds pass. "He's in hospice care. Doesn't always recognize his friends. And a stranger…" the General eyed Zachary. "I'm not sure you would get anywhere. He probably won't talk to you."

Zachary ground his teeth, holding back the words that rose to his lips. It wasn't easy to keep himself under control. Going through three different people to get to one who probably couldn't even remember his own name was not what he had been hoping for. He swallowed hard and kept his voice steady.

"I'd like to talk to him anyway. Give it a try. If he's in hospice, then I probably don't have much time. He might be the only one who can tell me anything, and when he's gone..." Zachary shrugged. "I really do need his help."

"You couldn't tell me what it is you're looking for? I've been on these streets for long enough..."

Zachary moved his feet around uncomfortably, not wanting to stand in one place. He wanted to get out of there. Too many memories were crowding around him and he had difficulty keeping his whirling brain and restless body under control. No one had told him he could trust this General, or Father Henry, or anyone else in the kitchen. He distrusted most people who worked with the homeless and destitute without a recommendation from someone he trusted. Good people existed, but so did people who only worked with vulnerable populations to give them access to new victims. Desperate, vulnerable people who couldn't safely go to the police or other authorities.

Zachary took another step back. He could return the way he had come, back through the corridors to the main hall and out to the street. Or there was another door on the opposite wall that appeared to be an outside door, where deliveries were probably brought directly into the kitchen.

"No need to get antsy," the General said, looking down at his potatoes rather than at Zachary. "We don't know you, either."

Zachary nodded.

"I'll point you in the right direction," the old man conceded. "But that's no guarantee that you'll be able to get in to see Freddie or that he'll be able to talk to you or give you the information you need." He shook his head. "This will probably be a dead end."

"It sounds like it," Zachary admitted. "But I'm desperate. I'll give it a try."

"Why does it matter? This thing that happened more than twenty years ago?"

"My brother needs to know. To put his mind at ease."

The General looked around at the others again, as if to get a read on them and figure out what information he should give Zachary. But he had already promised to point Zachary in the right direction.

"There's a hospice on Third Street," he said finally. "You know where it is?" He gave Zachary the details he would need to find the building without waiting for an answer.

"Thanks, I appreciate it," Zachary told him after scratching the directions down in his notepad. Though he was pretty good at remembering and finding addresses, and used to know his way around the neighborhood, he was shaky and anxious, and the information might fly out of his head before he even left the building.

"Good luck to you. I'm afraid it might be a wild goose chase." The General considered for a moment. "There may be other people who were around during that time. But I don't know what information you're looking for."

Zachary shook his head. "Thanks. I'll keep that in mind... if Freddie doesn't work out."

He could get the additional information from the General now, but he wasn't getting good vibes and wanted to get out of there. The General seemed like a nice enough guy and had provided Zachary with the information he needed, but Zachary wasn't getting a good feeling and had no desire to stay there and find out why.

He pointed to the door. "Is this an outside exit? That I could use instead of going back the way I came?"

There were several nods from the workers in the kitchen. Zachary headed toward the door.

"You're welcome to come back for dinner," Father Henry offered. "There's always enough to go around."

Zachary nodded and grunted his thanks. He hit the crash bar on the door and stepped into the cool, exhaust-laden air.

25

He was glad he had a bit of a walk to get from the church to the hospice. He left his car in the church parking lot and stretched his legs. The fresh air and exercise would help to banish the ghosts of the past. He walked briskly, alert, on the lookout for anyone paying him too much attention or for any trouble brewing. It was only early afternoon, so there shouldn't be too much to worry about, but he knew he had to be careful in downtown Clintock. It wasn't like walking in Kenzie's neighborhood in Roxboro.

Nobody seemed to be paying him too much attention. Zachary glanced behind him a few times, still feeling antsy after the discussion at the church. He knew it was only because of memories bubbling up to the surface. No one had followed him. They were all busy with their own work, preparing for the day's dinner. It was, as Zachary had told the priest, an important service. One that saved lives. They were good people. Selfless and community minded.

Not everyone who assisted the poor and downtrodden was a predator. Zachary had known some very good people over the years.

Checking the street signs to orient himself, Zachary pulled out his notepad and looked again at the address. It hadn't been a hospice when he had lived in the area. Just a house, he thought, or a small apartment building.

It only took a few minutes to get there. A repurposed fourplex. Foggy in his memory, but maybe an old drug house. He liked the idea of a drug den or crash pad being turned into a hospice or other charitable work. It was hard to fight back against the drugs, crime, and poverty on the streets, but that was one way to do it.

He wasn't sure whether it was the type of place he could just walk into, like a hospital, or whether it was more private. He looked for a buzzer or instructions on the front door but found none. He peered through the glass of the front door. It looked like there was a check-in or information desk a few feet away. Zachary tried the handle, and it turned easily in his hand. He pushed the door open and poked his head in. The woman sitting at the desk looked in his direction and smiled. Zachary took it as an invitation to enter.

"Uh, hi. I'm looking for a friend, and I was told he is here."

She studied him. Zachary had not shaved for several days and was dressed casually. He could easily be a homeless or down-on-his-luck friend. The nurse gave him a knowing smile and nod.

"I'm sure Freddie will be glad to have a visitor."

She took him to a room where she gave him instructions to wash up and gave him a gown and mask to wear before he went in to see Freddie. "I know it's a pain," the nurse said apologetically, "but we try to keep our patients away from germs as much as possible, since a simple cold or flu virus could take away what little time they have left. If he tells you to take off the mask, you can. It's up to him."

Zachary nodded. "Sure. That makes sense."

She then took him up a flight of stairs to a bedroom with a hospital bed. Sun streamed in the large windows, making it bright and cheerful, but it was still obviously a hospital or medical facility with the usual hospital-issue furniture and equipment.

"A visitor for you, Freddie," the nurse announced. She walked with Zachary to the side of the bed and checked on Freddie. He was awake and turned toward them. His face was pale and cadaverous, cheeks and eyes sunken in so that he was only a shadow of what he had been in life.

"It's Zachary," Zachary told Freddie confidently, as if they were close friends.

The nurse took a moment to check Freddie's pulse and smile at him, meeting his eyes. "He probably won't have a lot of energy," she murmured to Zachary. "He may drift off."

"Okay, thanks."

She nodded and left him alone with Freddie.

Zachary moved to where the nurse had been standing, close to Freddie's bed, where he would be able to see him.

"Hi, Freddie. How are you doing? They treating you good here?"

"Won't let me have any smokes," Freddie complained in a weak, raspy voice. "But the food is good."

"Yeah?" Zachary could smell the remnants of lunch, but there were no plates or trays in Freddie's room. "Nothing like three squares a day."

"That's right." Freddie squinted at Zachary. "I know you, buddy?"

"You might have known my brother, back in the day. It was Ella who told me to touch base with you."

"Ella?" his voice squeaked up slightly. "She's one fine lady."

Zachary didn't know whether he meant physically or as a person, but it didn't matter. He made agreeable noises.

"A long time ago, my brother was running in these parts," Zachary told him, pulling over a chair and sitting where Freddie could still see him. "Dumb kid. Drinking and getting himself into all kinds of trouble."

Freddie's chest rumbled with laughter before breaking into racking coughs. "Weren't we all," he told Zachary after recovering his breath.

Zachary chuckled. "This was about twenty years ago, a bit more. So, you would have been…"

Freddie didn't fill in his age or bother to do the subtraction. "And what you care about him messin' around twenty years ago?"

Zachary nodded at the question. "Well, it's one of the guys he was running with then. Robbie Elder." Zachary paused momentarily in case the name was familiar to Freddie and brought back some memories. But Freddie didn't fill anything in. "Another wild child." Zachary gave another small laugh. "I don't know what they were mixed up in, these kids. But one day... Robbie didn't make it home."

"Oh, no," Freddie said sadly, his eyes widening slightly. He nodded along with the story. "He ain't never come home."

Zachary sighed. "My brother never saw him again. He'd just disappeared. Nobody's seen hide nor hair of him ever since."

"Ever since then," Freddie echoed.

"But things have happened... it's a different world now, and maybe we can get some better clues. I've been looking around, talking to some people who knew Robbie. Seeing if maybe I could get a line on him after all."

"You can't do that. He's gone."

"Maybe. But someone still knows what happened to him. Someone saw it happen. Or heard after what had happened. People saw the car. They knew who he was and maybe who did it."

Freddie licked his lips. They were dry and chapped. Zachary picked up the cup from the table next to him and held the straw to his lips to allow him to drink. Looking around, he found some Vaseline and spread a generous amount on Freddie's lips.

"Thank you." Freddie smacked his lips a few times. "Thank you, son."

Zachary waited a few minutes, not wanting to push Freddie. So far, Freddie hadn't indicated that he knew anything about the incident Zachary was talking about. And maybe he didn't know anything. Zachary wasn't there to upset him or force anything out of him. After what the General had said, he wasn't expecting much.

"There were rumors of gang involvement," Zachary said after a few minutes of silence. "And somebody said that he'd been shot. In a car. He got in the back, and someone in the front turned around and drilled him. Somebody saw the vehicle after, upholstery soaked in blood. But he wasn't there anymore."

Freddie shook his head. "What a thing. What a terrible thing."

"Do you remember anything like that?" Zachary asked. "Anyone who said they saw it? Robbie Elder. He was seventeen. Living with foster parents. A dumb kid who got in over his head."

"A dumb kid," Freddie echoed.

"Yeah."

"Thought he could put the squeeze on the wrong person," Freddie contributed.

Zachary caught his breath. "Is that what happened?" he asked casually. "Put the squeeze on who?"

"Kids these days. They don't know how it works. How to check things out and ask questions before you do something like that. If you're smart, you always know who it is before you turn the screws."

"Of course."

"Those boys were messing in stuff way over their heads."

"Yeah," Zachary agreed. "Local gang? Cartel?"

"Family connections. Poor schmuck never knew what he did wrong. Got his gore all over that car."

Zachary swallowed, trying not to react to the words and image. This was what he had come here to get. This was why he had tracked down Ivy, Ella, the General, and Freddie. This was where the trail had led.

"You saw?" he asked Freddie.

"I saw that car. Like you said. Soaked with blood."

Zachary gave him another sip of water.

"You're sure it was Robbie Elder?"

"It was twenty years ago," Freddie pointed out with a cracked voice. "I was probably high as a kite."

And he hadn't even known Robbie Elder. The name might be in his memory somewhere, but it wouldn't have meant much to him. Why remember it after twenty years?

For that matter, the entire memory of the blood-soaked car might be something Zachary had just planted. Freddie might have never seen any such thing. The only new information Freddie had provided was that Robbie was trying to blackmail or pressure someone who had mob connections. Freddie might have easily made that up without even realizing he was doing so. Zachary had heard of such things, and he was usually more careful.

"Did you know his friend? Tyrrell? Tyrrell Go—Miller. Did you know any of the guys he used to hang out with?"

"They weren't a real gang," Freddie said, shutting his eyes. He didn't look like he was in any pain, just as though he was tiring. "They might have thought that they were tough—all'a those kids do. But they weren't players. They just got involved with the wrong racket."

"Were there any threats against them? Robbie was the only one they went after?"

Freddie made a murmuring noise in his throat, but it wasn't clear whether he agreed or disagreed.

Zachary waited, watching him for a minute. Freddie's breathing lengthened, and it was evident that he had fallen asleep. Zachary retreated, going back down the stairs toward the door.

"How was he?" the nurse asked.

"Pretty good, actually. I was afraid he wouldn't be able to remember anything."

She shook her head. "It's so unpredictable. He might be unable to remember what he had for breakfast, but remember something that happened decades ago with perfect clarity. Memory is something that we still don't understand well."

Maybe Zachary had just managed to get him at the perfect time. And he had been asking about decades ago, rather than what Freddie had for breakfast. He was lucky.

"Well, thank you very much for your help."

"I hope you'll come back to see us again."

Zachary didn't plan on a return visit. He shrugged and pushed through the front door.

The air had cooled during the time he had been visiting with Freddie, even though it had only been a short time. Zachary looked at the sky and saw approaching storm clouds. They would block the sun before long, and the temperature would drop even more.

He decided he'd better hustle if he wanted to get back to his car before it began to rain. He walked as fast as he could back toward the big church.

He wouldn't need to go back inside. He'd gotten what he needed from Freddie. There was no need to talk to the General after all.

26

As Zachary headed back toward the church parking lot, the hair on the back of his neck began to prickle. Zachary turned and looked behind him but didn't see anything or anyone who looked suspicious. He tried to walk a little faster, but he was already at his full speed. Any faster, and he would begin tripping over himself. He had done physiotherapy after a car accident that caused temporary swelling around his spinal cord, and he had practiced and done all the work necessary to retrain himself to walk again. But things like running and going up and down steps were more difficult. He hadn't practiced those as much and they still felt awkward.

Did he want to attempt a slow jog? He looked at the gathering clouds again. Then he scanned the streets around him for any threats. He was sure there were eyes on him. He tried to make eye contact with a few people who looked casually in his direction, but none of them met his eyes.

He didn't like the feeling. The closer he got to the car, the more anxious he became. Blame it on the time he had once been jumped by a group of skinheads as he left a gay bar. He knew that walking to his car could be a very dangerous prospect. Things could have ended far differently if someone hadn't stepped in to help him on that occasion.

He startled at a shadow in the entrance of a back alley and, when he turned his head to look, he saw a tall, solidly built man sheltering there from the wind that was picking up. A homeless man? Or maybe waiting for a cab, ride share, or friend to pick him up? He didn't make eye contact with Zachary, didn't smile or nod politely when Zachary looked at him.

Zachary swallowed and pushed on. After a few seconds, he looked back over his shoulder and saw the man coming out of the alley, looking in Zachary's direction. Zachary swore under his breath. It was just a coincidence. One of those things that happened a hundred times a day. Zachary had just happened to walk by while the man was getting ready to go in that direction.

Zachary pushed himself to go faster, and his toe caught on the edge of a slightly raised sidewalk block, tripping him up. He managed to catch himself and avoid doing a face-plant in the middle of the sidewalk. But he also had to slow down if he were going to make it to his car without an embarrassing accident.

He looked back again. The man was still coming. His legs were much longer than Zachary's and ate up the ground between them.

Zachary tried to measure the amount of time he would need to get to his car, unlock it, and get the car door open. He had an alarm. He could set that off intentionally. People would look, wanting to see what was going on. He wouldn't be alone. The man wouldn't do anything in front of witnesses.

But before he got into the church parking lot, there was a hand on his shoulder. Zachary jerked his shoulder away, turning and bracing himself against attack. He raised his hands to protect himself.

"Just chill," the man growled. He grabbed Zachary's other shoulder and spun him forcefully, his hand landing on Zachary's back as he pushed him into another alley. Zachary tried to resist, but was propelled forward.

"Hey!" he tried to protest. "What's going on? Wait. Who are you?"

He knew that none of the questions would be answered and that, in fact, none of them mattered at all. Words were not what the situation called for, but action. Pulling away. Fighting the man. Using his body for something other than just standing around and walking where the big man pushed him.

"Please!" he protested, trying to gain control of the situation. "I need… please don't!"

The man kept pushing him, burying him more deeply in the tomb of the deserted back alley, away from anyone else. Away from anyone who could see or hear him.

He hadn't listened to any of the warnings. He hadn't let himself be dissuaded by Ivy's or Ella's good sense. He had insisted that all he needed were a few answers for Tyrrell and that turning over old rocks to see what slimy things he could find underneath them would not attract the attention of anyone important. It wouldn't put him in any danger. No one would care about what had happened twenty years ago. It was all in the past.

He tried to turn and block the man's hands, to keep him from pushing Zachary any more. Then he would figure out how to extricate himself from the alley and get help.

The large man looked irritated by Zachary's flailing. "Will you just stop it?" he demanded. "Just be still and listen to me."

Zachary kept his hands up, but the man didn't move. Didn't slap Zachary's hands away or try to grab them and restrain him. He just stood there, glowering at him, waiting for Zachary to comply with his demands.

Zachary swallowed. He shook his head slightly and tried again to ask, "Who are you?" but the words wouldn't come out.

Seconds ticked by. Zachary's heart was hammering and his breathing elevated. But the man didn't hit him or grab him. Didn't do anything to him.

"What is it?" Zachary forced out. "Who are you?"

"You don't recognize me?"

Zachary blinked. He stared at the man, taking in his face rather than just his build. It was vaguely familiar. But it was certainly not the face of anyone he had seen regularly or knew intimately. He tried to think back. Twenty years ago. Who had he known that might be mixed up in this thing?

But it didn't fit. Zachary was sure that he had seen the man's face more recently than that. It was a face from the past, but not nearly long enough ago to have something to do with Tyrrell and Robbie Elder. He saw Joss in his mind and heard her voice in his ear. And that didn't make any sense at all. He hadn't seen Joss since they were kids. And then they were reunited just over a year ago. Where would he have met this man with Jocelyn? The only place he ever went with her was to the bookstore or coffee shop because she preferred to meet him away from home. The only man in her immediate orbit was Luke, a teen Zachary had helped rescue from human traffickers.

Zachary's head spun with the random connections. He rubbed the center of his forehead, trying to ease the pain of a growing headache and to think of what he was supposed to know. Where could he have met the big man before? He looked like a bouncer from a bar, but Zachary had never been to a bar with Joss. The only place he had ever been to with Joss that had required security built like the man was…

27

"You were... you were at Peggy Ann's," Zachary managed to get out.

The man chuckled. "You were a lot braver walking into a big-time cartel boss's house than you are in a back alley with me."

"Well... I had my sister with me there. And a plan. Or at least, half a plan. I was prepared for it. I wasn't prepared to be... mugged by some guy on the street today."

Zachary's mind worked at dizzying speeds, trying different theories and discarding them. Why would Peggy Ann be coming after him now? He'd had nothing more to do with her since the night that he and Joss had gotten Aster back. She had no reason to come after Zachary. Or any way to know that he was in Clintock. Or to care.

What would Peggy Ann care about what had happened in Clintock twenty years before? Had the murder of Robbie Elder had something to do with trafficking? With someone in Peggy Ann's stable? Twenty years earlier, she wouldn't have had the same status as now. She wouldn't have been as high up in the organization, if she was even a part of it yet. Zachary tried to remember the details he knew about Peggy Ann's ascent in the cartel. She had been a mid-level boss when Luke was first recruited by the trafficking ring, but had advanced as other people had been brought into the organization or had been killed.

Did that mean that the man or Peggy Ann had tracked Zachary down because of something unrelated to Robbie Elder? Something to do with Joss or Aster? Or Luke, who Peggy had good reason to be angry about losing. No trafficker liked to lose an asset like Luke, and they had done everything they could to get him back again when they had discovered that he was still alive.

"What does... what does Peggy Ann have to do with this?" Zachary asked, making a motion to take in the neighborhood and his investigation.

"Nothing," the man told him, folding his bulging arms across his chest. He looked down at Zachary. The difference in their heights made Zachary feel like a child. "I'm not with Peggy Ann anymore."

"Oh. Then who are you with?"

"We need to go somewhere we can talk."

"Uh..." Zachary had no idea why he would agree to go somewhere to talk to the big man. Somewhere more private where he could be beaten to a pulp and left for dead? Or just killed, with no one there to see and testify about what they had seen. Like no one had been able to testify about what had happened to Robbie Elder decades before.

"Have I done anything to hurt you?" the man challenged.

"Well, no." Zachary probably wouldn't even have bruises from being shoved around. He had been startled more than hurt, unable to defend himself because of his panic and the difference in their physical size.

"I could have just thrown you head-first into one of these walls and left you here to bleed out into your brain," the man pointed out helpfully. "If I wanted to hurt or kidnap you or whatever you're afraid of, I would have done it by now. I want to talk to you. Before you bumble into something that *does* get you killed."

"Like what?" Even though he asked, playing for time, Zachary knew that the man was talking about his investigation and the people who might hear about it. Zachary had not listened to those who had told him that he needed to be careful. Gangs were dangerous, more dangerous than individual people. Zachary hadn't thought that any of the gang members who had been on the street back then would care anything about what Zachary did now. They would all be dead or in prison, and someone else would have taken over operations since then.

Clearly, he had been wrong. He had stirred something up, stumbling into something that would cause him trouble. And this man was just the beginning.

"Somewhere we can talk," the man repeated.

Zachary nodded and swallowed. "Okay," he agreed. "How about the library?"

"The library? Didn't you get enough of that already today?"

Apparently, Zachary had been observed more closely than he had thought.

They would have to meet somewhere there were people around, so that someone would at least notice if he were harmed. But also private enough to talk without being overheard. The library had probably been a bad idea anyway. Too many blind spots where something could happen without anyone being the wiser. Until it was too late.

"What about the outreach center?" the big man suggested. "Looked like you had friends there."

Zachary wasn't sure about taking him anywhere near Ivy or her clients. He didn't want to put any of them in danger.

But the man stood there, unmoving, and what he had said was true. If he'd been there to hurt or kill Zachary, he could have done it by now and been gone. It would be hours or days before his body was found. If the man hefted his body up and threw it in one of the open dumpsters, it might go to the landfill without ever being discovered.

"To *talk*," he repeated, giving Zachary a hard look. "Let's go back to your friend's place and talk."

Zachary couldn't think of anything to do but nod. The man stepped back and motioned for Zachary to lead the way.

He still couldn't believe he wasn't being mugged or beaten up. He anticipated the big man grabbing him, laughing at him believing the obvious lie, and continuing with whatever violence he had planned. Bullies were like that sometimes. They wanted to manipulate emotions, see hope rising, followed by the inevitable crushing defeat. It was like a drug, that rush of power over someone else.

But the man didn't laugh or grab Zachary again. He followed Zachary out of the back alley and walked at his side. Having him there beside Zachary made the sidewalk feel crowded, but there was nowhere else to go. The street was quiet, most people anticipating the storm and racing for shelter, so they didn't have to give way to anyone coming in the opposite direction. Zachary walked back to the community outreach center and looked around, trying to decide if he was really going to take the thug in there. What if he put other people in danger? He should just get into his car and drive away. But his car wasn't there. He had left it at the church building. And what were the odds that the menacing-looking man would just let him go? He had already taken action and physically detained Zachary once.

"Let's go in."

Zachary looked at the sky as the first big raindrops splashed around them. He felt a few on his face and soaking into his shirt. He hadn't brought a raincoat or umbrella. There was nothing to do but go inside.

The man gave him a firm nudge toward the center, and Zachary finally moved, entering through the front door.

The front hall was bustling now, various programs and activities underway. Bruce noticed him from across the room and did a double take. He looked behind him, but Ivy wasn't there. He said something to the teenager he had been talking to and disappeared into a hallway.

"There's not really... anywhere to talk here," Zachary pointed out. As if he could get out of talking just because the center was too busy.

"I'm sure there's a quiet room we could use somewhere."

"There's a lot going on…"

"Talk to your friend. They must have offices. Places they counsel people."

"I don't know…"

Of course they did. They had years earlier. There was a whole warren of rooms down the hall Bruce had just disappeared into. Offices, meeting rooms, a workshop, weight room, and various multifunction rooms. If things were still the way they had been. And why wouldn't they be? They wouldn't get rid of the rooms. Maybe they would be used for something different, repainted, possibly a wall knocked down here and there to combine two rooms into one, but the space was still there.

He and the man made their way across the hall, moving around kids and adults busy with their programs. People gave them sideways glances but didn't stop them. Why would they? Just because they didn't know Zachary didn't mean they had any reason to challenge his right to be there.

Bruce came back into the main room, followed by Ivy. She looked at Zachary and the man following him across the room.

"Zachary?" Her voice was tentative this time, not the exuberant greeting he had received earlier. She tucked a tendril of blond hair behind her ear. "What's going on?"

28

U m..." Zachary looked at the big man, wondering whether he would jump in with an explanation or demand, but he didn't. "I was just wondering if we could use one of your meeting rooms for a few minutes. We needed to talk and... it's raining."

Ivy looked out the front doors at the rain pouring down from a dark sky. "Wow, is it ever. I..." she studied the man briefly and looked back at Zachary, shaking her head. "Who is this? I don't want trouble here. If you bring someone in here who's going to cause trouble..."

Zachary shook his head, but didn't know what to say to her. The big man was obviously trouble. But Zachary didn't have anywhere else to take him and he had to have this conversation. What else was he going to do? Run over to the church with no jacket on to retrieve his car and drive madly back home to Roxboro? The man was sure to follow him if Zachary made a break for it. They could meet at the church, but Zachary wasn't comfortable there. And he didn't want the man going with him back to Kenzie's house. He wasn't inviting anyone dangerous there.

Ivy was studying Zachary's face, not pleased by whatever she read.

"I'm a cop," the big man said, "I'm not going to cause any trouble."

Zachary's jaw dropped, and he couldn't close his mouth again. He stood there just gaping.

A cop?

The man hadn't shown any badge or told Zachary his identity. He could have taken Zachary to the police station for questioning if he were a cop. And Zachary had already talked to the local cops to ensure they knew what was happening. Why hadn't Detective Able left Zachary a message saying that another law enforcement officer was on his way to talk to Zachary about the case?

Ivy looked the guy over and apparently decided he might be a cop, even though he hadn't shown any badge to prove it. Maybe she didn't want cops flashing badges in the middle of the hall. There were always people at the center who didn't want anything to do with cops and would bolt the minute they identified one.

"Fine," Ivy said, shrugging. "Most of the rooms are in use right now. You can see by the signs on the doors. But nothing else is booked, so grab whatever is free."

She motioned to the hallway. Zachary and the alleged cop walked down the hall, looking at the doors that they went by. Each had a Vacant/Occupied indicator that could be slid back and forth, like the sign on an airplane lavatory door that changed when the lock was turned. Most of them showed the red Occupied status. They found one showing the green Vacant sign, and the man pushed it open. Lights flickered on, and Zachary saw that it was the weight room. He stood back, waiting for the man to close the door again and look for a meeting room with a table and chairs but, apparently, he decided the weight room was just fine and motioned Zachary in.

Zachary wasn't sure how he felt about meeting in the weight room. He had not been comfortable there as a teenager. He was too skinny and small and, if he had wanted to start lifting, everyone would have laughed at him. Only jocks and tough guys used the weight room.

But on the other hand, it might be easier to talk to the big man if they weren't staring across a table at each other. Zachary preferred to be on his feet. He could think better moving around, and he could decide how close to or far from the man he wanted to be for his own comfort.

Weights could be used as weapons. He immediately thought of all of the movies or TV shows he had seen where someone had been murdered with a weight. Bashed in the head or strangled by a too-heavy barbell landing on his throat while lying on the weight bench.

But there were weapons everywhere, and the man looked perfectly capable of murdering someone with his bare hands if he needed to.

The man stood there waiting, impatient. Zachary finally nodded and entered as well. They both moved into the room and let the door shut on its quiet pneumatic closer. The man hadn't turned the indicator sign to Occupied, and Zachary didn't either. It would probably look strange, two strangers to the center having a conversation in the weight room with the Occupied sign barring anyone else from entering.

The cop—if that was really what he was—moved over to one of the lifting stations, picked up a barbell already loaded with disks, and tested its weight. He did a few lifts with it and looked over at Zachary.

"I suppose introductions are in order."

Of course, he already knew who Zachary was, but Zachary gave his name anyway and waited for the man to introduce himself.

"You can call me Hal."

Zachary nodded briefly. "And are you really a cop?"

"Twenty-five years on the force."

Zachary couldn't help staring at the man's bulging muscles as he lifted and lowered the weight. It always amazed him what the human body could do when pushed.

"Why didn't you identify yourself out there?" Zachary nodded in the direction of the main hall.

"Maybe I wanted to keep my identity quiet until we were in private."

Which made perfect sense, of course.

"But you *were* at Peggy Ann's house. You were working for her, weren't you?"

"Undercover," Hal told him dryly. "Yes."

Which also made sense. "But you're not working for her anymore."

"No. Got out of that." Hal grunted as he replaced the weight, then he picked up a couple of large dumbbells and took them over to a weight bench, where he lay down and started pumping them up and down over his body. "I'd been in place too long. It gets dangerous after a while. Either you're in danger of being found out because you slip up, or you start to feel like you're really one of them."

And which had it been for him? Had he been comfortable as one of Peggy Ann's bodyguards? Too comfortable? Or had he been worried she would find out who he was?

"You remembered me?" Zachary asked. Hal must have witnessed hundreds of meetings between Peggy Ann and clients, employees, or rivals.

"You made an impression," Hal said with a smile. "Most people don't go there to make waves. People are afraid to face her, with good reason. They don't go to challenge her. And they don't succeed in talking their way into whatever they want. Getting one over on Peggy Ann." He shook his head briefly. "Does not happen."

Zachary shrugged. "It was Joss, not me."

"It was both of you. You could see that your sister wasn't getting anywhere with her. And you had… a quick mind."

There were a few seconds of silence. Zachary imagined Hal must be wondering what had happened to Zachary's quick mind on this occasion. Taking so long to recognize Hal. Unable to think of where to go to talk privately. And he hadn't exactly been glib when talking to Hal or Ivy.

"So… what exactly did you want to talk to me about?" Zachary asked eventually.

Hal's arms moved mechanically up and down with the weights, not appearing to tire. He wasn't out of breath or showing any sign of exertion when he spoke.

"You're looking into the murder of Robert Elder."

Zachary swallowed. "The disappearance. There is no proof that it was murder. It was reported as a missing person. I had Detective Able pull the file. He would have told me if it had been changed to a homicide file."

"Not officially. But we knew that it was more than likely a homicide."

"We?"

"Detective Robertson and I."

The name suddenly clicked in. Able had told him that the initial investigators had been Robertson and Delaney. Hal Delaney.

"You were one of the detectives who investigated it!"

Hal nodded and switched to a different exercise with the dumbbells. Zachary felt like a dumbbell himself for not realizing who Hal was sooner.

"Do you have your old notes on the file? What can you tell me about it?" he asked eagerly.

"Oh, now you want to talk to me." Hal chuckled.

Zachary had to laugh at himself. He felt a massive rush of relief. All of the tension drained out of him. He was out of breath like he had been running.

"Yeah. For sure. Now I want to talk to you."

"Well... what do you want to know?"

Zachary sat on another weight bench close to Hal, looking down at him. "Everything!"

29

H al chuckled again. "There isn't a whole lot to tell, unfortunately. There were… not a lot of leads to follow. The boy had been out drinking with friends and had not returned home. We talked to the friends. Talked to the parents, took a look around the boy's room and the house. But they didn't really know anything, and the friends were not forthcoming. Didn't have much more to say than that Elder had been fine when they had left him."

"One of the friends was my brother."

Hal pondered this. "I looked at my notes. That doesn't sound right. There wasn't a Goldman."

"No. He was adopted. Went by Miller."

"Ah. The best friend."

Zachary nodded. He didn't know for himself that they were *best* friends. He could speculate that they had been because Tyrrell still wondered what had happened to him twenty years later. Tyrrell had said several of them had hung out together, and so had the Weylunds.

Hal eyed Zachary. "It's been a long time, but I can see the resemblance."

"Tyrrell is my younger brother," Zachary said. "I was in foster care... other places. We were just reunited a couple of years ago. I want to help him out."

Hal did a few more reps, his lips pressed together. "He was bad news, that kid. Quite the troublemaker."

"Robbie Elder?"

"No. Your brother."

Zachary swallowed. He cleared his throat. "He'd been through some tough stuff when we were younger. Abusive home. House burned down and we were all sent to foster care."

"Was he the one who burned the house down?" Hal's tone was sarcastic.

"No. That was me."

Hal looked at him, pausing in his workout. "You?"

"It was an accident. Trying to make things nice for Chri—for the holidays. Lit the candles..."

Hal shook his head. "You're the one who should have been trouble."

"I got into my fair share. Tyrrell was lucky to be kept with the younger kids and adopted, but they didn't understand the trauma he had been through. He never got proper treatment. Became an alcoholic early on. I don't know how old he was when he started to drink. Maybe nine or ten."

"Like I said, he was bad news. Heavy drinker. Rebellious. No attachment to his parents, which meant he didn't have to do what they said. Thought he was a smart guy and could outwit the criminals who were wealthier and more powerful than he was. That's a bad combination."

Zachary leaned forward, trying to take it all in. He had never seen that side of Tyrrell. Tyrrell had repeatedly insisted that they had just been messing around. Just doing the kinds of things that all teenagers do. Zachary had imagined that meant graffiti and other minor vandalism, maybe ringing doorbells or setting off alarms to disturb people. Setting off fireworks within the town limits. Perhaps even shoplifting or stealing copper wire from construction sites. Maybe as bad as hot wiring a car and going out for a joyride. But serious trouble? Trying to outmaneuver more powerful criminals?

"What did you find out?" he asked Hal, trying to keep his voice steady.

"Teenagers think that they are invincible. They think they can get away with anything without serious consequences to themselves. That's why they do stupid crap like drinking games or jumping off cliffs. Or stealing from the members of criminal gangs."

Zachary's heart thumped. He remembered how it had been, watching the other boys get away with stuff because they were so brazen. Thinking how easy it would be to steal a fortune instead of having to make money of his own. Even when he was determined not to get into trouble, his impulsivity would get the better of him and he would find himself in the middle of a big mess with no excuse and no way out of it. And then the hammer would fall, and he would have to take the consequences for his actions, even if he felt the consequences were too severe.

"There were rumors that he was involved with a gang. But I didn't know whether they were talking about him and his friends running around together. Or whether…"

"They were a bunch of little hoodlums. Everyone knew that. But not an organized gang. But yes, they thought they were smarter than the gangbangers and the organized rings and cartels. Thought that they could hoodwink them. Steal from them, cause confusion, who knows what else. They wouldn't put up with it for long before taking them down."

"And you think that when Robbie disappeared…"

"I have no doubt he was killed."

Zachary had already suspected as much himself, but having the cop who had investigated it say so cut him to the quick. How was he going to tell that to Tyrrell? Tyrrell was already dealing with enough stuff with his addiction recovery, his failed marriage, trying to be an every-second-weekend dad. He didn't need Zachary to bring him the news that his juvenile rebellion had gotten his best friend killed.

"Did you have any confirmation of that at the time?"

"Only rumors. And you can't do much with that. Did you find anything out from your friend at the hospice?"

"He's not my friend, just someone who I was told might know—"

Hal had put down his weight to sit up and was making an impatient, rolling-forward motion with his hand. A clear "get on with it" gesture. He didn't care whether Freddie was Zachary's best friend or a complete stranger. He just wanted to know what Zachary had found out.

Zachary opened his mouth, but found it too dry to speak. He tried to swallow, to work up enough saliva to get the words out.

What proof did he have that Hal was a cop? Only his word, not even the flash of a badge. He knew that Hal had been working for a human trafficking ring. Maybe he was still working for Peggy Ann or another cartel member who had been around for longer. Someone even higher up the corporate ladder than Peggy Ann was. Gordo, whose territory stretched across Vermont and possibly into adjacent states. Or someone on a national or international level.

Zachary couldn't just give Hal what he asked for because he claimed to be a cop. It was a good sign that he hadn't killed Zachary or done something to hurt him, but that didn't mean he wouldn't.

Zachary's brain flashed ahead through various scenarios. He could challenge Hal to prove that he was a cop. Get him to show his badge or call Detective Able to confirm that he was on the force and give him a description or send him a picture so Zachary could verify his identity.

But any of those things showed his hand, which opened Zachary up for retaliation. They might be in a place that Zachary considered safe, the organization run by an old friend, but what could Ivy do to protect him while he met with this big man in a back room, away from all eyes? Hal could kill him or take him out the back door and torture him somewhere more private, where no one might overhear or see what was going on.

Zachary sighed. "Freddie has dementia. I don't know what he's in hospice for, but he wasn't very intelligible... and his memory is gone. Names, dates, remembering the old neighborhood... it's all gone now. Whatever he knew..."

Hal watched Zachary alertly.

Zachary shrugged. "Another dead end. I'm hitting a lot of those."

"We didn't have a lot of leads when it first happened," Hal agreed. "And that was twenty years ago. Things happen in that much time. Memories fade. Witnesses die or move on somewhere else. Physical evidence is lost."

"Did you have any physical evidence in the case? Something that could be reprocessed now for DNA, or new fingerprints in the criminal databases...?"

"No. What was there to find? The kid disappeared without a trace, if you were to believe Miller and the others. We had no crime scene. We picked up a few rumors on the streets, but nothing that anyone could verify. No body."

"Blood?"

Hal looked at Zachary, eyes narrow. "Blood?"

"Blood in the car. I heard that there was blood in the car he was shot in."

"Where did you hear that? That he was shot in a car?"

"From a source." Zachary wasn't about to tell Hal it was his little sister and have him showing up at her apartment to ask her pointed questions.

"You have any evidence of that?"

Zachary shook his head. "No evidence, only rumors. Somebody said that somebody had seen the car upholstery soaked in blood."

Hal reached down for one of the dumbbells and pulled it up and down in a regular beat. "No car, no blood, and no body."

"You didn't find anything?"

"No."

"There wasn't a car soaked with blood that you couldn't identify because there was no DNA testing yet?"

"No. No car soaked with blood. Vermont is filled with wilderness and lakes. It's not hard to get rid of a car if you're set on it not being found." He paused in his lifting. "Or torch it. That gets rid of blood evidence in upholstery pretty quickly."

Zachary nodded slowly, pondering this. No car soaked with blood. No physical evidence. Freddie had seen it, but Zachary wouldn't tell Hal he had found a witness. In another week or two, Freddie would be gone. He would never be able to testify about what he had seen and heard.

"I guess it's all dead ends," he told Hal. "I'm not sure there's anything else I can do."

"You're not going to investigate it any further?"

"You sound like you want me to." Zachary was surprised at Hal's tone. He had expected Hal to warn him off like everyone else. If Tyrrell had been stupid to think that he was smarter than a mobster and Robbie had been killed because of their mistakes, then wouldn't Zachary be that much stupider to think that he could find out the truth after twenty years? And to be able to figure it out without bothering any of the parties who had been involved in Robbie's killing or the disposal of his body.

Hal shrugged, pausing in his workout. "As a cop, sometimes a case sticks with you. A lot of us have one or two pet cases that we pull out every few years to look at again, hoping that we'll be able to move it forward again. Robbie Elder is one of those cases for me. It doesn't make any sense, because he was a stupid young punk who got what he asked for. But it's one that I just can't leave alone. One of the reasons I got into the organized crime unit was because I was hoping at some point to hear about what happened to him. Just to put it to bed. Someone somewhere knows what happened and can answer all the outstanding questions."

"So, when Able told you that I was looking into the case, you wanted to find out what I dug up."

"What? Yeah, of course. Sometimes a new set of eyes...

someone asking questions slightly differently than before... a family member who cares about the answer..."

Zachary nodded. That was what he had hoped. If he shook things up a little bit, went about it differently, saw something with his kaleidoscopic ADHD brain that others hadn't noticed, maybe he could find out what happened to Robert Elder.

"So you're stopping?" Hal asked again. "You've taken it as far as you can?"

Zachary nodded. "Yeah. I've done all I could."

30

Was Zachary going to stop? The question gnawed at his brain all the way back to Roxboro. Though he had chased down most of his leads so far, he wasn't convinced that he had found everything there was to find. Hal had given him information that he hadn't had before and, maybe with that, he could convince Tyrrell to tell him more about what had really happened that night.

He went back and forth on what to do next while keeping an eye on his rearview mirror. Hal could probably find Zachary whether he followed him or not, being with the police department, but that didn't mean Zachary had to make it easy for him. Zachary drummed his fingers on the steering wheel while he tried to figure out his next step. The rain pounded down on the windshield and the road, making it difficult to see. Ivy's friend Bruce had given Zachary a ride back to the church to get his car so he wouldn't get soaked. And it would just get worse as it got later and he lost the little sun that he had. Best to get home and relax for the night.

He gave his phone a voice command to call Jocelyn Goldman and waited for his sister to pick up. It rang a few times, and he figured it would go to voicemail, which was fine since he wasn't sure what he wanted to say to her. But then there was a noise on the line and Joss's voice.

"Hi, Zachary."

Though her greeting was brusque, it was better than the "Now what?" he usually got.

"Hi, Joss." Zachary raised his voice to make himself heard over the pounding of the rain. "How's it going?"

"Where are you? I can hardly hear you."

"Driving. It's raining, sorry."

"Maybe you could call me back later when I can hear you."

"I'll make it quick. I was just wondering if you know any of the guys who work for Peggy Ann."

There was silence from Joss, and Zachary looked at his phone to see whether she had hung up or was still on the line. Joss's name was still on the screen. He waited to see if she answered. Possibly she couldn't hear him well enough to know what he had asked.

"There was a guy working for Peggy Ann," he told her loudly, "bodyguard, security, whatever. Big guy, of course. Name was Hal. Do you know him?"

"What have you gotten yourself into now?" she asked in exasperation.

"I just… he doesn't work for her anymore. I ran into him somewhere else and wondered if you knew anything about him."

"Like what?"

"Like… whether he is trustworthy. I don't know. He told me some things, and I don't know whether to take him at his word or if he might be lying to me."

"How am I supposed to know that? You think I have anything to do with those guys? I wasn't part of Peggy Ann's stable, and I certainly didn't talk to her bodyguards if I was ever around them. You were with me when we went after Aster. We didn't talk to any of them then, did we?"

"No more than a few words," Zachary agreed.

"I can't tell you anything about this guy. I wouldn't even know him."

"Okay. Thanks."

"What is this about, Zachary? How many times do I have to tell you to stay away from these people? Do you want to end up killed? You don't want to be talking to them, or running into them. Just stay away from anything to do with trafficking."

"It wasn't on purpose. I was looking into something else. Like I said, I just ran into him."

"You didn't just run into him. You were poking around in something that wasn't any of your business."

"I'm investigating something for Tyrrell."

"What? What could he have you investigating that has anything to do with trafficking?"

"I don't know. I mean, I don't know that it is connected with trafficking. This guy... he said he was a cop. That he was undercover when he was working for Peggy Ann."

"All the more reason to stay away from him. The only thing worse than hanging out with traffickers is hanging out with cops. Especially cops messed up in the business. Why don't you just go back to nice safe PI work? Go find some missing persons."

"Well... that's what I was doing. Trying to find a missing person."

"I meant missing persons that don't have any criminal connections. Not one who is involved with a crime syndicate."

"He was seventeen," Zachary told her. Joss was tough, but he knew she had a soft spot for kids in trouble. Just like he did. "Whatever he was mixed up in... it wasn't really his fault. And the consequence shouldn't have been someone blowing him away."

"Seventeen," Joss's voice came back softer. "Who is Tyrrell looking for? It isn't... his kid, is it?"

"No. Someone he knew back when he was a teenager. It's a cold case now. How much trouble could I get into, looking into a twenty-year-old missing person case?"

"If I didn't know you, I'd say you couldn't get into much. But I've met you. And I know you will cause trouble no matter what case you're looking into."

Then it didn't matter if he was looking into something to do with trafficking or organized crime, did it? Zachary resented being told what he could and couldn't investigate, even though he knew Joss had his best interests at heart.

Joss sighed heavily. "Just be careful, Zachary, please. I don't want you getting into something over your head."

"I know. I'll try. I didn't think there would be any problem with me investigating this case."

"But now you know. If you've run into Hal in your investigations. That's too close for comfort. Just back off. Tell Tyrrell that you couldn't find anything and let it go."

"That's probably what I should do," Zachary agreed.

"You have to. Don't ignore me, Zachary. Listen to your big sister for once."

"Okay."

She made a growling noise, told him goodbye, and hung up. Zachary glanced over at the blank screen a couple of times, trying to figure out what he should have said or done differently. But he knew Joss. She would never be happy with him. She would always find something to criticize. Not because she was a bad person or hated him, but just because she thought he should do things a certain way, that he should think like Joss and do the things that Joss said. But the choices she had made in her life had caused her a lot more suffering than Zachary's slightly risky decisions in choosing which cases to take. Or when to stop.

He never was very good at stopping something once he got going.

31

Zachary was glad to get home after everything that had happened, well and unscathed, other than maybe a few bruises he had sustained when Hal had caught up to him on the street and waylaid him. Why he couldn't just call out to Zachary and introduce himself rather than grabbing him by the shoulder and shoving him into an alley, Zachary didn't know. Maybe he had spent too much time undercover, in dark alleys persuading people to do what Peggy Ann or whatever other cartel boss he was working for wanted. That kind of power could go to someone's head.

Everything seemed quiet and idyllic when he pulled up in front of Kenzie's house. No one walking or parked nearby appeared to be out of place. Lights inside the house told him Kenzie was home, relaxing or cooking dinner. It seemed strange that everything should be normal at home after all he had gone through that day in Clintock. It was like he had gone back in a time machine, and now returned to the present. He expected everything to have changed, but it was all the same. Everything was as it should be.

He got out of the car and locked the doors. He looked around again for anything that might be out of place. Any person who shouldn't be there. A longer look from one of his neighbors. A curtain twitching, indicating that someone was looking out at him. Nothing. He pulled up the handle on the door to ensure it was locked and pressed the key fob button again to arm the security system. He walked around the car, looking for any sign that anyone might have messed with it. He knew those boys had been hanging around it when it had been parked at the center. Could they have put a tracking device on it? Tampered with his brakes or any other system? He couldn't be too careful. It had happened before.

He bent down and looked under the car. He pulled out his phone and shone the light everywhere it could reach, then turned on his app to look for any radio signals or magnetic fields that should not be there. No smudges or scratches indicated that anyone had leaned on it or tried to jimmy the locks.

Zachary walked around it once more, looking inside to ensure the light was flashing to indicate that the security system was armed. He pushed the button again just to be sure.

One more look around the neighborhood, still alert for cars that didn't belong there. A kid rode by on a bike, and Zachary watched him ride up to his house, then looked around for any other movement. Everyone was probably inside having dinner. No one appeared to have taken any notice of his arrival.

Zachary slowly pocketed his keys and headed for the front door, where Kenzie stood in the open doorway, wiping her hands on a dishtowel and eyeing him speculatively.

"Everything okay?"

"Yeah. Everything is fine. Just... checking. Can't be too careful."

She smiled and nodded. But he thought he detected a little hesitance. A little reserve about whether he was pushing past careful into the realm of paranoia.

But it wasn't paranoia. It might not be one hundred percent healthy, but it wasn't paranoia. After the number of warnings he had received about what he might be stirring up, and past experiences both he and Kenzie had been through, he could not be accused of being unreasonably cautious.

Kenzie let Zachary pass into the house, then closed the door and keyed in the alarm code herself. Zachary stood there, hesitating. He was used to arming the security alarm when he got to the house, and coming home felt incomplete without doing it. He stared at the alarm panel. It said that it was armed and the indicator light was on. Kenzie looked at him and raised her brows.

"I armed it. All set."

"I just... forgot something." Zachary headed back toward the door. He opened the door, looked out at the car, and then closed the door. He smiled and shook his head, entering his code into the key panel to clear the front door open event. "Never mind. I forgot; I already brought it in."

Kenzie said nothing, heading back to the kitchen to continue with meal preparation.

"How was your day?" she asked after Zachary had checked his email on his laptop and then joined her in the kitchen.

"Well... it was interesting." Zachary fell into the usual routine, getting out the dishes, glasses, and cutlery to set the table. Filling a jug of water. Attending to anything else that he could see they would need.

"Interesting how?"

"I..." Zachary tried to sort it out and decide how to tell her everything. What was the most important or would be the most interesting to her? She certainly wouldn't be interested in all his movements throughout the day. The routine stuff wouldn't interest her and his return to the old neighborhood wouldn't have any significance to her as it did to him. "It was just different to go back to Clintock, where I grew up. I never lived in the same neighborhood as Tyrrell, so we never ran into each other by accident, but going downtown and seeing people and places that I used to know... it was weird after twenty years. Gave me a really weird feeling."

"Good? Bad? Nostalgic?"

Zachary rolled his shoulders, trying to release tension. "I guess... it was good to see Ivy Shane. I haven't seen her in forever and she's really nice. Good memories of her. She's running a neighborhood outreach program now, a really important person in the community, helping a lot of people."

"Good for her. What was she like when you knew her? Other than 'nice?' "

"She was homeless then. There were some other kids she hung around with. I saw her sometimes. I didn't bother her; she and her group had nothing to do with me. But I did take pictures of them sometimes. When I didn't think anyone noticed."

"You didn't *think* so?"

"I guess she did. But I didn't realize it at the time. And then... when I was able to help her out, to get her out of jail after she'd been arrested for that hold-up, that was when she talked to me the first time. To thank me and say that she knew who I was." Zachary shrugged. "She's still... I don't know. Very open. Direct. There's no... pretending with her. No masking."

"Pretty unusual in today's world. Maybe even more so for a woman. One working with indigent people, as she does. It seems like there would be a lot of circumstances where you would want to hide your natural reaction to people and show them... a more tolerant or acceptable attitude than what you were feeling."

Zachary nodded. "Maybe. But she's always been... very real."

Kenzie opened the fridge and tossed a bag of salad onto the counter in Zachary's direction. He tore it open and dumped it into a bowl.

"And then seeing the old soup kitchen, and a coffee shop that we used to go to, and the library. It was like... being immersed in that world again, but not being part of it. There and not there at the same time."

"Out of time."

"Yeah."

"Did you make any progress on the case? Find any clues?"

"Um... a few," Zachary admitted. "I don't know how much further I'll be able to advance my investigation, but I'll see what I can do."

32

Kenzie was quiet for a few minutes, continuing to work on the dinner preparations and letting Zachary think his own thoughts. They moved the serving dishes onto the table and sat down. Zachary carefully spooned portions of each dish onto his plate. He'd learned long ago in foster care to take everything he was served and to eat it whether he liked it or not. Kenzie knew he wasn't big on vegetables or some of the more sophisticated dishes she tried, but he always had some of each anyway. She encouraged him to eat a variety of foods and to tell her which vegetable dishes he liked so that she could make them more often, but Zachary wasn't sure if he would eat more vegetables even if she served just the dishes he liked. And the ones he liked tended to have more of the unhealthy stuff in them—sugar, salt, and fat to mask the flavor of the vegetables—so she didn't want to serve them too often.

That was the problem catering to the tastes of someone like Zachary, who for the first ten years of his life had eaten little more than junk food and packaged meals heated on the stove or in the microwave. He hadn't cultivated a taste for fresh fruits and vegetables, and just wanted his greasy burgers, Chicken and Stars soup, and boxed macaroni and cheese.

"I have a witness who saw a car," he told Kenzie, thinking about the case and what she might be interested in or what she might be able to help him with. "The upholstery in the back seat was described as being soaked in blood. Someone was allegedly shot there. So… how much blood would be involved?"

Kenzie shook her head. "I have no idea. Where was he shot? What caliber and type of bullet? Did it get an artery? Heart? Lungs? Gut? Shoulder?"

"If it was soaked in blood, then… there must have been an artery involved, right?"

"Possibly. Did it spray? Were there long splashes of blood on the ceiling of the car? Fine droplets? Or was it all in the upholstery? Do we have any idea of the caliber of the gun?"

"No." Zachary thought back to Freddie's words and the rumors Mindy had reported on. "I can't even tell you for sure that it was a handgun, though I assume it was."

"A shotgun or rifle in an enclosed space like that…" Kenzie trailed off.

"It would be a mess," Zachary agreed. "No one said anything about spray or spatter, or anything but the blood soaking into the upholstery."

"Then it's possible that there wasn't any arterial involvement. And that it was a small enough caliber that the bullet stayed in him. Very little spatter, no… *tissue* blasted around the cabin of the vehicle. But if it got a major vein or an organ like the liver, there would still be a lot of blood leaking out of him. And depending on how long he was in the seat…"

"Do you think he bled out? If there was that much blood loss, then his chances aren't very good, are they?"

"I have no idea how much blood we're talking about. What one person considers a lot of blood might just be a minor nosebleed. And was it soaked into the upholstery, or just into the top layer of the fabric?"

"Well… it sounded like a lot."

"We can't go by 'sounded like.' You need actual physical evidence. I can't help with a report of a lot of blood inside a car. It doesn't mean anything to me. You and I could interpret the same person's report completely differently. Without pictures or samples, I can't even guess."

Zachary chewed a bite of green salad, then added an extra glug of dressing onto the rest. Kenzie gave him a look, but didn't complain. They had discussed before how he covered up any flavors he didn't like with dressings, ketchup, or whatever other condiments were on hand. Except tartar sauce, of course. He couldn't stand the stuff. He would eat what she served, but that didn't mean he always enjoyed it. Now garlic bread... it didn't matter what she served if there was garlic bread on hand. Which was probably why she didn't serve it with every meal.

"What evidence would you look for in a twenty-year-old crime?" he asked, approaching it from another direction. "A murder, say, someone who was shot. But the body wasn't recovered and it happened twenty years ago."

"I don't think I would be looking for anything. What is there to be found? After twenty years, there are not many places where you would still be able to find blood evidence. They never found the car?"

"No. Well, not that I know of. If it ever was discovered, it wasn't linked to the crime."

"But with that much blood in it—if there was that much blood, they would have tried to connect it to something. They would keep samples of the blood to see if they could tie it to a person sometime in the future, even if they couldn't identify who it was at the time. Pre-DNA, it wasn't as easy to tie together a scene and a victim as it is today. DNA testing was just coming into use, and a little department in Vermont might not have access to testing. And without a body, anything to compare the sample to."

"So maybe they were dumped separately. The person and the car. And maybe the body was never discovered, but the car was. And they still haven't been able to tie it to any other case, any missing or murdered person."

"It's possible," Kenzie said carefully. "But I wouldn't assume anything. And they could tie the car to the original owner, so there would be at least one connection with your murder victim, or at least with the location. Assuming that the shooter or someone connected with him was the owner of the car. You might be able to tie the owner to the car, if not the car to the victim."

Zachary nodded.

"And how do you know that the body was *not* discovered?" Kenzie asked.

Zachary finished as much of the salad as he could stomach and moved on to the pasta to reward himself. He looked up at Kenzie. "What do you mean? If the body was discovered… then it wouldn't be a missing person anymore. They would close the case. Or it would be transferred to homicide."

"What if the body was found but not identified? They could never tie it to your missing victim. We have a lot more tools now than we did twenty or twenty-five years ago, when they might not have even had police departments in different towns connected to each other. A lot has changed in the past couple of decades. Even today, with all of our advancements, I still end up with John Does who can't be identified. And if they disappeared from a different county or state, I wouldn't know where to look. I can't check every missing person nationwide automatically. It takes legwork. I need something to compare the body to. DNA, dental records, fingerprints, medical history. If he disappeared twenty-odd years ago and then was discovered ten years ago, or even yesterday, how would we find his missing person report? And what would we have to verify his identity? Do the police have *any* physical evidence in this case?"

"Not that they've told me about," Zachary admitted. "I asked Able, and he said that they didn't have anything. I know with Heather's case… the physical evidence had been destroyed. They didn't have space to store everything so, if a piece of evidence wasn't thought to be useful…" He shrugged. "They didn't have the same retention policies as now."

"So, your missing person would likely remain a John Doe. Unless he was found in a place that was significant to your case, or he had identification on him, or something else that pointed directly at the victim's identity, we wouldn't know."

Zachary nodded slowly. "How do I get a look at any John Does that have been discovered in the last twenty years?"

"You don't, Zach. That's up to the police department and their cold case investigators. You can call and put a bug in someone's ear, ask them to look back and see if they can find any John Does that might fit your missing person's physical description. But it's going to be a long shot. Do you even have anything for comparison purposes? Fingerprints? Dental records?"

"His mother and brother are still alive, so we could do familial DNA."

Kenzie nodded. "Right. It's possible you could find—or the police department could find—a matching John Doe. If you can get them to look. But I wouldn't hold my breath. They don't have a lot of manpower to put into cold cases. They want their people focused on current cases that can be solved."

"Maybe Able could put in a request."

"Maybe. But don't pin your hopes on it. And what about New Hampshire or any of the other states we share borders with? It wouldn't take someone long to drive to another county to dump a body. And back then, it would be a far more effective way to keep the victim from being identified if he was found."

33

It took Zachary a long time to unwind before bed. His mind was still whirling with the possibility that Robbie Elder's body could have been discovered years ago and they just hadn't known who it was. And the appearance of Hal, who he still wasn't convinced was a cop or a safe person to confide in. And seeing Ivy again and the priest at the soup kitchen... There was just so much whirling around in his head. Watching TV and visiting with Kenzie, who was reading a book, was just not helping.

"How's it going?" Kenzie asked, looking up from her book and catching Zachary rubbing his temples.

"Hyped up tonight. Did a lot today."

"Yes, you did. You going to take something before bed?"

"I think I will," Zachary agreed with a sigh. He could see how the night was shaping up and didn't want to end up too short on sleep to function as sleepless nights piled up. Maybe if he could stop it before it started, he could avoid crashing.

Kenzie looked surprised, knowing how much he hated taking a sleep aid to get the rest he needed. And the way that he would feel in the morning, groggy and two paces behind everybody else. It would be hours before he would feel like he had kicked the effects.

But he was emotionally drained and needed the sleep he would only get if he took a pill.

She nodded and looked back down at her book. "You should probably take one now, so it starts to work by the time we go to bed."

She didn't get up to get one for him herself, as she might have done previously. Not after accidentally overdosing him one night, when she had given him one and then he had taken another later while already feeling the effects of the first, not realizing what he had done.

Zachary pushed himself up from the couch. He rubbed his eyes on the way to the bathroom. He should also put in eye drops and take a painkiller for his head. Then a sleeping pill to start slowing down his rapid-fire hamster wheel brain so that he could unwind and be relaxed when he got into bed.

Forty-five minutes later, when he and Kenzie had both finished their nightly rituals, Zachary still felt like his brain was going too fast, jumping from one thing to another as he reviewed his day. He took his notepad with him and put it down on the nightstand on his side of the bed.

"You're not still working?" Kenzie asked, frown lines appearing between her eyebrows.

"No. It's just that... I keep thinking of things. If I don't write them down, I might forget. Or else my brain will keep repeating it and repeating it, not letting me relax. If I write it down... then I've got it, safe and sound and, hopefully, my brain lets it go because I've already dealt with it."

Kenzie nodded. "Writing down all of your worries. Getting them on paper is supposed to help you to look at them rationally and to let unnecessary worries go."

"Yeah. Something like that. I know my brain, and it's... *sticking* tonight."

"Good for you. Sounds like a good strategy." Kenzie began dotting moisturizer cream on her face and smoothing it in gently. Zachary would still have a few minutes before bed while she did that.

Unfortunately, it wasn't just thoughts on the case that were spinning around his head, and he didn't like to write down the more personal stuff. He wanted the past to stay buried and not to have to deal with the emotions that it brought. What good was dredging it all up? It didn't help him, and it didn't help Tyrrell or Robbie Elder.

Zachary jotted a few more notes and then placed his notepad on the side table again. Kenzie looked at him as she put her night cream to the side. "All done? Are you ready for lights out?"

"Yes."

For now, anyway. But Zachary was pretty sure that his brain would keep throwing up barriers to sleep that he would have to get out of his head. He would use his cell phone light to note them down and then try again. Or he should thumb type them into his cell phone notes app instead of trying to juggle phone light, pen, and notepad.

Kenzie turned off the light, and Zachary snuggled up to her, kissing her hair lightly.

"You're doing okay?" she asked.

"Yeah. I'm fine."

He could feel the sleeping pill's effects when he lay down. He felt a slight sense of vertigo when he closed his eyes, and then felt darkness was gathering around him. Looming up and then enfolding him. It took a pretty strong sedative to settle him down. But a few more minutes, and he might be able to fall asleep.

34

He awoke with a start, both arms out in front of him to stop whatever was coming at him. He held them there defensively, trying to figure out why he had awakened so suddenly. He looked at the window. Was that dawn? Had he slept for so long? He never slept all the way through the night.

"What time is it?" he asked Kenzie.

She moaned and shushed him. Zachary thrashed, trying to get free of the grip of his sheets, and reached for his phone to check the time.

He'd been in bed less than half an hour. The light outside the window was just the streetlight. Zachary put his phone down, closed his eyes, and tried to snuggle back into the warm space he had been sleeping in and return to the blessed, blank silence of sleep.

He tossed and turned, too drowsy to get up but too anxious to find sleep again. He swore under his breath.

"Zachary?"

Kenzie's hand landed on his back. Zachary's body jerked like he'd received an electric shock. He tried to pull away.

"Hey, it's okay. Just relax..." Kenzie rubbed his back with soothing circles, but Zachary thrashed and tried to escape her touch, skin crawling, caught in a flashback. He couldn't bear to be touched.

"No, no!"

Kenzie withdrew her hand. "Shh. You're just having a dream. Wake up. It's okay."

"Not asleep," Zachary muttered into his pillow.

Kenzie's face drew closer to his. "Hey. Are you okay? You awake?"

"Need to... need to get out."

"Out of where?"

"Out... anchor me."

She moved still closer so that they were nose to nose, almost touching. He could smell her face cream and the conditioner in her hair.

"Five things you hear," she prompted, skipping over what he could see, since it was dark.

"The fan." Zachary listened intently, trying to identify some other sound in the bedroom where Kenzie was, where he needed to go. "You... breathing. Car on the road."

"What do you smell?"

"Your cream. Hair conditioner. Sweat." He took a deep breath in. "Popcorn." They'd had popcorn earlier in the evening, helping further cement the timeframe.

"What do you feel?"

That one was hard. It was all muddled with the flashback, so he didn't know what was current and what was past. He could still feel the hands touching him. The sheets, the too-warm air.

"Can't feel the fan," he murmured.

Kenzie sat up and adjusted the fan to blow over his body.

"Air. Bed." He grasped for Kenzie, finding her arm and wrapping his hand tightly around it, holding it hard, probably harder than necessary, to overwhelm the other sensations and convince himself that he was here and now, not stuck in the past. "You."

Kenzie didn't pull away from him. She didn't try to rub his back again.

"That's right," she whispered. "You're okay. You're here with me. In our room. Can you see the window? The light from outside?"

Zachary realized that his eyes were tightly closed, keeping him in blackness. He squinted and blinked, trying to get them open, to focus on the window with its streetlight shining through the vertical space between the two blinds, providing enough illumination for him to see Kenzie's face, still close to his. He let go of her arm and put his fingers over her cheek. Just touching, ever so lightly. Her skin was soft and silky-smooth under his tentative fingertips.

"Okay?" Kenzie asked again.

"Okay."

"Good." She relaxed into her pillow. She put her hand over his so that his was sandwiched between her face and her hand. She turned her face slightly under his hand, so that his hand ended up over her mouth and she kissed it. "All good. You're safe here."

"Thank you."

They stayed like that, touching each other, for a long time. Kenzie's breathing told Zachary that she was asleep, and he tried to match his breaths to hers, hoping it would help him settle down and sleep. He could still feel the effects of the sleep aid, but he was also still anxious, his mind jumping from one interview to another, trying to put everything together and to sort out the memories that insisted on bubbling up.

35

He had slept fitfully on and off all night, still restless even when asleep. When it started to get light out, he dragged himself out of bed. He still felt exhausted, but he couldn't stay in bed any longer. It was better to be up, even if he was tired. He could work on the case, distracting himself from the memories of his years in Clintock and hopefully uncovering the truth about Robbie Elder's disappearance.

By the time Kenzie left for work, Zachary had decided on the next course of action for himself. He stopped at the nearby coffee shop for donuts and a couple of large coffees and headed to Tyrrell's apartment.

It was Zachary's old apartment, which he had lived in before moving in with Kenzie. He had been ready to let it go, since he was now living full-time with Kenzie, at about the same time Tyrrell needed a new place after his latest binge and subsequent round of rehab. Zachary rented it to Tyrrell at a low cost so that he could still afford to pay for groceries and child support. Since he was now working at the Kirsch family foundation, he had a good paycheck. So he could start to pay for the other things that he needed.

He still had keys, so Zachary let himself into the building but knocked on Tyrrell's apartment door rather than letting himself in there. He was intent on seeing Tyrrell and having a good long talk with him, but he still had to respect Tyrrell's privacy.

It took a while for his knocking to rouse Tyrrell and get him to the door but, eventually, he opened the door and looked at Zachary, unshaven and bleary-eyed.

"Zachary? What are you doing here? What's wrong?"

Zachary held up the coffee tray and box of donuts. "We need to talk."

Tyrrell stepped back, allowing him in, but Zachary figured that was more because of surprise than that he actually intended to give Zachary permission to enter. He just wasn't wide enough awake yet to tell Zachary to stay out and mind his own business.

Zachary put everything on the table, then sat down, helping himself to one of the coffees. He wasn't sure he could stomach a donut yet. The sleep aid or his disrupted sleep the night before had left him feeling a little queasy.

Tyrrell slowly shut and locked the door and joined Zachary at the table. He picked up the other cup of coffee and had a sip.

"We have to talk about what?"

"Robbie Elder."

Tyrrell shrugged. "I've already told you everything I could about what happened."

"No, you didn't."

Tyrrell stared at him. "You weren't there. You can't say that I didn't tell you everything."

"I had a little chat with Detective Hal Delaney. Do you remember him?"

Tyrrell took a minute to process this news. As he came to realize what this meant, he tried to keep a flat expression that would give nothing away, but he was noticeably paler than he had been.

"I suppose. He was one of the cops on Robbie's case. He talked to everyone, not just me."

"What did you tell him about that night?"

"Same as I told you. We were out, drinking and enjoying ourselves, and when we finished, we went in different directions. And I never saw Robbie again after that."

"Delaney says that you were smart-ass kids who thought you knew everything and were making plans for bigger stuff. Stuff that involved squeezing powerful people for blackmail money."

Tyrrell jerked back as if he'd been slapped. "What? He never told you that."

"He knew what you guys were up to. That you were in way over your heads, and it backfired on you."

Tyrrell continued to shake his head, his mouth an angry red slash.

"Robbie getting shot that night was a direct response to you guys threatening the wrong person," Zachary said flatly. He made it sound like he was a lot more certain about it than he was. Not everything connected up as neatly as he wanted it to. There were a lot of gaps in his knowledge. But he tried to make it sound like he'd worked it out or been told all the details.

Tyrrell was shaking with rage or fear. He stared at Zachary, his eyes wide. He'd spent a lot of time denying what he had done, lying to himself about it. But Zachary could see the fear. The seventeen-year-old boy who hadn't been able to deal with what he had done and the disappearance or death of his friend.

"Did you see?" Zachary demanded. "Were you there when he was shot, or did you just hear about it afterward?"

"I don't know what you're talking about. Who said he was shot? He was never shot. He just disappeared. He went somewhere. Ran away. Got away from those stiffs who were supposed to be looking after him. Who wouldn't run from them? They were unbelievable. Didn't have a clue how to raise kids, how to make rules, talk to them, any of that stuff. And I thought the Millers were goody two-shoes! But they were nothing compared to Robbie's foster parents."

"He didn't run away. If he had run away, he would have shown up by now. He would have gone back to Clintock or Kingsley. Called his mother. Sent her a letter apologizing for running away. He didn't run away after bleeding out in the back seat of a car."

Tyrrell felt for the chair with shaking hands and lowered himself into the seat across from Zachary. There were tears in his eyes. Brimming up and overflowing down his cheeks.

36

W ho told you he was shot?"

"There were witnesses. People who heard about the shooting and saw the blood soaked into the car upholstery. Robbie never walked away from there, Tyrrell. He was dumped in a lake somewhere or showed up on some morgue table as a John Doe."

Tyrrell put his hands over his face. "You don't know that."

"Did you see it happen?"

Tyrrell shook his head. "I only heard about it after. I never saw, I never knew for sure if it was true, or if he just got away, decided to leave it all behind."

"Is that something he would do?"

"If his life was threatened…" Tyrrell started. Then he shook his head again, tears streaming down his face. "No. He wouldn't have just left. He wouldn't have left without saying goodbye to me. We were best friends."

"So, you knew he was dead when you hired me to look for him."

Tyrrell bit his lip. "I didn't know for sure."

"Why didn't you tell me what you knew? It would have been a lot easier."

"I didn't want to bias you. I wanted you to find out what you could on your own, objectively, to see if there was any evidence either way. The cops never wanted to find him. They never looked for him. They said he was just a stupid hood and would show up on his own sooner or later. They never did any real investigating to find him. He wasn't worth it to them."

"Who was he meeting that night?" Zachary asked. "Who killed him?"

"I don't know."

Zachary didn't believe that for a minute. Of course Tyrrell knew who Robbie had been planning to visit. They were in on the scam together. He still wasn't convinced that Tyrrell hadn't been there and witnessed the shooting himself. But then, why hire Zachary two decades later to find out what had happened to Robbie if he had seen it for himself?

Tyrrell had been drinking a lot at the time and maybe he had managed to convince himself that he hadn't really seen what he had. Or he had blacked out.

"How could you not know? Who was he going to see?"

"I don't know. We had a few marks, and I don't know which one got to him."

"He wouldn't have gone to see them without some backup, would he?"

"He loved putting the squeeze on these guys. Sometimes he would go see them on his own and come crowing to me the next day about what I had missed because I went back home to my family."

It was the first time Zachary had heard him refer to the Millers as his family. He felt a twinge of jealousy about Tyrrell growing up with a real family. One that didn't include Zachary. Of course, Mindy and Vince were Tyrrell's biological siblings. He hadn't abandoned his family of birth for his adoptive parents. They were the only family that Tyrrell had been able to stay with. But up until now, Zachary had only heard Tyrrell mention his adoptive parents in a distant way. Or heard from Mindy and Vince about how rebellious Tyrrell had been, how he hadn't been able to bond with them.

That had made Zachary feel good, something he would never have confessed to anyone. He felt proud that Tyrrell had not wanted to merge into his new family, that he had remained loyal to Zachary and the rest of his biological family.

But Tyrrell had been raised by the Millers, whether Zachary liked it or not, and they were the family that Tyrrell had gone back to that night. It was ridiculous to feel worse about Tyrrell calling the Millers his family than about letting his friend get killed and lying about it to Zachary.

But as he and Kenzie had observed more than once, people were not necessarily logical creatures, but emotional ones, making decisions based more on habit, emotion, and impulse than thinking them through and making the best choice.

"Why would he do that? See them without someone to watch his back and ensure he didn't get hurt?"

Tyrrell shook his head. "It was a rush. The power, the danger, being able to manipulate them. Robbie ate it up. He loved getting one over on these guys who were supposed to be so much more powerful and badass than a couple of juvies. It was a big thrill and Robbie loved it."

Tyrrell swallowed hard. He opened the donut box, looked over the variety of sweet confections, and didn't pick one out. Looking for something to do with his hands, more than actually hungry for breakfast.

"I feel so guilty," Tyrrell confessed. "It just eats me up if I let myself think about it. I should have been there. I should have stayed with him that night. He asked me to, but I was blotto and just wanted to be home in my own bed." He rubbed the corners of his eyes. "I wanted to make sure Mindy and Vinny were down for the night and that they were safe." He confided it as if it were something to be ashamed of. Going home to check on his little brother and sister, to make sure that they were being taken care of properly and were safe and sound for the night. Zachary was proud of him for that. For caring about them even in his drunken state, even when out "messing around" with Robbie and their other friends. He had still thought of his siblings and keeping them safe.

"If he went without you, knowing the danger, then that's not on you." Zachary rotated his coffee cup in a circle, staring at it rather than at Tyrrell. "You couldn't control his actions, what he did after you had split up for the night."

"I could have stayed with him. I could have kept watch and stopped it from happening."

"You could have gotten yourself killed as well. How would you have stopped it? By the time you knew he was in real danger from these guys, it would have been too late. He would have been dead."

"I could have done something," Tyrrell insisted stubbornly. "I could have stopped them."

"You couldn't have then. But maybe you can do something now."

Tyrrell raised his eyes to Zachary's face, questioning.

"You could identify who killed him, so we can track down the evidence to prove it and get him put away. Just because it happened twenty-some years ago—that doesn't mean that they can't still be convicted and sent to prison. Then, at least, there would be some justice. You would know that Robbie didn't die without anyone knowing or caring or doing anything about it."

"He wasn't just some animal, some scrap of meat," Tyrrell insisted, arguing with the cops who had refused to take a serious look at it, with everyone who had looked away and not cared that a kid had disappeared or been killed. "He was a person. My best friend. He was a good guy. They couldn't just gun him down like a rabid dog. But nobody cared! Not the cops. Not his guardians. Not his real family. Nobody cared what had happened to him."

"They didn't know what had happened to him. You didn't tell them what they needed to know."

"They still didn't care. Even if they didn't know that he might have been shot, they knew he was missing. That he hadn't gone home that night. Or the next day. That he never went home at all. How could someone just disappear like that, and no one cared?"

"You cared. And you couldn't let it go on any longer. You wanted to know what happened to him. To have it laid to rest at last."

"Did they just dump his body somewhere? Is that what you think?"

Zachary sighed. He took a long drink of his coffee, though he didn't taste it. "I don't know. I'm going to see if I can find out. If there were ever any remains recovered that might have been him. They didn't really have any DNA testing for missing persons back then. But now... it shouldn't be that hard to get a sample tested if we can narrow it down enough. It would be good to return him to his family, if we can find anything."

"They don't deserve to have him. They just threw him away like trash. He wasn't garbage. He was a person, and you don't just throw people away."

There was an ache in Zachary's chest at Tyrrell's words. He thought that he had dealt with his own abandonment issues long ago. He'd discussed them in therapy enough times that if talking about them helped, he should have been past them. But he knew why Tyrrell was so adamant about it. He and Robbie had shared the experience being thrown away by their biological families as if they didn't matter. As if they were worthless. Tyrrell and the younger children had grown up being told that their parents couldn't take care of them anymore. That their mother was sick and their father couldn't care for six kids alone. But Tyrrell had probably remembered enough to know that it wasn't true. They had been thrown out because their parents had never regarded them as anything more than a nuisance. As a ticket to more welfare money. And when the house had burned down—when Zachary had burned the house down—they had decided to throw them all away and be rid of them.

Even if Tyrrell didn't remember it consciously as a teenager, he had never gotten over those feelings of abandonment. No more than Zachary had.

37

W hen he returned home, Zachary saw that he had received a voicemail from Detective Able. He had called the night before, but Able hadn't been available then, and there hadn't been any urgency to reach him. A few hours, one way or another, wouldn't make any difference to Robbie Elder's case after so long. Able said that he was in the office and Zachary could give him a callback.

Zachary took a quick look at the email inbox on his laptop, then hit the link on his phone to call Able back. He leaned back into the couch, closing his eyes and trying to relax every muscle. He felt emotionally wrung out after his breakfast discussion with Tyrrell. He would have preferred to be able to veg the rest of the day, but he needed to keep himself busy and there was plenty of other work to be done even if he wanted to take a break from the Elder case, which he wasn't going to do.

"Zachary Goldman," Able greeted, obviously reading Zachary's caller ID on his phone screen. "So, what have you found out?"

"Well... nothing I have any concrete evidence for yet, but I'm working on it. From what I've been able to dig up so far, I think that Robert Elder was probably killed the night he disappeared. There were rumors and at least one witness."

"Killed. How?"

"Shot. It looks like he and his friends had set up a little black-mailing operation. He went off to meet someone that night, to put the squeeze on them, and he ended up getting shot for his trouble. His body was not recovered, so it must have been dumped some-where, in a way that it was never connected with the Elder case if it was found later."

"Sounds like a lot of speculation to me."

Zachary shrugged. "Well, I'm a private investigator, not a cop. I can speculate and follow as many rabbit trails as I like."

"Must be nice."

"Not always. There are a *lot* of rabbit trails."

Able chuckled. "I guess there are. Is that what you're calling me about, then? To report your progress so far? That you think he was shot and killed?"

"No. I was hoping to get some information on any John Does who were discovered after that, who might be related. See if I can find Robbie that way. Then maybe once I pin it down to a partic-ular set of remains... the police department could run his DNA. Even if you don't have any of Elder's DNA on file, his mother and brother are still living. A familial match could be made to identify his remains."

"You want what, exactly? Any John Does found in the months after Elder was killed?"

"Or since then... any remains that are old enough to be his."

"Every John Doe in the past twenty-odd years who could be Robert Elder."

Zachary cleared his throat. "Yeah."

"You want us to review every file to see if they match Elder."

"If they are a potential match, yes. You can eliminate any remains that were female, in the wrong age group, or weren't killed within the right time period... If you want to feed me the raw information, I can narrow it down myself, save you the trouble."

"Just give you the dozens of files and let you sift through them."

"I can come in at your convenience. I should be able to eliminate a lot of them in the beginning. Then I can drill down and focus on the possible matches. I know someone in the medical examiner's office here. She can help me figure out which ones can be eliminated."

"You have no idea how much manpower that would take."

"Just to pull the files?"

"Just to pull the files," Able agreed. "You're talking about paper files that need to be pulled out of storage when you're talking about investigations that old. And I can't just show them to you. You would need to file a freedom of information request, and then I'd have to review each file individually."

"Vermont is not that big a place. Especially if you limit it to the area around Clintock. I know that theoretically, the killer could have driven the body anywhere in the state or the surrounding states, but I doubt if they did. It was probably dumped pretty close by. You can't tell me that Clintock has *that* many John Does."

Able grunted. "Don't plan on getting anything from me. I'll send the request up the chain of command, but chances are, you aren't going to get anything."

Zachary let out a sigh. He should have known that was the response he would get. He might be able to go back through microfiche copies of Clintock newspapers, looking for any reports of human remains being found. It was a rare enough occasion that it should be reported in the papers. But that would take a lot longer than a computer search by the police department would.

"Well, do what you can. I'll do some more research on my own. I talked to Detective Delaney, and he—"

"You what?"

"Detective Delaney. You said he was one of the detectives who first investigated the missing person case."

"Yes, he was. But how did you get in touch with him?"

"I *am* a private investigator," Zachary reminded him, reluctant to admit that he hadn't found Hal, but the other way around.

"Yes, but…" Able didn't finish his thought. "The department has had some *issues* reaching former Detective Delaney."

"Former?"

"Yes. He is no longer with the department. But I'm sure he told you that."

"Uh, no. He didn't happen to mention that detail. He's retired?"

Able was shuffling papers in the background. Zachary waited for him to return and pay attention to the call.

"Where did you find Delaney, exactly?" Able asked.

"I met with him in Clintock. We talked at the community outreach center."

"Where is he living? Do you have his phone number?"

"No."

"How are you supposed to get back to him? Or how did you set up the meeting in the first place? You must have some information that allowed you to contact him and set up the meeting."

"What's going on? The police department can't reach him? Don't you have his current contact information? That all seems a little…"

"It is unusual," Able confirmed. "We have a few matters we would like to connect with him on. And if you've been in contact with him, maybe we can reach out to him through the same channels…"

"He heard that I was looking into the Elder missing person case and reached out to me. I thought he'd gotten that information from you. If not… I'm not sure where he got it or how to reach him again."

"Was he going to follow up with you?"

"No." Zachary hesitated to tell Able anything more, then decided to put his cards on the table. "I was a little nervous of him, to tell the truth. When he asked me if I was going to pursue it any further, I told him that I wasn't. So… he wouldn't have any reason to contact me again."

"What was it that made you nervous about him?"

"Just the way he acted. He didn't look or act like a cop. He never showed me his badge. Didn't introduce himself as Detective Delaney until later, so I wasn't even sure that's who it was. Could have been someone trying to pass himself off as a cop."

"I'll send you a picture. You can make sure your Delaney was really our Delaney."

"That would really be good, actually. I don't like to think that I might have talked to the wrong person... or said the wrong thing."

"Why would anyone else be looking into the case after so long?"

"Why would Delaney?"

"Well, he was one of the original investigators. I can see him wanting to know what's going on if he hears it is being investigated again. But he didn't hear it from me."

"Could he have heard about it through... underworld sources? Not the police department?"

"He could have heard about it from Robbie Elder himself. I have no idea where he found out you were looking into it."

"This isn't the first time that I've run into Delaney. The first time was actually when he was a bodyguard for Peggy Ann, a woman involved in human trafficking in Vermont. Pretty high up the food chain. Do you think... can you tell me if he was under-cover there like he told me, or whether he was really working for her?"

"I'm afraid that's outside my purview. All I can tell you is that he's not working for us now. And even that..." Able trailed off.

Zachary opened his eyes, his interest piqued. "Do you think he could still be undercover?" Zachary offered. "Maybe the whole thing about him being off the force and the department not being able to reach him is just another cover story? While he's working on something else?" Zachary warmed to the topic. "Maybe corruption within the police department?"

"There is no corruption within the department being investi-gated by Delaney or anyone else," Able told him firmly, an edge to his voice. "I can't tell you whether he is still undercover or if he is really off the force. If he's working a case, I won't be the one to screw things up for him. And you'd better keep your mouth shut too."

"But what if he's gone rogue and is working for Peggy Ann or someone else in the trafficking business? What if he's crossed the line and the police department is looking for him to rein him in?"

"You know what, Goldman? You ask too many questions. I don't have time for all of this. As a private investigator, it's your responsibility to stay out of the way of active investigations. And I'd say that *you've* crossed the line. I don't know what Delaney is up to but, whatever it is, you'd be well advised to stay away from him and not have any further contact. And if you do see him, tell him to call in and get things straightened out with the department."

"I'm still investigating the Robbie Elder case," Zachary spoke in a flat, even tone, not wanting to rile Able up, but also not about to give up on his case. "I'm happy to stay away from Delaney, if he'll stay away from me."

"What's that supposed to mean?"

"Just what I said. I don't want anything else to do with him. I won't be reaching out to him."

Able was silent for a few seconds.

"Fine," he said eventually. "Glad to hear it. Let me know if you make any headway on your case and stay out of the way of any of our investigators. Your PI license doesn't give you the right to stick your nose into police business."

"Are you going to look up those John Does?"

"I said I'll put the request in, and I will. But don't expect anything out of it. If anyone decides to take it on, it will probably be months before you see any results, if not longer."

38

Zachary made himself a sandwich for lunch. Then he wrapped it in plastic, stuck it in the fridge, and ate a donut instead. He'd paid for them. It would be irresponsible not to eat them, wouldn't it? Tyrrell hadn't been that interested in them after the emotional discussion and memories and, though Zachary had left a couple with him, he had ended up taking the rest home.

He paced up and down the hallway and around the living room, working through the case in his head and trying to figure out the next step. He had chased down most of the leads, but he knew he was not done. There were still a few other avenues to explore. Kenzie's suggestion of the John Does, of course. He would have to see whether she could request those files through the medical examiner's office if Able couldn't do anything to help him or would take months to do so. He didn't know whether Kenzie would have access to Clintock's records on her computer system or whether she would have to put in a special request to have them delivered to her. From what Able had said, not much of the information would be on the computer.

There was someone else who knew who had killed Robbie Elder.

Zachary could keep looking for witnesses, but there was another possibility.

Eventually, he put in his Bluetooth earphones and tapped Tyrrell's picture on his phone screen. It took a couple of calls before Tyrrell answered, his voice irritated.

"I'm working, Zachary. I thought you wanted me to get my foundation work done. I can't do that if I keep getting interrupted."

"I was thinking about this case and other ways to approach it. I need the names of the people you were blackmailing. All of them."

Silence from Tyrrell. Zachary stopped walking and listened intently to see if he could hear anything to indicate what Tyrrell was doing. He might not be able to interrupt what he was doing to give Zachary an answer. Or it might be something he hadn't thought about for so long that he needed time to recollect the names and make a list for Zachary.

"It might take some time," Zachary suggested. "I know you're busy right now, but could you put together a list for me?"

"No."

Zachary was surprised by the flat refusal. "If I have those names, I can narrow down who killed Robbie, and then I'll have a better chance of figuring out what they would have done with the remains. They won't be expecting it. They'll be relaxed after so long with no movement on the case."

"No, Zachary. I can't do that."

"Don't you remember? Do you have any notes or anything from back then? We could go over them and they might help you to remember…"

"No. I want you to back off of this case. You've done a good job. I feel better about it now that I've had a chance to think about it and look at what really happened. I can make my peace with it. I don't want you to take any more time on this."

"I think that with another day or two…"

"No. It's a waste of time. And I don't want you getting involved with something that could be dangerous."

"I'll be discreet in my inquiries. I can't just leave it, T. The kid deserves some justice. Like you said, he was someone; he was a person."

"No!" Tyrrell said more forcefully. "You need to leave it alone now. I'm not going to be responsible for someone coming after you."

"What's changed? This morning you still wanted to find out who had done it and where he was."

"I just had a chance to think about it. And I think... I knew all along what had happened to him. I just didn't want to face it. To remember. But now that we talked about it... it's all coming back, and I don't want to talk about it anymore or dig deeper. Especially if there could be consequences. It happened over twenty years ago, Zach. Let's just leave it alone now."

"I can't just stop in the middle of an investigation."

"Well, you know what, bro? This time, you're going to have to. Just let it go now. I don't want to do this anymore."

The call terminated. Zachary stopped short, ceasing his pacing, and pulled out his phone to look at it. He hoped there would be some error on the screen, showing that Tyrrell hadn't been the one to cut off the call. But there was no error. His brother had just hung up on him.

Zachary put the phone back in his pocket and looked out the living room window. He needed to do more than pace. The weather was reasonably nice; he needed to go for a walk outside. Then maybe he could get his thoughts back in order again and decide what to do about the case.

He lost track of time, stuck in his own head. That was one of the problems that medication didn't ever seem to help. Some of them increased time distortion, making it seem like time had passed very quickly or very slowly, but none of them seemed to improve his perception of time. He could think that he was only going to spend five minutes on a project, only to "wake up" from it hours later, unsure where all of the time had gone.

His phone was ringing and vibrating in his pocket. Zachary pulled it out and saw Kenzie's name.

"Oh, hi, Kenz."

"Hey. Where are you? Are you coming home?"

Zachary looked at the darkening sky, and then down at the phone in his hand. "Oh. I didn't realize it was so late. Sorry. I was just walking… trying to sort something out. I'll come home."

"Do you want me to pick you up? How far away are you?"

Zachary looked around him. "Not far," he told her with relief. "I should only be a few minutes."

She could look at the tracking app on her phone to see where he was, if she were concerned. And she might have done that before calling him and just not felt like letting him know that. But he didn't need to feel guilty, because he was nowhere near Bridget's house. His recent abduction had effectively put a stop to his ever going back to his ex-wife's house to try to catch a glimpse of her or the twin babies, more than any medication or therapy ever could have. He had such a strong aversion to going back there, it made him shudder just to think of it. A development that he was sure delighted Bridget and Gordon.

"Dinner soon," Kenzie told him. "Don't lose track. Come straight home."

"I will."

He hung up, took a few deep breaths to refocus his brain, and headed home. The sky was darkening and the temperature was dropping. He hadn't noticed it before Kenzie's call. A fine private investigator he was, wandering around aimlessly, totally oblivious to his surroundings. What if someone had decided to take advantage of his absentmindedness?

As he walked, he felt his phone vibrate again. An alarm or some other alert that he had set. Maybe Kenzie sending him a quick text to make sure that he was still heading straight for home rather than being distracted by something else. He ignored the phone and just kept going.

39

T hanks for coming straight home," Kenzie told Zachary when she greeted him at the door with a kiss. "How was your day? You must have been stuck on something."

She knew him too well, understanding how he needed to move his body to help keep his brain engaged when working on a difficult problem. Some tasks kept him hyperfocused without moving around. Watching a video or studying a photo. Research or testing that required him to do the same thing over and over again. What might seem boring and repetitive to someone else felt like an engaging ritual for Zachary, helping everything to click into place.

"Yeah, just trying to figure some things out on Tyrrell's case. Bobby Elder's, I mean."

"You could probably use a break. Sometimes it's when you pull away from it that your brain fires into gear and you get inspired."

Zachary nodded. He checked the burglar alarm, disarming and rearming it again quickly.

"How about you? How was your day?" he asked, trying to get out of his own head. She was right about sometimes needing to pull back before he could get anywhere.

"Not bad. But nothing exciting."

Zachary liked it when Kenzie had interesting things to share with him from her work. But not too *exciting*. He would rather things didn't get too exciting at the morgue. Visions of zombies or dangerous escaped viruses filled his brain.

"Go wash up," Kenzie told him.

Zachary blinked at her. "What?"

"Go wash up. Change your shirt. Get ready for dinner. I'll have it on in a few minutes."

Zachary looked at his shirt, which he had worn a couple of days in a row. But he hadn't spilled anything on it. There were no stains. He sniffed at it tentatively as he headed toward the bathroom. Kenzie was right, of course, it was time to change it. He threw it in the hamper and got a fresh shirt out but didn't put the new one on until he had visited the bathroom and done a quick cleanup, not just of his face and hands, but a too-cold sponge bath of his upper torso as well. He pulled the shirt on without properly toweling off first, resulting in it sticking to his damp skin.

Zachary's phone vibrated and he put it on the sink counter while he rolled on a little deodorant and dabbed on aftershave. He had voicemail messages. He didn't remember the phone ringing, but it must have at some point, and he hadn't answered it. Or maybe he had looked at the caller ID and not recognized it, so he had promptly forgotten about it. Or the messages had been left while he was talking to Tyrrell or Kenzie.

He touched the screen to play back the voicemail messages while he finished making himself presentable for dinner.

"How would you like that brother of yours to disappear just like his friend?" a guttural voice demanded. "Those who don't learn from history are doomed to repeat it."

Zachary stopped, staring at his phone with his mouth open. The phone automatically advanced to the next message.

"We know who you are and where you live."

Zachary tried to swallow, but his throat was as dry as sandpaper. He filled a cup with water and took several gulps, which made him feel nauseated. How could he have been completely oblivious when these calls came in? He shook his head, as if denying it would wipe them out. He listened to both messages again, and then a third played.

"Zachary, it's Dr. Boyle. Missed you this afternoon. Please call me back when you get this message and give me an update. Let me know if everything is okay."

Zachary's heart sank. He looked at the date line at the top of his phone screen. It was Wednesday. His regular therapy day. He'd also missed his calendar reminders, too lost in thought even to remember that he had any commitments.

He tapped the call-back button and listened to it ring as he returned to the kitchen. Dr. B answered as he reached the doorway, so he went into the living room instead of the kitchen to talk to her with a modicum of privacy.

"It's Zachary. I'm so sorry, doctor. I completely forgot what day it was."

"How are you, Zachary? Everything okay?"

"Yes, yes, it's fine. I'm sorry; I just lost track of time this afternoon and didn't see my reminders. It won't happen again."

"Taking your meds?"

"Yes."

"Good. How are you sleeping?"

"Restless. But I'm taking care of myself. Sleep aid on bad nights. Kenzie can confirm that I've been taking them."

"Good. I know how much you hate taking them, but it will help keep you balanced. It is easier to manage life's little hiccups when you get the sleep you need."

"Yes," Zachary agreed. "I'm really sorry. I don't know how the afternoon slipped by me like that. I'll be there on Saturday. I won't miss that session."

"All right. Thank you for calling me back. I appreciate not having to worry about what might have happened to you."

"Everything is good," Zachary confirmed again.

"See you Saturday, then."

Dr. B hung up. Zachary slid the phone into his pocket, shaking his head.

When he walked into the kitchen, Kenzie's head turned toward him, but she didn't say anything about the phone call.

"Talking to Dr. B," Zachary told her, though he was sure she had probably heard every word and been able to figure that out for herself. "I missed today's session. Don't know where my head was at."

"I know."

"You know?" Zachary frowned.

"She sent me a text when you didn't show up. I checked the app to see where you were… figured you were just distracted."

He was surprised she had not called him and kept calling him until he answered. Instead, she had waited until dinner was almost ready before calling him. If he hadn't answered then, Zachary supposed she would have gotten into her car and followed the GPS signal to his phone. It hadn't been that long since his abduction, when she had found his phone in the gutter where he had dropped it in the scuffle. He would have thought that not showing up at Dr. Boyle's and then not answering his phone would have sent her scurrying over to find him.

Kenzie shrugged and nodded. "I was a bit concerned," she admitted. "But I could see your little dot moving slowly. Too slow to be in a car. And not trapped in one place. So, I figured… just you out for a walk."

"Sorry about that. Sometimes… I get so focused on a problem…"

"I know you do. So did you work it out?" She placed the last serving dish on the table and Zachary sat down to help himself.

"What?"

"Your problem. Tyrrell's case?"

"Yeah. No, I didn't solve it. But I have some thoughts."

But now that he was getting threats, Zachary was reconsidering. He didn't want anything to happen to Tyrrell or Kenzie. Or anyone he was close to. Was it really worth pursuing the case to its conclusion if it put people he loved in danger?

Couldn't he just do as Tyrrell had said and leave it alone? Let Robbie rest in peace, wherever he was?

The trouble was, he wasn't sure he could.

40

Zachary didn't tell Kenzie about the threatening voicemails. He decided to put those on the back burner and not think about them for a while. Maybe whoever had left them would give up if Zachary didn't do anything to respond to them. He wouldn't go to the police and have them try to trace them. Getting the police *more* involved in the Robert Elder case would not be likely to please whoever was trying to get him off of the case. But maybe if he didn't make any more calls to the police or do anything too obvious, he would decide that Zachary had taken his threat seriously and would let it go at that.

It wasn't like there were a lot of avenues left to explore anyway.

It had been a long day, and he was at home with Kenzie and wanted to spend time relaxing with her and giving their relationship the attention it needed. He couldn't let it fall by the wayside.

They chatted some more about her work and random investigative and forensic topics that interested them both. Zachary had his laptop closed and the TV on, and Kenzie was reading a book, when her phone rang.

Normally, she didn't answer it in the evening when they were unwinding. But when she looked at the face of the phone for the caller ID, she raised her brows and swiped the call to answer it.

"Hi, Dad."

They exchanged some pleasantries. Zachary was glad to see her making an effort in the relationship with her father. While Walter was not a man that Zachary wanted anything to do with professionally, he did want Kenzie to have a good personal relationship with him. Family was important and, if she refused to have anything to do with him, she would regret it sooner or later.

It was different from his own situation, where the childhood relationship had been so toxic and abusive and Zachary's father was a drunk and a pedophile. Not someone he wanted any kind of relationship with. Kenzie's father was self-centered and would cross ethical lines to get what he wanted or thought was best, but he was a good person at heart and loved Kenzie and wanted to please her.

Kenzie was looking at Zachary, her expression questioning. Zachary realized he must have missed something she had said that had been directed at him rather than her father.

"What? Sorry?"

"Walter has… a question from the governor's office." Her voice held a skeptical, warning tone.

"Uh… for me?"

"Yeah."

"Uh…" Zachary wasn't sure how to handle this. "Okay?"

Kenzie tapped her phone screen and held the phone horizontally between her body and Zachary's. "Dad? You're on speaker now. Zachary's listening."

"Zachary," Walter greeted pleasantly. "How have you been?"

It had been a few months since Zachary had done a job for Walter, and that had not worked out well. He had resolved to listen to what Kenzie had to say about her father and never to take another case from him again. So he was cautious about whatever Walter wanted to tell him or what the governor's message was.

"Pretty good, Walter. How about you?"

Walter chuckled. "You don't need to sound quite so enthusiastic." He didn't sound offended by Zachary's cautious manner, though. He was probably used to that from people. As a lobbyist, he probably dealt with a lot of skepticism and caution from the people he called.

"You had a message for me?" Zachary asked.

If the message really was from the governor, then why hadn't the call come from his office? And why was Walter calling Kenzie's cell rather than Zachary's?

"Yes. As you probably know, Governor Smith is facing another election in November, so he is well into campaign strategies, dealing with staff turnovers before then, all that fun sort of stuff."

"Uh-huh?"

"He is looking for someone who can run point for him on background investigations for new staff members, as well as deep background on his opponents. Not just whether they have any convictions or scandals in their past, but relationships and back-grounds on family members and their opinions, where they stand on various election issues, any recent travel, what they have posted on social media, especially if they have hidden accounts… There's just a whole raft of these issues to be dealt with during an election, and after that too. There would be ongoing work to do for his office, not just pre-election work."

"Oh." Zachary thought about this. The governor could afford to pay well. And it sounded like a good number of hours of work, at least to start with. Some of the work could be done by Heather, leaving him free for the more interesting investigations that came to his door. It would be good, steady work, at least until the elec-tion. He wasn't sure how much work there would be after that. He would have to take Walter's word that there would still be more to do after the election. "Well, I'm flattered that he thought of me. Or that you recommended me. That was very nice of you…"

"I didn't do it to be nice. I know you're a good investigator, and that's what he needs. Someone who can really dig in, who has discretion, a small operation that won't be leaking all over the place. There are a lot of advantages to working with someone with an operation… like yours."

Did Walter mean *small*? That he liked Zachary for the job because he was a one-man operation—or two-person operation, if he knew that Heather worked on administrative files and computer work?

"I'll have to think about it," Zachary told him, not showing too much enthusiasm to Walter. Even if it was a really good job, it was best to make Walter think he would have to work to get Goldman Investigations for the work. It put him in a better bargaining position. "Is there a deadline? And is there a written offer outlining everything he would want done?"

"He's offering it to *you*," Walter emphasized. "Not to anyone else. There's no job posting, no other applicants. If you want the job, it's yours. But he can't wait around for an answer. He would need you to accept pretty quickly."

"Not tonight."

"No!" Walter laughed. "He can certainly wait more than a couple of hours. But you can't leave it for too long. You don't want to be leaving it for a week. I'd like to hear your thoughts tomorrow. I can answer any questions you may have. You can tell me what you are thinking, any concerns, just a good bull session to work through any possible friction."

"So, I have until tomorrow to give an answer?"

"You have until tomorrow to think through your options and let me know what direction your thoughts are going. Hopefully, by the end of the week, you'll be in a position to give him a positive answer."

Zachary looked at Kenzie to see her reaction to his offer and the pressure to decide quickly. Kenzie's lips were pressed together, and she gave her head a quick shake.

"I don't know if this is something I want to get involved with," Zachary told Walter. "It's not really my kind of thing. We could help you with the background searches on an hourly or per-file contract, but I don't want to sign on for the whole thing. I have other investigations going on right now that need my time."

41

"Zachary," Walter's tone took on a serious, disappointed tone. "This is a great opportunity. I talked you up. I think it would be really good for you. Don't just turn it down flat without considering it."

"I'm not. But if you want a preliminary indication of what I'm thinking, that's my answer. It really doesn't sound like my kind of thing. I don't want to have my time tied up with a political file."

"It's good, steady work. It's doing the kind of thing that you like to do, without any risk of the violence you've faced lately in other cases. You wouldn't have to worry about drumming up business from other sources."

It was probably unthinkable to someone like Walter that Zachary might not want the steady kind of office job that he was proposing. But Zachary hadn't gotten into private investigation because he liked to sit in front of a computer all day doing the same thing day in and day out. He liked varied experiences and clients, a range of different types of investigations, getting out and working with people, digging down into a cold case like Tyrrell's. The monotony of an office job would kill him.

"That's not really the kind of thing that I'm looking for. I enjoy working for a variety of clients rather than just one. I appreciate you thinking of me, but I am not looking for a change right now. I'm happy with what I'm doing."

"Zachary," Walter said firmly. "You need to think about this. You can't think you can afford to support a family just on what you make on these small files. You need to be thinking of the future. On how sustainable this model that you've been using until now is. You don't want to be looking back five years from now saying, 'I should have taken that job.'"

"Why the high pressure, Dad?" Kenzie interrupted. "It isn't like Zachary is the only one who is working. I've got a good job with a regular paycheck. And you have no idea what Zachary is making or how much will come in in the future. Or..." her voice took on a bit of an accusing edge, "what it is that he likes to do. What kind of work is good for him."

"I'm not pressuring you. I'm just saying that it's a really good opportunity. The kind of thing that you want to look at if there might be kids in the future... the demands of a family are very different than a couple of single people who decide to cohabit for a while. Don't you want a family, Zachary?"

If Walter knew Gordon, Bridget's partner, and Zachary knew he did, then he knew that Zachary wanted children and a happy family life. He wasn't content with just cohabiting for the rest of his life. But Zachary wasn't going to pressure Kenzie to have children, either. She had a job that she loved at the medical examiner's office. She wasn't likely to turn into a stay-at-home mom and abandon the career that she had been working on setting up over the past decade.

"Walter... give us some time to think about this and talk things over," he said eventually. "We need some time."

"Of course," Walter granted, maybe backing off a little at Zachary's concession that he and Kenzie would need to discuss it. "Let me know once you've had a chance to talk things through."

Kenzie said goodbye and terminated the call. She looked at Zachary, raising her brows. "Well, that was unexpected."

Zachary nodded slowly. "Did you tell him that I was looking for something? Trying to pick up some more contracts?"

"No, nothing like that. I don't know where this came from. I don't know if he's telling the truth or not. He could be, I guess." She sounded doubtful. "Maybe the governor was looking for someone, and Walter suggested you. They know each other, of course. And he wouldn't speak for the governor unless he had his agreement beforehand. You *can* accept it if you are interested, or ask him what the next step is."

"Not really the kind of thing I'm interested in doing," Zachary told her slowly, feeling his way through the conversation. She had told him before not to take anything her father tried to offer, explaining that he was always looking out for himself and not anyone else. Did she have a different opinion because it was the governor who was offering the job and Walter was just relaying it? Did she want him to take something that was more of a consistent, dependable source of income? Some desk work that would put bread on the table and not run any risks? "Sitting at a desk all day isn't really what I want to do."

"No, I know that. It sounds like you could do other things too, maybe, but… I don't know. I'd like to know how this whole thing came about. I don't believe for a minute that Walter is just offering something out of the goodness of his heart."

"Yeah." Zachary shook his head. "It just doesn't feel right."

They left it at that. Zachary didn't say that he was interested in the job, and she didn't push him to take it or, alternatively, tell him not to take it under any circumstances. Zachary could call Walter back the next day to tell him no, or he might just let it slide until Walter decided to push it further and call him back.

42

Thursday morning, after Kenzie left for work, Zachary tried to focus on his files. He still thinking about Walter and the offer he had made out of the blue the night before, and it distracted him from what he wanted to concentrate on. With everything else that was going on surrounding the Robbie Elder case, he couldn't help wondering if it was somehow related. But how could it be? No one had said anything about the case, and there wasn't any connection that Zachary could see. And how could the governor or Walter know anything about the case? It wasn't exactly public knowledge that Zachary was looking into it, and it was too obscure for anyone in any position of authority to care about it, especially twenty years later.

His phone rang, and he saw from the caller ID that it was Heather.

"Hey, Feathers."

"Hi, Zach. Have you looked at your email this morning?"

"Uh, no..." Zachary immediately felt guilty. He had been neglecting his email lately, assuming that Heather would take care of things or tell him if there were anything that he was falling behind on. "Sorry, is there something I need to see?"

"Well… yes, there is."

Zachary tapped his computer keys while he talked with her on the phone, and clicked the mouse to bring up his email login.

It looked like everything was under control. There wasn't a long list of emails that hadn't been dealt with. Heather took care of the invoices and bills, and moved emails into Zachary's to-do list if there were something he needed to follow up on personally. And anything personal and low priority, she moved into a separate folder that he could look at when he felt like it. Most of it was unimportant and just ended up in the trash when he got around to it.

"There are a couple up at the top there," Heather pointed out.

"Uh-huh?" Zachary clicked on one of them and opened his mouth to ask what Heather needed him to do about it. But when he glanced at the content, he didn't need to ask.

"They're pretty threatening," Heather said in a low voice.

"Yeah. Thanks. I don't think it's anything that we need to worry about…"

"Zachary, you've got people threatening to kill you! What's going on with Tyrrell's file? Are these the first emails like that you've gotten?"

"Yes. But… I did get a couple of voicemail messages yesterday," Zachary admitted.

"So, these guys have your phone number and your email address and they're threatening to kill you? You need to report this to the police. Get them to trace the emails. Find out who is doing this!"

"They've been run through an anonymizer service," Zachary said, looking at the header of the second email he opened. "The police can't trace that. They'd have to subpoena the records of the anonymizer, and most of them are overseas. They won't even bother for something like this."

"Death threats aren't important?"

"Death threats to a PI about his cases? No, they happen way too often for the cops to care about that, and they would probably be sending me threats themselves if they were allowed. In fact, this could have come from one of them." Zachary thought about Able. Just how intent was he on getting Zachary to drop the Elder investigation? Had he known or suspected that Zachary didn't intend to stop when he said he would? The threats hadn't started until after he had talked to Able, trying to get him to look into John Doe cases to see if he could identify one of them as Robbie Elder.

"But what if they're not just threats?" Heather demanded. "What if they follow through? Show up at your house?"

"We have a good security system. Hardwired into our security company. As soon as it goes off, they dispatch someone." He chuckled. "As I've found out a couple of times when I've accidentally triggered it."

"Well, that's good, but something could still happen to you before they arrived. I'm serious, Zachy; this is really concerning."

"I know. I'll look into it. See if I can figure out who it might have come from. Chances are, it's nothing. Just someone venting. An adultery case that I've reported back on. Somebody who doesn't like me interfering with his life. But it blows over. They make a threat or two and then go on with their life. Decide to shack up with the girlfriend instead, and decide that it was good that I turned them in so that they could rid themselves of a bad marriage. I've seen it happen a dozen times."

"You don't think they are really serious."

"They might think that they are. But no… I've rarely had anyone take any action. They prefer anonymity." Zachary motioned to his laptop by way of explanation. "They are hiding behind it. They're not ready to come out into the open."

"It really concerns me. Don't you think you should send it to one of the cops you know to check out? Just to make sure?"

"Maybe." Zachary tried to brush her off. "I'll look into it a bit more."

"It's Tyrrell's case, isn't it? I couldn't understand why he wanted to dig up something that was so old."

Zachary wasn't sure what was puzzling her about it, since she'd also asked him to look into her cold case. Sometimes people just needed to deal with the past before moving on. However, Tyrrell had apparently decided he didn't want Zachary to look into it anymore. Unless he had flip-flopped again.

"It might be Tyrrell's case," he admitted. "And if it is… then we don't need to worry, because I'm considering dropping it. Tyrrell didn't want me to pursue it any further."

If it *was* the Robbie Elder case, then why? Was he that close to figuring out who the killer was? Perched right on the brink of uncovering the truth? And how would anyone know that? The only people who knew where Zachary was looking now were Tyrrell, Hal, and Detective Able. Any one of the three of them could have decided to use anonymous messages to scare him off the case. But the chances that he'd really gotten that close to the perpetrator, who knew who he was and thought he was closing in on them, seemed pretty slim.

Zachary kept busy with other things, pretending the Robbie Elder case did not exist. Maybe Able would find something and let him know that it had all been sorted out, that a previously unidentified body had now been identified as Robert Elder, thanks to Zachary's investigation, and they were going to return him to his mother. She could have a memorial for him, and Tyrrell could go to that and find his peace, and everything would return to normal. There would be no need for any further investigation.

But did he really think he could let it go without knowing who had shot Robbie? That he could just forget that there was a man out there who had taken it upon himself to shoot a seventeen-year-old kid twenty years ago? He wouldn't call Robbie innocent. He knew he couldn't go that far. But he'd been young and stupid and should have been educated, shown how misguided his actions were, rather than being summarily shot.

Zachary had plenty else to work on. Heather emailed or texted him a few times, keeping on top of him to do other things. He suspected that she was intentionally distracting him from anything to do with Tyrrell. And for the time being, he was okay with that.

He almost succeeded in making himself forget about the case. Every time he started wondering about it again, he told himself to wait and see whether Able found anything. In a day or two, he would probably come back with either a yes or a no.

43

On Friday, Zachary couldn't wait any longer. He would go for a short drive back to Clintock to look around and ask a *few* questions. Maybe he would talk to Tyrrell's adoptive parents and ask them what they remembered from that time. Surely if Tyrrell had been involved with a gang and blackmail, they would have noticed. Maybe they had seen Tyrrell talking to some of their intended targets—though, of course, the Millers would never have known that was what they were up to.

It wasn't a very good plan, but at least it was something.

Zachary looked around before disarming and unlocking his car, watching for anyone watching him or sitting in a parked car. Everything seemed to be as it should be. People out walking dogs, going to work, or out for a run. All people that he knew, following their usual routines. No utility workers or city services. No white panel vans with tinted windows. No one with a camera or who was obviously making a recording of what he was doing.

All good. All perfectly normal.

Zachary turned his key in the ignition.

It didn't start. He let go of the key quickly and stared at it, heart pounding. He remembered his suspicions about the boys hanging around his car at the center. Had they tampered with it?

Allowed someone else to? Maybe they were angry at being confronted by Ivy and had retaliated by not telling them that someone had done something to it.

He didn't turn the key again. He didn't press the gas or do anything else. His heart pounded, and he just sat there, ears pricked for a ticking or the click of a switch. He'd seen all kinds of things on TV shows. Bombs that were triggered by sitting in the seat. By turning the key. Maybe a countdown timer had started and it was just a matter of time, or maybe it would happen when he tried to get up and out of the car.

Should he call Kenzie to hear her voice one last time? Or Bridget, since she couldn't do anything to him if he were blown to bits.

It would have to be Kenzie. He couldn't leave her thinking she mattered less to him than Bridget. That he didn't care about her when he knew he was about to explode.

But he didn't think he could pull it off. He wouldn't want to sound tearful or worried. He didn't want to scare her or for her to realize that he knew he was about to die.

Zachary pulled out his phone and looked at it. He still couldn't hear any buzzing or ticking, anything that indicated how much time he had left or that the device had been armed. He quickly scanned for radio waves or magnetic fields and couldn't find any. He checked Kenzie's location, something he had only done about a hundred times since getting the first death threats, to ensure she was at the medical examiner's office where he expected her to be. It was secure there. She couldn't be kidnapped. No one could get at her without talking their way past the guards, and they would know that something was wrong.

Except that Zachary didn't know how much corruption there might be in the Vermont police departments. He had suspected it before. He had known when they had rescued Madison and Luke from the human trafficking ring that someone in Roxboro PD was dirty. He had wondered whether Able had spread the word that he was looking into a cold case, and someone was worried about that. When Tyrrell and Robbie had been blackmailing gang members, had they crossed up some cops?

What about Hal? Was he a current cop or a former cop? He had shown up awfully quickly when Zachary had started looking for witnesses. How had he known? And how had so many other people known that he was a threat? People emailing and voice messaging him. Able and Tyrrell both telling him to back off. There had to be a leak somewhere.

Zachary's mouth and throat were dry. He tried to swallow, but he needed about a dozen bottles of water to irrigate that desert. Before putting his phone back away, he texted Kenzie.

Hope you're having a great day today. See you tonight.

There were dots on his screen almost immediately, indicating that she was sending him a reply. He breathed shallowly, waiting for it.

Remember that we have to go shopping tonight before date night

Zachary laughed. It seemed bizarre to think that there were such things as grocery shopping and date night in the future. When he might not have any future beyond the next few minutes.

He sent her back a kiss emoji and slid his phone into his pocket.

Waiting any longer wouldn't accomplish anything. He was just drawing out the inevitable. Zachary opened his door and swung his legs out. Still no click of a dead man's switch releasing, getting ready to launch him into the stratosphere.

He put his feet on solid ground and stood up.

Nothing happened.

But it still could. He might have started something. Triggered a countdown. Fulfilled some kind of qualification that started a series of events he could not stop.

Zachary leaned against the car, trying to catch his breath. His legs were so weak and wobbly that he could barely hold himself up. Anyone watching him would think that he was drunk. Or having a stroke. He'd embarrassed himself so often with panic attacks that he didn't care what people thought.

But he should put distance between himself and the car, just in case. He should call his mechanic and get it towed if nothing happened. Jergens could put it up on a lift and see if anything was attached before trying to start it again. Maybe it was coincidental, something as simple as a dead battery, but he couldn't assume it was safe. He couldn't put anyone else at risk.

He eased the car door shut, not letting it slam, just barely letting it click into place. Even that little click sent his heart racing. He didn't lock the doors or arm the security alarm, no matter how much he was tempted to. Any sequence of routine actions could prove fatal.

Zachary left the car at the curb and walked up the sidewalk to the house. He let himself inside and cleared the security alarm so it wouldn't go off. He did not need the klaxon blaring and private cops descending on his house this time. He couldn't manage anything like that. He couldn't see his car clearly through the peephole and was not tall enough to see through the little arc window at the top of the door. Instead, he went into the living room and looked at the car parked by the curb.

Everything seemed perfectly normal.

No firebomb. No concussion blast and windows blowing into the house.

It looked just like it did any other day.

44

Most of the day passed in a haze.

After watching the car through the window for an hour or two, Zachary was exhausted. But his heart was still pounding wildly, his muscles still tense. Being in a state of near-panic for hours was not healthy and rapidly drained his energy. He eventually gave in and took one of his anti-anxiety pills, knowing that it would reduce or reverse the state of panic and make him useless for anything else except sleep.

But as it was, he was useless anyway. What would he do, sit there watching his car for the rest of the day? Turn his back on it and check his email or his task list? He wouldn't be able to focus on it at all. If he did any work, it would be so messed up that he would have to completely redo it again the next day. The day was already a loss, so what did it matter if he took an anxiety pill and went to sleep for a while?

He took a pill with the remains of the cold coffee in his cup. He went into the kitchen to refill the coffee cup, but didn't get that far. There were still donuts on the counter from his breakfast meeting with Tyrrell. Kenzie was trying to avoid such fattening treats, so finishing them was up to him. And so far, Zachary hadn't been able to eat them all. He shouldn't have ordered a full dozen for the two of them. Maybe two donuts, or four, but a whole dozen? For him and Tyrrell to polish off in a breakfast meeting? That was ridiculous. He took one of the remaining donuts from the box and jammed it into his mouth. Fat and sugar to help him to relax after the tense morning too. His doctor would be happy that he was keeping his calorie count up. He always lost weight before Christmas, but if he could stay at his target weight for most of the year, he would be much less likely to get down to the lows he had hit the last couple of years.

He didn't get a plate, even though he could hear Kenzie's lecture about getting donut crumbs all over the house. He didn't have the energy to manage a plate. He would go to the bedroom and lie down. A few hours of sleep after the anxiety pill, and then he should be back on his feet again, ready to engage with an hour or two of work before Kenzie got home. Then grocery shopping together—which he was beginning to hate with a passion—and date night. Maybe take Kenzie out to a movie and then back home for some cuddling and possible intimacy.

It all sounded good in his head. He could even look forward to how he would feel after sleeping the effects of the anxiety pill away. Even though he might be a little fuzzy or muddled, he would feel fine. Normal. Like other people did every day. No more preparing for death. Just calm and relaxed and ready to spend time with his partner.

When he awoke, the sunlight coming into the room was starting to turn orange. There were noises in the house. Zachary forced himself to sit up, heart thumping wildly over his sudden wakening and hearing someone else in the house. He looked on his bedside table for his phone, but it was not there. He patted his pockets, not having any more luck finding it there.

Footsteps down the hallway. Getting closer. Zachary braced himself, looking around for a weapon. Hadn't he decided that he should get a taser to help to protect himself? What ever had happened to that decision? Once he was out of danger, it had just completely fled his brain.

He gripped the blankets of the bed. There was nothing else for him to do to keep from falling apart. If he wanted to stay in control, he needed to hold on to something.

The door opened.

Kenzie, looking at him quizzically. "Zachary? Are you okay?"

He nodded, unable to find any words.

"Are you sick?" Kenzie looked around the room.

Of course he never slept during the day unless he was sick or something was really wrong and he couldn't handle it.

"I just… Must have had too many donuts," Zachary invented. "I was feeling queasy. Laid down for a while. I'm fine now; you just startled me. I didn't realize how late it was."

Kenzie nodded slowly. "You're feeling okay now?"

"Yeah. Yeah, I'm fine."

"But I don't suppose you want any supper if you are just recovering from an overdose of donuts."

"No. Probably not."

45

Kenzie ate supper on her own while Zachary had a shower to wake himself up properly and get back on track. He had achieved nothing during the day. Now he needed to be available to Kenzie for their grocery shopping trip and date night. He wasn't sure how he was going to manage it. His anxiety level was still high, but he couldn't take another pill. He needed to be alert for the rest of the evening.

He looked out the window at his car through the bedroom window as he dressed and got ready to rejoin Kenzie. He called Jergens to see if he could tow it and have a look at it for any trackers or explosive devices. Jergens had been in the Middle East and seen enough IEDs in his day, but was amused at the idea of finding one in Vermont on Zachary's car.

"Buddy, we just don't see that here. Of course, I'll look for you, but I won't find anything."

"Good. Then you'll need to find out why it didn't start this morning. But check for a device first. I don't want you messing around with the ignition and setting it off…"

"Of course," Jergens agreed in good humor. "I know that much, at least. You don't need to worry about that, Zach. I'm just telling you; you don't need to worry."

"You don't know that. You don't know these guys. They could have done anything."

For that matter, Zachary himself didn't know who he was dealing with. But if they were powerful enough to know that he was looking into a twenty-year-old case the minute he started contacting witnesses, they had to have a good network with lots of eyes and ears on the street. Zachary's brakes had been tampered with during a previous case, and he didn't feel like another trip to the hospital. Or to the morgue, for that matter, unless it was to see Kenzie for something.

"Let me know what you find?" Zachary requested. "And be careful when you move it… putting the hook on it, putting it into neutral…"

"I'll check it out in place first. Make sure there is nothing suspicious before I tow it. And then I'll put it up on the lift and give it a thorough going over before I try to start it to see what is wrong with it. Okay?"

Zachary blew out his breath slowly. "Okay. And let me know."

"As soon as I can. But this isn't the next car on my list, so you might have to wait until tomorrow. Don't call me tonight demanding to know what I found."

"Okay."

Zachary left it with him. Jergens was a professional; if there were something to be found on the car, he would find it. Even if it was just a bug or a tracker. And if it was an explosive device, he was the one guy Zachary knew who would know how to handle it.

He slid his phone away and returned to the kitchen to see if Kenzie was ready. She put her dishes into the dishwasher, shut the door, and started it washing. She frowned at him.

"All ready to go?"

"Yeah. Sorry to be so long. Hard to get my motor running after an afternoon nap. One of the reasons I hate taking them."

"So you just… didn't feel good after you ate?"

He shrugged. He didn't want to lie to her and tell her why he had been so anxious, but he didn't want her to worry about his being blown up or something happening to him. Or to her. He would trigger the anxiety she had been dealing with since her abduction, brief though it had been.

"All right, let's go." Kenzie started to walk toward the front door.

"Uh—we'll take your car," Zachary interposed.

She turned and looked at him. "Yours has a bigger cargo area. We always use yours."

"I had trouble starting it this morning. Jergens is going to pick it up tonight and have a look at it."

"It didn't start this morning? You didn't say anything to me."

"You were at work. I found other things to do to keep myself busy today. And it will be taken care of. Jergens will sort it out for me."

Kenzie shrugged. "Okay. Sounds good. We'll take my baby."

She turned around and headed instead for the door to the garage. Zachary followed. He looked at the sporty red convertible before he got in, his stomach knotting. He walked around it slowly, looking for any sign that it might have been tampered with. She had driven it home, so it had started without any problem. But someone could have a remote detonation switch and just be waiting until Zachary was in the car before setting it off.

"What's wrong?" Kenzie asked, standing at her door watching him.

"It was parked in the police parking garage all day, right?"

"Yes. Just like always."

There was good security in the building. They wouldn't let anyone in who didn't have a pass and the proper identification. But was the police department safe? What if someone in the Roxboro police department was part of the conspiracy to bury the Robbie Elder case? A cop could have moved from Clintock to Roxboro. Or someone who was higher up in the food chain could have influence over one or more cops in the Roxboro police department. Hal himself had been involved in both the Clintock police department and Peggy Ann's organization. Zachary knew from experience that Peggy Ann had at least one cop in the Roxboro police department under her control. Who knew who might have touched Kenzie's car during the day?

Zachary pulled out his phone and ran through his usual checks for a transmitter on Kenzie's car. She stood watching him.

"What's going on?"

"I just want to make sure… that no one has tampered with it."

"In the police parking garage."

"Yes. You never know…"

"Why would someone have tampered with it in the police parking garage? And who?"

"I don't know who. They have moles everywhere. You can't know."

"Who exactly has moles everywhere?"

"Peggy Ann. Other cartels. I don't know for sure."

"Zachary…"

"I know she does," Zachary told her firmly. "I *saw* that when we rescued Madison and Luke. You know that. Just because you didn't see him doesn't mean he wasn't there. And we had to plant false information using Campbell, remember that? To make them think that Madison and Luke were dead and not tip them off as to where we took them?"

"Yes, but that was…" Kenzie shook her head. "That was ages ago. Why are you worrying about it again now? We haven't had any contact with the trafficking rings around Roxboro since then."

"But I saw Peggy Ann when I was in Kent helping Joss get Luke out of jail. She hasn't stopped operating. She's still running the same organization. Probably bigger now."

"What does that have to do with my car being tampered with in the police parking garage today? That was months ago."

"There was an undercover cop working for her back then. I saw him, but I didn't know who he was. And he contacted me in Clintock this week."

"An undercover cop."

"Yes."

"And you think he could have come to Roxboro and tampered with my car?"

"He could have. Or he could reach out to someone they had in the Roxboro police department and have them do it."

And Zachary had just established that Peggy Ann did have at least one mole in the Roxboro police department. She couldn't say it was outside the realm of possibility.

"Why?"

"Because they want me to stop investigating Robbie Elder's disappearance. His murder. I don't know how they're mixed up in it, but they could be."

"Now?"

Zachary nodded. "They want me off the case. Hal said he wanted to find out what happened to Elder, but that could be a smokescreen. I don't know if that's true. If he is working for Peggy Ann..."

"If he's an undercover cop, he won't do anything to hurt us. He's gathering evidence to be used against Peggy Ann, not working for her."

"We don't know that. He might have turned. It sometimes happens, you know. They get too attached to the people that they are supposed to be gathering evidence against and end up turning against the police department."

"I highly doubt that has happened. Especially where he contacted you in person. He wouldn't do that if he wanted to do something to harm you, would he? Let you know that he was there and that he was a cop, and then turn around and do something to my car?" She shook her head in irritation. "And even if he wanted to, wouldn't he do something to your car, not mine? He doesn't need someone in the police department to tamper with yours. It's sitting at the curb out in the open, and..." She cut herself off, turning and looking toward the street where Zachary's car was parked, even though the wall and the house blocked it from view.

"Is that why you won't use yours?" she demanded. "You think that someone has tampered with it?"

Zachary shrugged. He tried to get into the car to show that he was ready and wasn't concerned enough about the possibility that it had been tampered with to let it stop him from going to the grocery store with her. But he couldn't. He couldn't force himself to get into the car without being more sure of himself.

Kenzie was silent as Zachary went around to the back of the car and carefully felt along the inside of the bumper for any bug, tracker, or other device that might be attached. Nothing. It was smooth and untouched. He repeated the process on the front bumper. Those were the two easiest areas to access if someone only had a few seconds to attach something. Just a quick crouch down behind or in front of the car, slap a magnet-mounted device into place, and walk back away.

He tried to see under the rest of the car, shone his phone flashlight around for a minute, and then finally got into the car. He still had stomach cramps as he pulled the door shut and buckled his seatbelt, but they were manageable. It was still possible that someone in the police department could have tampered with Kenzie's car, but the saboteur would have had to scoot underneath it on his back. Far more likely to be noticed by the security staff than a quick crouch to slap a magnet under the bumper.

Kenzie settled into her seat without saying anything. She turned her key in the ignition. Zachary held himself stiff. It started with a purr. No click. No explosion. No sign that anything was amiss. Zachary breathed out slowly. He pulled out his phone and pretended to be checking his email, unconcerned. But he doubted he was fooling Kenzie. She was too good at reading him and recognizing when something was wrong.

46

"How long have you been worried about the cars?" she asked in a neutral tone, opening the garage door and backing out.

"I'm always concerned about them. But this... just since this morning, when my car wouldn't start."

She nodded slowly, as if that explained everything.

Zachary supposed that from her perspective, an event like that could trigger extra anxiety and maybe some level of paranoia.

They drove to the grocery store in silence. Zachary tried to act as if nothing was bothering him. He knew Kenzie's anxiety would likely be triggered in the grocery store. For some reason, it was an environment that always seemed to make her worried and jumpy.

He should have offered to do the grocery shopping himself this time. The whole point of their doing it together recently was to train him in what things she needed and where to find them, so that he would get it right when she gave him a list. They had gone together enough times that he was sure he could find what she needed and pick out the brands she liked. And to get both green and yellow bananas so that they could ripen through the week and not all go bad at once.

But she wouldn't have let him go in her car. She didn't let

anyone else drive her baby, not even Zachary. And Zachary could not have gone in his own car.

They should have put it on hold. Waited until Zachary got his car back and then he could go on his own.

He saw Kenzie take a deep breath before opening her door to get out. Not only did she have her normal anxiety to deal with, but now she had to deal with his. Zachary forced what he hoped was a reassuring smile. Everything would be fine. Nothing was going to happen while they were in the grocery store.

Zachary tried to keep his behavior under wraps and to be patient and solicitous with Kenzie while they were in the store, but that just seemed to make her bristle more. She didn't appreciate being "handled."

"Just give me some space," she snapped when Zachary tried to get the soup she liked along with his Chicken and Stars. "I need space."

He dropped back farther behind her, hurt. He was just trying to help. That's what he was there for.

Halfway down the next aisle, Kenzie was looking back for him, apparently irritated that he had backed off too far. "You don't need to act like that."

Zachary spread his hands and shook his head, not sure what she expected him to do. Kenzie scowled. "Why don't you go get the milk and eggs? You can do *that*, can't you?"

She had left out the words that the cutting remark was meant to include. You can do *that one thing right*, can't you?

"Sure," Zachary agreed, and walked away from her, headed to the opposite side of the store, far away from her. He would take his time. Give her as much time and space as she needed. And maybe make her think that he had gotten distracted and stopped to look at something else.

Carrying the milk and eggs, he walked back across the store to find her, looking down each aisle to see how far she had gotten. He saw Kenzie and walked down the aisle toward her but, in looking beyond her, he saw a familiar figure.

Hal.

47

What was Hal doing there? He didn't live in Roxboro. He had no reason to be there, in the grocery store with Zachary and Kenzie. No reason unless he had been following Zachary. He wouldn't know where Zachary lived or shopped unless he had tailed him. All the way from Clintock? Had he had a tracker on Zachary's car since then? Had he been sitting on the street, watching until Zachary and Kenzie got into her car and headed for the grocery store?

Kenzie looked at Zachary's expression and then turned and looked behind her. She couldn't see anything unusual, just other grocery shoppers. Hal stood looking at the cereal boxes as if deciding what to buy.

"What?" Kenzie asked, her voice low and hesitant.

"Go back to the car."

"But—" she gestured at the shopping cart that she had half-filled.

"I'll check it out. You go out first, so I know you're safe in the car. We'll get the rest of what we need another day. Go."

She seemed rooted to the floor. Zachary took a deep breath in, trying to regulate his breathing and keep his voice calm and soothing.

"It's nothing, I'm sure. I just want to be careful. Go to the car, lock the doors, and text me that you're safe and everything looks fine out there. Keep an eye out for anyone watching you or giving you more attention than they should. People should just be getting into their cars and walking away. If they're sitting there... be suspicious."

"Should I call the police? What's going on?"

"Just... someone who shouldn't be here. It's probably nothing. But please go and let me know you're safe."

Kenzie finally nodded. She separated her hands from the shopping cart as if the movement were painful, and backed away a couple of steps.

"Just act like everything is normal," Zachary told her, not wanting her to draw attention to herself by walking backward down the aisle, afraid to turn her back on Zachary and whatever danger he had seen.

Kenzie nodded and turned around. Zachary looked at the bags of coffee on the shelf next to him, pretending to be checking the prices. Hal was still standing there looking at the breakfast cereal. Determined, Zachary pushed the cart toward him. He stopped just inches away from Hal.

"What are you doing here?"

Hal turned his head to look at Zachary, then turned back to the boxes of cereal again. "Buying groceries."

"You're following me."

"You having any luck on the Robert Elder case?"

"I told you that I was going to drop it."

"Yeah. I didn't believe that."

"You're wanted for questioning by the police."

"On Robert Elder?" Hal questioned, looking amused.

"No. Detective Able said that you weren't answering their calls. They were looking for you and couldn't reach you."

Hal chuckled. "Yes, I bet they'd love to be able to talk to me, wouldn't they? In case he didn't tell you, we've had a bit of a falling out, and I don't want anything to do with them. So they'll have to get their questions answered another way."

"Are you investigating the police department in Clintock?"

"What gave you that idea?"

"Just speculating. I thought maybe you weren't really as retired as Able thought you were."

Hal shrugged. "Well, I wouldn't be likely to tell you, would I?"

"Are you the one who tampered with my car?"

"I didn't touch your car."

"Did you put a tracker on it? Is that how you followed me here?"

"You didn't drive your car here, so that would be difficult."

"But you could have followed it home to Kenzie's house and then watched until you saw us leave the house together."

"Why would I do that?" Hal took a box of Cheerios from the shelf and put it into his basket. He started walking away from Zachary.

"Hold on! I want to know what's going on!" Zachary insisted, following him. "You owe me an explanation! Why are you showing up here? Following me? Stalking me? You don't have any right to pry into my private life or interfere with my family. Are you the one who has been threatening me? You said that you wanted to solve this case, not that you wanted me off of it."

"I do," Hal said, turning toward him. "I'd be delighted to have this case solved. It's bothered me for a lot of years."

"Then you're not the one threatening me?"

"No. Who has been threatening you? How? Threatening you with what?"

"I've had voicemails and emails. Threatening to kill me. That wasn't you?"

"Why would I threaten to kill you?" Hal asked patiently. "I thought we just established that I want you to solve the case. That's why I'm here. To help you."

"You stalked me here so you could help me with the case."

"You don't think that a cop would be interested in justice? Why do you think I got into law enforcement in the first place? It certainly wasn't to sit around on my butt watching people be railroaded into crimes they didn't commit or murders of kids brushed

off and ignored. I wanted to see justice done. For your friend...
and everyone else."

Zachary didn't remind him that Robbie was Tyrrell's friend
rather than his own. It really didn't make any difference.

"So, who do you think is threatening me?"

"Could be anyone." Hal's eyes rolled up to the ceiling while he
thought about it. "I don't think that the police department cares
whether you solve it or not. Better for them to close it than for it to
sit open on the books for another twenty years. I may not see eye-
to-eye with them on most things, but I don't think Detective Able
is trying to block you."

"You don't think there is any police corruption? People inside
the department who might have had something to do with
Robbie's death? They certainly wouldn't want me to solve it."

"Of course there is police corruption... there always is. And
I've been in a position to see it. But I don't know about the Clintock police department having anything to do with Robbie's death
or trying to stop you from finding out about it. Why would they
care?"

"You said yourself that they were causing problems for gang
members. Organized crime. That could stretch to the police
department. I know Peggy Ann had a man inside the Roxboro
police department. Why not in Clintock? And if she had a man
inside, so could any other cartel or criminal organization. Right?"

"Yes," Hal agreed with a nod. "Could. But I don't think you
need to worry about cops. He'd have to make himself pretty
obvious to come after you."

"Unlike you." Zachary looked Hal up and down.

He laughed. "I don't have to report to anyone. To be anywhere
at a particular time. I don't have to write reports on my work, keep
a paper trail, or talk to a partner about it. I can come and go as I
like, like a ghost. But someone inside the police department doesn't
have that kind of freedom. There are a lot of other things they
would need to do to keep any kind of operation under wraps. Yes,
there are little things they can do when placed inside the department. Read reports. Pass intelligence along. Make a minor change

here and there to divert an investigation. But taking out the private investigator who's making a big fuss, broadcasting everything he is doing? A corrupt cop would have to make himself visible for that. And they do not have that much manpower. It's a small town. Hard to bury anyone there where he can keep operating but not give himself away."

Zachary looked at the groceries in his cart, but he was thinking about the cop who had questioned him when he had gotten Madison and Luke out of the apartment where Peggy Ann had them stashed. It was anxiety-producing just to think of how much danger they had been in, with Peggy Ann a minute or two behind them and the cop talking to them, delaying them, hoping to keep them in place until she returned from the building and dealt with them.

"I saw a cop here who was working for Peggy Ann."

"I know."

48

"You *know*?"

Hal nodded. "Sure, we heard how close it was. Peggy Ann wasn't pleased that he let you go, but there is only so much a cop can do and still keep his cover. Like I said. He'd have to blow his cover to come after you directly. I don't think you need to worry about a cop coming after you directly."

"But there could be others. People that Tyrrell and Robbie threatened to expose back then, who are still around now and still vulnerable to blackmail."

"Maybe even more vulnerable now, depending on how they are placed."

Zachary nodded. He looked around nervously. As if the dirty cop or whoever it was might come down the aisle pushing *his* shopping cart and threaten Zachary. But of course, he wouldn't. He would wait outside, maybe tail Zachary home and attack him there. They would assume that his house was less secure and they could get in.

He pulled out his phone to make sure that Kenzie had texted him to indicate she was safe in the car. He didn't want to leave her out there too long. It wasn't exactly a secure location. He'd wanted to get her away from Hal in case he was the threat, but he didn't seem to be. Not if he was telling the truth about wanting the case to be solved.

I'm waiting in the car. Tell me what's going on.

He slid the phone back away and looked around again. Hal watched him, amused.

"Getting a little paranoid, there?"

"I have enough anxiety without getting death threats."

Hal nodded as if he understood, but he looked totally relaxed. Maybe that was just his mask, his persona. The way that he kept Peggy Ann and anyone else from seeing his thoughts.

"I asked Able to let me see any John Does who might have matched up with Robbie Elder's death. He didn't think they would be able to give me any information, but he said he'd pass it on up the chain of command. If he starts to look at those John Does himself, is he going to find Robbie Elder?"

"Since I'm not the one who killed him or disposed of the body, I couldn't tell you. But my prediction? Yes. That boy is out there somewhere. And unless the killer did a really good job, the body always surfaces sooner or later. Identifying them isn't always easy, but methods have gotten better and better over the decades."

"That's what Kenzie was saying. That they had probably found the body and just didn't know who it was."

"She's a smart cookie."

"She works for the medical examiner's office. She knows what she's talking about."

Hal raised an eyebrow and nodded. So he hadn't looked at Zachary close enough to find out what his partner did.

"I need to go now. What are you going to do?"

"Buy some groceries. Find somewhere to hole up for a while."

"While you wait for me to solve Robbie Elder's case."

"Yeah."

"Why don't you help with that? You're the person who knows the most about it, other than whoever killed him. You're the one who knows all of the players and looked into it at the time."

"Are you saying you would be willing to talk to me about it?"

"I told you I wanted you to tell me everything."

"That's different. Are you willing to work with me?"

"I don't know. Maybe. Yeah." Zachary thought about Tyrrell wanting Zachary to drop the case just when he was starting to get some traction on it. "I need to talk to Tyrrell. See if I can get some more information from him."

"He's been holding back? Not a big surprise, considering."

"No. I guess not. Not if he was involved in blackmailing or stealing from these guys. But then he told me to back off; he didn't want me to investigate it anymore. Told me he'd changed his mind about it."

"What do you expect? He doesn't want you to find out all of the crap he was pulling. And if you are getting threats... chances are, he is too."

Zachary was feeling a little better when he got out to the car with the groceries. There were still things on the list that they needed to pick up, but they could either make do or come back in a day or two when it felt safer. Kenzie rolled down her window to talk to him as he pushed the cart up to the car.

"Is it safe? Can I get out?"

Zachary nodded. "Yeah. It's okay." He glanced around once, looking for anyone other than Hal who might have eyes on them. Just because he had dealt with what appeared to be the immediate threat, that didn't mean that there were not more. And if Hal *wasn't* the party who had been threatening him, then whoever had been was still out there. Still watching him and waiting for their opportunity. Maybe with eyes on Kenzie now, and her car, which had been left vulnerable in the parking lot while they had been inside.

"You can just stay there. I'll put them in," he offered, waving a hand toward the grocery bags.

Kenzie popped the lid of the tiny trunk and Zachary loaded it up with groceries. It was easy to crouch down and check the inside of the bumper. Again, it was clean. He ran a scan with his phone while standing behind the car with the trunk open, hiding him from Kenzie's sight. But he couldn't do much to keep her from seeing him checking the front bumper.

He did it anyway.

49

Saturday morning was Zachary's additional therapy day. Or, since he hadn't actually gotten to his Wednesday session, his make-up therapy day. He was embarrassed about having missed it and not sure how to talk to Dr. B about his increased anxiety with the death threats and his worries about the car. He didn't want her to think it was a symptom that needed to be medicated away.

As he prepared for his appointment, he looked out the window and realized his car was not there.

Of course. Because he had called Jergens to come and get it. And he wouldn't have driven it anyway, wouldn't have even tried to start it. What kind of a person would do something that risky? Not him. He wasn't going to take any risks this time.

So that meant that he would need to take the bus, a cab, or a ride share. Probably too late to catch the bus. He should have thought about it earlier.

"Do you mind if I come with you to your appointment today?" Kenzie suggested. "Then maybe we could pick up the rest of the groceries we need afterward."

That would solve the problem of alternative transportation. Zachary hesitated only a moment before nodding.

"Sure, that sounds fine. Since I don't have my car today."

Kenzie looked out the window. "Where is it?"

"I had my mechanic come by to get it and check it out."

She nodded. "Right. Of course. I could come in with you. To talk to Dr. B."

He looked at her. It wasn't one of their couple's sessions, so he wasn't sure why she suggested it.

"Umm…"

"If you're not comfortable with it, that's okay. I just wondered."

"Why?"

Kenzie pursed her lips, looking awkward. "You've been a little erratic lately. I wondered if it was something we should discuss with her together."

"I haven't been erratic."

She looked at him, raising one eyebrow.

Zachary shook his head. "I haven't. My car not starting properly and someone following us to the grocery store do not count as erratic behavior. Those are things that actually happened."

"But your behavior… I'm not sure that someone actually followed us there. Or that there was anything wrong with your car, other than it just not starting properly. It could be the battery. Or the starter. I don't know what."

"But it didn't start," Zachary emphasized. "I didn't just make that up."

"No. It doesn't mean someone tampered with it, either."

"It doesn't mean they didn't."

She threw up her hands in frustration. "This is exactly what I'm talking about. You don't see it because you don't see yourself that way. That's why I should come and talk to Dr. B about it. She can listen to both sides and either tell me to back off because you're being perfectly reasonable, or tell you that you need to pay attention because you're starting to go off the rails."

"You think I'm imagining things."

"I think that you might be headed for trouble. I think you're… interpreting things through a different filter. You and I can both see the same thing, but interpret it differently. That's not the same as hallucinating or imagining."

Zachary pressed his lips together, thinking about it and trying to figure out how to handle Kenzie's fears. He couldn't just tell her that she was paranoid, the same thing that she was saying about him. Neither of them was paranoid. They were just being cautious. Heeding the warning signs.

"Okay." He took a deep breath and let it out, trying to relax his muscles. "You can come in. Sure. I don't have anything to hide. We're in this together, right? Making this relationship work, which hinges on me retaining at least part of my sanity."

Zachary was quiet on the way to Dr. Boyle's office. He didn't know what else to say to Kenzie. There wasn't much point in his saying anything until they were in the session, or he would just have to repeat it. He already knew Kenzie's conclusion, that he was being crazy and letting his imagination run wild. *He* knew he wasn't crazy, and that was the important part, wasn't it?

She kept glancing at him as they drove, expecting him to begin the conversation or trying to think of ways to begin one herself. But they ended up just waiting. They would have plenty of time to hammer it out during the session.

Zachary did not like morning sessions, but Dr. B did not do Saturday afternoon sessions, so that was the time slot she had open for him. And he couldn't complain about it. She had a family life too. She needed time off to nurture her own relationships and to recover from whatever emotional wringer her patients put her through. While she had always seemed calm and relaxed during their sessions, even when Zachary broke down, he didn't imagine it was easy to listen to everyone's problems and not take on any of their emotional baggage herself. She must need time for unwinding and recreation after all of that.

But that didn't help him to feel prepared for a session in the morning, when he wanted to be at home relaxing and going over his files. He knew he needed to take action on Tyrrell's file, and that wasn't going to be easy.

Not with everything that was going on.

He didn't pace in the waiting room, though he wanted to. That would probably wind Kenzie up more. He needed her to be as calm as possible during the therapy session. If she were too upset, Dr. B might put more weight behind her words and not believe Zachary's reasoned explanations.

50

Elizabeth, the nurse receptionist, called Zachary's name and led him and Kenzie to the office where Dr. Boyle usually met with him. Even though it was a Saturday, it was familiar and comfortable and made him feel like he was in the right place. In a few minutes, he and Kenzie were joined by Dr. Boyle. She looked at Kenzie and raised a questioning eyebrow. Obviously, they all knew it wasn't a couple's day.

"Good morning. How is everyone today?"

"I have some concerns," Kenzie said without preamble.

Dr. Boyle sat down, nodding. She opened the file on her desk and made a couple of initial notes. The date and the fact that both Zachary and Kenzie were present, he assumed. He didn't try to read her writing upside down. He'd tried before and he couldn't decipher it. It was hard enough for Zachary to read print. Reading cursive, and reading it upside down, was beyond his ability most days.

"Do you want to begin with your concerns, Kenzie?"

"Sure." Kenzie looked at Zachary to see if he would jump in, but he had nothing to say. She wanted to be there; she had to confront him about what she saw as his paranoia, so she should begin. "I'm worried about some behaviors I have seen over the last few days. I know Zachary is having some problems, and I wanted to give my perspective and what I've been seeing. Not because I don't think he would tell you everything. I just think it might be useful."

"Go ahead," Dr. B encouraged.

"Zachary has been very anxious this week. The last couple of days especially. I think it is probably being triggered by the case he is working on. Maybe dealing with something from his childhood has resurfaced old memories and he is having problems dealing with those."

His day at Clintock had been difficult; seeing those places that harked back to his youth and dealing with the priest and the other volunteers and carers. He remembered the dream he'd had that night, breaking through despite his having taken a sleeping pill.

"Yes, there's been some of that," he agreed, keeping his tone flat and neutral. He didn't want to get emotional about it. That wouldn't help anything.

Kenzie looked surprised at this admission. She looked at Dr. B. "But more than just anxiety… I'm seeing a lot of paranoia and compulsive behaviors. His rituals over locking the car have gotten worse. Looking for tracking devices or…" She shrugged, looking at Zachary and waiting for him to complete her sentence. Zachary looked away from her and didn't. "Or car bombs," Kenzie finished, her face flushing.

Dr. B looked at Zachary. "How do you see that, Zachary?"

He tried to sort out a response. It was true that some of his behaviors were compulsive. Having to lock and check the doors more than once. Needing to enter his code into the home security system when he stepped inside the door, even if Kenzie had already done so.

But that wasn't why he was checking for trackers and bombs. He did scan for bugs and trackers in the car and the house regularly, as part of his daily or weekly routines, but having the car towed and Jergens check it over was not compulsive or paranoid behavior.

"The car didn't start. I had to make sure that no one had tampered with it."

"And installed a car bomb?" Dr. B asked.

"Yes."

She wrote something on the file.

"I'm not being paranoid. There was good reason to check. And if someone had done something to my car, then I had to make sure that no one had done anything to Kenzie's either. That's why I checked hers. And I still rode in it. Last night and today."

"So you were reassured that there was no danger?"

"I was reassured that… the danger was minimal."

"I see." She nodded. "What made you think your car problems might be related to someone tampering with it? Or that there might be a bomb?"

"Because of the threats."

"Okay. What threats are those?"

Kenzie looked at Zachary, eyebrows up, waiting to hear what he had to say. They thought that the threats were imagined. That he was being paranoid because of his increased anxiety left. But Zachary knew that it wasn't that. He was anxious about car bombs and tampering because they were very real threats.

He pulled his phone out and tapped a few times, navigating to his voicemail and eventually playing the voicemail threats on speaker.

51

"ow would you like that brother of yours to disappear just like his friend?" a guttural voice demanded. "Those who don't learn from history are doomed to repeat it."

"We know who you are and where you live."

Kenzie's mouth dropped open and her eyes widened. "When did you get those?"

"Uh… Wednesday. I kept busy with other things on Thursday. Friday, I tried starting the car, and when it didn't start the first time I turned the key… I was worried that it might be because of a bomb. I didn't want to risk setting it off by turning the key a second time, stepping on the gas, or popping the hood. I called Jergens to pick it up and have a look at it." He looked at Dr. Boyle. "He was military. With IED training. I told him my concerns. I wouldn't put someone else in danger."

"Do you know who those threats came from? Do you recognize the voice or the number?"

"No. The call display was blocked. And the voice is disguised. You can tell that they're talking below their normal register. Might even be a woman pretending to be a man."

Neither of the women said anything for a moment.

Zachary cleared his throat. "There were emails too. Also threatening. In more detail. Heather called me about those. Wanted me to go to the police. But they were run through an anonymizer service. The police wouldn't be able to trace them without a subpoena to the service provider, and they are usually overseas to protect them from any requests like that."

"You should still have taken it to the police," Kenzie insisted. "And you should have told me about them. And the voicemails. Why didn't you tell me? Why didn't you tell me about the threats?"

"I didn't want to upset you." Zachary swallowed. Obviously, not telling her had not kept her from being upset. It had just meant that she had seen his actions as paranoid instead of justifiably cautious. "I figured that you were safe when you were at work, and I could see on the phone tracker app that you were at the office. And I figured that you were safe when you were at home, because we have good security. The security company will be there in two minutes if the alarm goes off. We've... tested their response times before."

"Yes," Kenzie agreed, her mouth quirking into an expression that was not quite a smile. More of a grimace. "But you were still worried about my car. You checked it before we went to the grocery store and before coming back."

"Someone could have messed with it while it was in the parking lot. Put a tracker—or something else—under the bumper. It's very quick to do and no one would notice."

"As you know from experience."

"I'm a private investigator. I have had occasion to track cars."

And Kenzie knew he had tracked both her and Bridget without their permission. Kenzie finding that out when they had only been on one or two dates had caused some major fireworks. It was safe to say she had not been pleased.

But she didn't bring that up.

"And before we went to the grocery store?" Kenzie challenged. "When the only places I had been were in the police department parking garage and our own?"

"I told you the reason for that."

Kenzie looked at Dr. Boyle. "Because you think that there

might be members of the police force who are corrupt. Working for the cartels."

Zachary nodded.

Dr. Boyle looked at Kenzie, waiting for her response. "How do you feel about that, Kenzie?"

"I think… it's over the top. I know there is such a thing as police corruption, don't get me wrong. But I don't think anyone in the police department would go down into the parking garage and put a bomb on my car. That's… going too far. Especially if the concern is about Zachary's case, not anything I am doing."

Zachary nodded his agreement. "I think you're probably right. *Probably.* But I can't be sure. Why wouldn't I at least check before getting into your car? I don't think anyone would target you because of my investigation, but what if I found the bomb on my car or it failed for some reason? They knew that I would eventually be in yours."

"You think that someone would take the chance of killing me just to get you out of the way?"

"I don't know."

Dr. Boyle made a few more notes in the file. "What kind of case is this that you are investigating, Zachary?"

"A missing person. Which turns out to have likely been a murder. By someone powerful in organized crime or politics. Because they were being blackmailed and didn't want their activities to come to light."

He waited, looking at Kenzie and Dr. B, waiting for one of them to say that he was overstating it. Being paranoid about the case. That it couldn't really be anything to do with anyone who was in organized crime and would come after him to keep him quiet.

"I also think," Zachary spoke slowly. But he wanted to get this out while they were in a safe place, while Dr. B was there to help to control the reaction to his statement. "That the offer that came from Walter, supposedly from the governor, was something to do with the case."

"What?"

He shrugged, looking away from her.

"How could that have been anything to do with the case? Why are you saying that? I know that we are both pretty suspicious of Walter's motives, with good reason, but how could this have anything to do with Robbie Elder? No one said anything about him."

"I think it was just another attempt to get me to drop the Elder case. Pressure from various quarters and threats to my life did not appear to be working, so they thought they would try it from another direction. Give me a job that would take all of my time so that I would have to drop any more investigation into Robbie and just work on the governor's file."

"But why would the governor do that? You think that he's involved in some conspiracy?"

Zachary hated the word conspiracy. It conjured images of black helicopters, aliens, men with amnesia rays, and bizarre government experiments. It didn't capture backroom discussions between politicians, the swapping of favors, or a problem discussed over expensive cigars. He and Kenzie understood that Walter knew his way around these back rooms. As a lobbyist, he was used to looking for ways to influence people, to motivate them personally or professionally to take certain actions to ensure success. He was good at what he did. Zachary did not doubt that he could get whatever he wanted.

"I think... that if your father asked him if he could create a job for me, a way to use me within his organization, that Walter could get him to agree to it. He wouldn't necessarily have to give a reason. They know each other well enough, have been in each other's pockets."

"But why would the governor or my father want you to stop investigating this case? It doesn't have anything to do with either of them."

"I would agree if it wasn't for that job offer. If Walter hadn't come forward when he did to try to get me onto a big, prestigious file... I would agree. But it doesn't make sense. If the governor's office wanted someone to run all of those searches and background checks and to have some solid investigative work done on his employees and opponents… he would have gone to one of the big firms. Not to me."

"So now you think my father was involved in Robbie Elder's murder." Kenzie looked at Dr. B, waiting for her to write this down and agree that Zachary was paranoid.

"No. I think someone wants me to be quiet. And he or they are politically powerful. They know that Walter is connected through you. And he is someone they can ask for a favor, if they agree to support one of his lobbies."

"He wouldn't do something for a corrupt politician or crime boss because they promised to support a lobby."

"Maybe he would. Maybe he wouldn't. Maybe he doesn't know it is related to organized crime. He just sees the dollar signs. Or the success of a cause that he has high hopes for. You warned me before not to trust him. Are you telling me I should trust him now?"

"No. I just don't think he would get involved in anything like that."

"He probably doesn't know," Zachary emphasized. "He might think he is helping me, helping you out, doing the right thing for the state. Protecting us from some danger. He doesn't know it is to keep me from working on this case."

He and Kenzie sat looking at each other. Dr. B didn't jump in with any words of wisdom.

"Have you heard anything back from your mechanic?" she asked Zachary.

"Not yet. But he said he had other vehicles ahead of mine. That it would take a while. It isn't exactly a job I want him to rush. He needs to be careful and do it methodically."

"When do you think you'll hear back from him?"

"Later today, probably."

"Would you let Kenzie know what you hear back?"

Dr. B was assuming that Jergens would not find anything untoward in the car. Zachary would pass this on to Kenzie, and she could reassure him if he started showing more signs of paranoid behavior.

And report back to Dr. Boyle.

"Yeah. I'll let her know."

"Okay. I'm not going to recommend any med changes or any other changes this week. Let's see how this plays out."

Which meant she was suspending judgment. Giving Zachary the leeway to prove that he was reasonably concerned about an actual threat and not paranoid.

She and Kenzie would see that he was just taking reasonable precautions and not going off the rails.

52

It was not a call from Jergens that informed Zachary of the results of his mechanic's review of his car, but a loud knock at the door. Kenzie was working in her home office on the other side of the house. Not far away but, since he was the closest one to the door, he figured he was the one who ought to answer it.

He checked the monitor for the front door camera and saw a familiar figure standing there. He hurried to the door and opened it. Sergeant Campbell nodded to him and motioned to a couple of other, less-familiar figures to follow him. Zachary watched with consternation as each of them traipsed into the house. He hadn't actually invited anyone in. Campbell slapped him on the shoulder in a friendly manner.

"Well, Zachary, you always keep our lives interesting, don't you?"

"Uh... what's this about?" Zachary asked, mentally cataloging all of his current investigations and anything that might have triggered the attention of the Roxboro brass. The Elder case was based in Clintock, so he could understand getting a call from Able or someone else at his station to give an accounting of what he had done and whether he had found anything, but that should not have extended to the Roxboro police department, as far as he could tell.

"Had a call from your mechanic. Ex-army captain Jergens."

"Oh." Zachary swallowed. His mouth was suddenly dry. He went to the kitchen to get a drink to irrigate it. "Get you something?"

"I'll take one of those," Campbell said companionably, nodding to the water bottle Zachary removed from the fridge. Zachary handed him one. He cracked his own open and looked at the table.

"You want to sit down here? Or in the living room?"

"Anywhere is fine. Where is your car usually stored? In the garage, I assume?" Campbell nodded to the two other cops standing to the side, looking like they didn't know where to go.

"Uh, no. Just at the curb."

"You don't park it out of the weather?"

Zachary shook his head. "No... Kenzie's baby..."

Campbell grinned at this. Kenzie chose that moment to come down the hall from the office to see who had been at the door. She smiled at Campbell and greeted him with familiarity. "What's going on, Sergeant?"

Campbell took one of the kitchen chairs and sat down. Zachary sat down across from him. Kenzie tentatively pulled back a third chair and considered sitting.

"I am following up with a report made about Zachary's car," Campbell explained.

"A report made about his car?"

The two other cops headed outside to the curbside parking space, leaving the three of them alone.

"We may want access to your garage, too, even though I understand Zachary's car was not stored there?"

"No, never. What's going on? Did the mechanic actually find something?"

Campbell nodded. "He did indeed. I'm sorry to have to tell you this," Campbell looked at Zachary and met his eyes. "But there was an incendiary device in your car. Which means that it has been taken into evidence for the time being, until our lab guys can thoroughly process it for any evidence."

"It actually had…" Kenzie's voice was faint. "You're saying that his car had a bomb in it?"

Campbell nodded. "More or less, yes. Now, whether it was live and wired correctly and would have gone off and all of those other questions, I can't answer yet. All I can tell you is that there were explosives wired to the car. Jergens said they probably mis-wired the ignition afterward, which was why the car failed to start. Maybe they were interrupted, or maybe they didn't know what they were doing. The lab guys will be all over it. We'll see what they can tell us about who put it there and what we know about the perpetrator once they've had a chance to do their magic."

Zachary and Kenzie nodded.

"Like an autopsy," Campbell said with a smile. "Only on a car and bomb, rather than a body with a tumor."

"How long is that going to take?" Zachary asked, thinking about the long list of things he still wanted to do. He didn't like being homebound. He couldn't exactly take Kenzie's car. Aside from it being her baby and no one else being allowed to drive it, it was also not exactly the best vehicle for covert surveillance. It stood out like a sore thumb wherever they went. "And if I can't get the car back, can I at least get the equipment that was left in the car?"

"I'll check on that for you." Campbell gave a nod. "So, I need you to tell me how a bomb ended up in your car. How you knew it was there. Why you didn't call the police. Who you think was responsible for putting it there. All of those juicy details."

He pulled out a top-bound spiral notepad and started to make notations in advance of Zachary beginning his story.

"Well… I've had some threats the last few days," Zachary admitted slowly. He was glad he had already confessed this in front of Dr. Boyle so that it wasn't a shock to Kenzie, and she could nod and pretend that she had been in the know the whole time. "I didn't know whether to take them seriously or not. I do get threats sometimes, and usually nothing happens. People blow up, cool off, and go on with their lives."

Campbell nodded his agreement. Zachary was sure that the police must also experience this a lot.

"I was hoping that it would just blow over. But then when I got into my car to go to Clintock... and the engine didn't start when I turned my key in the ignition..."

He had another swig of water, remembering the terror of sitting in the car, wondering if it would be the final moment in his earthly experience. He hadn't exactly shared that bit with Kenzie.

"I immediately thought of a car bomb. I didn't try it again or press the gas or anything that you might do when your car doesn't start right away. Didn't pop the hood. I just... I was worried that it was an explosive and that anything I did might set it off. I got out of there and called Jergens to see if he would take a look at it for me. I knew that he had some experience in explosives."

"So he came and got it. And that's the extent of your knowledge."

53

Yes. I guess from what you said, he discovered the explosive... and called you."

"What you should always do if there is a bomb in your car," Campbell pointed out, his tone mildly critical.

"Well... maybe I should have. I just thought... no one would believe me if I said there was a bomb in it and no one could see one. I could just see some rookie cop deciding to try the key for himself and maybe blowing everything up. I knew Jergens was experienced. He would know how to handle it."

"We would have called in the bomb squad from Burlington, more likely than not," Campbell advised. "We don't have our own unit, but we would not advise our officers to try to start a car that might have a bomb in it."

"And I'm sure they would never do it," Zachary shot back.

Campbell shrugged. "You are probably right. It would be a risk. But you should have reported it to the police. Call me if you don't want to call 9-1-1. We've dealt with each other enough times over the years. You know I would give you the benefit of the doubt."

Zachary nodded. "I suppose so. I wasn't thinking that. I just thought... he's my mechanic and is the best one to deal with whatever car trouble it is having if something just needed maintenance, or with the bomb if there was one. I didn't even think he would call you, just that he would take care of it."

"It's a good thing that he did call us. We don't want amateurs—or even retired professionals—handling and disposing of explosives."

"Right. Guess not."

"So what case do you think this is related to? Adultery? Fraud? Insurance?"

"I'm dealing with a missing person case that I think was probably a homicide."

"Here?"

"No. In Clintock. More than twenty years ago."

"A cold case. How did you get involved in that?"

"My brother. It was someone he knew, and he had always wondered what had happened to him. So I said I would look into it for him. I wasn't expecting it to blow up into anything this big."

Zachary heard what he had just said and shook his head, pressing his fingers into his temples. "I didn't mean *blow up*."

"That's okay. Name of the missing person?"

"Robert Elder."

"Of Clintock? Is that where he disappeared from?"

"Yes." Zachary hesitated. "As far as we know."

Of course, Robbie could have been anywhere else in the state, or anywhere else in driving distance. He might not have had a car of his own but, if they were stealing from and blackmailing gang connections, he might easily have picked up another vehicle. He would have been halfway across the country.

But the witnesses had not said that. Mindy would have said if the rumor had been that Robbie had been taken to another state and killed, and Freddie would have said if he had been somewhere other than Clintock when he saw the car soaked with blood and heard what he did about the victim.

"Yes," he reiterated. "He must have been in Clintock. It doesn't make sense if it was anywhere else."

"And you think he was killed, not just a runaway?"

"It was treated as a runaway. But I have witnesses and rumors that say he was killed."

"Witnesses?"

"Haven't managed to find anyone who saw it happen yet, but the rumors were pretty detailed. And I do have one confirmed witness of the crime scene, a car, with blood soaked into the upholstery."

"And who is supposedly the perp?"

"Still working on that. Maybe a gang member. Someone in organized crime. Or someone who has powerful connections."

"Which is why they were able to make it disappear."

Zachary nodded. "He was a delinquent, so no one missed him too much or figured he was in any real trouble. Or no one thought it any great loss to society."

"I've seen it happen," Campbell admitted, not second-guessing Zachary's assessment. He had dealt with his share of missing teens, Zachary was sure. Most of them just out having fun, going back to their families after a day or two.

"But nothing closer than that?" Campbell asked. "No one you can point at and say that it was thought to be him, even if you don't have the evidence to back it up?"

"No. One reason I need my car is to make more inquiries. I really want to find out what happened."

"Do you think that is wise?"

"It's a cold case. In Clintock. *You're* not going to take it up."

"No," Campbell admitted. "You can't convince anyone in Clintock to take it on?"

"I've asked a Detective Able to have a look at it. See if we can find any John Does that might have been Robbie Elder. Do a DNA test to confirm. But... so far, he hasn't been too encouraging. That would be a lot of work, going through a lot of paper files. And no one wants to do that. Or to make copies, read through them, and redact everything for me."

"Doesn't sound like a lot of fun," Campbell agreed with a chuckle.

"Is this really happening?" Kenzie asked, shaking her head. "I can't believe that we're talking about a bomb. In Zachary's car."

"And somebody set it there. The setting of the bomb is now an active case, but I'm not sure how many resources we can put into it. Things like this usually burn bright for a moment and then die out. If you'll forgive an inappropriate metaphor."

Kenzie gave a soft snicker. She was used to gallows humor. But she still looked distressed.

"If we can find something, it is usually right away, within the first few hours. If not... I don't hold out much hope of finding the perpetrator."

"And so far, you haven't been able to find anything?" Kenzie asked.

"Well, this is my first interview on the matter, other than talking to Captain Jergens. And Zachary has been able to point me in one direction. Whether it is the right direction or not, only time will tell. If I can find someone involved in Robert Elder's world who has been hanging around Roxboro, or there are rumors of someone looking for or buying explosives, we might be able to sort it out."

Kenzie looked at Zachary.

"You have someone in mind?" Campbell asked, reading her expression.

"What about that guy at the grocery store yesterday?" Kenzie asked Zachary. "He seemed like the right kind of guy to do something like this. And he's involved with the case, isn't he?"

Zachary hadn't told her much about Hal, avoiding all the questions he could, but she had probably picked up on more than he had said.

Campbell and Kenzie were both looking at him expectantly.

"Uh... Hal Delaney," Zachary said eventually, addressing Campbell. "He's involved in the case, but not in the way you might think. I do have some concerns about him... following me here from Clintock and to the store. But... he is a cop."

"He's a cop?" Campbell repeated, looking down at the words

he had just written in his notepad. "I thought you said that the cop you were dealing with was Able."

"He is. And he said to look out for Hal. That he's not on the force anymore. There's some kind of rift between them, but I can't tell who is right or wrong in this case, or telling the truth or lying. Hal was undercover, and I don't know if he maybe still is now, and the animosity toward him and the Clintock police department is just a cover."

"So you have an ex-cop or undercover cop who wants to know something about this case. Why? What does he care about a delinquent who disappeared twenty years ago? Why would that be a case of interest to him?"

"He was one of the detectives who investigated the missing person case. He says that he could just never let it go. That he wants to know what happened to Robbie. So when I started investigating it, he just attached himself to me. He says he'll help, but he doesn't have much to offer in that way." Zachary sighed and shrugged. "I want to go back and talk to Tyrrell. Get him involved. He is the one who can tell me who the targets were. It has to be someone that they were targeting."

"Targeting?" Campbell repeated. "In what way?"

"Theft or blackmail. Or both."

"Kids," Campbell said with disgust, shaking his head. "They have no sense. No sense of their own mortality or where the line is. It's a wonder any of them grow up to be mature, responsible adults."

Zachary nodded.

"I'll talk to Tyrrell, if you don't mind," Campbell said politely. He put one of his business cards down on the table though, of course, Zachary already had his contact details. "Have him give me a call. We'll need to go over everything as soon as possible. Remember, it's what we can do in the first few hours after something like this. We don't want to leave anything too late. I want to talk to him today. Within the hour, if possible."

Campbell stood up from the table. He shook hands with both Kenzie and Zachary.

"And of course, call me if you think of anything you can share. I don't want to spend all of my time on a cold case when I've got a fresh one in front of me."

Zachary nodded.

"Good. Keep in touch."

"And can I get my equipment out of my car?"

"I'll let you know."

54

Kenzie was quiet after Campbell and the other cops left. Zachary was sorry that he had not told her earlier about the threats but, on the other hand, he wasn't, because it would just have given her more to worry about when there wasn't anything she could do about it. She was safe at home with their security system, safe at work with the security there and the police department operating in the same building, and he had gone out with her to do the grocery shopping, so she was as safe as she could have been doing that. What else could she have done except worry?

But Zachary was also concerned that her silence meant she wasn't speaking to him. Or that she couldn't think of what to say to him anymore because he had let her down. He never wanted to let her down, but it was inevitable that he would sooner or later, not just with his private investigations business and the trouble that it seemed to bring them, and with his mental illness and other foibles that meant he would always be letting her down personally as well. And she wasn't like Bridget, who would have let him have it. Kenzie didn't yell and criticize the way that Bridget did. She always tried to say things nicely and encourage him, not talk about all of the ways that he let her down.

"Do you mind if I have Tyrrell over?" Zachary asked.

Kenzie looked at him. She looked exhausted, even though it was still morning and she hadn't had to work all day at the morgue. He had assumed she would go to work for a few hours in the afternoon, but she had shadows under her eyes, and shook her head at the suggestion.

"Do you think we could leave that for another day?" she said. "I'm not really up for company right now."

"It's just… I need to talk to him about this case. If I'm going to get things sorted out, I need to talk to him. To get him to tell me everything."

"By sorted out, do you mean solving the case or getting rid of whoever it is that is stalking us and put a bomb in your car?"

Zachary shifted uncomfortably. It was obvious which of the choices he was supposed to make. But that wasn't what he had meant.

"I was hoping to kill two birds with one stone," he said. "If I can solve the case, then we get whoever is making the threats off our backs…"

"Or you get yourself killed."

"I'm not going to get killed." Even as he said it, he knew it was stupid. He could only control his own actions, not the consequences. He could do everything right and still get killed. He could make all of the safe choices but, even if he did that, there was no guarantee that it would keep the stalker from getting to him. He could tell everybody that he was off of the case. Not look at it any further. Dive into his task list and work on his regular, routine cases. Call up the governor and say that he would take his job. He could do all of those things and it still might not deter the stalker.

Kenzie gave him a look that combined anger, despair, and disgust. Zachary turned away, unable to look at the disappointment and fear in her eyes. How had he gotten so deep into this case that he couldn't get back out? Would he ever learn how to quit and escape a situation if it became too dangerous? Or would his obsessive brain always dictate that he finish what he had started?

"Do what you want," Kenzie snapped. She walked past him and retreated down the hall to her bedroom and shut the door.

He knew that "do what you want" did not mean that she was okay with his going ahead or that she trusted him to make the right choice. It didn't mean that she was good with company and it was okay if he invited Tyrrell over. He should follow her, reassure her, do what he could to comfort her, and make sure that she got the rest she needed to start recovering from the shock of having their lives threatened.

But he was going to invite Tyrrell over whether Kenzie wanted him to or not, so he would have to rely on the fact that she had told him to do what he wanted to defend his decision later, when the subject was bound to come up again. He sighed and sat down on the couch to make his phone calls.

55

It took a while for Tyrrell to get there, and Zachary was beginning to wonder if he had miscalculated, and his brother wouldn't come after all. But eventually, as he paced back and forth from the front door to the living room window and back, he saw Tyrrell's car pull up in front of the house, taking the spot that Zachary's car should have been occupying.

Zachary didn't wait for Tyrrell to reach the door and press the doorbell. He opened the door and stood waiting for Tyrrell to complete the walk to the house.

"Hey," Tyrrell greeted, his teeth gritted, not even trying to put on his usual smile of greeting. They both knew he was there against his will, so what was the point in pretending he was happy about it?

Tyrrell walked by him into the living room as Zachary closed the door and cleared the security alarm as usual. Tyrrell sat on the couch, leaning over, elbows resting on his knees, rubbing his face and cupping his eyes like he was tired or had a migraine.

"How are you doing?" Zachary asked him. He watched Tyrrell, worried about the possibility that he was hung over. Tyrrell had been under a lot of pressure lately, and his response to stress was to drink. Zachary was probably lucky that Tyrrell had come to the house instead of disappearing on a binge, waiting for the whole thing to blow over.

"I'm just great, Zachary," Tyrrell said grumpily. "What have you got to drink?"

"Water. Coke. Probably some kind of juice or powdered mix."

"You know that's not what I mean."

"I know. But you know I'm not giving you alcohol."

"Of course," Tyrrell agreed. He rubbed the bony ridge over his eyes. "Coffee?"

"Sure." Zachary moved into the kitchen to pour a cup for Tyrrell. At least the coffee was fairly fresh, brewed since Campbell had left. He poured himself another cup as well, noticing when he returned to the living room that he already had three cups clustered on the side table with various levels of cold coffee in them. He would need to clean them up and put them in the dishwasher before Kenzie reemerged from the bedroom. He glanced toward the bedroom, wondering if she would come out to say hello to Tyrrell when she heard his voice. Probably not. She was pretty ticked and had not wanted to have to deal with company.

Zachary handed Tyrrell his coffee, and Tyrrell sipped it, scowling at Zachary.

"So what is this about? I already told you I don't want you to pursue Robbie's case. So what am I doing here? Why haven't you moved on to something else?"

"I still want to know the truth about what happened to Robbie. And I think you do too. You're just too scared to go ahead with it."

Tyrrell raised his head for a moment to look at Zachary. "You got that, did you?"

"I wanted you to meet somebody."

"Who? What are you talking about?"

Hal came walking out of the kitchen into the living room. He stopped in front of Tyrrell, looking down at him.

Tyrrell stared up at him, a frown of concentration on his face. He started to shake his head and then stopped. "Wait a minute. Are you...?"

"This is Hal Delaney," Zachary introduced. "He was one of the detectives who investigated Robbie's disappearance back in the beginning."

Tyrrell shook his head. "What is he doing here? The investigation is dead and cold. No one wants to look into it any further. It's a waste of time and other resources."

"I'm not with the police force anymore," Hal told him. "This is my own time."

"Then what do you care? Why would you want to investigate it now when you didn't back then?"

"I did investigate it back then," Hal responded. "But I was the junior, and when there were other cases to be dealt with... I couldn't keep working on it forever. And you and your friends were not exactly helpful about the whole thing."

"Me and my friends?"

"You were a bunch of little hoodlums, and none of you would answer questions or tell us what had really been going on. Exactly how do you expect the police to solve a case when you lie to them about everything?"

"I don't," Tyrrell growled. "I just want everyone to leave it alone now. It was a mistake to ask Zachary to look into it. To get everything stirred up again. I should have left it where it was, dead and buried."

"It might be cold, but it's not dead and buried," Hal told him. "As long as it is unsolved, it is still an open investigation, no matter how old it is."

"It's dead and buried," Tyrrell insisted. "Just like Robbie."

Zachary sat down at the other end of the couch. "You don't know that Robbie is dead and buried."

"That's what you said, isn't it? You know he's dead. You know that they took his body and dumped it somewhere so that it would never be discovered. Dead and buried. And that's where he should stay."

"We don't have proof that's what happened. You wanted to know what had happened to him."

"Well, I don't anymore."

Zachary was silent, looking at him. Hal stood looking at the two of them and offered no argument for continuing the investigation.

"Did they threaten you?" Zachary asked finally.

Tyrrell looked at him. He took a couple of hard swallows of the scalding coffee, his eyes watering at the corners.

"Who?"

"Whoever it is that doesn't want us to continue with the investigation. Whoever… killed Robbie or made him disappear, I assume."

Tyrrell blinked a few times and looked away. He didn't deny it, at least. Zachary had expected at least one denial in the beginning.

"They threatened me too," Zachary told him. "They put an explosive device in my car."

Tyrrell looked at him, wide-eyed. "What?"

Zachary nodded. "Yeah. I had the police here earlier."

"They put a bomb in your car? Like an actual bomb?"

"Yes."

"Then why are you still doing this? What does it take to get you off the case? It's putting you in danger. Kenzie. Me. The kids. Why would you keep going when I took you off the case?"

"The kids?" Zachary repeated.

Tyrrell rubbed his eyes. "Alisha and Mason. They said that they would go after my kids, Zachary! At first, it was just threats to me, but they must have followed me when I went to visit my kids, because then they said that they weren't safe. That they would do something to them if I didn't listen and get you off the case!"

56

Zachary felt sick at the thought of someone threatening to harm his niece and nephew. He had never wanted to get anyone else in trouble or put them in harm's way. He was just trying to get to the bottom of a missing person case. Or a homicide case, as it appeared to be.

"They're not going to stop," he told Tyrrell. "You won't be safe if you tell them I'm off the case. You think that if I walk away from this, they'll leave you alone and forget all about it? They'll realize that they can't watch us both forever. They can't be sure that I'm actually off the case and not still investigating, but just keeping it quiet."

"If you get off of the case, the kids will be safe. We'll all be safe. Everything can go back to normal."

Zachary shook his head. Hal did too.

"I've worked with this kind of criminal for years," he said. "They never stop. They let the case go cold because no one was investigating it. They thought they were safe. But now that you've reawakened the police and witnesses, they will not be satisfied until everyone who is a threat has been removed."

"Why do you care? You never did back then," Tyrrell accused.

"I did. I just couldn't do anything about it."

"And you still can't."

"You're still just a punk. You don't care about your friend. You don't care what happened to him or how his family has been feeling for twenty years. All you ever cared about was covering your own butt. You're still just the same stupid little punk you ever were."

Zachary felt sorry for Tyrrell and how the cops must have treated him after Robbie's disappearance. Hal was menacing now, when the two of them were grown adults and it wasn't even his job to investigate the case. Back when Tyrrell had been seventeen and the police had been the authorities, so much bigger and more powerful than Tyrrell, he must have been terrified of them. They could accuse him of being involved in the murder. Arrest him for some crime if they found out what he and the others had been doing that night. Theft, blackmailing, whatever else Tyrrell and the others had been involved in.

As much as Tyrrell had wanted the police to investigate and find out what had happened to his friend, he had still had to protect himself and keep them from discovering what he and his friends had been up to. He was vulnerable, and so were they. And in the end, Tyrrell had broken. His parents had to send him away to boot camp to try to get his behaviors under control again. He must have been drinking heavily, trying to medicate himself and forget everything that had happened. To hide from the ugly truth and his part in it, and the guilt he felt over knowing that his best friend had likely been killed for something that the two of them had thought was a lark.

"Tyrrell," Zachary put his hand on the younger man's knee. "If you want to stop these guys, we have to find out who they are. And I can't do that without you. I need you to help me out here."

"I've told you everything I know. I just don't know any more, Zachary. I wasn't there when it happened. I didn't see, and I only heard rumors afterward. No one from our group saw it go down. Robbie went off on his own and he shouldn't have. He should never have done that."

"No," Zachary agreed. The ill-planned approach had cost

Robbie his life. "He shouldn't have. But look, you do know more. You know the person that he went to see that night."

"I don't know who it was. I told you that."

"Sure. But there are only a limited number of people it might have been. You didn't have dirt on everyone, only on a few people. There is only a limited pool to choose from."

"Well, yes." Tyrrell wiped his eyes with the heels of his hands and looked at Zachary. "But most of them are long gone. They're dead or I have no idea where they went or what happened to them. They could be buried just as deeply as Robbie." He sniffled and shook his head. "None of those people are around anymore, Zachary."

"You're not around. Because you're not in Clintock anymore. But some of them are. And even if they're not there, they may still be in Vermont. Someone heard about our investigation and didn't want it to go ahead. That means they are here, close enough to hear about it and close enough to be concerned about what we might find."

"You haven't found anything, though, have you? You haven't heard any names?"

"No. I've heard that he was involved with gang members. Whether those were youth gangs or organized crime…"

Tyrrell rolled his eyes as if he couldn't believe what he had done as a kid. "Organized crime." He gave a weak laugh. "Why?"

"Because you were a stupid kid," Hal said with a shrug. "Kids think that they are immortal. Or that it doesn't matter if something happens to them. They think that life is just childhood and that there isn't anything they would want to live for in adulthood anyway."

Zachary thought back. There might be something in the thought. When he was growing up, everyone had insisted that childhood was the best time of life and, once a person became an adult, it was just grinding work and responsibility, no fun, tethered to a family and a mortgage. He hadn't looked forward to it. He hadn't believed that he would ever have a fulfilling job, get married, or be able to survive on his own. Adulthood had seemed so daunting. He'd had no idea that it would actually be better than child-hood. He could see how Robbie might have thought that he was at the end of the line. His family had kicked him out. His guardians had given up on him. He wasn't going anywhere in his life. He could make some money and enjoy himself. He might die in the process, but did it really matter? Did anyone really care?

"What Robbie did is in the past. We can't change any of that. The only thing we can address is the present and this threat to our lives. We can't get police protection or around-the-clock body-guards. I've got good security here, but someone could still put another explosive device on my car and get it right this time. Or attack me while I'm out for a walk. You can't be in Riverbrook to protect your family. The only chance we have to stop this guy is to unmask him."

Tyrrell shook his head, but seemed resigned. "Like I said, I don't know where any of them are anymore. I didn't keep track. I wanted to put that part of my life long behind me."

"Well, let's make a list. All the guys you can remember being targets. Everyone you had dirt on or stole something from. It had to be one of them."

"How is that going to help?"

"It will. Trust me. Don't forget—I'm good at tracing people. I can find them, see what they're doing today, who would most likely be the stalker."

Tyrrell looked around him. "Do you have a pen and paper?"

Hal finally sat in the easy chair to watch them, no longer towering over Tyrrell. He looked satisfied, but still watched Zachary and Tyrrell warily, as if they might commit some misstep or try to get away from him. But he wasn't the one that Zachary needed to get away from. He was not one of their potential victims, so he was not the bomber. He was not the one trying to get Zachary and Tyrrell off the case. On the contrary, he kept showing up, trying to talk them into doing more so they could put the old case to bed. Zachary believed he was haunted by being unable to solve Robbie's disappearance or murder.

Zachary handed Tyrrell a notepad and a pen and sat near him

to watch the names as Tyrrell wrote them down and to answer any questions he might have about who to include.

"This is silly," Tyrrell insisted as he tried to dredge up all the names from his memory. "None of these people are going to be around still. Do you think I would ask you to look into it if I thought any of them might still be around to target you?"

"Someone is."

Tyrrell grumbled something else under his breath. Zachary didn't really need to know what it was.

After a while, Tyrrell shoved the notepad at Zachary. "That's everyone."

"You're sure?"

"Of course I'm sure. My kids' lives depend on it, don't they?"

Zachary conceded that was a good point. He put the notepad down beside his computer and started to type.

57

The nice thing about gangsters was that they were in a hazardous business and likely to die young. That made some of the names very easy to cross off. Zachary might not be able to figure out exactly who it was on the first round, but he could knock the ones who were dead off of the list.

Tyrrell watched him, making him nervous. "Why don't you go get a Coke?" Zachary suggested. "You know where they are. Ask Hal if he wants one too."

"I'm not thirsty."

Zachary made a shooing motion, and Tyrrell backed off a little, not leaning over to see what he was doing. After a few minutes, he did go into the kitchen to get himself a soft drink and a snack and to provide Hal with what he wanted. Zachary kept working the list of names, identifying who was still alive and in the state and, once he could establish that, whether he could track where they had been on particular days. Some of them were prominent enough to have been in the news, allowing Zachary to pinpoint whether they had been close enough to sabotage his car or to follow him from Clintock to Roxboro.

Tyrrell leaned over him again to look at the list and the number of names Zachary had scratched off. The list was getting very short. Tyrrell shook his head.

"I told you, everyone is dead or gone."

Zachary's eye was on one of the suspects, whose name he recognized from TV. He ran a few searches, looking for news of where he had been at various points in the last week.

"It's not going to be him," Tyrrell disagreed, watching Zachary's search. "He's no gangster. He's too soft."

"It could be. He could have influence over the governor. Or be able to ask him for a favor."

"The governor?" Tyrrell repeated.

Of course Tyrrell didn't know about the job offer from the governor's office. Zachary just nodded and didn't explain. But looking at the various appearances the senator had made over the week, he didn't see how he could have been involved in tracking Zachary or putting the explosives on his car.

Unless he'd hired someone else to do it, of course, which was always a possibility. Someone like that could have plenty of lackeys to do his bidding. But would he want to involve anyone in his personal business? Add someone else who knew he was involved in something shady and could point back at him? If he were trying to get rid of witnesses and get Zachary off of his trail, it wouldn't be a good idea to involve someone else.

"Maybe not," he said to himself, and looked down at the list again.

"I don't see how it could be any of these guys," Tyrrell said. He'd obviously been thinking things through. "They were people we had already touched. They paid up. If they paid up once, then why would they go after Robbie the next time? Kill him? It doesn't make any sense. Why wouldn't they just keep paying? It isn't like we went after them for too much money and they couldn't afford it. They would have just paid again."

"You're sure you weren't squeezing any of them too hard? Sometimes people look like they have a lot of money, but they don't. It's all a front, and they are up to their eyeballs in debt."

"No. We were just kids. The amounts that we were getting... they were big for us. We'd never had anything but a few coins before, and suddenly we could ask for a hundred bucks and get it. That was big for us. But these guys? A few hundred bucks was 'walking around money' for them. They could drop that without breaking a sweat."

"And you don't think that Robbie would have gone back and asked for more? Thousands? Hundreds of thousands?"

Tyrrell laughed and shook his head. "We didn't think in those amounts. You might as well ask for a billion. It was petty change for them. I don't understand why anyone would kill over that."

Zachary nodded. He looked at Hal. "What do you think? Who would kill for a couple of hundred dollars?"

Hal shook his head. "That's nothing. Even street kids like them could have raised that much," he said, nodding toward Tyrrell. "Knock off the grocery store. Grab a handful of jewelry at the pawnshop. Borrow it from a friend or swipe it from a parent's stash."

"Then..." Zachary was thinking it through. "Robbie must have gone after someone else. Not someone who had paid before. Someone who resisted. Who didn't wait to see what the cost would be or if they would keep coming back after him."

He looked at Tyrrell, who didn't seem to be following. "Somebody else?" Tyrrell echoed.

"Who isn't on this list?"

"Everyone is on the list. I told you that. I wouldn't leave anyone off."

"How did you get these guys? What were you guys doing to dig up dirt on them?"

Tyrrell frowned. "Taking pictures. Following them around and taking pictures when we caught them doing something that looked bad. Paying someone off, buying drugs or dealing, going behind a partner's back. Adultery. Whatever."

Similar to a hundred jobs that Zachary had done, following someone to see what they were up to. Only he had a client who was paying for the pictures; he wasn't going back to the subject to blackmail them.

"Where are the pictures?"

Tyrrell shook his head. "Where? They aren't anywhere. It was twenty years ago. They are long gone by now."

"Then what is anyone worried about?"

"Well... I guess they haven't thought it through."

"There is still evidence out there somewhere. If there wasn't any proof, no one would be worried."

Tyrrell shook his head slowly. "I don't know. Maybe Robbie got pictures developed that I hadn't seen yet."

Zachary leaned forward eagerly. "Where is the last roll of pictures you guys took?"

"He would have taken them with him. To show to the mark. So if there were pictures, they're gone now. They've been destroyed."

"Where are the negatives?"

Tyrrell stared at him. It had been a long time since they had been kids, taking pictures to the one-hour kiosks for development. Everything now was digital. It was hard even to find anyone who still did chemical development.

"The negatives," Zachary repeated. "Where would he have put the negatives?"

"In... we had a box where we threw everything. For safekeeping. I guess... if he didn't have the negatives on him, then they would have been in the box."

"Where was the box? His house?" Zachary wondered whether he could convince the Weylunds to talk to him again.

"No. Mine. The Millers."

Zachary nodded. "And where did it go after you moved out? Did you take it with you?"

"No." Tyrrell shook his head. "I never took much when I moved somewhere. I had a few papers, that's all. I never stayed anywhere long and wouldn't have any time to pack." Zachary had seen how Tyrrell left everything behind when he went on a binge.

Food rotting in the fridge, rent unpaid, he would leave the landlord to clean everything out. "Everything else, I just left with them. I imagine they would have been thrown out years ago."

"Can you find out?"

58

Tyrrell chewed on his lip. "Zachary... I haven't been in touch with them for the last few years. We weren't... we weren't really family, like you and Vince and Mindy. I broke ties with them."

"Do you want to protect Alisha and Mason?"

The question galvanized Tyrrell. He stiffened. "Yes, of course."

"Then who cares if you have been in touch with them or not? Now you need a question answered."

Tyrrell grimaced. "Just call them out of the blue? Mom and Dad, I need to know where you put my box of pictures and negatives?"

Zachary nodded. "They still live in the same place. They might have just shoved them into a closet. They wouldn't necessarily have had to get rid of them to make room. They went from having three kids at home to none. Plenty of extra room."

Tyrrell growled, not eager to do what Zachary asked.

"You can do it," Zachary encouraged. "Don't worry about what they will think or about your relationship. All you are doing is asking for some pictures that belonged to you. To protect your kids."

"And then what? We destroy them? We give them to whoever

this guy is? How am I going to protect the kids once we have them?"

"I don't know yet. Until we find out who it is, I don't know how to deal with them. It could be different for different people."

"Yeah. Gonna have to burn them, I bet. Video it. Send them the video."

Zachary shrugged. "Maybe."

Tyrrell had pulled his phone out and was fidgeting with it. He knew he needed to take the next step, but obviously was not eager to do so. He met Zachary's eyes and looked away again.

"Don't judge me. You never had to do anything like this. Going back to your adoptive family. Because you didn't have one."

"No, I didn't," Zachary agreed.

"They're going to have all kinds of questions and I don't know how to answer them all."

"Just tell them you'll deal with that later. Right now, you need those pictures."

"Why?"

Zachary didn't know how to answer. He gestured toward Tyrrell with an open palm, referring to the conversation they had just had.

"I mean... why do I tell them I need the pictures? What's the big emergency after they've been laying there for decades?"

"Do you have to give them a reason?"

"I'm going to have to give them some kind of explanation."

"Uh..." Zachary rolled his eyes ceilingward, trying to come up with a good explanation. "You are... working on the twelve steps and you are on the one that talks about making amends."

"Step nine," Tyrrell supplied.

"Step nine. And there is something in those pictures that relates to an amend. You need to see who was at a party or who you took a picture of when you shouldn't have. I don't know. You can come up with something."

"That's pretty good," Tyrrell admitted. He swallowed. "I can tell them I'm sorry at the same time. Since I'm making amends."

Zachary grinned. "Two birds with one stone. Why not?"

Tyrrell wiped his phone on his pants, wiping off sweat from his hands. "I don't want to have to go over there. If I have to visit with them, tell them a lie face-to-face... I can't do that and tell them that I'm making amends at the same time."

"Take it one step at a time."

Tyrrell nodded. He wiped the phone again and then tapped the screen. He looked at Zachary and Hal and walked into the kitchen, where he kept his voice as low as possible so they wouldn't hear him. Zachary turned to Hal to involve him in conversation to keep himself from listening in on the conversation.

"So, what about you, Hal? Do you have a family? I guess when you were undercover, you wouldn't have been able to be with them, so..."

"Some people are still able to see their family members while they are undercover. For others... it's like going off for a tour of duty. You tell your family you'll be back in a year, or whatever, and hope that things don't fall apart while you're gone."

"So do you?"

"Have a family? No." Hal pondered. "I'm not exactly an easy guy to get along with. I'm not the 'family man' type. I don't think I would do a very good job of that scene."

"So, it's just you? Or do you have a roommate or a team that you meet up with? Some kind of social life?"

"What, do you think I live in a cave?"

"No... I figured you must have some kind of life. That's why I asked."

Hal shook his head and waved the question away. "I'm not interested in sharing my private life with you."

Zachary nodded and didn't pursue it. He doubted whether Hal had a roommate. If he'd been living with someone, the police department would have been able to use them to get in contact with Hal. Pass a message on to him, at least. But maybe they had, and Hal had still refused to engage.

Tyrrell returned from the kitchen. A very short conversation. He looked relieved. "Well, that's that."

"You couldn't get them?" Zachary asked.

"I got them. But they're out of the country. On a big vacation."

"Oh."

"But the stuff that was in my room is in the attic." Tyrrell said it stoically, then smiled and nodded. "So, we can get it while they're gone."

59

There were a few logistics to organize. Zachary didn't have his car back, but Tyrrell and Hal had theirs. They discussed the positives and negatives of going in two separate vehicles, and eventually agreed that Zachary would ride with Tyrrell and Hal would follow behind. Zachary suspected that the main reason Hal volunteered to be the follow car was to keep an eye on Tyrrell and make sure he didn't do anything like taking off to get the pictures on his own or chickening out and going the other direction.

Tyrrell now seemed just as determined to find the negatives and figure out who was threatening them as he had previously been to drop the case and stick his head in the sand. As Zachary had said, it was the only way to guarantee they would be protected. With the stalker behind bars, they could all relax.

Zachary didn't bring up any of his misgivings to Tyrrell. If the guy was organized crime, such bosses were known to keep running their criminal enterprises from prison, and putting such a person behind bars was no guarantee that it put them out of his reach. And there was the time it would take the police and prosecutors to conduct their own investigation and build a case against him. And bail. Someone like that would definitely be able to make bail, too.

Far from being behind bars and unable to hurt anyone, they might just be poking the bear and then releasing it to see what damage it could do.

What was important was to uncover the truth. That was what Zachary had always believed, and that was how he had always operated. Frequently there were negative consequences, but he honestly believed that revealing the truth would always work out for the best in the long run.

Just as long as he didn't get himself killed in the process. Or someone else close to him.

He was more cautious acting with Tyrrell than he would have been on his own. Tyrrell was a father, and Zachary was attached to his niece and nephew. He didn't want them to lose their father again, as they had when he had gone on binges, but permanently this time. He could never forgive himself if that happened to him.

The situation would have to be managed delicately.

Blackmail was a dangerous business.

Tyrrell talked a little as they drove to Clintock, talking about what it had been like growing up with the Millers and how different they had been from Zachary's and Tyrrell's biological parents. That very difference had made Tyrrell distrust them.

"You should be able to trust someone more if they are nice to you, right?" Tyrrell asked, shaking his head already to negate his words. "But I couldn't. If they had acted like our mom and dad, I would have at least understood and known what was coming. But I couldn't understand what they were doing. I always figured they were trying to fool me, to get around my defenses somehow. And they *were*. Only, not because they were looking for a way to hurt or control me."

Zachary nodded. He'd had a few good foster parents as he had grown up. There had always been a mix of good and bad parents. Or parents who were not perfect, but all had different flaws. Most of them had been trying to do the right thing and to raise him properly. But Zachary had been too old and too damaged to change. He couldn't alter the way that he thought and his brain chemistry or the genes and learning disabilities that he had been born with.

Lorne Peterson had been nice and, even after Zachary had left there, they had kept in touch. But he and his wife had been unable to help Zachary when he had lived there. Over the years, Mr. Peterson and Pat had taken the positions of Zachary's chosen parents, but he had never lived with them. Even if he had, things would not have turned out much differently. Zachary and Tyrrell were both destined to be damaged children who grew up into damaged adults.

And Tyrrell was a prime example of the fact that no matter how much love, attention, and good intentions his adoptive parents had lavished on him, no matter how hard they had tried to do the right thing by him, they could not heal the damage, prevent the alcoholism, or force him to be a mature and responsible teenager instead of one who went out at night looking for trouble and finding it.

"They were good for Mindy and Vince, though, right?" Zachary asked.

Tyrrell nodded. "I think so. As a kid, I always tried to get between them. To be a buffer between Mom and Dad and Mindy and Vince. That didn't help them. I thought I was doing the right thing, but I think I just made things harder for the younger kids. They had to choose between listening to me or listening to Mom and Dad. Or to convince me that listening to Mom and Dad wasn't a bad thing and could turn out okay. I could never believe that. I always knew that there would be tears in the end. Something would go wrong and, no matter how much they tried to convince me that I was wrong and things would be okay, I didn't believe it."

"They seem like nice people. But I think Mindy relies on Vince a lot for making decisions. She always wants to know what he thinks about things."

"Yeah. They've always been really close. But she's afraid of making decisions on her own."

"It's good that they're close and were never separated. That all three of you got to be raised together."

"When I wasn't off at boot camp or some residential treatment program," Tyrrell said, rolling his eyes.

"Yeah."

Zachary watched the ribbon of pavement stretched out in front of them, trying to capture and hold the feeling of peace and calm he usually got from highway travel.

Tyrrell looked in the rearview mirror to ensure Hal was still on their tail. "I hated this guy so much when I was a teenager. He was so full of himself. So confident that he was right and I was keeping things back from him."

"Well… you were," Zachary pointed out.

"I know, and that just made his confidence all that much more irritating! How did he know I was lying or keeping something back? Why didn't he believe what I told him, like everyone else? People are usually happy to believe what you tell them. They want to believe that you're a good person and you're telling the truth, and you can tell people the wildest stories and have them believe that they are the truth. It's crazy."

"But Hal didn't."

"Hal. I can't believe that you call him that. For me, he'll always be Detective Delaney. And Detective Delaney will always be this hard-nosed cop who knew I was lying and wouldn't listen to any story I told him. He knew too much, figured things out too quickly. He was just a young guy back then, probably had barely made detective. But he was as sharp as a tack. I could see the way his partner looked at him. Delaney just picked up on everything and left Robertson in the dust."

"He seems like a bright guy."

"Oh, he is. I swear he's like a human lie detector. He just looks at you… and he knows whether you're telling the truth or not. And probably knows what the real story is, too. He never believed it when I told him I didn't know what had happened to Robbie. I said that Robbie was just going straight home… but he knew that wasn't true."

"He said he knew about you guys stealing things and trying to blackmail gang members. That you guys thought you could outsmart everyone else."

"Yeah. That's what we thought. And initially, it worked. But eventually... well, eventually, it all came crashing down. I couldn't believe it. Even when Robbie didn't show up that first day, I thought he was late or off making trouble somewhere else and would be back. He was just out drinking or with a girl, had found something more important, for the moment, than meeting with his friends. Then I thought that those foster parents must have sent him away somewhere. I'd already been sent a couple of places, so I knew what it was like and that he couldn't do anything about it if they put him into some closed program. I went to his house, expecting them to tell me they'd sent him away. But they didn't know anything about where he was."

And that was when the bottom had fallen out for Tyrrell.

60

Zachary jolted awake. He hadn't even realized that he had drifted off partway through the highway drive. He thought he had been getting enough sleep, but apparently had not.

Tyrrell was looking at him, grinning. "Have a nice nap, Sleeping Beauty?"

Zachary rubbed his gritty eyes. A headache was starting to coalesce behind his left eye. He groaned. "I can't believe I fell asleep. I'm not usually one of those people who falls asleep the moment you put them into a car."

"You must have needed it. Head back, snoring to beat the band."

Zachary was embarrassed. "You should have woken me up."

"Why? I know how little you sleep."

"Is this it?" Zachary looked out the window and at the nondescript house. White siding, like most of the houses down the block that were all of similar size and shape. All with smooth-looking green lawns and a few trees and flowers. Some of them had short picket fences, and some of them did not.

"This is it," Tyrrell agreed, looking at the house. Zachary

wondered if he was overwhelmed with memories and, if so, whether they were good or bad.

There was the sound of a car door slamming, and Hal joined them.

"You have a key?" he asked.

Zachary hadn't wanted to ask. He doubted that Tyrrell would still have a key after that many years. Especially since he had lost almost everything more than once when he had disappeared on a binge. He was estranged from his parents. It would have been weird for him to hang on to their house key for twenty years.

Tyrrell shook his head. "No, but I know where to get one."

Zachary thought he might go to one of the neighbors to ask someone who had lived next door over the past few decades. But Tyrrell led the way to the side gate and the backyard. There was a sunny wooden deck that raised Tyrrell's eyebrows.

"This is new!" he commented.

But it didn't look new. It looked like it had been there for at least ten years. New to Tyrrell.

Tyrrell looked around the rest of the yard, taking in the decorative little gardens. Eventually, he stooped down and picked up a rock. Turning it over in his hand, he revealed the hidden key compartment in the base, which slid open at his touch. A house key lay in place, as it obviously had for years.

"Small towns," Tyrrell said. "Probably everyone in the neighborhood knows that this is here."

"And probably everyone in the neighborhood has one," Hal said. "Unless they don't bother to lock their doors at all."

"Well, they're away on vacation, so they did lock it this time." Tyrrell put the rock back in the garden and climbed the deck steps to the back door. He tried the key in the back door, where it needed a little wiggling and jiggling before finally giving way and allowing him entry.

"Just like always," Tyrrell said. "It always was a little sticky. You have to know how to coax it."

Zachary looked around before following Tyrrell into the house. The raised deck gave him the advantage of seeing over the neighbors' back fences so that parts of their yards were visible. But he didn't see anyone working in their gardens or watching out the windows, stepping closer to the windows that faced the Miller house to see who was entering through the back door. Everything was quiet and, apparently, no one was keeping a close eye on things.

Hal waited for Zachary to enter, then took a look around the yard just as Zachary had, confirming that they were safe, before following on Zachary's heels.

Zachary was so used to keying his code into the burglar alarm at home that he looked around for a keypad as soon as he stepped in the door. But there was no security alarm keypad in the Miller house, where they left a key out to make it easy for strangers to get in whenever they wanted to.

"And you've probably never had a break-in," he said to Tyrrell.

Tyrrell looked at him for a moment, as if not comprehending what he had said, then shook his head. "Not that I know of. But then, how would we know, unless they left a big mess? There were certainly times when I was accused of stealing something from the parents, when it could have been Vince or Mindy, one of our friends, or anyone who had walked into the house while we were gone."

"Anything like that happen after Elder disappeared?" Hal asked.

Tyrrell frowned, pondering this, as he headed for the stairs and looked up. "I don't know. I don't remember a lot of what happened around that time. But... yeah. I don't remember being accused of stealing anything that time, but messing things up, yeah. I didn't do it. Unless I was so drunk at the time that I blacked out and couldn't remember it later. I figured it was probably Vince or Mindy and covered for them. Said that it was me, even though I didn't know who it was."

"Did either of them ever thank you for it?"

"No. I don't think anyone ever said anything. I probably got grounded for a week. But I never stayed grounded. They couldn't physically stop me from leaving the house. And I was still supposed to go to school. So being grounded wasn't really anything more than words."

"So, it could have been an intruder, and no one knew it."

"Yeah. I guess."

"Could it have been someone looking for pictures?"

"I don't know. Nothing down here," Tyrrell looked at the thick photo albums on a shelf in the living room. "It was my and Vince's room. I just figured… he had a tantrum and threw things around. Or left things out after he'd been playing. I don't know. It wasn't like he usually did those things."

"So, your bedroom was rifled."

"Maybe."

Tyrrell started to climb the stairs. Zachary motioned for Hal to go before him, bringing up the rear. Climbing stairs always felt awkward for him and he didn't want Hal behind him, analyzing what was wrong with him.

"What about your sister's room? Was it rifled too?"

"No. Just mine. Like I said… I thought it was just Vince being messy. I didn't think it was any big deal, and I just covered for Vinny so he wouldn't get punished."

Just as they always had at home before the fire, when the punishment was a lot more severe than just telling a kid that he was grounded. Or even sending him away to a weekend reformation camp.

61

Tyrrell stopped at the first door in the upstairs hallway and peeked inside. "This was the boys' room. I guess it's a guest room now."

The room was perfectly tidy. Clearly not used unless there was company. Not a wrinkle in the perfectly-made bed. Not a speck of dust on the side table or lamp. Tyrrell pulled the door closed again, walked down the hall, and opened the next one. "This was Mindy's. Now... Mom's office." There was a small writing desk with space for a laptop on an articulating arm. And a stationary bike in the corner. Office and gym.

Tyrrell skipped over the next door, probably the main bathroom, and opened the door at the end of the hall. "Here's the master. Mom and Dad's room."

It wasn't as clean as the guest room, but still relatively tidy. A few things were left out that Zachary would have expected to be put away. Maybe things that had been accessed at the last minute as they packed their suitcases for their vacation.

"It's very nice," Zachary said honestly. He'd lived in a lot of different houses, and this was a pleasant one. Not ostentatious and not a wreck. Just a tidy, middle-class home, where the owners were currently on vacation. His profession had led him to enter a number of houses where the owner was not present, and it was always interesting to see what secrets the homeowners hid—or did not hide—from sight.

Tyrrell took them to the attic access panel, which incorporated pull-down stairs. Zachary had seen them in TV movies but rarely in real life. He hoped it meant the attic was finished, or at least not full of mice, insects, and itchy fiberglass insulation.

He stayed at the end of the line, with Tyrrell ascending first, followed by Hal, and then Zachary climbed once the other two had disappeared into the ceiling. It wasn't finished, but there were plywood panels laid across the ceiling joists, which made it possible for a few archive boxes of miscellaneous items to be stored. And there was a bare light bulb that Tyrrell had turned on. Zachary watched Tyrrell and Hal move slowly around each other, careful not to both step on the same piece of plywood at the same time and possibly put too much weight on it. No one wanted to fall through the ceiling.

"Over here," Hal said, pointing out a stack of boxes labeled *Tyrrell's Room.*

Tyrrell nodded but didn't get any closer to them. But it wasn't because Hal was already on that piece of plywood. Hal stayed well back so Tyrrell could approach and open the boxes himself.

Zachary and Hal both looked at Tyrrell, waiting. But his energy for finding the man who was stalking them seemed to have flagged. He was back in his childhood home, somewhere he had good memories, and maybe he didn't want to contaminate his good memories with the discovery of the stalker's identity. The *killer's* identity, if they were right about what had been done to Robbie.

"Do you want to take them somewhere else?" Zachary suggested. "We could get a hotel room and go through stuff there, if you don't want to look at it here."

Tyrrell continued to stare at the boxes without saying anything. Zachary waited, giving him some time. If he were dealing with flashbacks or trying to get his thoughts straight, it could take a little while, and pressing him to hurry would slow down the process instead of making it faster.

Hal looked back at Zachary, raising his brows questioningly. Zachary made a motion for him to wait and be quiet. To his credit, Hal didn't act the hard-nosed cop and plow on ahead, demanding action from Tyrrell.

Eventually, Tyrrell moved toward the boxes like a zombie. Zachary watched his feet anxiously, worried that he would step off of one of the plywood boards without even realizing what he was doing. But Tyrrell reached the small stack of boxes safely. He looked over at Zachary, blinking rapidly.

"Do you want help?" Zachary asked.

"No... don't want to put too much weight in one place."

"I'm pretty light. If you want a hand."

"I can do this." Tyrrell swallowed. "What is there to be scared of? It's just a bunch of junk that I had as a kid."

Zachary nodded. "Nothing to be worried about," he assured Tyrrell.

But it was still a few minutes before Tyrrell opened up the flaps of the top box. He pushed the contents of the box around gently without commenting on what he had found. Then he closed it and set it beside the rest of the stack. He investigated the next box down.

"I didn't even realize I left so much stuff here," he observed. "I never went home after college. And I had another life then."

He had already taken everything he wished to from home. Maybe the rest brought back too many memories. He had not had an easy time living with the Millers, even though they had tried their best to help him.

Tyrrell shook his head and put the second box on top of the first. He looked at the third box. "If the photo box isn't in here, then what do I do?"

"It could be in another box," Hal said, motioning to the other stacks of boxes. "It could have been mislabeled or left in the closet of the wrong room. Or they might have gone through them and merged them with their own photo library."

"But there weren't family photos in there."

Hal shrugged.

Tyrrell opened the last box with his name on it and moved around the contents. He reached in, digging down deep, his fingers scrabbling at the bottom of the box to get a purchase on whatever he had seen. In a minute, he pulled out a metal box. Zachary leaned toward him, trying to get a better look at it.

"Is that it?"

Tyrrell nodded. "Well, it was, anyway," he said nervously. "If no one has messed with anything…"

He made his way back toward the stairs, where Zachary was still standing. Zachary backed down slowly—which was even more awkward than climbing stairs—and got out of Tyrrell's way. Hal followed Tyrrell and pushed the stairs back up to the ceiling when they were all down.

"Where do you want to look at them?" Zachary asked. He didn't particularly feel like sitting in the middle of the hallway floor to do it and didn't imagine Tyrrell did either.

And Tyrrell's safe space, his bedroom, was no longer his, but had been converted into something that wouldn't make him feel comfortable and at home.

"Kitchen table?" Zachary suggested.

Tyrrell nodded his agreement and led the way back downstairs and to the table. The afternoon sun filled the room with a warm glow. He looked around the kitchen as if making sure everything was in the right place and it hadn't changed into something he didn't recognize anymore.

He sat down at the table and put his hand on the lid of the box to open it. Zachary saw that it was a collector's box for hockey cards. Had Tyrrell ever collected hockey cards? Or had Mr. Miller hoped to interest him in them? Tyrrell looked at Zachary.

"Can you get me a drink? See if there's something in the fridge?"

Zachary obediently opened the fridge and though it was mostly empty, there were several cans of pop. He gave one to Tyrrell and offered one to Hal. Both men accepted and popped the tabs open. Tyrrell was probably wishing he had something quite a bit stronger to satisfy his thirst, but it would have to do.

Tyrrell put down the can and again prepared to open the box. Again, he stopped.

"Just do it quickly," Zachary advised. "Without thinking about it or the consequences."

"I know." Tyrrell nodded.

62

H e took a deep breath, still thinking about it. But he managed to pull the lid off of the box.

There were a couple of stacks of developed photos, but the box was mostly filled with strips of negatives.

Zachary was a hobbyist photographer as well as needing to take pictures for his work, and it warmed his heart to see all of those recorded memories. He had lost most of his negatives in an apartment fire, and most of his current work was digital rather than on film, so he didn't have many negatives.

Tyrrell picked up a random strip and held it up to the light. "Yeah... these are my photos," he said, as if there had been any doubt. "But it's going to be really hard to look through them all and to recognize anything." He shook his head. "How are we supposed to do this? It will take hours!"

"I can speed it up a bit," Zachary offered. He sat down at the table, his phone out and ready. "I need your phone too," he told Tyrrell. Tyrrell hesitated, then finally held it out to him.

"What are you going to do with it?"

"I'm just going to use yours as a light box," Zachary advised, and navigated to an online video that was just a white screen. He maximized it, giving himself the backlight he needed. Tyrrell and

Hal watched him position a negative strip over the screen, letting the light shine through the negative and light it up.

"Well, that's a bit better," Tyrrell admitted, but he still squinted at it, scowling about not being able to identify all the blobs clearly. Zachary then booted up an application on his own phone and held it over the negative strip. It magnified the film and inverted the colors so the photo suddenly jumped to life on Zachary's screen.

"Whoa!" Tyrrell leaned over it. "That's perfect!"

"It's not a dedicated negative scanner, but it does the job in a pinch," Zachary agreed.

They started going through the stacks of negatives, with Tyrrell sorting through them and handing negatives to Hal, who slid them over Tyrrell's phone screen while Zachary held his phone above them so that they could all see what the pictures were.

Tyrrell started to get into it, remembering where and when particular pictures had been taken so that he could more quickly eliminate the photos taken too long before Robbie's death to have had anything to do with it.

They got down to a few strips of negatives that Tyrrell handled carefully, his body language telling Zachary they were important. He knew they were getting to the pictures that might be meaningful. The ones that might hold the key to solving Robbie's disappearance and possible murder.

Zachary held his phone steady over the strip as Tyrrell placed it on the makeshift light table.

It was a low-light picture and therefore somewhat grainy, but clear enough to make out two figures in bed, a man and a much younger woman. She was probably underage. More blackmail photos, not that different from the ones they had looked at already. But he had not seen the man's face on any of the other rolls.

Zachary looked at Tyrrell for his reaction.

Tyrrell was staring, his eyes wide with shock. The photo definitely meant something to him.

"Do you know who it is?" Zachary asked. "Did Robbie ever tell you that he was going to go after this guy?"

Tyrrell shook his head. He was pale, looking like he had just seen a ghost.

"The girl. She's Sofia Costa. She was... she and Robbie liked each other."

"Liked each other? Did he know that she was sleeping with someone else? An older man?"

"No."

Zachary wondered what the situation was. A pretty young woman who had a young man already. Was he a john? A sugar daddy? Was she with him of her own free will, or was coercion involved? It could be a past relationship, but Tyrrell had known Robbie well and he seemed to know that this was something he had never seen before.

"If you haven't seen this picture before, and Robbie didn't take it, then who did?"

"Might still have been Robbie," Tyrrell said, his voice weak. He cleared his throat and tried to continue in a stronger tone. "He might have just taken the pictures and then tried to figure out what to do once they were developed. Maybe he wasn't sure who it was until he blew them up." He shrugged. "Or one of the other boys might have taken them and then brought them to his attention when they realized who the girl was."

"And when he saw this picture and realized who it was... do you think he would have gone and confronted this guy right away?"

"Oh, yeah. Definitely."

"Because she was Robbie's girlfriend."

Tyrrell nodded his head.

"Do you know who the man is? Was it someone you recognize from back then?"

Hal looked over Zachary's shoulder, leaning in for a closer look. He looked at Tyrrell, and then back at the picture again.

"I know who that is. And your brother does too."

"Who?"

Neither of them answered at first. It was Hal who finally spoke.

"Victor Costa."

It took time for the words to compute. Zachary looked at Hal and then at Tyrrell, the words playing back in his mind. Sofia Costa and Victor Costa. He hoped that Victor Costa was a distant relation. A second or third cousin. Or maybe not even part of the same family, but someone who shared a popular Italian surname.

But that wouldn't explain Tyrrell's expression or the gray tone that his skin had taken on.

"They're related?" Zachary asked softly.

"Her father," Tyrrell answered.

Zachary swore under his breath. He stared at the young woman and older man, their faces and intertwined bodies, trying to make something else of it than what he saw. But there was no other way to interpret it.

Of course Robbie had gone after Victor Costa. Of course he hadn't been able to ignore it. And Victor Costa's response? He wasn't going to pay blackmail money to cover up the taboo. It was too explosive. It wasn't a situation where his wife might forgive him an indiscretion or his business partners would just roll their eyes and say that men had needs to be filled. And if he was running for office, even the whisper of incest would instantly turn the voters against him. He couldn't take any chances of the photos getting out to anyone.

"Was Costa organized crime?" Zachary asked Hal.

Hal gave a curt nod. "Yeah. He was mob. *Is* mob."

"He's still around?"

"He's still around," Hal confirmed.

"So, if this came out now..."

"He'd be ruined." Hal's lips pressed tightly together for a moment. "The organization will put up with a lot of things. They have their own ethics. But this would not be tolerated."

"Not to mention prison and the chance of being convicted of murder," Zachary observed.

"Those concerns would be much lower on the list. This is what

he did not want to come out. Not that he might have had something to do with Elder's death."

Tyrrell ran his hand down his face. "What are we doing to do
now? How do we handle this? How do we get Victor Costa off of
our backs? We're dead meat. He's not going to back off for
anything. His only choice is to wipe us out, just like he did Robbie.
He won't even hesitate if he gets in the same room with us. Or he'll
send his thugs after us. There won't be any more car bombs that
don't detonate." Tyrrell looked at Zachary. "What have we done?"

"If we drop it… destroy the pictures… make it look like they
never existed… start spreading the word to everyone I've talked to
that it was a dead end and I have no way of getting to the truth…"

Tyrrell stared at him, his eyes not believing what Zachary was
suggesting. "You would never do that."

Zachary swallowed. He had always thought that honesty was
the best policy. That only by digging up the truth could justice
really be served. If he dropped it like he said, Sofia Costa and
Robbie Elder would not be avenged. Everybody would go on as if
nothing had happened, Sofia a broken woman living with a dark
secret in her past. Robbie dead and buried. And Victor Costa living
high on the hog, satisfied that he would never have to face the
consequences for what he had done to his daughter.

Tyrrell was right. He would never drop it like that. But he
could lie to Victor Costa about it.

63

"We need to see Sofia," Tyrrell said finally.

Zachary and Hal looked at him. "See Sofia?"

Tyrrell nodded slowly. "I don't know what to do. I need to talk to her. She's his daughter. Who knows how she will want it handled? Or what is the best way to deal with her father. No one else will know how to handle him like she does."

"Was she his only child?"

"Yeah. Daddy's little girl." Tyrrell grimaced, looking at Zachary's phone and shaking his head in disgust. "I always thought he just spoiled her. Gave her whatever she wanted, but then tried to control her life too much. Like parents do."

Was that how Tyrrell saw his parents' rules and efforts to moderate his behavior? As being too controlling? Zachary had never appreciated the control that his caregivers had tried to wield over him. He, too, had just wanted to break free of the rules and live his own life. But as he had been a teenager, the foster care system had something to say about that.

"Do you know where she is?" Zachary asked Tyrrell.

"I guess... she's probably not still living with her dad. She'll have her own house now. I haven't kept track."

"He put her up in her own little place," Hal advised. "A little villa. I don't know exactly where it is, though."

"Give me a few minutes. I'll see if I can figure it out," Zachary told them. His stomach turned at the thought of Sofia's father still controlling her life. No longer living in forced proximity with him, maybe, but was she still at his beck and call, making herself available whenever he made demands? Was the little house of her own just another way of ensuring she was where he wanted her to be and remained under his control?

He switched apps on his phone and ran a few searches to narrow down Sofia Costa's location. She had credit cards, so getting a credit report listing her recent addresses wasn't hard. She didn't appear to have moved in the past twenty years.

"This looks like a good address." He read it out to Tyrrell and Hal. "Unless that's a post office or delivery address."

They both shook their heads. "No, that's definitely an out-of-town estate," Hal said. "Sounds like it is the actual physical address."

"Do you want to call her?" Zachary asked. "Let her know that you are coming?"

Tyrrell scratched the back of his head, considering. "No, I don't think that would be any benefit. At best, she'd say come on over, and at worst, she'd lock us out or take off."

"Less likelihood of her taking off if we just show up," Zachary suggested.

"Yeah," Tyrrell agreed. "I have no idea what her schedule is like. If she works or vacations during the summer months. She might not even be around."

Zachary scanned the details on her credit report. "It looks like she has other credit cards that she uses overseas. She hasn't used them in the past few months."

"So, she's probably still here."

Zachary nodded. "That would be my guess. We won't know for sure until we go over there. Or call."

"Well… I guess there's no point in putting this off," Tyrrell said with a huge sigh. "The longer I think about it, the harder it will be to follow through." He met Zachary's eyes. "Right, bro?"

Zachary nodded. "Exactly right. We don't have time to make a detailed plan, because we don't know if she will be there and how she will react. So the best thing to do is… be bold and improvise."

Hal looked amused at this. "Is that what you call what you did when you went to talk to Peggy Ann?"

"Well… it worked out, didn't it?"

"She could just as easily have killed you. Or left you in that basement room until all hope was gone."

"Wouldn't you have intervened at that point? I mean, you're a cop, so you can't just let someone commit murder and not do anything about it?"

Hal folded his arms and shook his head. "I would have had to break cover to do that."

"You would have just let her kill us."

"I wouldn't have done it myself. But if I couldn't stop it without breaking cover, then no, I wouldn't have done anything to stop it."

Zachary shuddered, remembering being locked away in that basement cell. What if Sofia had a room like that in her basement? But she wasn't the actual gangster. That was her father. And hopefully, he would not find out about them before they'd had a chance to develop their action plan.

"Are we going to talk, or are we going to go?" Tyrrell demanded.

"Let's go," Zachary agreed with a nod.

64

What Hal had referred to as a "little villa" was nothing of the kind. Small towns like Clintock tended to be filled with small, older houses. Middle class. Sometimes neglected. Zachary could think of areas that were poorer, the houses smaller and more badly neglected, but he couldn't think of anything above what he would have considered a "large house" in Clintock itself.

But as they left town and entered the beautiful Vermont wilderness, it was another story. There were acreages and farms that were modest or quaint. And there were huge estates with mansions nestled among the green trees. Tyrrell was following the directions on his GPS, which they hoped would lead them to Sofia's home. Hal had left his car at the Millers' house, deciding that it was more important for them to stay close together than to have two separate means of transportation. He sat in the back without a seatbelt on, leaning forward in the space between Tyrrell's and Zachary's seats to keep an eye on the road.

"It should be just around this curve," Tyrrell predicted, one eye on the GPS.

He rounded the curve and they saw the tall iron security gate, and a sprawling white stone mansion with slate-roofed turrets at the end of the driveway.

Tyrrell stopped the car at the gates, and they all took a collective breath looking at it.

"I can't believe she lives here," Tyrrell said, shaking his head. "When we were teenagers... I mean, she lived in the neighborhood and went to school with us. She might have had a little more money than most of us, nicer clothes, but she was still... just upper middle class."

"Things change," Hal pointed out. "Especially when you are talking about a mob boss. He doesn't make his money running a grocery store. The kind of money someone like that makes as he moves up the ranks..."

Zachary thought back to Peggy Ann's mansion. It too had been breathtaking. He couldn't comprehend what having that much money would be like. To be able to do whatever he wanted to? Buy a home that was ten times as large as anyone needed to live in, multiple luxury cars, staff or servants, food and clothing and jewelry that surpassed anything he could have imagined.

And this wasn't even Victor Costa's house, but the one he had gifted to his daughter.

"Hello?" a woman's voice issued from the speaker beside the driver's window, crisp and efficient. A maid or housekeeper? Personal secretary?

"Uh... I'm here to see Miss Costa. My name is Tyrrell. I'm an old friend."

There was no reply from the speaker, and they all sat waiting, sure they would be turned away.

"Please drive up to the house. Miss Costa will meet you by the pool."

Zachary was surprised that it was so easy. He had expected Tyrrell to have to argue his way in. To make up some story to convince Sofia to allow him in.

But then, maybe Sofia would have something else to say about their visiting. She might just send them away again.

The gate opened slowly and Tyrrell drove through. He took his hands off the steering wheel one at a time to wipe them on his pants.

They were all alert as they drove down the long lane. It curved past the house toward a long garage with several open bays. Tyrrell parked in front of the house.

"Where do you think the swimming pool is?"

A large, black, shiny limo was driven out of the garage. Its windows were darkly tinted, so they couldn't see the chauffeur until he opened his door and stepped out. He looked in their direction and then away again.

Zachary tried not to stare at him. He was a big, well-built man with white skin and dark hair. He wore a uniform, including a peaked cap. The cap and the large, mirrored sunglasses hid much of his face from their view. But they did not wholly obscure the extensive scarring of the lower part of his face. Deep, jagged scars that made it look like fireworks had blown up in his face.

Or, since they were talking about organized crime, maybe it hadn't been fireworks.

Zachary thought about the explosives left in his car and his gut clenched. He was lucky to have escaped injury himself. If things had turned out differently, he could be lying in bed in the hospital with burn dressings swathing his face and much of his body. Or worse, lying on a slab in Kenzie's morgue or in state at the funeral home.

He pulled his eyes away from the chauffeur's destroyed face, trying to stay focused on the rest of their surroundings. He needed to be aware of everything. Danger could come from any direction. His head swiveled this way and that, watching for any more members of the staff.

Tyrrell looked at the house, and then at the chauffeur. "Can you point us in the direction of the swimming pool?"

The mirrored sunglasses turned toward them. He considered the request, then answered gruffly. "Follow me."

They all fell in behind him, not wanting to get too close, needing the buffer between them. Hal looked the most confident.

He was, of course, far more used to these sorts of situations than Zachary and Tyrrell.

The chauffeur led them through a gate beside the house, following a cobblestone pathway around the perimeter until they arrived at the pool. Zachary glanced at the clear blue pool and surrounding deck. Sofia Costa was not yet there. But the voice over the intercom had said that she would join them here.

"Have a seat," the chauffeur said through his teeth, motioning toward the seating area closest to the house.

A suspicious bulge suggested he was packing a gun under that uniform. He was not just a chauffeur. Not with scars like that. Not with a gun. The chauffeur did not return to his car. He was more than likely a bodyguard or some kind of security for Sofia, who apparently needed to be protected even in her home.

65

Zachary followed Tyrrell's and Hal's example and walked over to the seating area the chauffeur had indicated. Tyrrell and Hal sat as instructed, but Zachary was too anxious and restless to sit. He stood close by, pacing a few steps now and then, trying not to attract too much attention to himself. They all exchanged nervous glances every few minutes, waiting for Sofia to join them. Tyrrell tilted his head toward one of the other seats, encouraging Zachary to sit down. But he preferred to keep his feet.

A sliding door opened, and a woman walked out.

The girl in the photos had been about the age of Tyrrell and Robbie at the time, seventeen or so. Slim and coltish. Pretty, but not someone who would have garnered more than a casual look. Zachary had been expecting a mature woman with a hard face and waifish figure, for whom the years had not been kind. Knowing that she was abused from a young age, that her father was involved in organized crime, and that she had probably led a hard-drinking lifestyle, he had not expected to find any great beauty.

But Sofia was a late bloomer, or she'd had some work done. She was now curvy, her figure flawless under a tiny bikini. Her skin was golden, with no visible scars or birthmarks. As she drew near them,

Zachary thought her eyes and hair were probably her most arresting features, despite her perfectly-proportioned body. Her dark brown hair was wavy, forming into a few ringlets around her face, highlighted with gold. Her brown eyes sparkled with life. Not the tired, dead eyes of someone who had led a hard life. Sofia Costa was in the prime of her life, looking twenty years younger than her chronological age. Totally breathtaking.

Tyrrell bounced to his feet as she walked up, his jaw dropping. "Sofia? Holy cow!"

She laughed, showing off perfect teeth, and then put on large, round sunglasses that obscured her eyes. She didn't offer her hand or a hug and kiss to Tyrrell. She wrapped a thick terry cloth robe from one of the lounge chairs around her. Having shown off her beautiful body, she was now content to protect it from the slight chill in the air as the sun lowered in the sky. Sofia stretched out on the lounge chair, making herself comfortable.

For a few seconds, they all just looked at her, stunned. Zachary supposed that in their minds, they had all been expecting to meet that middle-class, abused seventeen-year-old. But Sofia Costa had grown up.

The chauffeur had still not returned to his car, but stood nearby, his face pointed toward Sofia. Chauffeur or not, Zachary was sure he enjoyed the view as much as anyone.

"What brings you here, Tyrrell?" Sofia asked, going directly to the purpose of their visit. No idle chit-chat, talking about the weather or what had happened over the past twenty years. No catching up or pretending that they were great friends who had just lost touch with each other.

Tyrrell stared down at her, his eyes moving up and down her curving figure.

"We were... my brother Zachary..." Tyrrell motioned awkwardly toward him. "He's a private investigator."

Sofia Costa lifted her sunglasses slightly to look at Zachary, then dropped them into place again.

"What do I want with a private investigator?"

"I asked him if he would look into Robbie's disappearance all of those years ago."

"Robbie?" Sofia practically spat the name out. "Why would you do that after all this time?" She looked over at the chauffeur, and then back at her visitors.

"I just hoped… I thought he might be able to figure out what had happened and put him to rest…."

"What happened to Robbie? You know what happened to him. It was not that big of a secret."

Zachary swallowed. His mouth was dry. He wished that she had offered them poolside drinks.

"I never…" Tyrrell too seemed to be finding it difficult to swallow and speak coherently. "There was never any proof. I was hoping that Zachary would be able to find something. Evidence. So that we would know for sure. And I could let his parents know what had happened to him…"

"You know what happened to him. He was killed."

Tyrrell sat back down on his chair, but he sat at the edge of it, leaning forward, looking like he might jump back out of it any second.

"Maybe you knew… because it was your father."

Her expression didn't change. "It was my father what?"

"I think that he killed Robbie. All of those years ago, I didn't know who it was. I didn't know who he had gone back to see that night. But now…"

She shook her head slightly. "How would you know that? What makes you think it was anything to do with Victor?"

"Because we went back… Robbie had taken pictures… pictures of you and Victor."

She bit her lip. Zachary looked for other signs of emotion. It was hard, with the sunglasses covering so much of her face. He thought she had lost some color. Her jaw and throat worked, even though her voice was perfectly controlled and steady.

"What are you talking about? Pictures?"

Tyrrell lowered his voice. "I didn't realize it at the time. I never looked at the negatives that Robbie had left in our box. But we went back today, and I have the negatives of the pictures that Robbie took of you and your father... *together.*"

Sofia's hand flew up to her mouth to cover her expression. She sat up, no longer lounging back in the chair, and she pulled her sunglasses off. Her eyes were wide, the skin around them white.

"You have... those?"

"Yes." Tyrrell frowned. "I'm sorry, Sofia. I never knew. I would have tried to help you back then, if I had. I didn't know who Robbie had gone to. I didn't realize that you were... being abused." He swallowed. "I would have tried to do *something,*" he insisted.

"What could you do?" She demanded. "You'd do the same as Robbie and get your face shot off? How would that help me? How would that change anything?"

"I don't know," Tyrrell admitted, his voice strained. "But I could have tried. I could have done something. Or gone to the police about him, get him put in jail for killing Robbie. Then at least... you wouldn't have been under his thumb for all these years."

Sofia's face hardened. She put her sunglasses back on. "What do I care?" she asked. She motioned to her surroundings, the house and the pool and the lush green setting. "I have all of this. What else do I need?"

"To be free of him?" Tyrrell hesitated, looking uncertain. "Is he still..." He flashed a look over at Zachary, looking for assistance. But Zachary didn't know what to say or do. They couldn't assume that Sofia was still being victimized by her father all these years later. He might have lost interest in her as she grew older and had other, younger conquests he pursued now. He had no idea how to ask Sofia what the situation was now. He shook his head helplessly.

"That is the past," Sofia insisted, pointing at Tyrrell. "Don't come in and mess up my life now."

"We're not here to make trouble for you. We want to help."

"I don't want help."

"And also..." Tyrrell shifted uncomfortably. "Your father has been targeting us since Zachary started the investigation. Making threats. He even put a bomb in Zachary's car. We need to stop him.

If he's not hurting you anymore, then we don't have to worry about that, but... we need to stop him from doing anything to harm our families."

Sofia shook her head. She looked around. "That's your problem, not mine."

"He's threatened my children," Tyrrell said desperately. "I have a daughter and a son. I can't let anything happen to them. And Zachary and Kenzie." He indicated Zachary with a flip of his hand. "He's my brother and was just helping me out because I asked him to. Kenzie's been so good to me. She helped me through rehab and got me a job. I couldn't bear it if anything happened to them."

"That sounds like a *you* problem."

Tyrrell stared at her, his mouth open.

66

Y ou don't think he should have to pay for what he did to you?" Hal asked Sofia.

She looked at him, frowning. She clearly didn't have any idea who he was.

"I was one of the detectives who investigated Robbie's disappearance," Hal explained.

The chauffeur turned his head to look at Hal, then back toward his boss, watching for any sign from her that the cop was a threat. She made a waving-away motion, not concerned about this.

"You're not a cop anymore," she told Hal scornfully.

He looked surprised that she knew anything about this. He looked at Zachary. Zachary was the private investigator, and he hadn't known this. Did Sofia know because she still lived in Clintock and heard the gossip? Or maybe her father had kept track of the detectives who had investigated Robbie's disappearance in order to guard his own back, and had let her know. But it still seemed odd that she should be so well-informed about Hal no longer being a member of the police force and yet not know anything about Zachary investigating it again.

"I don't care if he has to pay for what he did," Sofia informed Hal, answering his question. "You live in a different world than I do, where people are always supposed to be punished for doing things against society's rules. I don't live in that world."

"Maybe not, but what he did was against the rules in the world you live in too. I know that wouldn't be tolerated if the other people in your father's world knew about it."

"The past is the past," Sofia insisted. She turned her head to look in Tyrrell's direction. "If you want to deal with my father, go see him."

"We can't exactly walk into his house and demand to see him."

She shrugged. "You did to me."

"Well..." Tyrrell blushed, looking away from her. "You and I knew each other once. I never knew him. I don't have any prior relationship to call upon."

"I'll tell him you are coming. People in my world appreciate honesty and plain speaking. If you have something to tell him, then tell him yourself."

The direct approach had worked with Peggy Ann. But would it work with someone who was even more experienced and deeply entwined in the criminal underground than she was? Would someone as powerful as Victor Costa see them and listen to what they had to say? Or would he just do as he had done to Robbie, and shoot them on the spot for daring to approach him?

"Would you tell him we will not pursue this further?" Zachary suggested. "Tell him that we're done and there isn't any need to threaten or take any action? We'll leave it alone."

She shook her head emphatically. "I told you, if you have something to say, you go tell him yourself, directly to his face. I'm not carrying messages for you. Or anyone."

Zachary looked at Tyrrell and Hal to see what they thought of this. If they believed it was a bad idea to visit Sofia, they were bound to think seeing Victor Costa was an even worse one. But what if it worked? What if telling him that he didn't have anything more to worry about would put an end to the threats?

And could they just let it go? Sofia Costa didn't want justice. Or not their kind, anyway. Maybe she felt like it was justice that she had been given the "little villa" and all of the other luxuries she enjoyed.

Giving it up would mean they didn't get any justice for Robbie Elder, either. But there wasn't actually any *proof* that he had killed Robbie or had anything to do with his disappearance. Just because he had disappeared after seeing the pictures of Sofia and Victor together did not mean that it was Victor or one of his men that had killed Robbie. Just as the rumors of blood in the car he had gotten into were not proof that he had been killed. It was an unsubstantiated rumor that Zachary would never be able to gather the evidence to prove. It had been too long ago, and any witnesses were dead and gone or, in the case of Freddie, on the way out.

Sofia could have her peaceful life. Robbie's mother wouldn't know anything more about his disappearance. Tyrrell had accepted that Robbie was, in fact, dead, and maybe he would be able to put it behind him now.

"You can call Victor and tell him to expect us? Get him to let us in?"

Sofia tossed her hair. "I can't promise he'll let you in. But I can tell him that I'm sending you over."

The three men looked at each other, deciding they would have to be happy with that. They wouldn't get anything more out of Sofia and, at least, an introduction to Victor Costa might ensure that they weren't killed the instant they set foot on his property. If they could convince him that they would leave the case alone… maybe there was a chance he would call off the dogs and not do anything else to threaten or harm their families.

"You know where it is?" Sofia demanded.

"No." Tyrrell shook his head.

"Just go down the highway like you were doing before you turned in here. Another three miles. There's a sign for Castello del Costa. That is where you turn in."

"Is there a security gate like there is here? You'll tell them to let us in?"

"There is no gate," she said, smiling. "Do you need a gate to keep people out of the lion's den?"

Zachary swallowed. How many times had he been told not to rush into dangerous situations? This time, it wasn't an impulse. But it seemed like the only way to protect his loved ones was by confronting the lion face to face on his own ground. Not exactly the type of situation he should be rushing into.

"Goodbye, Tyrrell," Sofia told him, unsmiling. "You were a good friend to Robbie."

Zachary wasn't sure whether she was being sincere or sarcastic. It was offered flatly and without inflection, and he struggled with her body language. He had been since she had arrived there, and it couldn't just be the fact that her sunglasses covered much of her face. He was used to being able to read people, but Sofia was closed off, very careful to give nothing away. He had to doubt whether even what seemed to be spontaneous reactions could be taken at face value.

They all stood and headed back toward the front of the house where the car was parked. The chauffeur backed up to let them walk past, then followed them out.

Zachary and the others stopped when they reached the car and looked covertly back at the armed chauffeur. Another person who was not what he seemed to be.

"Don't come back here," the man growled, his voice deep and rough. Zachary wondered whether his throat and voice box had been damaged in the explosion that had destroyed his face.

"We don't plan to," Tyrrell assured him. Sofia might have once been a friend, or the girlfriend of a friend, but they were no longer in the same circles. Sofia Costa was probably very different as a sophisticated adult with loads of money from what she had been as a gawky teen, just growing into her body and exploring the world for the first time.

67

Victor and Sofia lived on adjacent properties. Or Victor had subdivided his property or built a second mansion for her use. However it had been handled legally, Sofia still seemed to live very much under Victor's careful supervision.

"Do you really think we should do this?" Tyrrell asked in the car.

Zachary pulled his seatbelt across to buckle himself in as Tyrrell turned the car in a circle and took the driveway back out to the highway.

"It's probably a pretty bad idea," Zachary admitted.

"But are we going to do it?"

"How else are we going to get him to stop?"

"Do you think he will stop? And not just kill both of us on the spot?"

Zachary swallowed and cleared his throat. "At least the others would be safe."

Tyrrell looked slightly green at this comment and did not respond to it. Zachary looked over his shoulder at Hal to see if he had any thoughts. He was an ex-cop, after all; if anyone should know how to handle something like this, it should be a cop like Hal. Experienced, used to handling criminals, even organized crime figures. He wasn't the type of cop who went into a situation guns blazing, like the cops in the police shows on TV. He used intelligence and reason and found ways to manipulate the situation to his benefit. He was just the right kind of cop to have on a mission like this.

Only he didn't seem to have anything to contribute. His suggestions had been pretty minimal. Like he was just along for the ride, seeing what would happen.

He had worked for crime bosses before. What if he was working for Costa this time, just pretending to be an ally to Zachary, only pretending that he cared about solving his first missing person case? Maybe he had been watching Zachary all along, reporting back to Costa. Zachary didn't like the fact that Sofia had known that he was no longer on the police force.

As Sofia had said, there was no security gate at the driveway for Castello del Costa—just a long sign hanging from an arch over the driveway. There was no guard station or obvious security. But there could be surveillance cameras, motion detectors, or other electronic devices that were too small to be seen from the car. In Zachary's experience, a criminal like Costa would want to know if someone was approaching his house.

Tyrrell glanced aside at Zachary and kept going. There was no point in second-guessing now. They were committed. Sofia had announced them and, if they didn't actually show up at Costa's house, Zachary had no doubt that he would send someone out looking for them.

They were quiet as they drove the long lane up to the house. Victor Costa's house was farther back from the road than Sofia's. Zachary looked at his phone to see if he still had a signal and sent off a couple of messages. The sky was getting dark. He hoped he would be home for supper.

When they reached the house and got out of the car, the door opened, and a couple of refrigerator-sized men exited the home to inspect them and escort them into the house. Zachary had no gun or weapons. Neither did Tyrrell. The goons did take a gun off of Hal and carefully checked him for any more.

"I'll want that back when I leave," Hal told the man who removed it from its holster.

The man chuckled at this.

They were escorted into the house through a large hall and some areas that were obviously for entertaining guests away from the more private rooms occupied by Victor and his family or staff. There was a security door and then a private office.

"Your guests have arrived," one of the thugs announced in an amused tone.

Victor Costa was not a handsome man. He hadn't had any work done to make him more attractive, as his daughter might have had. He had a couple of scars on his face, a nose that had been broken at least once before and, all in all, he looked like a brawler. He studied the three of them, his small, dark eyes glittering.

"So, you are the men who visited my Sofia? She said you were coming over, but I'm afraid I didn't understand why. What exactly do you have to say to me?"

Tyrrell seemed reluctant to start. He had been able to talk at Sofia's, to someone he had known in his younger days, but he would not have had more than a passing acquaintance with Sofia's father. Tyrrell had probably known who he was, but he would not have talked to him.

"I think you know who we are," Zachary said, using as strong and firm a voice as he could muster. "Since you have been threatening us and trying to scare us off."

"Oh, I have, have I?"

"Yes." Zachary rubbed his palms on his pants and glanced around, trying to figure out how to tell the story. "I'm Zachary Goldman, and I've been investigating the disappearance of Robert Elder, a friend of Sofia's back when she was a teenager. You remember him, of course."

Costa raised his brows, looking politely surprised. "Oh, I do, do I?"

"He and Sofia were a couple. Which I gather you did not approve of."

"She did not make the best choices."

"And when Robbie figured out that you were having an illicit relationship with your daughter and confronted you about it, you killed him."

Costa stared at him. "I assume that if you are going to throw around accusations like that, you have some proof?"

"We have the negatives of the photos taken of the two of you together."

"My daughter and I are very close," Victor said with a shrug. "Photos can be misconstrued. You don't, I gather, have pictures of this alleged murder?"

68

Zachary forced himself to keep looking at Victor rather than looking at Tyrrell or Hal for help. He didn't answer the question, deciding that silence was his best response. Let Victor sweat over what evidence Zachary might have gathered during his investigation. Despite his response, he obviously was concerned about Zachary getting too much evidence, or he would not have threatened to silence him.

"You don't have pictures of the murder because there was no murder," Victor said, shaking his head, his heavy jowls wobbling.

"He got into the back seat of your car, and you shot him," Zachary maintained, keeping his eyes and voice steady. The most important thing was showing confidence, no matter how uncertain he felt. "He bled out, his blood soaking into the upholstery. You dumped the body. Pretended it never happened."

In the back of his mind, there was a tiny, niggling doubt. Why would Victor pretend that it had never happened? Wouldn't he have wanted to use Robbie's death as an example? *This is what happens to people who mess with me.* He was a crime boss. Why would he have hidden it?

But he hadn't been as big back then. Maybe it was too dangerous for him when he was still a minor criminal. But then, wouldn't it have been even more important to use it to build his reputation?

"This is ridiculous," Victor said, rolling his eyes and sitting back in his chair as if bored by the proceedings. Letting them all know that they were inconsequential to him. He didn't care if they knew about the murder. He didn't care who knew about it. They could go blab to the police if they liked, it would have no effect on him. He'd gotten rid of the body and all other evidence decades before.

But *had* he? Then why the threats?

"Give me one good reason I shouldn't follow your suggestion and just waste all of you here and now?" Victor demanded. "You come here trying to threaten me? What is stopping me from eliminating this threat?"

"Because I still have the pictures," Zachary told him emphatically. "You've been trying to stop us from finding them, but I have them. I have proof of your abuse of Sofia. And there's no statute of limitations on that. Charges could be brought against you at any time."

"You would have to have her cooperation. Without it, you would be nowhere. Besides…" He shrugged. "I kill you now, you can't share any pictures, even if you have them, which I highly doubt. Those pictures, if they ever existed, were destroyed years ago."

"The pictures might have been, but the negatives were not, and I have them."

Victor held his hands up in a "who cares?" gesture. Again drawing Zachary's attention to the fact that if Zachary was dead, he could not share them with anyone.

"I scanned them on my phone. They are saved to the cloud, and other people can access my account. If something happens to me, they'll go straight to my cloud drive to find out what I was working on. And there you are in all your glory." Zachary shook his head. "You and your own daughter."

Costa's face turned a shade redder, but he gave no other indication that he was at all concerned by this possibility.

"As a blackmailer, you are an amateur," he derided. "You are crude and show all of your cards. You don't have any finesse, like my Sofia."

Zachary couldn't help a glance at Tyrrell in reaction to this comment. Was he interpreting Victor too literally? Had he really meant that Sofia was better at blackmail than Zachary? Or that she was much more clever and subtle than he was in other areas, and he didn't like Zachary's direct approach?

Tyrrell's eyes widened slightly, clearly wondering the same thing.

It would make sense that Sofia was blackmailing Victor. Who knew what proof she might have of his abuse, and she was the only one who could say what she would do if he were charged. Would she deny it and refuse to cooperate with the prosecution, using all her resources to protect him? Or would she be leading the charge, giving the prosecution all the evidence she might have gathered and kept safe from him?

She lived in a beautiful home with every luxury she could want. Gifts freely given to her as the only child of a wealthy mob boss? Or the fruits of twenty years of blackmail?

Victor watched him, clearly trying to read his expression, analyzing whether his words had hit their target. Seconds ticked by as Zachary's brain raced, trying out one scenario after another. He should have waited before confronting Victor. Made sure that he had as much evidence as he could possibly get, creating an airtight case against the man. As it was, simply squashing the three of them would put an end to any personal threat to Victor.

"If you try to use those pictures," Victor said in a slow rumble, "the consequences will be dire." He paused. "You have no idea who you are dealing with."

Zachary swallowed. He had made a direct approach to Victor, hoping that it would stop any threats against Kenzie, Tyrrell's children, or anyone else he loved and held dear. He had thought that the man would admire his frankness. That was the way that mob bosses were always portrayed on TV. They liked people who were daring. They were impressed. But that was apparently not the case. Once again, TV crime fiction had not prepared him for real life.

Victor chuckled and shook his head at Zachary. "You have no idea," he repeated. "I know you don't have a picture of the murder *because there was no murder.*"

Zachary stared at him, trying to comprehend this statement and how it all fit together. Did he mean that it had not been murder, but an accident? The gun had discharged when it wasn't meant to? Or that it had been manslaughter, something done in the heat of the moment, in a fury at being exposed, rather than premeditated murder?

Or did he actually mean that there was no murder? That he had not killed Robbie. That Robbie had not, in fact, been killed at all?

Zachary felt his eyes widen, and his brain squealed into an even higher gear, weighing the possibility against everything else he knew about the case.

There was no body. There was no proof that Robbie Elder had been killed. The police had looked into it at the time and had found nothing. Able was, hopefully, looking into the unidentified murder victims of twenty years ago, looking for a body that might match.

But what if a body had never been found because Robbie Elder had never been killed?

But he had never again taken up his old name. He had never contacted anyone using that name again. Or even made a phone call or sent a postcard to his mother. He had left no trail.

Not using that name.

Could he still be somewhere close by using an alias? Was that who had been threatening Zachary and Tyrrell, giving credence to Victor's assertion that they had no idea who they were dealing with? That it was literally not Victor who had been trying to stop them, but someone else?

Sofia's words to Tyrrell came to Zachary's mind with brilliant clarity. *How could you help me? Do the same as Robbie and get your face shot off?*

She had not said that Robbie had been killed. She'd said he got shot in the face. Zachary had assumed that would mean certain death. But despite all of the blood, there had been no body in the car. And no body in the morgue. Why remove the body from the car and dump them separately, rather than just driving the car into a lake with the body inside? Zachary knew from experience that bodies were heavy and awkward to move.

If Robbie had been shot in the face and survived...

69

Zachary swore under his breath as it all came together. In his peripheral vision, he could see Tyrrell and Hal turning to look at him, curious about what he had just figured out.

"Sofia's chauffeur," Zachary said, stunned. He looked directly at Tyrrell. "Sofia's chauffeur... is Robbie Elder."

Tyrrell's mouth dropped open. His eyes could not get any wider than they already were. He shook his head, hesitated, and shook it again. "It couldn't be. I would know him if I saw him."

"After this long? With all of the scarring and reconstruction he would have had after being shot in the face? He wouldn't necessarily be recognizable."

"But I would still know him. He would know me. His voice, the way that he talked and moved..."

"He told you never to come back."

"Yeah."

"Maybe that was your answer. You found him, and you never needed to go back there again."

"I would have known his voice," Tyrrell insisted. "I'm good at voices."

"He didn't use his natural voice. He disguised it to be lower and deeper. Or it was damaged by... the shot." Zachary turned his head to look at Victor for confirmation. "Is that his normal voice now?"

Victor stared back. "I have not seen or spoken to Robbie Elder in over twenty years."

"Sofia's chauffeur? You've never...?"

He shook his head. He gave Zachary a small smile. "You think she would bring him here? Allow me to see him? She believes she keeps me in my place by threatening to reveal that I killed him twenty years ago. She keeps *him* in his place by telling him I can never know that he lived." Victor chuckled to himself as if impressed by his only daughter's genius. "She gets everything she wants. Daddy in his place, giving her the best that money can buy. A secret lover who she knows will never leave her side because of the danger to his life. And then along come Tyrrell Miller and Zachary Goldman, stirring everything up, looking for 'the truth.' There is nothing Sofia wants less than the truth."

You have no idea who you're dealing with.

It wasn't Victor threatening them. It wasn't Robbie, still in hiding. It was Sofia, worried that everything she had built up for herself would collapse if they revealed that Robbie had been hiding for the past two decades.

Tyrrell was still staring at Zachary. "Robbie is alive?"

Zachary nodded. Tyrrell leaned on the back of one of the chairs in Victor's office, looking as if he might collapse. Zachary reached over to squeeze his shoulder and reassure him.

"He's alive? He's been alive all this time, and I thought...? And he never contacted me, never let me know he was okay?"

"Sorry." Zachary wasn't sure why he felt the need to apologize for this. Tyrrell had been tortured by his memories for years, thinking he was responsible for his friend's death. He had fallen apart when Robbie had disappeared and Tyrrell had believed the rumors that he had been shot and killed. Maybe without that trauma, Tyrrell could have avoided the spiral into alcoholism. Or maybe not. They would never know. Zachary rubbed Tyrrell's back and shoulder.

"You can talk to him now," he suggested. "Find out... how he has been since you saw him last. It looks like he hasn't lived such a bad life. He lives a life of luxury with the woman he loves. Or a girl he had gone out with in school."

How had he felt about the woman Sofia had turned out to be?

"He told me not to go back there."

"We can find a way to reach out to him."

"He doesn't want me to."

Zachary looked at Victor. "I think... he's been held prisoner there for a long time. It might be time... to let him out."

Victor didn't seem concerned about it one way or the other. "You need to be careful of that one," he warned. "If you cross her..."

She was the dangerous one. Victor might be a mob boss, but he didn't care about Zachary or any minuscule threat he might pose. It was Sofia who would control how far any accusations of sexual abuse or attempted murder would go. Without her cooperation, anything Zachary did would just fizzle out.

Zachary had concerns about Tyrrell being the one to drive them back to Roxboro after the visit to the Costa estate. Tyrrell walked like a zombie, his mind in another world entirely. When they reached Tyrrell's car, Zachary reached toward him. "I'll drive."

It was several long seconds before Tyrrell responded, looking down at Zachary's outstretched hand. "I can drive."

"You've had a shock. I think it's better if someone else does. Until you've had a chance to think things through."

"I can drive my own car, Zachary."

Zachary kept his hand out. "Come on. You can relax. We'll stop at the burger place before we head home. Do they still have that fantastic onion ring burger?"

Tyrrell looked baffled. "I don't know."

"Let's go see."

Tyrrell deposited his keys in Zachary's hand and sighed, walking around to the passenger door.

Hal gave Zachary a nod of acknowledgment, tucking his gun back into its holster.

"You like burgers?" Zachary asked him brightly.

"Yeah. Sure. They got milkshakes?"

"They got milkshakes."

With the car filled with the smell of onion ring burgers fresh from the deep fryer and the cup holders full, Tyrrell seemed to be reviving slightly. He ate a few bites of his burger, leaned back in his seat with his eyes closed and moaned.

"This is exactly how I remember them."

"They're perfect," Zachary agreed, his mouth full.

They returned to the Miller house to drop Hal off to get his car.

"What are you going to do?" Zachary asked him.

Hal raised an eyebrow. "About what?"

"About the cold case. The open file."

"I'm not concerned about it anymore."

"But will you tell them everything? Fill them in?"

"I'm not on the police force anymore."

Zachary wanted to persist with more follow-up questions, getting a promise from Hal that he wouldn't do anything that might backfire on Tyrrell. But he ended up just smiling and nodding his confirmation. Zachary couldn't stop Hal if he wanted to go to the police department. But he didn't think that Hal would.

Their trip back to Roxboro went smoothly, without any arguments or emotional breakdowns. Zachary wasn't sure what to expect from Tyrrell once it all started to sink in. But Tyrrell seemed lighter, not despairing over all the time he had lost in feeling guilty about what had happened to Robbie.

It felt late when they got back home. Kenzie was up, making some tea and a sandwich. She looked at Zachary and Tyrrell, studying their faces and tilting her head slightly.

"Things went okay?" she asked tentatively.

Zachary nodded. "They went well. We just need to figure out our next step. T, you want to stay here the night? Grab the spare room?"

He should have asked Kenzie's permission before making the offer, but didn't think about it until the words were out of his mouth. She nodded her agreement, smoothing it over and adding her approval to the request. "You look beat, Tyrrell. You know where everything is. Just help yourself."

He had lived with them between his last binge and Kenzie getting him into a treatment program, so it was, Zachary hoped, like a second home to him. Tyrrell hesitated before accepting the invitation. Kenzie sat down at the table to drink her tea, and Zachary walked down the hall with Tyrrell to the spare room as if checking to see if he needed anything.

"The next step?" Tyrrell asked, frowning at Zachary.

Zachary nodded. "We're not done."

70

Zachary first used the transit system to follow a random path around town. Before leaving the house, he had checked for bugs or trackers in his luggage and clothing, so he was confident that no one could follow him electronically. He slipped his phone into a Faraday bag. Following someone on the bus was not easy if they were on the lookout for you, and he kept well aware of his surroundings and anyone who might be trying to keep eyes on him.

When he was sure no one could be following him, he got off the bus and walked around until he found a car rental place. He paid cash for the vehicle, though he did have to show them his identification and let them photocopy both his driver's license and his credit card in case there were any issues with the car. But the rental agent assured him that those details would never make it to the computer unless there was a problem.

Then he hopped into his new, nondescript white compact rental car and headed back to Clintock. He didn't know how long it would take for them to achieve their purpose. It might be several days before they could make contact with Robbie Elder.

But fate was on their side, or maybe Robbie had gotten restless after they had shown up at the villa and couldn't stay trapped there all day. When Zachary saw him show up at the gas station with one of Sofia's luxury vehicles, he called Tyrrell on the disposable phone he had purchased. Then he approached Robbie as he filled the tank of the big, sleek car.

"Fancy meeting you here."

Robbie was startled. His eyes shot daggers, and he looked around him quickly to see if anyone were watching them. "What are you doing here?" he growled.

"Looking for you. Glad you decided to gas up today and didn't make me wait a week."

"What? You can't *be* here. I told you not to contact me!"

"No. You told Tyrrell not to go back to the villa, so he didn't. But as far as never contacting you again..." Zachary shrugged. "We needed to talk to you."

Robbie looked around again. "Where is he?"

"He's on his way."

"You can't do this. What if someone sees me?"

"They've seen you before. Sofia knows where you gas up, I'm sure. If she wants to have eyes on you, she will."

Of course, that didn't help Robbie feel any better, but that hadn't been Zachary's intention.

"I need to get back to the villa. I'm not supposed to be gone any longer than I have to be."

"Well, you're not even finished gassing up yet, so I don't think you're out of time."

Tyrrell pulled into the gas station parking lot with a slight squeal of tires. He parked haphazardly and jumped out, hurrying over to Zachary and Robbie. He had clearly been worried that Robbie would be gone by the time he got there. Robbie looked down at the gas nozzle in his hand, holding his face away from them at an angle. Something that he often did to avoid stares, Zachary suspected.

"You're attracting attention," Robbie hissed.

Tyrrell stepped in too close. "I had to see you," he said. "Is it really you? I can't believe it. You just stood there while we talked to Sofia about what had happened to you. You didn't even say a word."

"What do you expect me to say? You weren't supposed to know I was there. How did you figure it out?"

"We might not have, without Victor's help," Zachary told him.

"What?" Robbie's voice went from a deep, gravelly bass to a squeak. He looked around them as if Victor might be hiding behind them or in one of the cars. "What are you talking about? Victor doesn't know!"

"That might be what Sofia told you, but it's not true."

"Victor pointed us right to you and Sofia," Tyrrell said. "*You* were threatening me? And my kids?"

"I wouldn't do that," he said with a quick shake of his head.

"And tried to kill me?" Zachary demanded. "You put a bomb in my car?"

Robbie's face flushed, though the effect was stripy due to the starburst of scars on his face. "I didn't try to kill you. The bomb didn't go off, did it?"

"Putting it there is still attempted murder. Maybe even terrorism."

"I wasn't trying to kill you. Just to warn you off. I knew it wasn't wired to detonate." He gave a bitter laugh. "You think I don't know how to do that after all these years?"

"Why didn't you contact me?" Tyrrell asked, his tone wounded. As if Robbie hadn't been doing it to save his own life. Did Tyrrell think that he'd disappeared just for fun?

"I had to keep a low profile. I wouldn't have survived this long if I hadn't learned how to keep my mouth shut and keep people from noticing me. Luckily, they don't really look at you once you put on a uniform," he indicated his dark suit. "And when they do look at me, all they see is the scars. They can't... recognize me from before."

Tyrrell nodded his head in agreement. "I can't believe I walked right by you and didn't even know it."

"You're not the first. I've learned how to disappear into the background."

"You could have done something. Sent me a note that you were leaving town and not to look for you. You could have done something to let me know that you were still alive."

71

The gas pump stopped, and Robbie returned the nozzle to its place on the pump.

"I couldn't do anything. For the first year... I wasn't alive. I shouldn't have made it. Should never have survived that. For a long time, I was just trapped... inside the pain, all of the surgeries and rehabilitation... I couldn't think or do anything for myself."

Zachary remembered what it had been like after the fire. How the pain from the wound debridement and other treatments would overwhelm him. He'd healed reasonably well in a few months. But his injuries had not been as severe as Robbie's.

"But after that..." Tyrrell protested.

"You don't know what it's been like. I couldn't have contact with anyone. No one could know that I had survived. Not you. Not my family. I didn't even go to my father's funeral. They don't know I'm alive. If Sofia's father ever figures it out..."

Zachary grimaced in sympathy. "He figured it out a long time ago," he said. "He just didn't tell Sofia."

"But she's been..." Robbie cut himself off and pressed his lips together as if Zachary and Tyrrell couldn't guess what she had been up to as long as he didn't say anything about it.

"He was letting her blackmail him. He probably would have given her everything as gifts anyway. But by pretending he didn't know that you had survived, he held something over her. She was still tied to him. Close to him all the time. And afraid of giving anything away. She didn't dare talk about what he had done to her, because it would lead to someone finding out about you. About the attempted murder, and her rescuing you and nursing you back to health. The lies kept her from escaping from him."

"He didn't know. He couldn't."

"You think that she could show up a year later, or whatever it was, with a man who'd obviously survived an explosion to the face, and he wouldn't figure that out?"

"It wasn't a year later. It was a long time. Five years? Maybe more. It all runs together. I couldn't keep track. And even then, it was under caps and behind glasses. I never left the car. Didn't take her over to his house. I stayed out of his way, I don't think he's ever seen my face. Why would he? I'm just her employee."

"He knew all along," Zachary insisted. "Where did he think your body went? Did she tell him that she'd disposed of you herself? Why would she do that? He would know that wasn't possible anyway. He's the kind of guy who actually knows how hard it is to lug around a body or to find a place to hide it where it will never be found again. What did he think she had done with you?"

"She told him that she had hidden the evidence, but could still produce it if she had to. That she would turn him in if he didn't do everything she wanted him to."

"And I'll bet he resisted and made her negotiate every step," Zachary suggested.

The man gave him a puzzled look. "Yes. I don't think he ever made it easy. She always had to work at it if she wanted something else."

Zachary nodded. "If he made things too easy, she wouldn't have believed she was exerting power over him. She would want to know why he was just giving her what she wanted. But as long as he resisted and negotiated, she thought it was because she was good at getting what she wanted. That he was still afraid of the threat that she could produce your body or evidence of your murder."

"He was."

"No, he wasn't. Because he knew you weren't dead. Maybe he knew a doctor that attended to you. Maybe he had someone following her around to see where she was going. Searching everywhere she had been for the body. But he's known for a long time that you weren't dead."

Zachary could see Robbie thinking this through. He had been kept prisoner for more than twenty years by the fear that if he joined the real world, leaving his pleasant prison behind, Victor Costa would track him down and kill him, like he had initially meant to, all those years ago. And Victor had known all along. He could have chosen to kill Robbie anytime, but he hadn't.

"You don't need to go back to her," Zachary said. "You can get into this car and drive away. What's she going to do about it?"

"She could tell the police I stole her car, for one."

"A dead man stole her car? How will she explain that you've been missing for over twenty years? What will she do when you tell them what happened to you? That she's been holding you prisoner for decades? It's false imprisonment. She could go away for a long time for that. And she couldn't keep it a secret from everyone. People saw you there. She couldn't pretend it didn't happen."

"I could have left there any time. I loved her. I could have left."

"Then why didn't you?"

"Because of Victor."

"Because of a threat. A lie."

Robbie shook his head. He put his hand on the door handle. "I couldn't leave. After all this time, I couldn't just leave her alone. And if I did...? I would be starting with nothing! I don't have anything of my own."

"People start from nothing all the time," Zachary told him. "I've done it. Tyrrell's done it. You just start building. Let your family know you're alive. Get new identification. Look around for a job. There are a lot of agencies that can help."

"Just pretend that nothing happened? He'll come after... *she'll* come after me."

"She can't keep holding him over your head. You know that he's in on the joke now. What can she do? You know about her and Victor. About the relationship between them. About the attempted murder and the blackmail. You have something on both of them. And all you want in return is your own life. You stay out of their way, and they stay out of yours."

Robbie opened the car door and sat down behind the wheel of the car. He looked around him as if seeing everything for the first time.

"Tyrrell will be happy to help you," Zachary said. "He works for a foundation that is involved with all kinds of organizations. Medical, mental health, homelessness..."

Robbie rubbed his fingers over his scarred face. "They can't do anything about this."

Zachary shrugged. "Plastic surgery can do a lot. It's pretty amazing now."

"And expensive. I would never be able to afford to have work done."

"Victor shot you. I'm sure the money to fix you up would only be a drop in the bucket for him. Give you a new face, a new life, in exchange for your silence. You carry on with your life and let them carry on with theirs."

Robbie still seemed undetermined. Going through the familiar motions of turning the key in the ignition and checking his mirrors.

"What did you mean, their relationship?"

Tyrrell looked surprised at this. "You took the pictures. You know what... he was doing."

"But that's not..."

"Victor said that he and his daughter are very close," Zachary interposed. "I actually think... that their relationship has persisted over all these years. He puts her up in a house right next door to his? Keeps her right there all this time? When she was supposedly blackmailing him? Why would he do that? Would you want to keep a close relationship with someone who was blackmailing you?"

Maybe Robbie was the last person he should ask, considering that he had been kept under Sofia's thumb for all of this time. He had chosen to keep a dysfunctional relationship going, at the very least.

Robbie stared out the windshield. "I always thought she was seeing someone else. She would come home, and I could tell. The way she acted. I could smell him on her. She would laugh and say she had just been to see her dad, and I thought she was using him to cover up for whatever affair she was having. For some other man."

Zachary just looked at him. Robbie didn't meet his eyes. "The whole thing is sick. But I can't get out. Can I?"

"How will you know if you don't try?"

Robbie chewed on his bumpy, scarred lip. "I could... just leave."

"Yeah. I think you could."

EPILOGUE

*Z*achary walked up to the door of his old apartment, wondering how he would feel about it. He'd been happy when he'd gone back to see Tyrrell in the past. Each time, things had changed a little more. Tyrrell was slowly erasing Zachary's imprint from the place and making his own. And that was good, because Zachary had moved on and it was Tyrrell's now, and Tyrrell needed to have his own place and to be happy, or he might go off the rails and run away again. Zachary didn't know if he could stand to go through that uncertainty again.

As he stood outside the door, he could hear voices inside. Laughing, cheerful voices. But not Tyrrell and his children. He knew their voices. He tapped on the door. Too tentatively for Tyrrell to hear him at first. Then more loudly. The voices stopped, and Zachary heard a soft footfall approaching the door, and then assumed that Tyrrell was looking out the peephole, checking to make sure he knew who it was before he opened the door to a stranger. Then the bolt snicked back, and Tyrrell opened the door.

He smiled at Zachary. "Hey, bro, come on in!" He stepped back, giving Zachary space.

Zachary looked in through the open apartment door, and

could see another man in the apartment, sitting at the kitchen table.

No chauffeur uniform, this time. A t-shirt and jeans, no hat, and no dark sunglasses that covered half his face. His scars were stark, but Zachary didn't find them ugly or frightening. They were just… a piece of history. Something that had happened to Robbie in the past that had left its story on his face.

Robbie looked away from Zachary at first, raising his hand to hide the worst of the scars from Zachary's sight. Zachary stepped closer, not staring, but not flinching and looking away, either. He sat down in one of the other kitchen chairs. He knew that if Robbie looked at him, he could also see scars on Zachary's face. While Zachary had mostly succeeded in shielding his face from the fire when he was ten, he'd obtained other scars throughout his teens, and a couple of new ones since then.

He pushed up one of his sleeves so that Robbie could see the scars there too. Scars where he'd opened his wrists, as well as scars from the fire, still visible even after the skin grafts. Robbie looked them over, and Zachary waited to see if he would ask questions about them. But then Robbie shrugged and asked Tyrrell a question about an upcoming football game.

They all had scars.

They all had parts of their stories written on their skin.

Did you enjoy this book? Reviews and recommendations are vital to making a book successful.

Please leave a review at your favorite book store or review site and share it with your friends.

Don't miss the following bonus material:
Sign up for mailing list to get a free ebook
Read a sneak preview chapter
Other books by P.D. Workman
Learn more about the author

UNLOCK ACCESS TO
ZACHARY GOLDMAN'S CASE FILES!

Get a peek inside Zachary's case files and see what other intriguing tales are in store!

CONFIDENTIAL

Zachary Goldman
Case Files

SCAN TO UNLOCK OFFER

books.pdworkman.com/sign-up-zg

PREVIEW OF SHE WAS OUT OF REACH

1

Zachary had been surprised that Rose Bircher wanted to meet him in her lab rather than at home. Most women in her circumstances would have been at home, unable to focus on work. They would take a leave of absence until things could get straightened out.

But maybe that was an unjust judgment. He hadn't known many parents in her circumstances and supposed that a mother could want to bury herself in her work just as much as a father.

He only waited in the reception area for a couple of minutes. There was a lot of white. White walls, white tiled floors, a sign on the wall with the lab's name in silver letters mounted on a shiny white surface. It made him think of a school or hospital. Not a restful place. Somewhere important work was being done and people were all focused on their projects.

The door into the inner workspace opened and Zachary got his first glimpse at the woman who wanted to hire him.

Rose Bircher was casually dressed. No white lab jacket. She was a thirty-something woman, on the thin side, with straight brown hair and a pleasant face. She wore dark-rimmed glasses and an aqua polo shirt with the company logo. She looked at Zachary, giving him a quick once-over, then held out her hand.

"Mr. Goldman?"

"Just Zachary."

"Rose. Thanks for coming. Follow me." She turned away from him, back toward the door. "You want coffee?"

"Sure."

"Good." She led him first to a breakroom with a coffee machine, stacks of mugs, and a couple of vending machines. The smell of freshly brewed coffee filled the air. "We go through the stuff like water around here. And it's pretty good."

She poured them each a mug and handed one to Zachary. He followed her farther down the hall, through a bullpen with lots of cubicles and young people pounding away at keyboards, their eyes intent on their screens. Few looked up to see who was walking by as Zachary followed Rose to the meeting room.

Rose poked her head into one of the meeting rooms to make sure it was vacant and then motioned Zachary in. There was nothing special about the room. He'd seen a hundred like it before: a table, chairs, and a small side cabinet with supplies. A whiteboard on the wall. There was a projector and screen controlled by a remote and currently recessed out of view.

Rose sat down and motioned for Zachary to do the same.

"I really appreciate you coming."

Zachary nodded.

Studying her, he could see the signs of stress on Rose's face. Puffy skin under her eyes testified that she hadn't slept well, though a layer of concealer kept the dark shadows from being visible. Faint lines across her forehead. Her hand shook as she raised the coffee mug to her mouth.

"I was told that you have investigated missing children before."

Zachary nodded. He'd had a little experience in that area. Usually teenagers, though he had also rescued his ex-wife Bridget's twin babies.

"I have some experience in that area, though I don't do a lot of missing persons," he told her honestly. "It is your daughter who is missing?" He asked it tentatively. She was too young to be the mother of a teenager. But she was not frantic like he expected the parent of a missing baby to be. But Rose had already surprised him in several respects.

"Yes." she swallowed and stared past Zachary at the wall. "My daughter Claire. She is five."

"Did you report her missing to the police?"

He had learned not to take this for granted. Not because it was like on TV where kidnappers for ransom told the parents not to call the police or FBI *or else*. Many parents did not report their children missing to the police because they knew who had taken the child. Often a family member. And they just wanted the child found and returned with the least disruption possible. Without making family business public or making a parent or grandparent look bad in front of their friends. People preferred to keep personal business quiet, even when it involved a child being taken.

"Yes. I talked to the police. They think that it was Claire's father."

That explained why he hadn't seen anything about it on the TV or internet news. Parental abductions were routine, of little interest to the public unless there were some unique, attention-grabbing details.

"Are you married? Or were you?"

"No. I met him in school. We lived together for a while. But we weren't really compatible. It didn't work out."

"Does he have shared custody? Visitation?"

"No. He didn't want anything to do with Claire, and I respected that. He has never been involved in her life."

"And that hasn't changed lately? He hasn't come to you asking if he could see her? Talk to her? Maybe he offered to pay something for child support?"

"No. We have some mutual friends, so I've kept track of him from a distance for the last few years. Occasionally, we've ended up at a party together or something like that. He asked for a picture once."

"Recently?"

"How long ago is *recent?*" She held her palms up questioningly. "It was... maybe a couple of months ago."

Zachary pulled out his notepad. He made sure that the date was filled in at the top of the page and wrote down Claire's name and the fact that her birth father had asked for her photo a couple of months before. That could be significant. He *had* shown some interest in her recently. Depending on what kind of a picture it was, he might have been able to repurpose it for a passport photograph or other identification. Or maybe just a phone picture flashed at someone to prove that yes, he was Claire's dad, or he wouldn't have her picture on his phone, would he?

Rose watched him and didn't make any comment about his messy, nearly unreadable handwriting.

"Does that mean you're taking the case?"

"Let's get a few more details first. Why do the police think Claire's father has her? Have they talked to him? Where did she disappear from?"

"Such a high percentage of kidnappings are non-custodial parents or family members; that's just what they assume from the beginning unless you have eyewitnesses who saw her being taken. And no one did. We were at a kids' play place at the mall. I was… on my phone. You can't keep an eye on your kid the whole time; there are all kinds of tunnels, slides, climbers, and ball pits. Your kid just gets swallowed up by this place with all the other kids…"

Zachary nodded. He had seen places like that. A great adventure for kids. Playing tag or dare with their friends, running off excess energy, exploring.

"How did he get her out of there? Don't they have ID to make sure you can only take the kid you arrived with?"

"Yes. I don't know how anyone could get her out of there. Some of their security cameras were down. I always thought they had really good security: guards, monitors, sign-in logs, all that kind of thing. But someone got in there and got my daughter out without anyone noticing. I called her and looked for her. I got frantic. They thought I was just being a helicopter parent and freaking out because she was out of sight. But when they made announcements and had their staff members walk around looking for her, no one could find her."

Rose swallowed hard and sipped her coffee. Zachary wasn't sure why she felt it necessary to mask her emotions, to make it look like this hadn't affected her. Most mothers cried. They weren't afraid to show him just how upset they were.

"How long has she been missing?"

Rose looked at her watch. "Three days." She put her palms over her eyes, warming them. After three days with minimal sleep, she was undoubtedly feeling the strain. Scratchy, sticky, swollen eyes. A fatigue headache. Brain fog.

"Have the police talked to her father?"

"No. They tried to track him down to talk to him. But he's out of the country. They haven't been able to talk to him or to get other authorities to talk to him." Her tone was flat.

"Out of the country? Where?"

She stared down at the surface of her coffee. Her eyes glittered with unshed tears, but she didn't let them fall. She just stared as if mesmerized by the reflection of the light on the surface of her drink.

"Saudi Arabia."

2

Zachary's heart sank. He wasn't going to be able to do anything for Rose Bircher. *Saudi Arabia?* If Claire's father had taken her there, there wasn't much that Zachary—or anyone else—could do about it. That was one of the countries where non-custodial fathers liked to take kidnapped children—a country where he had all the rights, and Rose had virtually none. The authorities there would not cooperate with US authorities. They would not deal with the child's mother.

"I'm not sure there is anything I can do to help you," he told Rose gently.

She didn't look surprised, her expression unchanging.

"I was told that you were unconventional. And stubborn. That you could get results where the police couldn't."

"Well... sometimes that has been true. But I can't always find something helpful. The police are your best bet. I just... sometimes I can find something else that they missed or follow up on a hunch. But... Saudi Arabia is a long way away."

"I know it is. But the police will only follow their specific protocol. And if they think that the child is out of the country and in a place where they can't reach her... they just issue whatever paper they do to tell the government that they believe she is over there and object to them not helping with the kidnapping case… and that's it. Then they just put a flag on his passport so that if he ever comes back into the country, they can pull him aside and talk to him."

He wasn't going to bring her back. If he had taken his daughter to Saudi Arabia, he intended to keep her there. He wasn't going to bring her back to the US.

"What is his name? Claire's father?"

Rose looked at him for a moment before answering, considering his response. Zachary examined it himself. If he couldn't do anything for Rose and didn't intend to take the case, then why ask for his name?

"Amir Osman."

"Is he from there?"

"No. He was born in America. But I guess… with his family name he could get a visa or whatever you need to immigrate there." She rubbed her temples. "I don't know all the details of that kind of thing."

"So he had been planning this for a while. He asked for her picture. He had to apply for whatever paperwork he needed to take her there."

"I suppose."

"Do the police have confirmation as to whether she was traveling with him?"

"He had a child with him. But a different name. Not Claire Bircher. He was also traveling with a woman. The child is supposed to be hers, not his."

Zachary nodded. Just enough obfuscating to make it effective. If an Amber alert had been issued under the name Claire Bircher, no one would have connected her with a child of another name. Until it was too late.

And because Amir hadn't had anything to do with his biological daughter before that and had never said he even wanted a visit with her, there was no reason for her mother to mention him when Claire went missing from the mall. It wasn't a case of a non-custodial parent not returning her on time after a visit. There had been no reason to suspect that her biological father had any interest in her until it was too late. And getting a child back from a country like Saudi Arabia... Zachary had heard stories.

"I'm not sure what you're hoping I can do for you," he told Rose. "The police have done everything they can, and I assume you've talked to experts in this kind of case. I don't have a lot of familiarity with international kidnapping and certainly have no experience flying to another country to try to get her back."

Rose took off her glasses and rubbed the bridge of her nose.

"There hasn't been much of an investigation into this case," she said slowly. "I mean, on the surface, they've done everything they should. They locked down the mall and made sure that no one could get her out but, obviously, she was gone by the time that happened, because there was no sign of her. They set up roadblocks. They did a search with K9s. They talked about an Amber Alert, but it didn't go out until quite a bit later because they didn't have a description of the kidnapper or the vehicle. But once all that preliminary stuff was done and they found out that I am... estranged from Claire's biological father, they decided that it was him. They put out all those travel alerts and searched to see if he had left the country during the window from the last time I saw Claire until they stopped him from traveling outside the United States."

"And that was when they found he had already fled with his daughter."

"With his girlfriend's daughter. They don't have any evidence that it was Claire."

Zachary was starting to get a feeling for what Rose was getting at. "Do they have any footage of Amir with Claire?"

"No. They have a few fuzzy airport surveillance pictures of him... but there's no way to tell if the girl with him is Claire or someone else. The girl in the picture is dark-haired."

At Zachary's look, she pulled out her phone and, after finding a picture, turned the screen around to face him. A little girl with long, blond hair and an impish smile.

"He might have dyed her hair."

Rose nodded. "Of course. And that is what the police are assuming. They all assume that the girl Amir had with him when he left the country was Claire."

"No full facial views"

"No. I thought all the airports had those check-in terminals that take a picture of you. But I guess they don't. Or they don't take pictures of kids who are too small to reach it, just their parents."

Zachary nodded slowly. There were holes in airport security procedures, despite what the officials would have people believe. People still traveled under forged documents. And the holes for children were even bigger than those for adults. Children weren't terrorists. They were vulnerable, but they were not a danger. It was a different mindset.

Zachary scratched a few more notes into his notepad and turned his eyes back to Rose.

"So there have been no confirmed sightings of Claire since you last saw her at the play place."

"Yeah. Exactly."

So, was she taken by a stranger? Or had she been taken by her birth father, passed off as another child, and flown out of the country? Without putting eyes on her, they couldn't be sure. The police might be right. They probably were. The ex-spouse or the child's non-custodial parent was the number one suspect in any child abduction case. It was far more likely to have been committed by a parent or other family member than by a stranger.

But Amir had not been part of Claire's life. He would only know where to find them if he had been following them.

"How many times have you seen Amir in the last six months?"

Rose shook her head. "Not at all. Well, maybe once, I guess. When he asked about a picture."

"You said that you sometimes run into him at events. You have mutual friends? Or are you in the same profession?" Zachary looked around him. "What exactly do you do here?"

"Like I said, I met him in college. We were both in computer science together. He went into industrial applications and I went into research, so we didn't exactly follow the same path. But we were both techies. And... yeah... some mutual friends."

"Have you talked to any of those friends about him? About Claire being missing?"

She shook her head. "No. Do you think I should?"

"If you could give me names and contact numbers, it might be better if I reach out to them. An unbiased third party rather than the mother accusing her ex of doing something."

"Okay." Rose didn't argue about it or say Zachary wouldn't find out anything talking to them. But if she'd been told by whoever referred her to Zachary that he was unconventional and dogged and might be able to find something out, then Rose would be more open to giving him whatever he needed without question. She looked at her phone. "Do you want me to read them out to you?"

"Why don't you just share the contacts with me from your phone? Then I won't get any digits reversed."

She nodded her agreement and spent a few minutes reviewing her contacts list and texting some of them to Zachary.

"Maybe Amir would have talked to one of these people about Claire," Zachary said. "If we can even get confirmation that he has been talking about her in the last few months, that would be a start. And if he has been saying that he wants to be a part of her life..."

Rose shook her head. "If he wanted to be a part of her life, then why wouldn't he come to me and ask me about seeing her?"

"That would be the logical approach," Zachary agreed. "But people make choices that aren't logical. Maybe he figured you would say no, and he didn't want to tip his hand. Easier to get away with it if he never let on that he wants to be in her life."

"I guess," Rose agreed. "If he'd been trying to get visitation or custody and then she disappeared from the mall or anywhere else, then he is the first one I would have thought of. It wouldn't have been hours before the police put a stop on Amir leaving the country."

Zachary nodded his agreement. "Who was the first person?"

"What?"

"You said he would have been the first person you thought of. As being her abductor. Who *was* the first person you thought of?"

"Oh… well, I just thought of someone who had been hanging around the play place. Some perv who went to watch the kids and was watching for a little girl to be by herself. A stranger, like on TV. I know parental abductions are more common, but I never thought of Amir as being her parent. I'm the only parent she's ever had in her life."

"What about your parents? Is there anyone else who helps to take care of her?"

"They're in New York. They only see her now and then when they come for a visit. And they don't babysit."

"Do you have a caregiver? Who looks after her while you're at work?"

"She's in school now. I have a woman who does after-school care until I can get there. But it's only an hour or so. A woman in the neighborhood who looks after a bunch of kids."

"A day home."

"Like that, yes. But just for after school."

"Can you give me her information?"

Rose shrugged and conceded.

"Did you see anyone at the play place you were suspicious of? Uncomfortable around?"

"Well, like any other mother, I kept a pretty close eye on any men who were there without a wife or girlfriend. The play place isn't supposed to let people without kids of their own in. You know, it's supposed to be a safe place where pedophiles can't hang around watching kids. It's just kids and their parents."

"I don't imagine it's too hard to get around that. Tell them that your wife and kid are already there. Point someone out and say you're with them. Or go with your sister or best friend and her kid."

Rose sighed and nodded. "It's great if everyone is honest and follows the rules, but the people who really want to get around the rules will."

"Like gun registration," Zachary suggested. "The people who

follow the rules are the ones who are not planning to break the laws. Those who are planning to use their guns for illegal purposes are the ones who *don't* register them."

"Right."

"Was there anyone at the play place that day that stuck out to you?" Zachary waited a few seconds to see if she would answer before prompting her further. "Anyone you felt was watching Claire? Or watching you?"

She hesitated, then shook her head. Zachary raised his brows. "Who did you just think of?"

"No one. I didn't think anyone was watching Claire."

"Someone watching you?"

There was another instant of hesitation before Rose shook her head. "No."

"Did the police get any surveillance video from the play place?"

"Some. But they said that only a few of the cameras were recording." She pressed her lips together and shook her head. "I always thought they were much more secure than they really are. There are lots of cameras around and signs saying that you are on camera. I don't know if they were even all real cameras. But only a couple were maintained."

"Did they show you any of the surveillance videos? Show you any pictures of men who had been hanging around that might have been suspicious? What did you tell them when they first arrived?"

"They didn't show me anything. I guess they must not have found anyone suspicious."

"I'll see if I can get copies of them. You never know. The police might have missed something." He'd been able to spot tiny details on videos before. Details the police had missed or not thought important.

"What did you tell the police when they first arrived? That Claire had disappeared? That she was gone? That she had been taken? What did you think had happened?"

"I said... that someone must have taken her."

"You'd never had any episodes with Claire before? When you

lost track of her for a few minutes, thought something had happened, and then found her again?"

"No... maybe when I lost sight of her for a minute, but I always found her again. She stayed close by. She'd be on the other side of the clothes rack at the department store. Or looking at a toy or snack she wanted to buy. Something like that."

"And at the park? School? The play place? What did she like to do? Did she ever play hide-and-seek? Play a prank on you?"

"No. She was a pretty easy kid. Lots of energy, but she was a good girl. Mostly, she followed the rules. She was never far away."

"So when you couldn't find her, she didn't come back to you, didn't come when you called, you believed that someone had abducted her."

Rose nodded. "Yes."

"A stranger. You never thought that someone you knew might have come and... taken her out for ice cream or taken her because they didn't think you were a good parent. Or Amir because he wanted her to be a part of his life and didn't think you would allow it."

Rose shook her head slowly. "None of those things ever occurred to me."

Zachary looked at the notes he had written down while they talked. The girl was missing. The police thought the case was solved, but the girl was out of their reach.

But there was no proof that Claire was with Amir. He understood why Rose felt so unsettled about the case. Not angry because Amir had come and stolen Claire away, but full of questions and not sure the police were right about what had happened to her little girl.

"Okay." Zachary dug a card out of his pocket and laid it before her. "Those are my rates. I'll need a small retainer to get started. I will see what I can dig up."

She let out her breath in a long sigh. "Thank you. I needed somebody in my court. I really don't think Amir took her to Saudi Arabia."

She Was Out of Reach, Book #17 of the *Zachary Goldman Mysteries* series by P.D. Workman can be purchased at pdworkman.com

ABOUT THE AUTHOR

P.D. Workman is a USA Today Bestselling author and multi-award winner, renowned for her prolific output of over 100 published works that span various genres. With a knack for crafting page-turners, Workman captivates readers with everything from cozy mysteries like the Auntie Clem's Bakery series to gripping young adult and suspense novels.

A prolific reader and writer since childhood, P.D. Workman crafts emotionally powerful stories that don't shy away from hard topics. Her books tackle mental illness, addiction, abuse, and trauma with raw honesty and compassion, giving voice to the often unheard. If you crave authentic, character-driven page-turners that hit deep and stay with you long after the final page, you're in the right place.

With each new release, fans eagerly anticipate another thrilling blend of thought-provoking storytelling and relatable characters that define P.D. Workman's brand as an author of unforgettable page-turners—gripping tales that leave a lasting impact long after the last page is turned.

> P. D. Workman, does not shy from probing the deep psychological scars of childhood trauma, mental illness, and addiction. Also characteristic of this author, these extremely sensitive issues are explored with extensive empathy, described with incredible clarity, and portrayed with profound insight.
>
> ——KIM, GOODREADS REVIEWER

Some of Workman's titles have been translated into Spanish, French, Portuguese, German, and Italian.

Workman began writing at an early age and is a prolific reader as well as writer. She is also passionate about teaching and learning, expresses her creativity through art and cooking, and loves exploring the Calgary parks and green spaces where the Parks Pat Mysteries are set. She was a legal assistant for many years and has done extensive charitable work.

Workman was born and raised in Alberta, Canada, and is married with one adult son.

————

Please visit P.D. Workman at pdworkman.com to see what else she is working on, to join her mailing list, and to link to her social networks.

————

If you enjoyed this book, please take the time to recommend it to other purchasers with a review or star rating and share it with your friends!

tiktok.com/@pdworkmanauthor

facebook.com/pdworkmanauthor

x.com/pdworkmanauthor

instagram.com/pdworkmanauthor

amazon.com/author/pdworkman

bookbub.com/authors/p-d-workman

goodreads.com/pdworkman

linkedin.com/in/pdworkman

pinterest.com/pdworkmanauthor

youtube.com/pdworkman

Find P.D. Workman's books at

PDWORKMAN.COM

Scan the QR code below

www.ingramcontent.com/pod-product-compliance
Lightning Source LLC
Chambersburg PA
CBHW030810260626
47169CB00001B/270